"MASTER, RUN SAVE YOURSEL

Nightfall watched helplessly as the sorcerer yelled something uninterpretable and pointed his finger at Prince Edward.

"Run," Nightfall shouted again, as he tried to force his way through the swamp muck he was trapped in.

Prince Edward drew his sword and ducked, using the gelding as a shield. Something radiant struck the side of the horse's head, back-splashing in sparks and droplets like iridescent liquid. The horse went still, his eyes locked wide with raw terror and shock. Frost formed on ear hairs and whiskers. Then the magically frozen head shattered into fragments on the ground, and blood pooled from a neck that seemed more glass than flesh.

For an instant, time stood still. Then Nightfall grabbed desperately in the mud for any object of substance to hurl at the sorcerer. But even as his hand found something in the sludge that surrounded him, the sorcerer began to mumble, apparently tapping captured souls for another spell.

"Run!" Nightfall screamed. "Run! Save yourself, or he'll kill us both. Just run!"

**Be sure to read these magnificent
DAW Fantasy Novels by
MICKEY ZUCKER REICHERT**

THE LEGEND OF NIGHTFALL

MICKEY ZUCKER REICHERT

THE LEGEND OF NIGHTFALL

DAW BOOKS, INC.
DONALD A. WOLLHEIM, FOUNDER
375 Hudson Street, New York, NY 10014

ELIZABETH R. WOLLHEIM
SHEILA E. GILBERT
PUBLISHERS

DAW TRADEMARK REGISTERED
U.S. PAT. OFF. AND FOREIGN COUNTRIES
—MARCA REGISTRADA
HECHO EN U.S.A.

Printed in Canada

To Roger Moore
A loyal friend forever.
A true inspiration.

ACKNOWLEDGMENTS

I would like to thank several other Moores, unrelated to Roger, whom I love dearly: Mark, Benjamin, and Jonathan. Also Jackie Moore, who unwittingly supervised every word.

Also many thanks to the Pendragons, past and present, as well as to Sheila Gilbert, Jody Lee, Jonathan Matson, and Adonrivel.

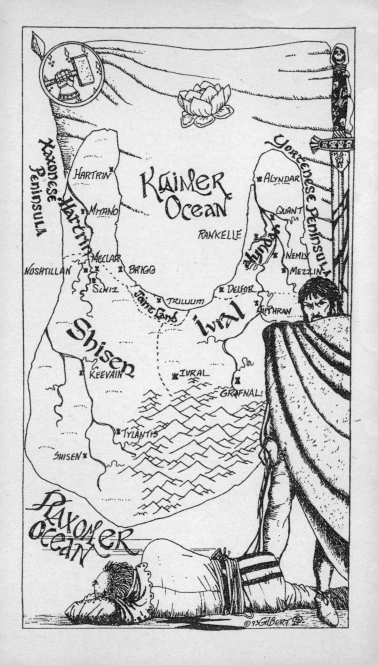

Chapter 1

A demon wakens with the night,
Reviling sun and all things bright.
Evil's friend and virtue's foe—
Darkness comes where Nightfall goes.
　　　　　　　—"The Legend of Nightfall"
　　　　　　　Nursery rhyme, st. 1

The ketch, *Raven,* tossed in the rhythmic swells of the
northern Klaimer Ocean, her bow christened with white
water. Nightfall propped his booted foot against the gunwale, toe touching the handrail, and reveled in the fresh,
salt aroma of the wind that filled *Raven's* sails. He shook
hair dark with dirt from his eyes, brushed back his scraggly beard, and watched foam spirals curl in *Raven's*
wake. In the distance, twilight colored the bloated shadow
of the Kingdom of Alyndar. On the deck, a sheet clamp
clanked against the mast. A sailor cursed harshly.

Bored of shifting with the eternal movement of the
deck, Nightfall trebled his weight with a thought and
stood steady as the lead raven that ornamented the ship's
prow. Though controlling his mass with a thought would
have shocked the other eight sailors aboard *Raven,* it
seemed commonplace to Nightfall. The ability had come
to him at birth, a congenital gift he'd long ago recognized
as a curse. It had complicated an already over-
complicated life, rescuing him from many a tight situation, yet also drawing sorcerers who would murder him to
seize his natural talent. Sorcerers gained their magical
abilities only by slaying one of the rare people endowed
with such a power, and their method required ritual
slaughter and taking possession of the victim's soul.

The captain's voice floated across the bulwarks in a
musical parody of friendship. "Maaaaarak!"

The call seized Nightfall's attention at once. The name
had grown familiar during his years in the country of

Nemix. Marak, Etan, Balshaz, Telwinar, Frihiat, each of those men had a vastly different appearance, diverse skills, and individual personalities that Nightfall never confused, though every one was himself. And not even the night-stalking assassin called Nightfall bore his true appearance.

"Maaaarak!" the captain called again, closer now.

Slowly, Nightfall returned his weight to normal, resuming his dance with the swaying stern. He tipped his head slightly, and an ice-grained breeze flicked strands of hair from his face. Otherwise, he gave no response to the captain's summons.

The captain's footfalls rang on the deck. Others followed, like echoes. "Marak?"

Nightfall lowered his foot to the deck and turned unhurriedly. He fixed his blue-black stare on the captain, noticing with alarm the half circle of sailors who flanked him. Dark curls swarmed the captain's head and chin like ivy. Flesh wizened by sea air and sun peeked around the tufts of hair. Eyes black as diamonds met Nightfall's glare, then rolled guiltily toward the deck. The captain stank of sweat.

A wave crashed against *Raven*'s hull, suddenly jolting the deck sideways. Staggered, the sailors righted themselves awkwardly. Briefly, Nightfall doubled his weight, drawing some satisfaction from the sailors' antics. His gaze locked with fanatical interest on the captain's uneven, yellowed teeth.

The captain gestured. The last dying rays of sunlight flashed from his sapphire ring, flinging blue highlights across the deck. "Marak." The captain expelled the name in a blast of foul-smelling breath. "I didn't know I let a fugitive aboard."

Nightfall retained his composure, aware he had committed no crime in the name or person of Marak, nor of any other alias except Nightfall. Familiar with violence, he let the early stirrings of adrenaline soothe him. "Neither did I." His gaze swept the sailors, and he spoke with sarcastic formality. "Which of them might you be speaking of, sir?" He searched his memory, trying to recall which of Nightfall's offenses might have fallen upon

Marak, and knowing none could. He covered his trails too well.

The captain shifted his bulk to the rhythm of the swells. Light winked and sparked from his ring. He cleared his throat. "I received a message from King Rikard of Alyndar, by courier dove, concerning the detainment of a murderer known as Nightfall." He stared, studying Nightfall's reaction.

Nightfall parodied confusion. "So? What does that have to do with me?" His mind raced. Never in his thirty-four years had anyone crossed his aliases. And only one person, a dancer named Kelryn, knew Nightfall and Marak were the same man. Despite his danger, he pictured the woman he loved: short, white hair flying around plain features, her slender body hardened into muscle that formed taut, perfect curves. *She betrayed me.* Shock and denial tainted the image. *She couldn't have betrayed me. She wouldn't. And yet, there's no other answer.* He felt chilled in all parts of his body, and more alone than he had at eight years old on the day of his mother's death.

The sailors shuffled nervously, closing the gaps in their ranks. The captain pursed his thick lips briefly. "King Rikard described you quite unmistakably." He waved, and the ring of sailors tightened.

Nightfall adopted an expression of shocked outrage. "This is insane!" He glanced over the sailors, finding no weakness or support among the men. "I've never been to Alyndar in my life."

"Get him," the captain said quietly.

As one, the sailors lunged for Nightfall.

Unable to run forward, Nightfall leapt over the handrail to the gunwale, doubling his weight to keep pace with the swaying ship. His eyes measured holes in the semicircle of men.

A wave of arms buffeted and dragged at Nightfall. Off-balance, he rolled back over the handrail and crashed to the deck. Pain lanced through his chest. He lurched to his feet and dove through a crack in the sailors' guard. The instincts of a thief showed in his movements. Even as he dodged through the wall of men, Nightfall swerved toward the captain. Two fingers caught the sapphire. A practiced twist freed it with no more force than a whisper. Then, a kick sent him sprawling, and he cursed himself for the split second lost to an unnecessary theft.

Callused hands gouged Nightfall's leg. A steel toe smashed into his side, driving air through his teeth. Nightfall twisted, whipping his knife from his boot. He struck with blinding suddenness, driving the blade into a fleshy thigh. A man screamed, and the grip on Nightfall's leg went lax. Scrambling to his feet, he sprinted across the deck, sheathing his dagger as he ran. Every breath jarred pain through his chest. He quartered his body weight, sacrificing coordination for speed. The shouts behind him mingled to an unrecognizable din.

Waves bounced from *Raven*'s prow. Her deck bucked. Again, Nightfall vaulted the rail onto the gunwale. His momentum threw him toward the water; only an abrupt weight increase and a side step saved him from the sea. Gradually, reason eclipsed the need for escape. He had learned to swim as a child, yet chunks of ice floated like seabirds in the waters. Though he would not drown, he could not survive the freezing temperatures of the northern Klaimer Ocean, and the famed Alyndarian lobsters would feast on his remains.

Shivering, Nightfall turned, beard flicking across his mouth, leaving a taste of dirt and salt. Like sharks eager for the kill, the sailors rushed him. With a wild cry, Nightfall dove back over the railing. He hit the deck in a roll. The maneuver shot agony through his lungs, and he realized he had cracked a rib in the earlier scuffle. The thought angered him. He struggled to his feet and ran. A sudden backward jerk and a lurch of the ship unbalanced him. He surged forward. His shirt tore in a sailor's grip, and he fell free. His momentum crashed him into the mast, sending another stab through his chest.

Hugging the mast, Nightfall regained his bearings. Frigid air dried the sweat on his back. The eight sailors had split, forming a ring around him. One man's thigh trickled blood through the gash Nightfall had opened in his pants leg. *No place to run.* Points of light obscured Nightfall's vision; dizziness nearly felled him. The wood felt cold and damp beneath his fingers. The circle of sailors closed, driven by action to a murderous frenzy. Bereft of alternatives, Nightfall caught the lowest cleat, dropped his weight to a minuscule fraction, and scrambled up the mast. The weight shift eased the stress on his rib as well.

Shouts arose from the sailors. Sea-wet air bit through the hole in Nightfall's shirt, prickling his skin into goose-flesh. The click of sheet clamps and the flap of the sail drowned out the whispered plans beneath him. Nightfall's options paraded before him. Clinging to the mast, he would succumb to exposure; or, when numbness and fatigue overcame him, he would plummet to his death. Surrender to the crew would cost him his freedom, but that could be regained. Apparently, King Rikard wanted him alive. So far, Nightfall had not killed or seriously wounded any of the sailors, which meant he still had an excellent chance to make it to Alyndar without a fatal "accident."

Still clutching the pole, Nightfall redrew his knife and let it fall. It tumbled harmlessly through the air, clattering to the deck. "I surrender," he said.

King Rikard Nargol the Hammer-handed perched upon his high-backed chair, surveying the Great Hall of Alyndar. The array of tapestries and paintings covering the stretches of stone wall between peaked windows had grown familiar, seldom rearranged in the thirty-eight years of his reign. A shield decorated with his crest, a fist clutching a hammer, hung over the entryway door. A guard dressed in Alyndar's silver and purple escorted a young emissary between rows of benches and toward the dais.

Waiting for the men to traverse the aisle, Rikard studied the nobles who sat on the nearest benches. As always, Prince Leyne, the elder of his two sons, sat stiffly in the front, alert and interested in the proceedings. A perfect copy of Rikard's shrewd, dark eyes stared back at him from the face of his heir. Leyne also sported his father's sharply-defined cheeks and thick, war-trained musculature, though there the resemblance ended. Instead of his father's brown curls, now turned gray, Leyne had inherited the late queen's golden locks and handsome features.

Now twenty-six, Prince Leyne could marry any woman he wished; but, instead, he had committed himself to combat training and court affairs. Other gentlefolk lounged around the Great Hall, but most of these had lost interest in the matters of state. They had broken into huddled groups, their conversations a dim hum of background.

Guards with polearms and swords stood at attention around the perimeter, their demeanors brisk but their drooping faces betraying boredom. Only one man sat with the king. At his right hand, Chancellor Gilleran poised on his seat, gaze fixed on the approaching messenger and escort. Short hair framed pale, blue-gray eyes. Each strand lay in its place, so straight and neutral brown as to appear to have no color or texture at all. Though fifteen years younger than his king, Gilleran had entered his forties. Crow's-feet etched his eyes and age had coarsened his features, making him look as dangerous as being a sorcerer made him in actuality.

Rikard knew that other kings, earls, and barons would have balked at the idea of allowing a sorcerer in their castles. Most feared the ritualistic slaughter that users of magic performed to gain their powers, ritual that, by report, required the sorcerer to consume his victim's beating heart. But to Rikard's knowledge, Gilleran had never slain any of Alyndar's retinue or its citizens. The sorcerer's powers served the kingdom well; his reputation, though unproven, kept the stewards and lesser retainers briskly efficient; and his guile complemented Rikard's own wisdom.

The messenger and his escort stopped before the dais. Now, King Rikard could see the white eagle symbol on the blue and red tabard that marked the young stranger as an emissary of King Idinbal from the southern country of Hartrin.

The messenger bowed deeply.

King Rikard gestured to him to rise.

The emissary obeyed, studying the king respectfully through green eyes beneath wide, dark brows and a fringe of reddish bangs. "Sire, I bring greetings from Hartrin and my lord, King Idinbal, as well as an agreement. I believe, sire, that you will find it generous and satisfactory."

Rikard nodded with guarded courtesy. Rising taxes against his own goods arriving in Hartrin had caused him to boost tariffs against Hartrin in kind. Affairs had spiraled nearly into economic warfare, and he had as much desire to see the situation defused as Idinbal. Alyndar's fur and lobster trade into the south lands gleaned more profits than Hartrin's spices and perfumes in his own lands. Still, Idinbal had a reputation as a cunning and frugal strategist, and not only on the battlefield.

The emissary continued. "King Idinbal has agreed to pay a quarter of his profits as tariff."

King Rikard's brows arched, then beetled as he waited for the other shoe to fall. As usual, Chancellor Gilleran sat in expressionless silence. Prince Leyne leaned forward attentively.

"His Majesty, King Idinbal, has agreed to pay half his profits for the following six months provided he can trade freely, without tariff, over these next six months. Sire, he has asked that you do the same." Message finished with an efficiency that all but demanded an impulsive consent, the emissary lowered his head, awaiting a reply.

Rikard watched his elder son's face as he deliberated. The young features crinkled in thought.

Rikard allowed his own mind free rein. Spring had come only recently. Ice chunks still cluttered the Klaimer Ocean, making ocean passage difficult, but no longer impossible. Hartrin's sleek ships would cross the channel heavily over the spring and summer, disappearing as late autumn and winter clogged the water with floes. Meanwhile, Alyndar's fur trade would flourish in the colder months when the animals came into full coat, and Alyndarian wagons would lurch overland through Nemix, Delfor, Trillium, and Brigg into Hartrin. While Alyndar did its briskest trade, Hartrin would do little in return.

King Rikard glanced at Leyne. The prince frowned, shaking his head, and it pleased the king to see that his son had thought the matter through, arriving at the same conclusion. "Thank your lord for his most ..." He paused to draw sarcastic emphasis onto the next word.

". . . generous offer. But Alyndar has no interest in this agreement—"

"Father, wait." Leyne rose.

Every eye darted to the prince. Hartrin's negotiator turned to face the young man directly.

"Perhaps we can work this agreement, with one minor change." Leyne addressed the Hartrinian directly. "Are you in a position to speak for King Idinbal on this matter?"

The emissary nodded. "Yes, Sire, I am."

Prince Leyne looked back to the king, apparently realizing he did not have the same authority. "I understand King Idinbal's need to wait for his payment; you've had a difficult winter. But our coffers are currently full. Perhaps my father would agree to your trade if Alyndar paid Hartrin in the coming six months and Hartrin paid us in the ones following."

King Rikard smiled, pleased by his son's negotiating. Compromise always worked better than direct refusal of an offer, and he had trapped Hartrin neatly. To decline the concession would almost require an admission of deceitful intentions, and Hartrin did more overland winter trade than Alyndar did in the summer. "Quite correct. I would agree to this."

The emissary paled, turning back to the king. "I . . ."

The door to the Great Hall whipped open suddenly, slamming against the far wall with a jolt that dislodged the hanging shield. Prince Edward Nargol strode into the aisle, flanked by his personal steward and two members of the guard. The shield plummeted in Edward's wake, missing the harried steward by luck alone, crashing to the floor at his feet. The sound of metal striking stone rang through the room. The steward leapt backward, eyes round as coins, hands clutching at his chest.

King Rikard groaned, wondering what moral cause his impetuous eighteen-year-old had chosen to champion this time.

Prince Edward stormed down the aisle, his golden hair flying, his beautiful, round face too gentle-featured to reveal his rage. "You can't do business with Hartrin, Father. It would be wrong." He wore the padding of the practice field, straps and laces dangling where he had begun to remove his gear.

The emissary spun around to face the prince stomping toward him. His expression mixed fear and uncertainty.

The steward stepped around the shield, trotting to catch up with his charge and the two-guard escort.

The Hartrinian emissary skittered aside as Edward clomped to a halt before the dais. "Father, Hartrin keeps slaves."

King Rikard reined in his temper with difficulty. Though familiar, his younger son's interruptions had become nearly intolerable over the last few years. "Ned, this isn't the time. We'll talk later."

Edward's expression lapsed into righteous distress, now devoid of rage. "Not the time? But how can it ever not be the time to right an evil against mankind?" He pounded a gloved fist into his palm with each point. "I'm talking about every man's basic right to freedom. I'm talking about every man's right to respect and to dignity under the almighty Father. I'm talking about elemental, fundamental morality—"

"Ned!" King Rikard shouted over his youngest son's tirade. *I'm talking about you rambling in my court!* He kept the chastisement to himself. Over the years, he had gained a reputation for fairness and saw no reason to tarnish it by humiliating the prince in public. *No matter how much he deserves it.* "Ned, I'm not going to warn you again."

Prince Edward fell silent, his blue eyes bright, his brows raised, and his forehead creased with surprise.

"When I'm finished here, we'll talk. Until then, find something constructive to do. Outside my court!" Rikard jabbed a finger toward the exit, looking to the escort to carry out his command if it became necessary.

The guards shifted nervously, apparently loath to manhandle the prince.

But Ned made their interference unnecessary. He turned with a pensiveness that alerted his father to trouble, then marched back down the aisle the way he had come. The steward scrambled after his charge.

King Rikard sat back with a sigh, watching his son's

retreat. The youth moved with long, solid strides, the pudgy steward jogging after him, requiring a step and a half for each of Edward's. The prince sported his father's iron-boned frame, firmed by weapons training, dance lessons, and horse riding. *Wasted. All wasted.* The king shook his head, wishing he had interfered more with his wife's attention to her younger child. *May she dance forever in the Father's light, she meant well; but tutors, poets, and storytellers do not make a strong man or a competent ruler. Ned has no understanding of reality.* Rikard had wished his younger son to become a warrior in his brother's service, a pursuit that well-matched his temper and size; yet the good queen had leaned toward the artistic and scholarly. *I should never have let her hire Zakrao to teach him.* He pictured the tutor, a lanky Rankellian who talked as much with his hands as his mouth and whose idea of "fairness" was based on the wants, not the worth, of a man. Zakrao would take the side of a slackard for no other reason than that no one else would and consider it justice only if the fool got his way. Now, Rikard shook his head at the memory and at his son's retreating back. As the exit swung closed behind Prince Edward and his entourage, the king turned his attention to Leyne. *Thank the gods, one of my sons will make a good king.*

The Hartrinian emissary retook his position before the throne, waiting with his head lowered and his hands folded across his abdomen.

The king turned his consideration back to the emissary. Before Prince Edward had arrived, he had the Hartrinian well trapped into a deal that would benefit Alyndar. Now, the mood had disappeared. "Does Hartrin agree to the new arrangement?" he asked with little hope that it would be the case. The emissary had had plenty of time to consider the deal, detail its flaws in his mind, and think of a suitable escape from his corner.

The emissary cleared his throat. "With all respect, Sire, I was not authorized to make that particular deal. I am, however, permitted to agree to having both countries pay ten percent of profits as tariff, year round."

"Done." King Rikard nodded once, keeping all evi-

dence of his relief from his outward expression. He had
tired of Idinbal's games. Ten percent closely approximated trade agreements with the other two kingdoms.
"Dismissed."

Pivoting, the Hartrinian left the Great Hall. King
Rikard watched as the nobleman departed, waiting for the
finality of the closing door.

But the Great Hall door remained open. Two soldiers in
the lavender and gray of Alyndar's prison guards entered,
their lighter uniforms conspicuous against the deeper purple and silver of the royal guard. Rikard recognized one
as the chief of the dungeon guards, a compact redhead
named Volkmier. Then, the door clicked closed behind
them.

King Rikard's pulse quickened. He saw the prison
guards only rarely. Considering his last instructions to
them, he knew they must bring news of Nightfall. Yet he
also realized the facts would far more likely prove disap-
pointing. Named for a night-stalking demon in a child's
nursery rhyme, Nightfall had become more notorious than
the legend that spawned his name. Likely, he had committed only half the crimes attributed to him over the last
twenty years; but if he had committed just a quarter, it
was still more evil per moon cycle than most men could
perpetrate in a lifetime.

Volkmier and his companion marched down the aisle,
their approach interminably long. Rumors claimed that
Nightfall heard every whisper spoken to the night wind.
Those who wanted an item taken, a person slaughtered,
an enemy discredited or killed need only let the dark
breezes carry the message. Then they must be prepared to
pay, if not in gold or money, then with their own blood.
Many believed Nightfall was the demon of fable come to
life, but Rikard knew better. The rhyme was older than
his own childhood, but the man who haunted the nights of
every country on the continent had earned his reputation
a scant twenty years ago and probably began his spree of
crime no more than a decade before that time. Captured
swagmen, fronts, and smugglers swore that Nightfall was
a single man. To the one, they described him as dark and
imposing, a bearded man with a wickedly scarred face, a

gravelly voice, and eyes the color of blackened steel. And, somehow, Chancellor Gilleran had discovered the connection between Nightfall and a Nemixite called Marak.

The prison guards stopped before the dais. Eager for details, King Rikard addressed them before they could execute the customary formalities. "What news do you bring, Volkmier?"

The chief prison guard poised, halfway bowed. "Majesty, we have Nightfall in custody."

Joy thrilled through Rikard, tainted by caution. He glanced to his right. Even Gilleran's usually blank face held a tight-lipped smile. The king leaned forward, hands clamped to the armrests of his chair. "*Raven* turned him over? He's in the prison?"

The first answer being self-evident, Volkmier skipped to the second. "Majesty, we placed him in the security cage under three locks and three separate keys."

The other guard completed his bow. "And, Sire, we still have the manacles and shackles on him from the ship."

"He didn't give you any trouble?"

"None at all, Majesty," Volkmier said proudly. He straightened. "We had a contingent ready when he arrived. The crew had him tamed. He came as meek as a kitten. We stripped him down carefully, took everything the sailors missed . . ."

Rikard frowned, assailed by doubts. *Something's wrong. This doesn't sound like the Nightfall who's haunted men's nights for two decades.* Prince Leyne's face mirrored his father's suspicions.

Volkmier continued, undaunted. ". . . including these." He pulled a pouch from beneath his cloak, opened the drawstring, and carefully jiggled three daggers onto his palm. Sunlight streaming through the windows glinted from razor-honed edges. Though simply crafted, the hilts did not detract from the crisply-tempered steel.

Seized with a sudden urge to test their stability, King Rikard opened a hand to reach for the daggers. Before he could move, Volkmier answered the unspoken question.

"Perfectly balanced for throwing, Sire."

His curiosity addressed, King Rikard redirected his gesture, tapping the chair arm with an open hand. The knives meant nothing; any sailor or traveler might be expected to carry a utility blade or two. But most sailors could not afford even a single knife of the quality of those that sat in Volkmier's hand. Still, he wanted more convincing evidence. "What else did you get from him?"

Volkmier flexed his arm, flicking the daggers back into the pouch. "Just clothing, Majesty. Filthy and ragged."

Rikard stroked his sculpted, gray beard thoughtfully. "I want to know what and who this man is. Use the torturer if necessary, but sparingly." *We only need him to admit to one murder to justify execution, but I don't want an innocent man whipped into a confession.* "I want the truth."

Volkmier bowed.

"Dismissed."

Volkmier and his companion headed away from the Great Hall.

King Rikard did not bother to watch their departure. Instead, he turned his attention to Chancellor Gilleran. The sorcerer's face had returned to its expressionless mask, yet his eyes burned like pale flames and the hands that lay in his lap were tensely clasped as if in anticipation.

The king conferred softly with his adviser. "You've met this Marak/Nightfall before?"

Gilleran shook his head, not bothering with words.

"But you'll know him when you see him?"

"Within a few sentences, Sire, I will know him." Gilleran made a routine gesture of reverence, though his attention seemed elsewhere. "And I hope, my king, you will leave Nightfall's execution to me. An assassin of his ilk deserves to have his soul writhe in agony for eternity." A slight smile flickered across his features and disappeared. By the time he fixed a grim stare directly on the king, his features had again lapsed into a pall. "Don't you agree, Sire?"

The cold cruelty of Gilleran's tone sent a chill through King Rikard despite the obvious logic of his words. He was seeing a side of his adviser he had never seen before. And he was not at all sure he liked it.

* * *

Alyndar's dungeon reeked of must, mildew, and lingering disease. Dressed only in the loincloth the guards had left him, Nightfall crouched at the far side of his cell, the wall stones cold and damp against his back. Through the bars, he could see shifting figures in the faint light that penetrated cracks in the ceiling and a few guttering torches among as many spent ones stuck in brackets on the wall. The whispers of the other prisoners came to him in garbled bursts, liberally sprinkled with his demon name.

The locks on his fetters had proved little more than an inconvenience. The shackles and manacles were heaped in a pile at his side, a gash across his ankle and a flap of skin abraded from his forearm the only evidence that they had once held him prisoner. Blood beaded the arm wound; its constant, sharp sting helped him ignore the rhythmical stab of the broken rib into his lungs with every breath. He clamped his hand against his oozing wrist to staunch the bleeding, skittering toward the cage door to assess its security.

As Nightfall moved toward the cell entrance, the other prisoners in Alyndar's dungeon fell silent, apparently straining to watch his techniques. A torch flickered and died. A thin wisp of smoke curled from the blackened wood. In the fading light, Nightfall assessed the three locks. They appeared intricately crafted, a barrier that would require a locksmith's tools and, even then, might thwart his professional skills. He retreated to his crouched vigil at the back of the cell, too thoughtful to become concerned.

Methodically, Nightfall checked walls and bars, assessing them with a touch. The granite seemed stable, the bars flawless, solid, and firmly welded. Other than the shed fetters, the cell was empty. Not even a wooden bowl or a straw pallet interrupted the cold expanse of stone. Nightfall's mind analyzed every detail automatically, seeing the shackles and manacles as weapons, the sapphire ring he had swallowed as a potential bribe, once he passed it. Even the tense whispers of his prison mates became duly noted as a possible tool. Their fear and awe of his reputation could serve him in some way, should the need arise.

Nightfall rolled his beard between his palms. Having fully surveyed his surroundings, he let his thoughts wander, and they riveted instantly on Kelryn. Again, the dancer filled his mind's eye, unconsciously dredging a thrill of desire. Moonlight striped her white hair and sparkled through muddled green-brown eyes, her plain features somehow beautiful, her every movement as graceful as her swaying, swirling dances. Never before had Nightfall fallen prey to the guiles of a woman, the goadings of his heart, or the preaching of his conscience. But that night he had told her everything: sworn his love, admitted his identity and his profession, confessed his deepest fears, his most foolish dreams. And she had accepted his flaws, loved him for them, and conceded a few of her own. She was a prostitute, yet, to the son of a prostitute, this meant little. And the rumor he had started that she carried sexual diseases had put an end to her seedier career, a loss of income that he had supplemented with stolen silver.

The mental image warped and faded. Nightfall's love prodded him to believe that someone had overheard them that night, that some peeping stranger had sold his identity to Alyndar's king. Yet logic told him otherwise. No one had spied on them. He had assured that with the same caution as he used in his thefts and murders. Twenty-six years of crime had gone unpunished because he never dropped his guard, not even in sleep. He had ensured their privacy before the talk and chosen the clearing for its openness. Had anyone come within hearing distance of their whispered heart-to-heart, a deaf leper would have known of the intruder's presence.

Nightfall crushed his knees to his chest, lightening himself to take weight from the injured rib. The jabbing pain eased only slightly, but he hoped the lessening of mass-stress might quicken healing. Another memory surfaced, the vision of a face he had not seen for longer than two years. Soft, dark eyes studied him from beneath a tangled mop of sand-colored hair. Though only nine years older than Nightfall, Dyfrin had served as the only father he ever had: "Marak, you have to trust some people some time," the older boy used to say with regularity. "You may make it without friends; but, with them, you can do anything."

Nightfall settled into a more comfortable position, his legs stretched in front of him. Though he appeared relaxed, he could lunge to his feet in an instant. Dyfrin's companionship and advice had taught him to seek pleasures in life when his mother's neglect and cruelty had taught him only how to survive. Dyfrin had offered a friendship that Nightfall had never found again, until he met Kelryn. The older boy had seemed to read his every need and mood, knew when to press and when to back off, how to approach an issue without offending and when to let the matter lie in pensive silence. When Dyfrin's lessons on morality failed, he could make the same point with logic: "If you can't mourn the orphans and widows, think instead of the enemies random killings create. What good is silencing a witness if his twelve brothers and ninety-three cousins hunt you down?"

The image of Kelryn superimposed itself over Dyfrin, strengthening until the vision of the man disappeared, wholly replaced. *She betrayed me. I can't believe the bitch betrayed me.* Agony trickled through Nightfall's chest, overriding physical pain. *Finally, I dared to trust someone, and she betrayed me.* Grief melted into outrage, then flared to fury. *I should have trusted my instincts instead of my heart.* Hatred warped the picture, and Kelryn's features disappeared from his thoughts. *She's taught me a lesson I won't forget. And when I get free of here, I'll teach her a lesson she won't be alive to forget.*

Footfalls clicked down the stone hallway of Alyndar's prison, seizing Nightfall's attention. Vengeance could wait. For now, escape must take precedence. He concentrated on the noise, recognizing the clang of keys and the faint rustle of mail links. *Guards.*

As the noises drew closer, Nightfall sifted out two separate pairs of bootfalls. Quietly, he kicked the chains and fetters into the darkest corner of his cell and restored his weight. Moving into the dappled shadows toward the center, he put his hands behind his back and pressed his legs together as if still held in place at the ankles.

Voices wafted to Nightfall, becoming louder as the guards' approach hushed the hissed exchanges of the other prisoners. ". . . hold him back while I open the locks."

"No problem. This is one killer I ain't letting near that door till we've got a good hold."

The conversation dropped off as the guards came into sight from the gloom of the corridor. They wore long chain shirts, belted at the waist, and wool dyed lavender and gray peeked between the rings. The taller one, a narrow-faced blond, clutched a clip of keys. The other was a solid man with handsome features and a fluffy ball of black hair that seemed to perch atop his head. They stopped just outside Nightfall's cell.

Nightfall rose with feigned awkwardness, simulating shackles. He kept his hands poised, crossed against the hollow of his spine. A burr knotted into his beard scratched his throat; and, from long practice, he resisted the natural urge to dislodge it.

The dark-haired guard drew his long sword and angled it for a stab between the bars. "Stand where you are, Nightfall. You move, you die."

Nightfall went still, assessing the two men in front of him. Both held the wary stances of seasoned warriors, their muscles taut from combat training. He felt confident he could best either with speed, and equally certain they would prove stronger and more skilled with weapons. His weight-shifting ability obviated the need to develop power in order to climb, and few of his thefts involved heavy objects. For killing, he relied more on surprise and aim than thrust and parry. He glanced from one guard to the other, trying to look nervous while he assessed them. Each carried a long sword. The telltale bulge of a dagger displaced the smooth line of the blond's boot. "I told your people before. My name is Marak."

"Save it for the torturer." The shorter guard made an abbreviated jab with his blade.

The taller one separated a key from its mates and thrust it into the lock. He twisted. The mechanism gave with a click.

"Torturer?" Nightfall shrank away, his fear not completely an act. "What do you mean, torturer? What's the charge?"

The blond let the key fall and selected another, fitting it into the second lock.

The other guard answered over the snap of its opening. "What's the charge?" An incredulous half-smile spread across his lips. "The charges, if I remember correctly, include forty-seven acts of grand theft, nineteen murders, two counts of treason, one assault, and more than eight hundred and fifty misdemeanors. And that's just in Alyndar."

The number of killings sounded high, the robberies low, and Nightfall doubted he had assaulted anyone without finishing the deed. Yet, otherwise, the charges seemed appropriate. He continued the conversation to keep the guards watching his face so they would not notice the missing fetters. "That's impossible. I've never been to Alyndar in my life. You're mistaking me for someone else. . . ."

The blond exchanged his key for another, working on the last lock. He snorted. "First time I ever heard that defense. How about you, Rylinat?"

Rylinat laughed merrily, as if his companion had actually said something funny.

"Ready?" The blond hooked the key clip over his belt.

Rylinat nodded. Sheathing his sword, he back-stepped, leaving room for the door. It swung open with a squeal of rusted hinges, and the two guards scissored toward Nightfall, alert to his every movement. "It'll go easier if you cooperate." A slight quaver in the smaller guard's voice revealed apprehension. Apparently, the legends had affected even him. "Come here."

Nightfall remained in the shadows, pleased that the guards' discomfort kept them focused on his face and arms. He kept his features slack, trying to appear innocent and scared. Hesitantly, feigning the awkward shuffle of shackles, he edged toward the guards.

Rylinat caught Nightfall's right arm, the companion his left. Nightfall kept his fingers laced together to prevent the guards from pulling his unmanacled hands apart. Docilely, he allowed them to lead him, in small steps, from the cage and into a dark tunnel of hallway.

Nightfall's mind kicked into memory, retracing his route to the cage. To the right, the long corridor led to a moss-slicked stairway which spiraled upward to a wooden door. Once through it, he would be free. Only one other barrier stood in his way, a gate that spanned from hallway floor to ceiling like a cold, steel web. His gaze strayed to the key clip at the guard's belt, the answer to the door locks.

Rylinat traced Nightfall's attention. Too late, the thief realized his mistake. The guard's stare slid past his companion's waist to the floor and the shackles missing from Nightfall's ankles. He opened his mouth to speak.

Instantly, Nightfall jerked, trebling his weight.

The blond stumbled. Thrown askew, Rylinat loosed a startled cry in place of the warning he had planned. He scrambled for balance, losing his hold on Nightfall's arm, nails raking his prisoner's naked shoulder. The sword on his left hip bumped Nightfall's thigh.

Nightfall seized Rylinat's hilt. He drew, twisting for momentum. As the blade rattled free, he spun, slashing open the blond's neck.

Impact quivered through Nightfall's hands and flung the blond guard to the floor. Blood splashed Nightfall's cheek. He whirled back to Rylinat, whipping the blade in a blind strike at the place the guard had stood.

Rylinat leapt back, pawing at his empty sheath, the sword nicking his tunic and sending the links into a rattling dance. "Here!" he screamed. "Nightfall's free!"

Shouts of encouragement rose from scraggly prisoners in the other cages.

Nightfall swore, knowing the noise would draw the attention of any sentry who had not already responded to Rylinat's shout. He let the sword sag, leaving space for the unarmed guard to retreat. *He's already alerted the others. Speed is more important than silencing him now.*

But Rylinat rushed Nightfall, apparently trusting his superior size and training, unable to know Nightfall now weighed as much as a boulder.

As the guard bore down on him, Nightfall sprang backward, flicking up the sword.

Too late, Rylinat tried to swerve. His own momentum carried him onto the sword, impaling him to the hilt. He crashed into Nightfall, meeting resistance as solid as the granite wall. Shock crossed his features. Then his mouth gaped open, emitting agonized screams. He slid to the floor, smearing blood across Nightfall's torso.

Nightfall cursed his own incompetence. Now that he had killed the guards, escape was no longer a matter of timing; it had become instant necessity. And Rylinat's shrieks had turned a difficult evasion into an impossible one. Ignoring the writhing guard, Nightfall shifted his attention to the motionless blond. Grabbing the keys and the boot knife, he dodged around Rylinat and ran for the exit.

Rylinat's screams dropped to sobbing moans, revealing the echoing slap of running footsteps and the pleading promises of convicts begging freedom. Nightfall measured the confusion released criminals might cause against the time it would take to free them and found the need for haste more driving. In the same situation, he knew Dyfrin would have loosed every one, expecting no reward, though he would receive it. One might assist him in a barroom brawl. Another might later supply information he needed for a heist. Still another would warn him when an enemy threatened his life or well-being.

Dropping his weight to normal, Nightfall continued his sprint down the hallway. Prisoners called to him from the cells, marking his passage. Ahead, the guards' footfalls rang louder, mixed with shouted commands. Nightfall whisked around a corner, probing the keys for the one that felt most correct from his momentary assessment of the lock.

The gateway flashed into sight. Six guards aimed loaded crossbows between the bars, three kneeling and the others standing. More guards in mail and Alyndarian uniforms huddled behind the bowmen.

Nightfall skidded to a stop.

"There he is!" one shouted. An overeager crossbowman released. The quarrel sailed toward Nightfall who sprang aside. Its point struck the wall. The shaft shattered, plunging a splinter deep into Nightfall's arm.

"Fire!"

Nightfall hurled himself to the floor, tucked and rolling. The bolts rained around him, just beyond accurate range. Retreating as he floundered to his feet, he darted off the way he had come.

Vulgarities chased him down the hallway. A sword struck the metal wall, the sound ringing deafeningly down the corridor.

Nightfall ran, weaving through puddled shadow, skirting the semicircles of torchlight. He kept his run sinuous, avoiding jerky movements that might attract attention, hoping to become lost to sight in the pervading darkness. Never having gone in this direction, he had no idea what to expect or where to go, so he trusted his instincts to lead him toward an exit. Behind him, the sound of the opening gate jostled and creaked through the hallway. Ahead, bootfalls hammered the granite, accompanied by a chorus of clinking chain links.

Mercifully, the prisoners seemed to have lost track of him, their shouts muddled into a wild chaos that no longer gave away his location. Directly before his own cell, Nightfall stepped over Rylinat's now still form, reassessing his strategy in the moments before the guard contingents sandwiched him. To remain in place was folly. Enraged by his escape and their companions' deaths, Alyndar's prison guards would surely beat him to oblivion or beyond. Yet to run in either direction meant colliding with a rushing herd of sentries. From the noises, he guessed the guards from the unexplored direction would reach him well before the other group. Already, he could see the leader's mail reflecting a beam of sunlight from a slit in the roof.

Nightfall seized the bars to his cage. Rust bit his fingers, flaking into his palms. He lowered his head, dropping his weight as low as possible, and scrambled like a squirrel to the top. He took a deep breath that jabbed the rib into his lung with enough force to make him dizzy with pain. He clung, not daring to exhale.

Within seconds, fifteen guardsmen dashed beneath him.

Their four ranks swept the corridor from side to side leaving no space for an escaping convict to slip past. The ones in the lead jerked to an abrupt halt before the body of the blond, and the others pulled up as suddenly. One in the back veered, stumbling to his knees. "What the hell?"

"Holy Father," one of the leaders said.

Spots filled Nightfall's vision. His lungs ached.

Another guard crept forward, checking first Rylinat, then his companion. "They're dead." His tone went ugly, though welling tears softened the curse. "The ruthless bastard. I'll rip him apart with my own hands."

Nightfall's lungs gasped spasmodically for fresh breath. He fought the urge for an explosive exhalation, letting spent air trickle silently between his lips.

Several guards glanced into the empty cell, but not a single one looked up.

"There's nothing we can do here," another guard said. "We've got to keep moving or he'll get away." Skirting the corpses reverently, they continued down the hallway.

Nightfall waited only until they passed, then slithered down the bars and dropped lightly to the ground. Gasping in a quiet breath, he ran in the direction from which the guards had come. Behind him, he heard the shouted exchange as the two contingents met.

"Where is he?"

"He's not this way!"

"Well, he's certainly not that way!"

"You idiots!"

The footfalls resumed behind him, growing louder as they spun back in his direction. They paused briefly as the new group found the corpses, gaining Nightfall several paces of lead.

The hallway branched into winding byways. Nightfall chose his course at random, guessing he ran toward the palace, yet finding no place to reverse direction. The pursuit grew more sparse as the guards broke into groups, but still they followed him consistently, never losing distance, yet never gaining.

The run taxed Nightfall. Deep breaths shot agony through his chest so he reverted to rapid, shallow patterns that lapsed into a doglike pant. The pain radiated into a nearly crippling side cramp.

Nightfall massaged the ache as he ran. Suddenly, the left wall fell away, revealing the black mouth of a stairwell. The guards had hauled him down steps to enter the dungeon, so it seemed only natural to ascend. Whipping around the corner, he started up the steps.

Nightfall's toes met slime-covered granite, interrupted by the passage of metal and leather. Encouraged by obvious signs of use, he sprinted upward, probing each slippery step briefly before trusting his weight upon it. From behind, the sounds of pursuit continued, the guards' boots slamming solidly on each stair.

On entering, Nightfall had been too busy trying to catch each of the guards' words and intentions to count steps. Now, the stairway seemed endless, and he wondered whether to blame the sensation on a poor choice of direction or his own impatient desperation. Just as he considered turning and trying to sneak past the guards, he came to a landing and a twisting hallway. He ran on, the sentries closing the gap behind him.

Shortly, he came upon another gloomy funnel of steps. Now committed, he took the stairs two at a time. Within a dozen paces, he came to a dead end, discovering the bottom of a trap door above him. Two keyholes admitted light in parallel bands.

Damn. Nightfall studied the locks, separating the correct keys by touch. He had no way of knowing where he would find himself once through the trapdoor, presumably in some well-traveled chamber of King Rikard's castle. Below him, the clink of armor grew louder. He flicked the first key into the lock and spun, then inserted the second.

"He's up there! I hear him." A voice floated up the stairway, closer than Nightfall expected. He could hear winded inhalations beneath his own and counted at least six sentries.

Nightfall cursed his gasping breaths and the injured rib that made them necessary. Exchanging the keys for the dagger, he slammed his shoulder against the trapdoor, prepared for a fight.

The panel swung open. Chilled air washed over Nightfall, startling him. *Outside. How?* Catching the sides of the opening, he hauled himself through, studying his surroundings. The moss-stained wall of Alyndar's castle rose beyond him, and a nearby pair of sentries whirled, alerted by the sound of the swinging door. To his left and right, a stone ledge adorned with gargoyles jutted to the height of his waist. The sun beamed through a cloudless expanse of sky.

As Nightfall swung to the pathway, a hand enwrapped his ankle. Thrown off-balance, he staggered, twisting. The gash from the shackles reopened, slicking his skin with blood. The fingers slipped off, but their tug sent Nightfall crashing to the ground.

The sentries near the castle ran toward him. From the trapdoor, a grim face appeared.

Nightfall rolled, scrambled to his feet, and leapt to one of the low walls. Behind him, guards sprang through the trapdoor opening. Ahead lay a vast void of air. Nightfall grabbed a gargoyle's head for support. Far below, easily three times the length of *Raven*'s main mast, the leaf-covered tops of oaks and hickories waved in the breeze. *Not outside! We're on the parapets!* Realizing his mistake, Nightfall whirled.

The guards advanced with the same predatory look as *Raven*'s crew, clutching swords and crossbows. "Get him," one shouted.

Cornered and prepared to fight, Nightfall brandished his knife, dropping his center of gravity. Several guards charged. Nightfall dodged. His ankle cracked against a gargoyle. Stone gave beneath his foot, pitching him backward. For an instant, he seemed to hover in midair. Then he plummeted from the parapets.

Nightfall screamed. Wind sliced through his loincloth, spinning him like flotsam beneath errant waves. Desperation scattered his wits. Helplessly, he clawed air. Within seconds, tree branches scratched his face and hands. Limbs shattered, knocking him sideways. Then, logic returned. He channeled all thought in one direction, driving his weight downward until his loincloth became heavier than his body.

Air resistance slowed Nightfall's descent. Branches brushed aside harmlessly, and he floated toward the forest floor little faster than the leaves his fall had dislodged. He hit the ground, breath driven from his lungs, staring through intertwined branches at a distant line of loaded crossbows.

Nightfall lay still, his consciousness wavering, aware any sudden movement would hurl him into blackness. Despite his dangerous occupation and his gift of weight shifting, he possessed a normal man's fear of heights. Never before had he tested his talent so abruptly nor relied upon it so completely. *Have to run. Gotta get out of here quickly.*

Something struck the ground near his head. Painfully, methodically, he swiveled his neck toward it, staring down the shaft of a bolt to its purple and silver feathers.

"Don't move, Nightfall." A red-haired commander spoke. He knelt on the ledge of the parapet, a crossbow leveled at Nightfall's head. "I don't know what demon blessed you. I don't know how you survived that fall, and I don't want to know. The king wants you questioned. Hell take your wicked, ugly, disgusting, murdering soul, I'm going to see that his will is done. But if you so much as quiver . . . if you give me the slightest excuse, I'll shoot you dead and revel in it."

Though he had landed relatively lightly, Nightfall felt bruised all over. A double stab of pain told him he had broken another rib, and his back ached badly enough to warn of a possibly serious injury. Vertigo gripped him. Closing his eyes, he surrendered to oblivion.

Chapter 2

Eyes darker than the midnight shade,
Teeth sharper than the headsman's blade.
When he smiles, a cold wind blows—
Darkness comes where Nightfall goes.
                    —"The Legend of Nightfall"
                    Nursery rhyme, st. 2

Prince Edward Nargol wove through the garden pathways of Ayndar's courtyard, too preoccupied to notice the buds of the first spring flowers poking through the dirt or the ever-present steward who chased him, huffing in his wake. *Slavery.* The evil inspired by the thought sent a shiver through him. His chest clenched in sympathy for the men and women forced to toil for moldy scraps unfit for hounds, driven to work beneath the broiling summer sun or shivering as frigid winds cut beneath their ragged clothing. *Owned like animals. Beaten and cowed like wild asses broken to plow. No one deserves that.* The last plot disappeared behind Edward's ground-eating stride. He kept to the trail, headed for the main gate and its hovering, attentive retinue of guardsmen.

"My lord, wait. Please." The steward pleaded, his voice a wheeze.

Edward paused, giving the steward sufficient time to draw to his side. "Elfrit, it's not necessary to follow me everywhere I go."

The slighter man stopped half a pace behind his prince. Sweat trickled from his gray-flecked, brown hair. "It's my job, lord."

"Not for long if you kill yourself doing it." Edward smiled. Elfrit had endured as prince's steward for four months, longer than any other attendant since Edward had turned thirteen. "Here, I'll give you the day free."

Elfrit adjusted his tabard, his breathing falling to a less painful-sounding pant. "And I thank you for your generosity. But, with all respect due, lord, I work for your father, not you."

The prince laughed. "I hardly think my father would object to my giving my own steward some time to himself."

Elfrit's cheek twitched as he suppressed an exclamation that Edward would never hear. He avoided the prince's stare, hunched and concentrating on each slowing gasp.

Impatiently, Prince Edward smoothed his red satin shirt and tugged his patterned breeks into a more comfortable position. "Well?"

Elfrit straightened, his breaths normalizing. Pulling a handkerchief from his pocket, he wiped his brow, leaving spirals of hair plastered to his forehead. "Where are we going, lord?"

Resigned to Elfrit's presence, Edward resumed his walk. "Out to do the king's bidding."

"And that is, lord?" Elfrit broke into a trot so as not to fall behind again.

The gate loomed closer. The six guardsmen before it snapped to attention as the prince approached. On the wall above, the other two sentries crossed their halberds.

"To do something constructive outside his court, of course." Edward waved the guardsmen to an "at ease" position. "Open the gate."

Elfrit groaned almost inaudibly.

The nearest sentries seized the iron portals, pulling them open. A third crossed his wrists in a gesture of respect. "Prince Ned, we will escort you." He inclined his head toward the guardsman directly across from him who imitated the deferential motion.

"That won't be necessary." Edward stepped past them and through the gates before the panels came fully open, Elfrit bundling after him.

Despite Edward's instructions to the contrary, the pair of guardsmen trailed him through the opening.

The prince strutted across winter-barren ground studded with the earliest blades of grass. Ahead, sparse evergreens interrupted a farmer's field, its irregular surface not yet plowed, its dirt boulders softening in the thaw.

Just beyond sight of Alyndar's castle, Edward knew he would find the Hartrinian camp.

Abruptly, he whirled on the guardsmen. "I told you, your presence is unnecessary."

The sentries exchanged meaningful looks as their companions closed the gates behind them. "We insist, lord," the first one said.

"And I insist otherwise." Prince Edward had tired of the interference. In the past six months, the guards had trailed him like puppies. "Thank you for your concern, but I'd rather be alone." He glanced at Elfrit. "Or as alone as my too-loyal steward allows."

The guards hesitated, trading uncomfortable glances.

Prince Edward turned, continuing in the direction he had been walking. This time, the guards remained in place. Edward could hear their whispers, garbled to nonsense, until even the buzz of their conversation became lost beneath the hiss of wind-whipped needles.

Elfrit jogged along beside his prince. "Lord, don't you think it might be wise to tell your father where we're going?"

Prince Edward did not skip a pace. He entered a small cluster of pines that he knew sheltered the Hartrinians' meadow camp. "Are you questioning me, Elfrit?"

That being clearly evident, Elfrit dodged the issue. "I'm only concerned for you, lord."

"Well, stop it." Edward threaded between the trees. "I'm quite capable of taking care of myself."

Elfrit muttered something unintelligible.

"What did you say?" Edward brushed through a brace of evergreens, the sight of the Hartrinian camp fully capturing his attention. Horses grazed piled hay, surrounding an array of tents. Smoke curled from the center of the camp, the fire obscured by the encircling canvas. A gaunt man in tattered homespun groomed a mare. A leather collar looped around the man's neck, abraded skin showing scarlet above and below the band. As the horses' questing noses flung hay to the ground, two other slaves raked it back into neat stacks. Otherwise, the prince saw no people.

Elfrit did not answer, nor did Edward notice his steward's sudden silence. He stepped from the trees and approached the slave.

The man turned, clinging uncertainly to his brush and the horse's mane.

"You're free now," Edward said. He reached for the collar.

The slave shied away.

Grief welled in Prince Edward's heart as he sensed the man's terror. Surely, no one had ever made a kind movement toward the slave. "I'm not going to hurt you. I'm going to set you free." Gently, he reached for the man, catching a trembling shoulder. Tears stung the prince's eyes. Carefully, he unclipped the collar. The leather fell away, revealing scaled skin, grime, and callus.

"Lord," Elfrit warned softly. "I don't think . . ."

Edward ignored his steward. "You're free now. A free citizen of Alyndar."

The slave stood, utterly confused. Edward stepped past, gesturing the other two toward him. "Come. I'll free you, too."

They approached hesitantly, tossing nervous glances at the tents with each stride.

Suddenly, a heavyset, darkly-bearded man ducked beneath a hanging flap of canvas and emerged from a tent. He wore Hartrin's eagle on blue and red. A sword swung at his hip, and a whip coiled in his fist. "Hey!" He galloped toward the prince. "Who are you?" He glanced at the collarless slave. "And what the hell are you doing?"

Elfrit shrank into the foliage. Edward turned to face the stranger, his shoulders squared and his head proudly aloft. "I'm letting these people live the life the gods intended."

The slaves huddled, still. The Hartrinian stared. "What are you rambling about?"

"The Father never meant men to be used like animals. Freedom isn't a privilege. It's every man's right."

The Hartrinian whirled toward the gawking slaves. "You! Get back to work." Fast as a snake, he snapped the whip, the lash catching the two nearest across the back. One dropped to his knees with a cry of pain.

Outrage flared through Prince Edward. Springing forward, he hammered a fist into the slave master's cheek.

The blow landed squarely. Bone snapped beneath Edward's knuckles, and the force sent the Hartrinian staggering backward.

Brush rattled as Elfrit ran back toward the castle. Edward caught the downed slave's arm to help him rise.

"You stupid bastard!" The slave master surged toward Edward. The whip thrashed forward.

No one had ever attacked Prince Edward before, except in spar. Caught completely off-guard, he dodged too slowly. The scourge slashed his face, opening a stinging gash across his lips and cheek. Before he could speak, the whip whistled toward him again.

Knocking the slave from the path of the thong, Edward threw up an arm in defense. The whip stung, coiling around his sleeve. Seizing it near the base, Edward tore the handle from the slaver's hand. His mouth ached, and he tasted blood, but the rage boiling inside him came wholly in defense of freedom.

Voices sounded from the direction of the tents. Four swordsmen in red and blue dashed toward them.

Now holding the whip, Prince Edward turned on the slave master. "Gods! Have you no decency? Don't you know what you're inflicting?" He swung at the Hartrinian, hoping to give him a mild taste of his own cruelty.

But the slave master lurched for Edward as he talked. The wooden handle caught the Hartrinian a clouting blow across the ear. His eyes snapped closed. His knees buckled, and he collapsed, limp, to the ground.

The slaves skittered away. Shocked, Edward dropped the whip, wanting to assist the man he had not meant to knock unconscious. But the rushing Hartrinian guardsmen forced him to tend to his own defense. He crouched, fumbling for his only weapon, the utility dagger in his pocket.

Before he could draw it, the two Alyndarian sentries burst from between the trees. "Halt!" one shouted at the Hartrinians.

Two stopped, crouching in defense. The others slowed, glaring at Prince Edward. The guardsmen on both sides hovered, a single sword stroke from an act of war.

The slave master lay still. Blood darkened one ear, his head awkwardly twisted.

To have arrived so swiftly, the guardsmen must have followed Edward against his orders, yet that seemed the least of his concerns. No one moved, and the silence grew heavy with tension.

"Men, at ease," Edward commanded his soldiers.

The Alyndarian guardsmen fell back, but they did not lower their swords nor drop their guard. With the situation partially defused, one of the Hartrinians sheathed his blade. He crept toward the slave master, his movements deliberately without threat, knelt at the man's side, and felt for a pulse. Shortly, his lips creased into a frown. "He's dead." He rose to a crouch.

Dead. Guilt ground through Prince Edward, and tears turned the scene to a damp blur. He had never seen sudden, violent death before. Though trained for war, he had no experience with combat and valued life, any life, too much to take one without just cause. He never expected his first glimpse of killing to be an accident by his own hands. *I killed a man. I can't believe I killed a man.* He stared at the fist that had held the whip as if it belonged to someone else. "I'm sorry," he said sincerely. "I'm really sorry."

"Sorry?" The Hartrinian guardsman's face purpled. "Sorry? You murdered him in cold blood. By our law, we could execute you here and now."

The Alyndarians bulled their way between the Hartrinians and their prince. One spoke, "This is Alyndar. King Rikard determines the law here." His tone dropped to a snarl. "Besides, the man you so blithely condemn is Prince Edward Nargol. And I think the king may have something to say about the wound your man cast across his son's face."

The Hartrinian lapsed into silence. But another shouted, his anger not so easily quelled by thoughts of consequence. "There'll be blood price to pay!"

The other Alyndarian soldier replied sharply. "And perhaps there will be. That's for King Rikard to decide." He held a dignified, nonaggressive pose, but his tone made it clear he would fight to protect his prince, right or wrong.

"The prince's steward ran to fetch His Majesty and your ambassador. Until then, there's nothing any of us can do except wait." He let his sword sag slightly, watching until the Hartrinian did likewise before letting his blade drop to a less defensible position.

In increments, the other guards followed suit.

Prince Edward remained, letting the tears course down his cheeks, salt burning his wound. In his heart, he knew his cause was right, though a man lay dead. King Rikard was a just man who would see justice done, even if he did get too preoccupied with court matters to remember to champion the poor. *That's my job. And so long as my soul is pure and my causes noble, the gods will see them done.* Edward bowed his head in remorseful prayer and waited for his father to arrive.

Nightfall awoke, sprawled prone on a floor that reeked of stale urine. A mildewed dampness chilled his chest and abdomen, dulling the pain of each sleep-deepened breath. He did not move, ignoring the grimy curtain of hair that covered and tickled his face and the aches that pounded through every part of his body. With effort, he kept his breaths heavy, sluggish, and methodical, not wanting to alert anyone who might be watching that he had awakened.

Carefully, Nightfall explored his surroundings, using other senses than sight. The odor of excrement and sweat convinced him he was back in the king's dungeon, and the pervading coldness completed the image. He heard slight, low movements to his left, the metallic chitter of tightly-linked chains accompanied by the swish of fabric. *Guards.* Nightfall counted breaths. *Two of them. Crouched or sitting sentries.* Detecting no other movement, he knew that he must have been placed in a different cell. He was no longer in the main body of the dungeon amidst its other convicts.

The sentries seemed to pose no immediate threat, so Nightfall turned his attention to himself. The sharpest pain still radiated from the cracked ribs that stabbed his lungs. Nothing else seemed broken; but he ached in all parts, not just those that had struck the ground when he fell. Clearly, someone had battered him while he lay unconscious. Despite his predicament, the irony did not escape him. *Afraid to face me awake, so they pounded me while I was senseless. Not a great way to get information, but it's safe.*

One of the sentries spoke. "I still can't believe Rylinat and Dinnell are dead."

His companion made an ugly noise. Mail clinked as he moved, apparently rising. Something wooden scraped the floor.

The butt of a weapon, Nightfall guessed. He focused on every motion of the second guard, still feigning sleep.

Accepting the wordless noise as a response, the first guard spoke again. "What do you think the king'll do with the murdering bastard?" A sleeve whisked as he gestured, presumably in Nightfall's direction.

"If he's got any justice, he'll hack the demon into pieces and feed them to the dogs." Metal clanged against rusted steel.

Nightfall tried but failed to identify the sound. Inwardly, he tensed, seized with a sudden, intense sensation of being studied.

The scrape of wood against the bars was his only warning. Nightfall opened his eyes in time to see a spear butt racing toward his face. He dodged backward. His body protested the abrupt movement, sparking pain. The spear pole struck him a glancing blow across the shoulder. Lurching forward, he seized the wood and jerked.

Caught by surprise, with his momentum still forward, the guard scrambled to reverse direction.

"Holy Father!" The other sentry leapt to his feet.

The spear rattled through the bars, the guard surrendering it an instant before the sharpened tip would have torn through his palms.

Now, Nightfall got a good look at his prison. Three of the walls were solid granite, the fourth a barred door opening onto the hallway where the guards stood. Though single, its lock appeared every bit as complicated as the ones on his previous cell. Torches lined the walkway, guttering in a wisp of frigid breeze.

Nightfall crouched, brandishing the spear. The guards

skittered to either side of the cell's door, safe from a direct thrust of the weapon. The first speaker, a tall, slender youth, stared at Nightfall through dark eyes contrasting starkly with a blanched face and the taut line of his lips. The spearman, a meaty blond with a homely face, motioned to his companion. "Get Volkmier. He should be on his way."

The youth looked uncertainly from his companion to Nightfall.

Nightfall went statue-still. For now, he had no intention of using the spear; killing guards gained him nothing until he found a way to open the lock. In the distance, he heard the sound of footsteps approaching at a leisurely pace.

"Go!" the older guard insisted more loudly. "Get Volkmier!"

The voice of the red-haired chief prison guard wafted from the hallway. "I'm here, and I'm with His Majesty. What's the problem?"

"Nightfall's armed," the youth called back. "He's got a spear."

Volkmier swore violently, the tirade transforming to an abashed apology in mid-word. He ran up the hallway alone. His footsteps stopped briefly, and Nightfall heard the click of a drawing crossbow. Then Volkmier stepped into view.

Nightfall recognized the commander as the one who had threatened him from the parapets. Now, as then, the guard aimed his crossbow at Nightfall. Gaze locked on the prisoner, Volkmier crept around the younger sentry to stand directly before the cell door.

Though it seemed foolhardy, Volkmier's position was obviously carefully chosen. It gave him as clear a shot at Nightfall as Nightfall had at him. To attack, Nightfall would need to lunge, leaving the commander more than enough time to trigger his bolt. Even if Nightfall had had room to gather momentum to throw the spear, it would move slower and more awkwardly than the arrow.

"They say you're quick, Nightfall." Volkmier stood steady as a cliff, his feet braced and the crossbow well-aimed. "Let's see if you can drop that spear faster than I can shoot you."

Nightfall plunged to his haunches, releasing the spear. The metal head sparked against stone, then the pole thunked to the ground.

The head of Volkmier's arrow followed Nightfall's movement, but the guard did not fire. "Very good. Now, gently, kick the spear to the bars."

Nightfall scrutinized Volkmier's every motion. The guard seemed quick and confident, not at all the type to bluff. To resist now was folly. Even if he managed to slay Volkmier, he would still be trapped in Alyndar's dungeon, unlikely to live more than a few moments longer than his victim. He prodded the pole with one bare toe. Holding his hands away from his body, he indicated helpless surrender, using the edge of his foot to flick the spear to the edge of the bars.

Volkmier made an all but imperceptible movement with his head in the younger guard's direction. "Take it from him."

The youth scuttled forward, nervously raking at the spear through the bars.

Still menaced by Volkmier's crossbow, Nightfall resisted numerous opportunities to regain his weapon.

The sentry worked the spear from the cell, then moved well beyond reach. All three guards relaxed noticeably, though Volkmier's weapon remained steadily trained on Nightfall's chest. "His Majesty and Chancellor Gilleran wish to talk with Nightfall in private. You and I are going to patrol the hallways and see to it they're not disturbed." He addressed the sentries, though his attention never strayed from Nightfall. "As to you, Nightfall, if you do anything to threaten King Rikard, I'll see that you die in the worst agony I can devise. Then, I'll find you in hell and do it again. Do you understand?"

"I understand," Nightfall said, his voice controlled to a maddening calm.

Volkmier lowered the crossbow, and motioned the sentries off in opposite directions. "We'll talk later. I want to know how in hell he got that spear. And you'd better have a good answer."

The elder guard cringed as the two sentries rushed to obey their chief's command.

Volkmier scrutinized the lock and bars for tampering. Satisfied, he followed the younger sentry in the direction from which he had originally come. Beyond Nightfall's sight, a brief exchange followed. "Majesty, I can stay with you while you talk."

A rumbling tenor replied. "Thank you, Volkmier, no. Chancellor Gilleran and I can handle this ourselves."

A brief pause indicated hesitation, though the words that followed were spoken with brisk efficiency. "Yes, Sire. If we can be of service, you need only shout."

"Thank you, Volkmier," King Rikard repeated. A heavy pair of boots trod the corridor toward Nightfall's cell, accompanied by one who walked with a swifter, lighter step. Volkmier's clanking movements faded down the corridor.

Nightfall flattened his spine to the back of the cell, crouching beyond reach of the king and his minister. He dropped his mass to take the pressure from his aching legs, lungs, and abdomen. He had only glimpsed Alyndar's king from a distance. Rumor claimed the chancellor was a sorcerer, and Nightfall thought it best to keep his distance. Death in a normal fashion might send him to hell. But soulbound to a sorcerer, he would live on in eternal torment, his life-force chained to the sorcerer's will, his innate talent ripped from him and used again and again. Careful research had made him fairly certain that sorcerers found their victims by bribe, coercion, and eavesdropping or by studying the populace for the one in a thousand with a natal ability. The sorcerers did not seem to have any supernatural sense that allowed them to identify the gifted ones without information or demonstration.

As King Rikard Nargol and Chancellor Gilleran came into view, a thought froze Nightfall's blood in his veins. *Kelryn knows about my weight shifting. If she sold my identity, why not my talent as well?*

"So this is the notorious Nightfall." Rikard stared at the hunched figure, smashed to the back of his cell.

Nightfall returned the king's gaze, assessing both men. Though gray in hair and beard, Rikard had retained his densely-muscled frame, and his dark eyes sparkled with vigor and evident wit. Beside the imposing frame and striking coloring of his king, Chancellor Gilleran looked small and nondescript. Only his eyes disrupted the image: pale, squinting, and cold as death.

A long silence followed the pronouncement while Nightfall regained enough composure to speak with his usual boldness. "Sire, my name is Marak." After all that had happened, it seemed ludicrous to try to stay with his original lie, yet he had few alternatives. "I'm a sailor, not a criminal. Your men made a mistake."

The king glanced at his adviser, who shook his head, frowning.

Cued by the king's attention to Gilleran at a time when it made more sense to watch his prisoner, Nightfall studied the exchange.

Rikard turned to the convict again. "You deny being Nightfall?"

"I would be a fool to do otherwise." Nightfall combed dried blood from his beard with his fingers.

Again, the king looked at Gilleran.

The chancellor scowled. "Certainly, Sire, he speaks the truth." He opened his mouth, revealing straight rows of ivory teeth. "But that doesn't change the fact that he *is* Nightfall."

That explains why the king keeps consulting him. Some sort of truth detection, Nightfall presumed. *No doubt, a skill wrenched from some innocent.* He imagined a child writhing in the terror of a prolonged, sorcerous death, its soul shackled into a limitless agony of service.

"Who are you?" King Rikard directed another question at his prisoner.

Nightfall said nothing. Even if the query had had an answer, he would have chosen to sit in silence. *If I say nothing, the sorcerer can't tell if I'm lying.*

"Who are you?" Rikard repeated.

Another lengthy pause, the hush interrupted only by the rhythm of their breaths and the mottled shadows created by the flickering torches.

The king loosened a sigh of resignation. His manner became direct, and his tone matched the change. "Look,

Nightfall . . . Marak . . . whatever your name is. You have
nothing to gain by silence. Even if we drop the other
charges, you killed two of my guards. For that, I have the
right to execute you without trial and in any manner I
wish. I'm not stupid. I won't let you out of that cell until
you're dead. If you insist on ignoring my questions, I'll
call Volkmier and order him to fill you with arrows
through the bars." He glared at Nightfall, tolerance
clearly waning. "It's not as bloody as he'd like, but I
think he'd enjoy doing it slowly."

Trapped, Nightfall lowered himself to the floor. "And
if I do talk? You'll free me?"

This time, the king did not bother to consult his chancellor. "Actually, that's a possibility."

Nightfall kept his hopes in check. To believe such a
thing was absurd, futile at best. "Forgive my doubts, Sire,
but you did just remind me that I killed your guards.
What possible reason could you have for letting me go?"

"Personal reasons." King Rikard's brow furrowed and
his features darkened, as if he considered some distant
annoyance. "But first, I need some information from you.
Specifically, the truth."

Nightfall looked away.

"You have nothing to lose by honesty. And nothing to
gain by lying. Now, who are you?"

Nightfall considered. Silence or lies would seal his
fate. He dared not believe the truth might buy him freedom; but, at least, it might buy him time. "Call me
Marak. Call me Nightfall. What does it matter?"

King Rikard continued to press. "But who are you?
Who are you really?"

The question was nonsense. "I'm Nightfall. I'm Marak.
I'm a dozen others as well."

Gilleran examined Nightfall with the intensity of a
peasant choosing the plumpest chicken in a market
square. No emotion escaped his set jaw and rock-steady
gaze.

The king ignored his adviser, clinging to the question.
"What does your mother call you?"

"My mother is dead."

Rikard narrowed in. "What did she call you *before* she died?"

An image filled Nightfall's mind, blurred by time. He pictured the frail, slender form of his mother, her dark hair combed to a sheen, a red dress hugging curves sharpened by hunger. To him, she looked beautiful, yet her pinched features warned him of coming violence. He shrank from the image. "She called me 'Boy' mostly. Sometimes 'Rat' or 'Stupid.' "

King Rikard glanced sharply at Gilleran, who shrugged. "Your *mother* called you those things?"

Bitterness tainted Nightfall's words. "Some of us don't grow up on hugs and kisses and silk."

The king seemed to ponder the words far too long before returning to his original inquiry. "But, surely, she gave you a name."

Nightfall searched his memory. Twenty-six years had passed since his mother's death and thirty, at least, since she had used his name. "I believe it was Sudian, Sire. Though I haven't heard it since I was a toddler."

"Then it should work just fine," King Rikard announced cryptically. He pulled at his beard, looking thoughtful. "Sudian what?"

Nightfall stared. The question made no sense to him. "Huh?"

The king copied Nightfall's defensive tone. "Well, forgive my growing up on hugs and kisses and a family name. But isn't it customary in most countries to give a man a second name based on his parentage? Sudian some man's son?"

Nightfall drew his knees to his chest, centralizing his balance. "Sudian Nomansson."

"No man's son? Are you protecting your father? There's no need. It's not his fault his son is a murderer."

"I have no father." Nightfall stated it definitively, hoping to end the conversation, yet with little doubt it would continue. About Nightfall's history, the king's curiosity seemed relentless.

As expected, Rikard pressed. "Every man has a father."

"Not me," Nightfall said shamelessly, catching and holding the king's dark gaze. "My mother was a prostitute. Any man could be my father." The memories surfaced, the years robbing them of emotion. He recalled lurking in the shadows of the street, huddled against the cold, his thin, unpatched homespun of little comfort against the wind. He remembered trailing his mother and her latest client to the bare, dusty room scarcely warmer than the alleyways, watching them writhe and moan between threadbare sheets. By two years of age, he had learned to disappear before the session ended to avoid his mother's teary-eyed rages against her lot and the child who, she insisted, cost her dearly in food, money, and time, though she gave him none of those. By the time he was three, he had learned to search her clients' pockets for crumbs and spare change, inherently knowing that to take too much might turn their wrath against her.

"A prostitute," the king repeated. "Hardly no man's son. I should think that would make you every man's son."

The cavalier observation raised a wave of malice. Instantly, Nightfall's thoughts were flung backward to the winter of his eighth year. Then, he had returned home from seeking food to find a stranger battering his mother while he ravished her. Nightfall had witnessed the final blow to the throat that turned her breaths to terminal gasps. A quarter of a century later, he still pictured the man with a vivid detail that could not be erased from memory. *That pig and ones like him will never be my father.* "No man came forward to claim me as his, and I am no man's son."

The king and his chancellor waited, eyeing Nightfall expectantly.

Grimly, Nightfall completed the recollection, as his mind always did. His mother's murderer had become Nightfall's first victim, slaughtered by an enraged eight-year-old with a table knife and a lucky stab. The memory would remain for eternity: blood splashing, warm and chokingly thick with an odor like sea things dying on a beach; terror and fear robbing him of anger, yet leaving the dull triumph of revenge.

Oblivious to Nightfall's crisis of memory, King Rikard

finished. "Well. No man's son, then. More importantly, are the charges against you true?"

Nightfall glanced at Chancellor Gilleran. The sorcerer stood with his arms folded and his legs crossed. A half-smile played about his lips. He nodded slightly, as if to feed the answer to the prisoner.

"Some of them," Nightfall admitted.

"You have killed?"

"From necessity." Nightfall kept his attention on Gilleran, awaiting a reaction. Necessity depended on definition.

Gilleran stared blankly. He did not challenge Nightfall's claim.

"You've stolen in every country in the world?"

Nightfall nodded once, not liking the direction of the questioning, yet knowing the king already had enough proof and reason to execute him.

"So you would say you're familiar with every land? Their ways, their laws, their geography? The ways to avoid or escape trouble?"

The sudden shift in King Rikard's approach surprised Nightfall. He raised his brows, trying to read the king's intentions, though he suspected he did not have enough information to do so successfully. *What does he want to hear? What do I have that he wants?* "Sire, I could map them in detail with a stick and a handful of dirt. But I won't reveal my secret haunts or name those who have helped me. I'd rather die in agony."

The king pursed his lips, rocking in place. His hands dropped to his sword belt, and he hooked a thumb over the leather. "I have more questions, Sudian Nomansson. But, in the meantime, I have a proposition."

Nightfall rose to a crouch, instinctively finding the more defensible posture preferable, even for wholly mental pursuits. He knew too much of street scams to fall prey to subterfuge, but trapped and slated for instant execution, he currently found himself in the worst position for bargaining.

King Rikard paced before Nightfall's cell. "As you may know, I have a son."

"Prince Leyne Nargol," Nightfall supplied.

Rikard smiled, stopping in his tracks, but he did not bother to look at Nightfall. "My younger son. Edward. Ned, we call him. A good boy with the best intentions, but terribly inexperienced and naive." He resumed pacing. "Yesterday, Ned accidentally killed a man, a member of a diplomatic entourage. And that cost me too much."

It seemed odd to Nightfall that the king would disparage his son to a criminal. Yet he supposed any discussion with one soon to be executed made no difference.

King Rikard came to an abrupt halt, seizing the bars in both hands and staring directly at Nightfall. "I paid blood price and quieting fees, but the gold means nothing. The problem is Ned."

Nightfall remained crouched and ready as a cornered animal, yet the direction of the king's needs confused him. He doubted Rikard wanted his son murdered, though the ways of royalty sometimes pitted reputation against propriety. He waited for the king's narrative to clarify his needs.

"Ned has cost me esteem, potential allies, thirty-six personal stewards, and my patience. Evidently, too much hugs and kisses and silk." He amended. "More to the point, too much time spent with philosophers and idealists." Having passed nearly beyond Nightfall's vision, the king spun about and resumed his walk in the opposite direction. "Luckily for Alyndar, Ned has no claim to the kingdom nor any of her lands. My mind is made up. I'm sending him away to get himself propertied and, hopefully, to learn a little reality at the same time."

"And free the kingdom of the consequences of his good intentions." Chancellor Gilleran traced the king's route with his gaze, otherwise completely still.

Nightfall waited, still seeing no need for his services.

"Don't misunderstand me. I love both my sons." Rikard turned at the far end of his course and headed back again. "If I send Ned out, I have little doubt he'll get himself killed within one moon cycle. If he doesn't fall prey to footpads or schemers, his own overbearing virtue will offend the wrong person." He halted directly in front of Nightfall.

Nightfall could see potential in the king's words, but he

found it impossible to translate theory to practicality. *Apparently, he wants me to protect Ned from the world and himself. But no one could be stupid enough to trust his son's life to me.*

"I want you to become Ned's squire."

Nightfall blinked. Otherwise, he made no sound or motion. *This is too good and too easy to be true.* Immediately, his mind boggled with possibilities. It would prove simple enough to rob and murder the young prince. Once free, Nightfall would never be caged again.

"There are conditions, of course."

"Of course." Nightfall waited, seeing no reason not to promise anything, except for Gilleran's truth spell. Still, he might get away with any carefully worded vow.

The king back-stepped, gesturing at Chancellor Gilleran. "As you may know, my adviser is a sorcerer."

Nightfall hid his aversion.

"He has a spell with a strange name I can't pronounce. I call it oath-binding. The way it's worked in the past, you and I agree to terms and Gilleran seals it with his spell."

Nightfall clutched his knees, now bothered enough to consider refusing the king's offer on principle. He hated magic and sorcerers, and not just their abominable methods of gaining skills. Despised and feared by nearly everyone, sorcerers seemed devious, cruel, and twisted by the nature of their abilities and the obtainment of them. Yet his other option was certain death.

The king continued, "Should either of us break a condition of the spell, his soul would die by sorcery. As I understand it, that means eternal torment for the spirit, which would become the property of the sorcerer." He glanced at Gilleran, and Nightfall thought he saw Rikard shiver.

Gilleran remained still, looking like a washed-out caricature of a man, though his eyes revealed strength and joyful cruelty.

Nightfall presumed all of the terms of the oath would be placed on him, leaving no opportunity for the king to break a promise nor die in magical agony. "And these conditions?" he asked, not at all certain he wanted to know.

King Rikard pulled a rolled parchment from the pocket of his robe. Opening it, he read. "First, you will serve Prince Ned with his long-term, best interests in mind at all times." The king looked up. "You will be obedient to Ned. You will address him always as 'Master' and, to others, use his full name and title."

Nightfall frowned.

"But, where Ned's judgment fails, your obedience to his welfare must always take precedence over obedience to his words, no matter the personal consequences."

I'm not calling any man "Master." Nightfall found the suggestion distasteful. "In other words, I have to do what's best for him, even if he whips me for it."

King Rikard gave a wry chuckle. "Whipping is the last thing you have to worry about from Ned. He may try your patience to the edge of eternity, he may command you to do things that have no basis in any reality that supports common sense. But he won't physically abuse you. That I can promise."

Gilleran tapped the king's arm in warning.

"But I won't," Rikard amended quickly. "For the purposes of the oath-bond, it would be best if I made no vows." He looked back at the parchment. "Second, you must see to it that Ned gets landed by Yrtish's Harvest Moon."

Five months. Nightfall knew survival. He had paid no attention to methods of obtaining land and had little experience with politics, but he thought it better not to reveal his ignorance. Apparently, the king felt confident of Nightfall's abilities and with good reason. *If anyone could keep Ned alive and landed, I could.*

"Third, you cannot harm or willingly cause or allow to be harmed Ned, Leyne, myself, Gilleran, or any noble, servant, or guardian of Alyndar's court. And fourth, Nightfall is declared executed. You take a new name, identity, and appearance, and cannot tell anyone who you used to be."

"That's it?" Nightfall asked sarcastically.

"That's it," the king acknowledged.

Nightfall immediately found the gap in the plan. "And, once I've finished serving your son, you execute me."

"If you fulfill the provisions of this oath, if Ned is landed by Harvest Moon, the oath-bond is automatically dissolved. You become a free man with no debts or obligations and a chance to start life fresh. Since all conditions of the agreement disappear once the oath is gone, I can't force lasting demands on you. It's in my best interests to keep you happy, to give Nightfall no reason to re-emerge. Do you agree to the terms?"

Nightfall considered. If he refused, he would die. He found the thought of serving a guileless fool unpalatable; yet, at least, he would be a living servant. Possibly, he could find a way of escaping the terms of the oath-bond if he found himself unable to fulfill them. *And I have to consider the possibility that the king is lying about the workings of the spell.* That last thought haunted Nightfall, but magic was rare and every spell as different as the innate ability from which it sprang. Having no experience with this particular spell, he had no way of guessing its weaknesses. "May I ask some questions?"

"You may."

"When Ned becomes landed, I'm free of all parts of the oath-bond?"

"Correct."

"Am I also acquitted of all crimes?"

King Rikard hesitated. "Yes. At least in Alyndar, though that doesn't give you freedom to commit more. So long as you take a new identity, I don't think the other countries will try you either. They'll take my word that Nightfall's dead. And, in a manner of speaking, he will be. As I said, it's in my best interest to keep you happy, to see that you have enough money and stature to prevent the need for murder or theft."

That had an undeniable appeal. Survival had driven Nightfall to an unprecedented spree of crime. Status and wealth would mean he never had to sin again, and a new identity would end decades of running.

"What if one of us dies? Or the chancellor?"

King Rikard deferred the question to his sorcerer.

Gilleran cleared his throat. "Once cast, my life has no

connection to the spell. My death or that of His Majesty, may the gods prevent it, will not affect the bond. Your death, of course, would dissolve it." He barely moved his mouth as he talked, expressionless as a corpse, his eyes hollow and unrevealing. "Though it would gain you nothing."

Except a chance to die a normal death, instead of becoming a tormented soul bound to a sorcerer. Nightfall kept the thought to himself, though Gilleran answered it naturally.

"Don't get **any** ideas about taking your own life the day before the deadline. Suicide violates any oath-bond. Your spirit would still belong to me."

The words chilled Nightfall, all the more effective for their deadpan delivery and timing that made it seem as if Gilleran had read his mind. "I need time to think."

"Very well," the king said. "I'll give you time. You have until I count to twenty." He took a deep breath. "One. Two . . ."

Sighing, Nightfall let King Rikard's words disappear into the rhythms of his thoughts. He had become too dedicated to survival to choose death over life, no matter how conditional.

". . . Five. Six . . ."

Rising, Nightfall approached the bars. "What do I have to do?"

Chapter 3

A week after its casting, the oath-bond still tingled through Nightfall like blood flow returning to an awakening limb, the feeling a constant, nagging reminder of its presence. Alone in a room in Alyndar's castle, he perched on a wooden chair, studying his distantly familiar face in the mirror. A series of scouring baths had removed the grime and dyes that had become a constant feature of so many of his personae. The ever-present beard was gone, his hair trimmed into a fashionably short style. The soft, thick locks glistened mahogany brown, wound through with reddish highlights, so different from Nightfall's black curls, Marak's dark tangles and Frihiat's bleached curtain, a color Nightfall had not seen since his childhood. The olive skin tones were replaced by his natural, fair coloring. The missing scraggle of beard revealed a strong chin, and the unkempt froth of head and facial hair no longer hid his straight nose and ears. The painted scars that distinguished his various characters had washed away, leaving a face without Balshaz's pocks, the slashes from Telwinar's plowing accident, or Nightfall's crisscross of ancient dagger wounds that made him look so frightening.

Even Nightfall's body seemed different. He had never worn a country's colors before, and the royal purple and silver of Alyndar's tabard gave him a regal air that seemed horribly misplaced. Without padding and a wicked aura of confidence, he had lost Nightfall's imposing build. Telwinar's limp had disappeared, and playing polio-stricken Frihiat had required a hundred masterfully twisted performances. Though accustomed to a myriad of different appearances, Nightfall found the reality of Sudian Nomansson more striking and frightening than any alias. Without the scars, squints, affectations, and beard, he looked a decade younger than his thirty-four years and as frail as the mother who had borne him. Stunted by starvation in his youth, he stood a hand's breadth shorter than most men and never seemed to eat enough to pack weight onto his narrow frame. Long, silent stalks, chases, and escapes had endowed him with quickness and agility, but his mass-shifting skill had obviated the need for bulk.

Only Nightfall's eyes seemed familiar to him. Feigned drooping lids, roving irises, and shaven lashes had not changed their color nor the striking resemblance to his mother's own. Crowded by sodden tangles of hair and a coiled, filthy beard, they had appeared more black. Now, the openness of his face and the pallor of his skin accentuated their deep blue, lending him a dashing innocence that inspired a chuckle of amusement. *Even my old friend, Dyfrin, would never recognize me.* Thoughts of the sandy-haired father-figure turned Nightfall's laugh into a smile. He could not help but consider the advice Dyfrin would have given him now:

"Don't think of it as doing the king a favor; he's done you one. By removing your identity, he's removed all your enemies. He's given you a chance at a new life and a noble cause."

A noble cause, indeed. Using my knowledge and experience to keep a spoiled fool alive. Faking loyalty to a child pampered and admired for no better reason than his parentage and with no understanding of human nature or the real world. Nightfall sighed, the grin disappearing into a wash of bitterness. It bothered him to have a hand in gaining power for another noble ignorant of his followers' needs, a leader who tended to politics and power while his peasants suffered from hunger, disease, and violence. And, to Nightfall, Prince Edward seemed the worst kind of ruler, a crusader who championed causes he did not and could never understand in ways that accomplished nothing but death and an earful of moralistic raving.

A week trapped in a castle room and daily sessions with Chancellor Gilleran, during which he learned general servant behavior, had left Nightfall anxious to leave Alyndar despite the persistent pain of fading bruises and broken ribs only partially healed. He kept his weight low to assist the healing process and resisted the urge to unlock the door and escape. The warning jangle of the oath-bond made him certain he would not get far. Although temporary freedom, such as a nightly study of the castle hallways, would gain him information about its layout and, perhaps, its rashly impulsive prince, it did not seem worth the risk. Hampered by mending wounds and ignorance, he dared not chance an encounter with Alyndar's guardsmen now, in Sudian guise. Cooperation, or at least its appearance, might gain him freedom. Causing trouble or ruining his disguise would seal his death.

Nightfall glanced away from the mirror, turning his attention to the now-familiar furnishings. A simple, wooden table supported the mirror. A stiff-bristled brush, a square hand mirror the size of his palm, and a bowl of water lay on the table's flat surface. A straw pallet filled one corner of the room, draped with a blanket. Nightfall's seat was the only other piece of furniture.

A key rattled in the door lock in a pattern Nightfall recognized: left, right, left, followed by a click as the tumblers fell into place. *Gilleran.* No one else had entered Nightfall's room since they had moved him from the dungeon after a private "execution" attended only by the king and his chancellor. Nevertheless, he scrutinized every sound, identifying patterns. Once certain of the other's identity, he rose, back-stepped, and lowered his center of gravity. The oath-bond would keep him from harming the sorcerer, but he still felt more comfortable in a fighting posture.

The door swung open. Gilleran slipped inside, then closed the panel behind him. He wore tailored silks in royal colors more vivid than Nightfall's linens, and he carried a staff decorated from head to base with carven fists. His frigid stare went straight to Nightfall, and a slight smile stirred the corners of his lips. "Prepared for another lesson?"

Nightfall did not trust any of the customs Gilleran had taught; though, so far, they seemed logical. The sorcerer had every reason to sabotage his education. "What I'm prepared to do is leave. I've wasted a week of my five months already."

"Ah." Gilleran slumped onto the chair, glancing at his own innocuous features in the mirror. "Impatience has killed many men."

"So have I." Nightfall remained in position. "But some things can't be avoided." He spoke with casual simplicity, but he doubted Gilleran missed the underlying threat.

Gilleran loosed a grunt that might pass for laughter. He spun the staff, letting it strike his opposite palm. "Avoided, maybe not. But detained. . . ?" He grinned openly, not bothering to finish.

The comment only emphasized what Nightfall had already surmised, that Gilleran wished to delay the task as long as possible in order to increase the chance of failure. The urge seized him to methodically slice the grin from Gilleran's face, but the first spark of such thought tightened the oath-bond like a vise. Air seemed to leave the room, and pressure crushed in on him from every side. He dropped the image before the sensation could intensify from discomfort to pain, and he forced himself to take deep, calming breaths. The poke of healing ribs into his lung seemed accustomed and natural in the wake of the oath-bond's warning.

Gilleran studied Nightfall's silence, demanding no response before speaking again. "We can't send you off injured. It'd be cruel. You're still hurting." Suddenly, he swung the staff for Nightfall's chest.

Nightfall caught the staff and ducked beneath the attack. He jerked the weapon from Gilleran's hands, instinctively gathering momentum for a return strike. The oath-bond caught him low, spearing, red-hot, through his belly. He collapsed, dropping the staff. Wood thunked to the floor, rolling with a hollow clamor that seemed endless. Pain stole all thought of violence, then both waned to angry memory, leaving him only the background tingling of magic and the ache of old injuries incited by sudden motion and the fall. Nightfall staggered to an awkward crouch.

Gilleran retrieved his staff, deliberately stomping on Nightfall's hand as he moved. "I'd delight in staying to talk, but I mustn't be late for Edward's farewell banquet. Of course, I'll have to let King Rikard know the prince's squire won't be fit for travel for another *month*." He turned his back on Nightfall deliberately, as if goading an attack.

Nightfall ignored the challenge, rising with caution meant to appear cowed. His fingers throbbed, but he did not acknowledge the pain. He would not give Gilleran the satisfaction.

Alyndar's banquet hall buzzed with conversation. Seated at the head table, King Rikard hid annoyance behind an expressionless mask. It would not do to display discomfort to a roomful of Alyndarian nobles and foreign dignitaries and ambassadors; but he could not keep his gaze from shifting repeatedly to the empty seat at his right hand. The guest of honor, Prince Edward Nargol, was inexcusably late to his own farewell celebration.

Flowers from the courtyard gardens decorated the seven tables in a rainbow of colors. Servants had twined them into vivid chains broken, at intervals, by clusters floating on silver bowls. Though striking, their varied perfumes paled beneath the rich aroma of roasted pork, beef, and pheasant. Over the last hour, Rikard had watched his guests' moods pass from eager to curious to restlessly hungry. Irritation would have to follow, one that would not bode well for his future dealings with these people, whatever those might be.

King Rikard glanced to his left. Prince Leyne met his father's gaze, one raised brow indicating a silent question propriety would not allow him to voice aloud. Rikard returned an equally subtle shrug. Edward's delay would require a satisfactory explanation he knew, from experience, he was unlikely to get. Bothered by his current line of thought, Rikard concentrated on the competent routine of the rest of his retinue. Guards ringed the periphery of the banquet hall, his personal half-dozen forming a rigid semicircle at a comfortable distance that left room for the serving staff. Servants scurried through the hall, tending pre-dinner needs and weathering the aggravation of nobles kept waiting inappropriately long. Though busy, they wasted no movements, their charges predetermined, their tasks shared without argument. He saw pattern to their every effort that defused some of the raw tension and reminded himself to discuss bonuses for every one with the chief organizer of kitchen help.

Across the hall, the double doors to the banquet hall slammed open. One panel clipped a passing serving boy, sprawling him. The goblet he carried rang against the boards, splashing a wild arc of wine across a tapestry. The guards nearest the door snapped to attention, glaives falling into position, hemming the entryway in case of danger. Caught off-guard, the guest-announcer skittered behind the guards, then craned his neck to identify the newcomer.

Rikard bit his lip and stifled his rage, knowing who had to stand behind any act of monumental embarrassment. He felt the reassuring pressure of a hand on his arm, and he appreciated his elder son's perception and sympathy.

Younger Prince Edward Nargol stomped into the banquet hall, half-leading, half-dragging a middle-aged peasant in rags who seemed bewildered and more than a bit frightened. A troup of guards trailed him. Their varied constituency convinced Rikard they had joined him in singles and pairs over time, each trying to avert disaster in his own fashion. The king saw no sign of Edward's steward. Either the long-legged prince had left Elfrit far behind or the attendant had quit like so many others.

The prince shoved through the crossed polearms, never losing his grip on the peasant's sleeve. The sentries withdrew their weapons and stepped aside respectfully. "Prince Edward Nargol," the announcer called unnecessarily though Edward had already passed him.

Rikard sighed and rose, considering the best way to alleviate the situation. Only his practiced composure rescued him from blinding fury.

All conversation ceased. Even the servants went still as

Edward strode toward the head table, sweeping the ragged stranger through the aisles between tables. Rikard's guards tightened toward their king, though surely their colleagues had already insured that no weapons would enter the banquet hall. Even Prince Edward's authority and impetuousness could not have brooked this formality. Rikard waved his own sentries back. He would have preferred to speak with Edward alone, leaving the peasant with his guards, but the scene the younger prince might create if he tried did not seem worth the trouble. He trusted his instincts as a warrior, and those told him the stranger could cause him no harm even should he wish to attempt such a foolhardy and obviously suicidal action. Since no open food or dishes yet sat on the table, he did not need to fear poisoning either.

"Father," Edward called as he approached, strong voice booming over the hush.

Rikard kept his wince internal, waiting until the prince reached polite speaking distance before giving a soft but firm reply. "Edward, sit." He gestured to the chair to his right. A lecture and explanation would come only after the guests had food. He would not prolong their wait beyond the delay his errant son had already caused.

As usual, however, Edward would not let the matter drop. "Yes, Father, but not until a chair is brought for Dithrin." He back-slapped the shaggy peasant who looked greenish and shaky, as if he might vomit at any moment. Brown eyes dodged the king's gaze and came to rest at his feet. The peasant bowed with an exuberance that nearly sent him crashing to the floor, and Edward's sudden grip was all that saved him from collapse. "He's an Alyndarian subject, and he's hungry." Edward looked pained. "Father, there are hungry people under your rule."

Is this the first you realized that? Shocked by his son's profound ignorance, Rikard turned his attention fully on Edward. *More sheltered than even I thought.* His arrangement with Nightfall pleased and pained him at once. Education and experience could only help Edward, yet he could not help feeling as if he were throwing a crippled lamb to the mercy of wolves. The stares of a hundred silent courtiers seemed to burn into his flesh, awaiting his next words; and the need to face such scrutiny made him certain. *It changes him, or he dies. Either way, it improves the kingdom.* He felt a twinge of guilt at the thought. Hard as he tried, Rikard could not apply his usual ruthless justice to the situation. The features of the queen he had loved, so clear in Edward's face, haunted him. Somehow, he felt as if she judged him from the holy Father's paradise.

Dithrin's demeanor relaxed slightly now that he no longer stood beneath the king's scrutiny. Prince Edward seized on his father's quiet. He glanced about, apparently for a servant. Finding none, he directed a guard instead. "Please fetch a chair. He can sit by my side."

"No," Rikard commanded.

The guard remained in place. A shiver racked Dithrin, and he trembled in anticipation.

Rikard continued, regaining command with an accustomed, quiet dignity. "Seat Dithrin at the seventh table." He pointed toward the gathering of nontitled folk, those of the lower class invited because of favors performed or distant ties of blood. "And feed him as any guest." He turned his attention to his younger son, temper trickling free of his control. Better to get the boy out of his sight than to risk a shouting match or loss of self-respect. "Ned, go to the tower chapel. We'll talk." He jabbed a finger toward the exit, turning his back to make it clear he would hear no argument. He addressed a guard. "Tell the kitchen to start dinner. We'll not wait for Prince Edward any longer."

The guard hurried off to relay his message to the proper servants. Dithrin scarcely waited for his escort, apparently eager to escape the thoughtful gazes and the presence of a king within his right to slay him for intruding. Prince Edward headed for the door, pausing only long enough to assure himself that Dithrin was properly tended to before disappearing into the hallway. As the guests returned to their own conversations, Rikard gave one last, whispered command. "See to it Ned makes it to the chapel and causes no trouble along the way."

The guards who had accompanied Edward rushed to a task Rikard did not envy. The king glanced at his chancellor, who sat at Leyne's left hand. Gilleran shrugged, then shook his head with an indulgence reserved for teenagers. The wordless communication brought the first stirrings of calm, restoring the composure Rikard would need to bring the visitors comfortably through a banquet interrupted by a family fight and an absent guest of honor. As usual, he appreciated the sorcerer's presence; few gentry had served him better or longer. Their association had spanned enough years that Gilleran seemed not only a competent adviser with a broad perspective, but one able to anticipate the decisions and needs of his king as well.

The arrival of food preempted any need for King Rikard to announce excuses for the prince's behavior. Disgruntled impatience turned to contented exuberance as servants piled plates with steaming vegetables and meat.

Rikard had only just taken his first mouthful when a servant addressed him from the place Edward would have occupied. Though so low no one else could hear, the voice startled the king. Apparently, the servant had been standing there for quite some time, waiting for the king to acknowledge his presence.

"Wine, Sire?"

King Rikard nodded without bothering to look. He heard the light splash of liquid filling his glass. Then the sound ended, but he still felt the man beside him. He took another mouthful of turnips, chewed, and swallowed. The servant remained in place, his patience or sluggishness becoming an annoyance. Rikard surmised that the servant could not have paused as long as it seemed, or his guards would have interfered. He turned his attention to the wine-server, his shrewd, brown eyes meeting blue ones so dark they bordered on black. He had seen the face twice, but once so different he would never have credited it to the same man had he not had a hand in the transformation. Surprise tightened every muscle, his mouth fell open, and his eyes widened.

Nightfall lowered and raised his head in a gracious nod. Mahogany hair spilled around his face, hiding his features. He had combed it across his forehead and straight to the sides, in a manner more suited to a young page, yet he managed to wear the style without appearing silly.

King Rikard set his jaw, eyes narrowing, cursing himself for his lapse. There was a strategy to dealing with strong men, whether allies or enemies, and displaying astonishment did not bode well for maintaining an upper hand. "What are you doing out?" he hissed.

"I'm sorry, Sire." Nightfall's tone did not match his words, the title spoken more from forbearance than respect. "And I'm sorry to disrupt your dinner. I just wanted to let you know I'm ready to leave whenever you wish." He added carefully, "And I'd hoped to catch a glimpse of my charge." The dark eyes made a quick scan of the head table. He smiled briefly during the search, just about the time his gaze fell on Gilleran.

Rikard remained steadily focused on Nightfall, locking his features into the blandest expression possible, though the precaution seemed ill-timed. He had already lost the advantage by allowing Nightfall's abrupt appearance to so obviously startle him. In his present state of mind, he would have preferred to send Edward out immediately, even despite the banquet; but to do so would not only violate etiquette, it would further tip the balance of mastery into Nightfall's favor. That idea irked him more than any of Edward's antics. "What about your injuries?"

"I've suffered worse, Sire."

King Rikard did not doubt the words, but Chancellor Gilleran had brought the news that Nightfall requested more healing time only an hour previously.

"If wounds alone could hinder me, my flesh would have poisoned vultures long ago." Nightfall added, "Sire." At least Gilleran's lessons in procedure had not been fully wasted.

King Rikard considered the death euphemism only momentarily. In Nightfall's case, it seemed apt. He had more concerning events to ponder: Nightfall choosing to remain imprisoned in a room he apparently could have escaped at any time, his sudden decision to leave so soon after his insistence on delay, the unassuming mannerisms that had not yet raised the concerns of the guards against a servant tarrying overlong at the king's side. *Trying to keep me off guard with unpredictability.* It seemed plausible. Chaos could unbalance any man. For the hundredth time, King Rikard worried about his arrangement, though not for long. Nothing remained to consider. Once Gilleran had cast the oath-bond, the time for choices had ended and only the fulfillment of the magic's constraints remained.

Nightfall did not move, head lowered, a curtain of hair hiding his face and making him seem more harmless child than demon.

The benign image unnerved the king more than the hostile glances they had exchanged in the dungeon. He cleared his throat, delaying to keep anything but command from entering his tone. "Very well, then. If you go straight back to your room and stay there, I'll send an escort for you in the morning." Finally, he spotted the means to regain the edge in their unofficial spar for dominance. He raised the glass of wine Nightfall had just poured and took a long sip. Though a simple action, it displayed his disdain for Nightfall's dangerousness, reminding him that the oath-bond left him unable to poison Rikard or any of his entourage.

Nightfall raised his head, a flicker in his eyes all that revealed acknowledgment of the king's bold gesture. Without another word, he headed toward the exit.

Nightfall awakened early the following morning, preparing himself for travel with an ease that seemed a mockery of his previous routine. He searched the room for loose fixtures. King Rikard had promised to fully outfit him with traveling gear and weapons, but old habits would not die. His pockets, he knew, held several handkerchiefs and the sapphire ring he had stolen from *Raven*'s captain. He knelt, examining the only chair. It stood steady, its legs composed of neatly rounded and sanded bars. Four support dowels spanned the distance between them. Aware the chair would still balance missing two or three of the inner rods, Nightfall pulled them apart and secreted one in his pocket. Rising, he took the smaller mirror and the brush as well.

Satisfied, Nightfall crouched on the pallet to await the

escort who would introduce him to Ned. He wondered how the prince would look and act, but he did not dwell on the thought or waste time forming a mental image. Soon enough, he would meet his master. Preconceived notions served no purpose. His thoughts could not change Ned's appearance or attitudes; they could only mislead him.

Again, Nightfall let his mind wander to Dyfrin and his last lecture before business had led them in opposite directions: "Marak, you've got to make yourself another friend sometime. It's not that hard, and it's worth the trouble. First, treat everyone—lord, lady, idiot, or slave—as an equal. Power and knowledge live in unexpected places. Second, never lend your coppers, but give them freely. Few things make friendship faster than kindness and nothing destroys it quicker than obligations. And lastly, never give a man reason to doubt your loyalty."

I followed your advice, Dyfrin. I found a friend, and look where it got me. Nightfall lowered his head, mind suddenly filled with Kelryn's visage. His hands balled to fists, and the vision disappeared beneath a red veil of rage. *Befriending her cost me my freedom, my dignity, decades of perfecting identities, nearly my life, and possibly my soul.* Trusting in no one had spared Nightfall the pain that his mother had inflicted through his childhood, the mixed messages of love and brutality, the compliments that, in the same breath, twisted into belittling insults and shouted obscenities. *Loyalty unreturned is only service. Money unreturned is simply stolen. And I'll treat a man as an equal the day he outwits me. Anyone who can't is nothing more than a victim waiting to be parted from his riches.* A smile touched his lips, every bit as cruel as Chancellor Gilleran's. *Whatever else I accomplish in my five months of freedom, I will make Kelryn regret her betrayal. She won't cross me or anyone else again.*

A knock on the door dispelled Nightfall's train of thought. A man's voice wafted from the hallway beyond. "Sudian?" He did not wait for confirmation. "I've been told to take you to Prince Edward."

Nightfall sprang from the pallet and crossed the room,

taking one last glimpse of the stranger in the mirror as he passed. He straightened his breeks, readjusted his tabard, and opened the door.

A middle-aged steward confronted him. The man's dark eyes rolled downward as he glanced over his charge, then returned to Nightfall's face. His chin tilted upward, his disdain tangible; he was obviously unimpressed with what he saw.

In the last twenty years, Nightfall had had little experience with this sort of treatment. In the guise of Nightfall, his reputation and appearance inspired terror at worst and, more often, grudging respect.

"Come with me." The steward turned, gesturing to Nightfall to follow.

Nightfall trailed the steward in silence, making a game of noting the myriad openings the man left for his own murder. Having exhausted imagining the objects in his own pockets as the weapons, Nightfall quietly identified the steward's belongings through creases and bulges in his clothing. When the steward paused beneath an ornate chandelier, the support for which spanned the wall near Nightfall's hand, the oath-bonded squire found suppressing his laughter all but impossible. And, by the time they exited into the courtyard, Nightfall had relieved his guide of two pocket knives, a pouch of silver, a tinderbox, his wedding band, and a candle molded in the shape of a frog. Nightfall was just considering removing the man's vest without his knowledge when the doors swung open and the activity in the king's courtyard seized his attention.

The oath-bond seemed to shudder, aching within him. Men in servants' livery scurried between three horses, heaping packs and objects onto a rangy dark chestnut and a sturdy bay mare. The third horse, a white gelding, carried only one bundle behind its jeweled saddle. It pawed the ground repeatedly, tossing its head in sudden bursts that sent the groom clutching its halter into a staggering dance.

Nightfall disliked the pale riding horse at once. Like many animals chosen for beauty, it had few manners, and its beacon coloring and grandeur would preclude evasive actions and draw the eye of every highwayman. *Might just as well paint "I'm wealthy; please rob me" across its side.* Another thought surfaced. *That'd actually be safer. Most bandits can't read.*

Several paces from the activity, King Rikard stood amid a half-dozen nobles. Beside him, Chancellor Gilleran watched the bustle with his arms folded across his chest, his face its usual empty mask. One broad-shouldered youth wore a mail hauberk and leather leggings beneath a meticulously pressed purple surcoat and a silver cape. A broad sword graced his belt. A helmet dangled from one gloved hand. Golden hair covered his head, sheening white, every lock neatly combed and tended. Round, pink cheeks betrayed him as a teenager, yet his thick frame bore no trace of adolescent gawkiness. Still, trained to notice subtleties, Nightfall recognized a mild tremor of excitement and an uncertainty to the youngster's motions that would smooth with age and experience. Only the straight line of a healing scar across the prince's face marred the picture. The other three nobles were strangers to Nightfall.

King Rikard glanced in Nightfall's direction. A welcoming smile flashed across his features and disappeared before he turned to the youth in mail and said something Nightfall could not hear. King and prince looked toward him together. Breaking from the group, they headed in his direction. Rikard's face held an expression of discomfort and warning.

Idly, Nightfall wondered whether the king anticipated trouble from Edward or himself and dismissed the thought as unimportant. Magic seemed to tingle and churn within him, as real as the shouted commands and scattered conversations around him. In the king's presence, Nightfall had no choice but to endear himself to Prince Edward.

As the noblemen approached, Nightfall dropped to one knee and lowered his head. Later, he could search for loopholes in the oath-bond. For now, it seemed safest to obey it to the letter, if only to convince the king.

King Rikard drew Edward to a halt before Nightfall. "Rise," the king said.

Nightfall obeyed, glancing into the prince's eyes and finding them as clear and blue as a crystal lake. Righteous innocence fairly radiated from him.

Accustomed to winning stare-downs in seconds, Nightfall lowered his gaze respectfully before the prince could look away.

"Ned," Rikard's voice boomed. "This is your squire, Sudian."

The crowd of servants and nobles lapsed into whispers. Acute of hearing and accustomed to the garbled syllables of varying dialects, the ill, and the aged, Nightfall managed to sift comments from the all but inaudible hubbub: "Who is he?" "Where'd he come from?" "Of course, he's a stranger." "No one who knows Ned would squire to him, no matter how desperate . . ."

Nightfall dismissed the throng, remaining silent so that Prince Edward could speak first. He considered his next move, basing it on descriptions of Ned, the courtiers' reactions, and his own brief but thorough appraisal of the man before him.

"Sudian." Edward studied his squire disinterestedly, obviously too accustomed to his stewards resigning to bother becoming attached to a servant. His gaze strayed back to the horses.

King Rikard relaxed, apparently pleased with the natural ease of the union.

But Nightfall saw a potential he could not resist exploiting. *This prince is like a newborn puppy. If I can gain his trust, I've got a tool any con man would envy.* He fell to one knee again with a crisp abruptness that seized the prince's notice, as well as that of every other man in the courtyard. "Master, it will be the greatest honor of gods and men to serve you."

Every eye locked on Nightfall.

"Since I turned twelve, Master, I've had the same dream over and over." He rose, gaze distant, arm making a grandiose sweep that implied divine interference. "In the dream, the almighty Father tells me to seek a golden prince of great beauty and moral insight, and to serve him without fail to the depths of my soul and the end of my life."

Quiet descended over the courtyard, interrupted only by the prancing gelding. The king looked startled.

"Master, I will see that your every need is met and that no harm comes to you. It would gladden me to throw myself before your dangers, to take your pain onto myself, even to trade my death for yours. Master, the gods themselves have sanctioned me as your squire. I will not disappoint them or you."

Nightfall locked a sincere expression on his face, glancing up to see the results of his fabrication. The king scowled in warning. His squinted eyes made it clear that he thought Nightfall was mocking the situation. The stunned crowd remained still and hushed, awaiting the prince's reaction.

As Nightfall expected, Prince Edward delighted in the excessive performance and the compliments. He became stiffly earnest. "Sudian, your presence at my side will be welcome. Should your loyalty prove as fierce as your desire to give it, you will be handsomely rewarded." He raised a gloved hand.

Nightfall suppressed the urge to dodge the coming blow.

The prince clapped a firm hand to his squire's shoulder with a force that ached through his healing bruises. Then, turning grandly, he headed toward the horses. "Pittan! Fetch Sudian the weapons and armor of his choice."

Caught gawking, the liveried servants scurried back to work.

King Rikard's eyes had darkened to black. He cast a surreptitious glance in all directions before addressing Nightfall softly. "Very clever. Just don't forget the terms of the oath."

"How could I, Sire?" Nightfall turned to confront an approaching servant, apparently Pittan. In fact, the conditions seemed to burn in his mind, presumably due to the nature of sorcery. He felt sure the magic would hold him to the intention as well as the letter of the agreement. At the time of casting, he had focused on the obedience aspects of the king's decrees. Only later, as the provisions became a settled constant in his thoughts, did he realize that the more important condition was his vow not to allow harm to come to Ned. *I'm bound to dive between the idiot and death, even if it means dying myself. A true death is preferable to the hell threatened by violating the oath-bond.*

Pittan bowed to the king before addressing Nightfall. He explained, though everyone had heard Edward's command. "Prince Ned asked me to find out what weapons and armor—"

Nightfall cut him off. "No armor. I'll take a sword. Something sharp, but not too bulky. And as many well-balanced knives as you can spare."

Pittan gave Nightfall an odd look but did not question. He rushed toward the castle.

The discussion of weapons reminded Nightfall where he might find the finest daggers in Alyndar. A split second glance at King Rikard confirmed that the king carried three knives on his belt. Taking a natural half-step closer, Nightfall relieved Rikard of the blades, pleased to discover they were the ones he, as Marak, had carried on *Raven.* Unable to resist the challenge, he acquired a few extra items from the king's person.

As a grizzled servant lashed a spade to the top of the chestnut's packs, Prince Edward clambered into the white charger's saddle. "Sudian, mount up. That one's yours." He pointed at the heavily laden bay mare that Nightfall had taken for a packhorse.

Nightfall took a step toward the horses, arrested by the king's hand on his arm.

"Here," the king whispered. "You might as well have these." His hand fell to his sword belt. "They're unadorned, so no one could recognize . . ." He trailed off, his hand patting his hip. He stared at the place where the knives had hung.

"I have them, Sire," Nightfall admitted, keeping the smirk of amusement from his face.

Rikard growled.

Not wishing to further enrage the king, Nightfall reached into his pocket and returned a misstamped gold coin, a writ from a Briggian merchant, and the king's signet ring.

King Rikard's face shifted through an array of reds to

settle on a purple nearly as royal as Nightfall's tabard. "It's not too late to execute you," he hissed.

"Sudian!" Prince Edward called. He gestured to the bay with a jabbing flourish.

Nightfall smiled. "With all respect, Your Majesty. I think it just might be." He trotted toward the bay. Accustomed to fast mountings on bare-backed horses, he lowered his weight and leapt into the saddle without bothering to use a stirrup. He took the reins into callused fists.

Shortly, Pittan approached with the sword and half a dozen daggers.

Nightfall thought he heard the king swear.

Prince Edward Nargol perched upon his snow-white gelding, his head high, blond hair flying in the breeze of its movements. His beauty and regal bearing made him look like a living sculpture; only patches and rivulets of sweat ruined the image. ". . . a chance to see the world! A chance to experience the lives of a thousand strangers. A chance to teach them . . ."

Riding at his side through evergreen forest, Nightfall let "The Legend of Nightfall" run endlessly through his mind, the familiar tedium of the nursery rhyme distracting him from Edward's idealistic ramblings. As the day wore on, the white gelding had become docile with fatigue. Overburdened, Nightfall's bay and the packhorse had begun to stumble, each misstep jarring pain through his healing wounds and further darkening his temper.

The stretches of sky visible between the trees dulled to pewter and lengthened as the forest became more sparse and clearings more plentiful.

Hunger descended on Nightfall, tearing at his guts. *Sleep,* he thought. *Sleep would feel almost as good as food.* He became suddenly, intensely aware of Prince Edward's stare upon him.

". . . do you think, Sudian?" The prince shook back his sweat-tangled locks, his silks now damp and spotted with dirt and pine needles.

Having heard only the last four words, Nightfall answered the only question he could. "Yes, Master, I do."

Prince Edward accepted the response. "Very good." He reined his horse, clambering from the saddle. As he landed, his knees buckled, and he crashed to the ground.

Obviously not used to riding for hours. His own knees aching, Nightfall sprang from his bay, turning a laugh into a cough. He ran to Edward's side, reaching out a hand to help the prince to his feet. "Master!" Despite the humor of the situation, he managed to sound concerned. "Are you hurt?"

"No, no. I'm fine." Edward accepted Nightfall's support, throwing his weight onto the smaller man as he rose. An abrupt increase in mass spared Nightfall a tumble, and he eased Prince Edward and twenty pounds of mail hauberk to his feet. "I just need to walk around a bit." He paced a careful circle, Nightfall hovering over his every step.

Prince Edward whirled. Finding himself nearly on top of Nightfall, he back-stepped. "Sudian! I said I'm fine." He winced, the abrupt movement apparently sparking pain through overtaxed muscles. "Unload the horses and see what you can make for supper. I'll start on the camp."

Nightfall nodded, turning to obey, though he did not understand the division. *If I unload the horses and cook, what does that leave as camp for him to start on?* Though accustomed to action and pushing himself to the limit, Nightfall could feel his thighs and buttocks stiffening from the ride. Movement had worked the kinks from his knees. Though he still hurt from bruises and the familiar jab of healing ribs into his lung, he knew tomorrow morning would bring an aching agony of cramped muscles. *Combat training or none, Ned's going to feel even worse.* He stripped off the white horse's bridle and unlaced its pack. Hefting the bundle, he staggered under its weight, managing a single step before the pack plummeted to the ground amid a muffled clamor of clothes and armor. Anticipating Edward's rage at the manhandling of his personal effects, Nightfall glanced toward the prince who seemed too engrossed in freeing the spade from the top of the bay mare's load to notice his squire's mistake.

Step one, lighten the load. Nightfall dragged the bundle

aside, pitying the horses. *He's packed for a plague-damned army.*

Having obtained his spade, Edward set to work digging.

Nightfall continued pulling pack after monstrous pack from the backs of the chestnut and his own bay. Discovering several weeks' worth of rations, he selected the items that would not keep for travel: fresh meat, corn, onions, squash, and peas. He also found bread and honey. Unable to resist, he smeared a slice with honey and took a bite, the sweetness enhanced by hunger. Pawing through the packs, he searched for a pot.

Edward set the spade aside, his ditch forming a shallow arc around the horses. He wiped his brow with the back of his fist. "How's supper coming?"

Caught with his mouth full, Nightfall chewed and swallowed hastily. "Just getting started, Master."

"Are you eating already?"

Prince Edward's tone suggested surprise and displeasure. Still, Nightfall could not imagine that the prince wanted him to starve. "Yes."

Edward clambered from the ditch. "Don't you know it's impolite to eat before a superior?"

No. In starvation situations, the rule made sense. *But we're carrying enough to feed every hungry family in Nemix and still have leftovers for the rats.* Dedicated to his act, Nightfall covered. "Master, of course. I was just testing it for you."

"Testing it?" Edward selected an ax from the piled supplies. "What do you mean, testing it?"

"Making sure the honey was good, the bread fresh enough for you. Taking the first bite in case your enemies poisoned it."

"Poisoned?" Edward looked aghast. "Poison? But I have no enemies."

Nightfall passed the piece of honey bread. "Those are the worst kinds of enemies. The ones you don't know you have."

Prince Edward stared at the bread and its semicircular defect, crenellated with Nightfall's teeth marks. "But my father's own men packed this food. And it's been on our person since then."

"The second worst kind of enemies are the ones who can poison your supplies without you knowing it."

Edward seemed to accept that. He took a bite, chewing with relish. "Best honey I've ever had."

Nightfall nodded agreement. He had never eaten better; but he suspected that, in Ned's case, hunger had more to do with the superlative than quality. Nightfall heaped another bread slice with honey for himself.

Holding his food in one hand, Edward hefted the ax. "You keep working on unpacking and dinner. I'll get started on the turf blocks and wooden stakes."

Turf blocks? Wooden stakes? Nightfall had no idea what Prince Edward was proposing. Still, he grasped his own instructions, so he did not need to question. As night came, enwrapping them in darkness, he sent the horses to graze, built a campfire, and prepared a stew. He followed Edward by the thunk of his ax into wood, the discomforting crack of a trunk's last supports breaking, and the swish and slam of lower trees and branches snapping beneath its fall. Then Edward hacked and shaped each trunk, over time acquiring a neat pile of stakes.

Nightfall waited until the prince headed off to acquire another tree, swiping a handful of the fashioned timbers for firewood. The prince's stamina after a full day's ride surprised Nightfall. While the stew thickened, and the night darkened to pitch speckled with white stars, he sorted their gear into a tiny pile of necessities and useful items, a voluminous stack of extraneous niceties that had to go, and Edward's personal items consisting mostly of battle armor and far too many clothes. Now equipped with daggers and sword, Nightfall ditched the chair dowel he had taken in Alyndar's castle. He tossed the flammable items from the superfluous pile onto the fire. Then, he drew two logs near the flames to serve as seats.

Ned's stack of sharpened poles grew.

Finally, running out of ways to amuse himself, Nightfall plucked wooden bowls and spoons from the useful pile, repacked the items according to his new system, and ladled stew into the dishes. "Master, supper's ready."

Prince Edward wandered over and sat on a log. The firelight glittered from beads of perspiration on his forehead, and sweat trickled along his nose. Exertion flushed his cheeks. Branches had gouged rents in his silks where they poked from beneath the hauberk. Evergreen needles decorated his hair, and he smelled of pine tar and bark. He accepted the stew bowl eagerly. Rising, he rolled his log away from the fire's heat.

Maintaining consistency, Nightfall took the first spoonful. Meat more tender than any he had ever tasted slid warmly into his pinched and rumbling gut. "It seems safe," he said with all seriousness.

Prince Edward started to say something, presumably to mention that poisons did not act that quickly. Then, apparently recalling that he had just argued against the possibility of sabotage at all and too hungry to worry about details, he ate.

For some time, dinner took precedence over conversation. Then, contentedly full, Nightfall pushed his first bowl aside while Prince Edward was still devouring his second helping. The squire stared at rows of lumber and the partially finished ditch, watching moonlight glimmer from the spade and the axe's blade. Unable to contain curiosity any longer, he phrased the question as respectfully as he could manage. "Master, what are we going to do with the sticks?"

Prince Edward stared at his squire as if Nightfall had asked the stupidest question ever uttered. "Build the camp, of course."

Nightfall glanced from the logs around the roaring campfire to the horses contentedly grazing on leaves, brown vines and new, young grass shoots, to the neatly sorted packs. It was already the largest, most comfortable camp he had ever seen. "Forgive my ignorance, Master, but why do we need carved wood to build the camp?" The question of how long it would take seemed infinitely more important, but he saw no tactful way to ask it. Besides, the answer should become obvious once he understood the prince's intentions. If Prince Edward planned another ride like yesterday, they would need more than half a night of rest.

Prince Edward politely swallowed his mouthful of stew before replying. "For the fences and the palisade."

Obviously, Nightfall's surprise showed clearly, because Edward continued explaining.

"I learned how to build a strong, defensive camp from my lessons. I'll teach you."

Nightfall suppressed a groan. *I don't believe this. Prince Silk Sheets is going to teach me how to sleep outside.* Then realization struck him. *His lessons. His history lessons. His "how to be a war general" lessons. By the Father's crown, he's building a pissing fortress!* The image of a towering buttress filled his mind, along with the weeks of hard labor it would cost for two men to erect it. The picture threw him over the edge. No longer able to restrain his amusement, he broke into a raging torrent of laughter.

"What's so funny?"

The somberness of the prince's tone only tripled the humor. Nightfall howled.

"What's so funny," Edward demanded, his voice breaking as he started to chuckle himself. Within seconds, they were both laughing hard enough to burst. Every few moments, Edward caught his breath to ask the source of the laughter again, and each time the question began a new wave of mirth.

Finally, they both sat, gasping, beneath the moonlight. A long time had passed since Nightfall had laughed except with cruel satisfaction in the wake of an enemy's death. Despite the pain in his lungs and exhaustion, he felt good.

The pause gave Edward the time he needed to fully regain his composure. "Sudian, why *are* we laughing?"

At you, you ridiculous simpleton. We're laughing at you. Nightfall passed up the straight line. "Master, we're both overtired to giddiness. As much as it pains me to leave work undone, it might be best if we both got some sleep."

"Without defenses? And let something attack us in the night?"

Nightfall wondered what Prince Edward would think if he knew his squire was the most horrible and dangerous thing in the forest. "Master, what good are defenses if we're too tired to fight?"

Edward's eyes narrowed. All humor left him. "Sudian, are you questioning me?"

Nightfall stared, annoyed by the malice in his prince's tone. "Master, are you asking me if I asked you a question?"

Now Edward seemed startled. "I'm pointing out that you're questioning my judgment."

"Is that a crime in Alyndar?"

"Yes." Edward retrieved his bowl of stew. "Well, no, not a crime actually." He gripped the bowl, fingers white with frustration. "It's considered rude. You're a servant. You can't just run around questioning nobles' judgments."

"Master, I don't understand." Nightfall adopted a wide-eyed innocent look. "My loyalty is to your welfare. If I see you making a decision I think might hurt you, I should say nothing?"

The prince chewed another mouthful of stew, swallowing before replying. "You have to trust that I see things you don't."

"Master, I trust you. I trust you more than anyone." *And if you believe that, you galley-clod, you're even stupider and more naive than I thought.*

Edward softened. "Very well, Sudian. I appreciate your loyalty. And you do look tired. Why don't you get some sleep. I'll take first watch."

"Master, thank you." Nightfall managed to turn his back before the smile overtook his face. Curling on his side in the clearing, he fell asleep almost instantly.

A movement awakened Nightfall. He opened his eyes to the darkness of wee morning and an exhausted Prince Edward headed in his direction. Beyond the campfire, the prince had gathered a pile of pine needles to serve as a bed.

"Ah, Sudian, you're awake. It's your turn to take watch. Can you handle it?"

Nightfall sat up quickly, giving an enthusiastic gesture of respect. "Master, I'm alert and ready for anything."

"Very good." Prince Edward sprawled across his make-shift bed, turning his back to his squire.

In thirty-four years, nothing has ever approached without waking me from the soundest sleep. Nightfall lowered his head, curling back into a ball on the ground. *You could have spared yourself the watch. I'm more wary in my sleep than you are awake.* He waited until Prince Edward's gentle snores wafted across the camp, memorized the normalcy of its sound and the layout of the clearing, then swiftly returned to sleep.

Nightfall awakened to the numbing chill of sunrise. He sat up, curling a leg to his chest, and a soreness in his inner thighs and buttocks reminded him of yesterday's ride. The pain brought a familiar satisfaction. In his years as Etan, the laborer, stiffness at sunrise always followed a day of noteworthy accomplishment. *But, this morning it only means I've got a fool for a master, one who doesn't know when to ride and when to rest.*

Nightfall sighed, glancing around the camp. The fire had burned to piled charcoal splattered with a few red coals. Prince Edward lay on his back beneath a blanket, with one arm thrown across his forehead. Nightfall had often heard that people looked innocent in sleep, and he found it fascinating to think that Edward could appear more guileless than he did awake. *If he became any purer, I'd have to diaper him.*

Not quite ready to rise for the day, Nightfall stared between the trees. Early sunlight reddened the gaps between branches, filling the sky with waving patches of scarlet, green, and gray. He crouched, watching the colors change as the sun inched upward. The tatters of sky between needled branches diffused to pink.

Oddly, of all his personae, it was Nightfall, himself, who liked to watch the dawn. He recalled nights in his childhood, when his mother or her client had barred him from the room, and he had hidden from the world and its dangers between the wheat stalks of a farmer's field. He would awaken to sunrise creeping over a billowing sea of gold, mesmerized by the rainbow parade that preceded the sun. Legends spoke of the seven sisters on horseback towing the burning chariot across the sky, chasing night's demons over the world's edge and back into their hell. The young Nightfall would pretend that the twilight beauty was the sisters' gift to him; that, one day, they would carry him across the horizon to a land where bowls of food sprang from the ground, where summer stayed all year round, and where the same man slept in a woman's bed every night. The sisters would all be his mothers, playfully arguing over which loved him more, though he loved them all the same.

The pinkness faded, intertwined with, then replaced by, a pale, blue-white expanse, back-lit by yellow. Standing, he chuckled faintly at the reverie. *Back in the days when I was as unenlightened as my master.* He glanced at Prince Edward, watching the youth twist in his sleep, tangling himself into the blankets. Shaking his head at the spectacle, Nightfall amended. *No. I think I was born more worldly than he is now.*

Trotting to the pile of wooden stakes, he collected a handful and tossed them on the coals. Smoke poured from beneath one of the logs, then trickled into oblivion. Leaving the coals to smolder against fresh wood, Nightfall prepared a breakfast of bread, cheese, and fruit, leaving it in place for Edward's awakening. Then, quietly sating his hunger on a slice of bread and a handful of winter berries, he finished preparing the packs for travel.

The horses stood in a row, alternating head to tail, swatting flies on one another's faces. Still disliking the beacon whiteness of Ned's gelding, Nightfall considered driving it away. But that would mean piling its share of the load onto the other two, already overburdened, horses. He combed the tangles from his red-brown hair, then set to grooming the mounts.

By the time Prince Edward awakened, all trace of dawn had left the sky. The fire flickered, orange and gold, over logs no longer recognizable as stakes. Nightfall had washed and shaven, the latter action taking the place of the ritual disguising that had grown so familiar over the years. He appreciated the time saved, though his face felt cold and his identity nakedly vulnerable. Despite years of perfecting his agility and sense of touch, he had only shaved a few times and appreciated the hand mirror he had taken from the palace. For clothing, the king had granted him only tunics, tabards, and breeks in Alyndar's colors, apparently to remind him of his duty to Edward. *As if this ceaseless grind of magic would let me forget.*

Edward disentangled himself from the blankets. "Good morning, Sudian." He sat up, his silks twisted, his yellow hair hanging limply into his eyes, and a pine cone stuck into the locks above one ear.

Fighting laughter, Nightfall paused longer than decorum demanded. "Good morning, Master." He passed the brush and mirror. Surely, Edward carried toiletries of his own; as heavy as the prince's pack had seemed, Nightfall wondered if he had dragged along an entire vanity table. Still, the squire knew his manners would lose to humor if the pine cone remained in place too long. "I've got breakfast ready. And the horses. When you're ready to leave, I'll tie up the gear."

"Very good." Prince Edward accepted the objects, flipping errant strands back into place. The pine cone tumbled from its perch. Its touch made the prince jerk away with a suddenness that changed his expression from pleased to pained.

Just noticed the riding soreness, Nightfall guessed. He moved to the fireside, stirring a green twig through the embers, watching the prince from the corner of his eyes for no better reason than amusement.

In obvious discomfort, Edward lurched to his feet. Yet, though he moved with a painful slowness, he still managed to change into a fresh set of linens, replace his hauberk, and cover it with a woolen cloak without a single moan or complaint. Then, he wandered off toward the stream to wash.

Nightfall folded the blanket, replacing it with Edward's effects. He seized on the prince's absence to examine his personal gear. Plates of armor sandwiched a collection of folded clothing and spare boots. A book lay protectively wrapped in a pair of linen britches. A sack held a matching brush and comb encrusted with tiny pearls, a vial of perfume, leather soap, and sword oil. A waterskin sloshed, smelling of an exotic wine unfamiliar to Nightfall. A tooled leather, drawstring purse held twenty or thirty silver coins, five years' wages to a laborer.

Nightfall closed the pack, securing everything except the pouch of silver which he left for Edward to carry on his person. Again, he sat by the fire just as the prince returned, clean and wet from the stream, his own morning ritual completed.

Edward took a seat on the log by the fire, starting in on the breakfast Nightfall had arranged. He stopped with a bite of cheese halfway to his lips. "Did you want to test it first?"

"Master, I've done that already."

"Fine." Edward put the food in his mouth, chewed, and swallowed. "Aren't you going to eat?"

Thinking it wiser not to confess that he had already done so, Nightfall accepted an apple and munched slowly. The warmth of the fire made a pleasant contrast to the morning breeze. Fully risen, the sun beamed through layers of needles. Comfortably full of rich bread and fruit and reasonably well rested, Nightfall felt content. *Perhaps the king did do me a favor.* The thought raised a sudden, goading stab from the oath-bond. *Now all I have to do is figure out a way to get this child some land.* Aware Edward did not like being questioned, Nightfall turned his query into a statement. "I was wondering where we were headed."

Edward tore a chunk from his bread, kneading it between his fingers. "East," he said. "We're headed East."

Since Alyndar occupied the westernmost tip of the Yortenese Peninsula, the direction seemed obvious. "Well, I was just wondering if we had a certain place in mind. A city? A barony?"

"No." Edward clutched his bread, his gaze becoming distant. "We'll go where the winds take us, spreading goodness where we can, enlightening the ignorant to the Father's greatness, to the dignity and worth of all men and women."

Nightfall rolled his eyes. *What star are you from?* "I thought our mission was to get you landed."

"That's secondary." Edward put the bread into his mouth.

To you, maybe. Nightfall was beginning to remember why the king's oath-bond was anything but a favor. *Ned, would it save you any trouble if I just went mad right now?* "Master, forgive my ignorance. But I always thought a king's son was given land."

Prince Edward swallowed. "My brother, Leyne, is the crown prince. He inherits everything."

"That's more land than any one man can handle. Can't he share?"

"That's not how it's done."

"Oh." The ways of royalty made little sense. *To have so much, yet still not enough for his brother.* Nightfall understood that men's greed and covetousness expanded to cover all that they had, apparently no matter whether it was a crumb or a kingdom.

"My mother always planned for me to become part of Leyne's household as a scholar. But Father believes I should prove myself worthy by winning land of my own." Prince Edward rose, holding the bread slice in one hand and drawing his sword with the other.

Nightfall skittered out of the way.

Caught up in his own heroics, Edward no longer seemed to notice his squire. He raised the blade in a salute to the gods. "And I would have it no other way. The kingdom of Alyndar has many brilliant thinkers, Father's wisdom, and Leyne's talent with words and weapons. Somewhere . . ." He gestured with the sword to indicate the world. ". . . out there is a kingdom, a barony, perhaps only a village that needs a leader like me."

Nightfall crouched, heart still pounding from the prince's sudden lunge with a drawn blade. *You mean, I presume, a kingdom starved for buffoonery.*

Prince Edward sat, returning his attention to his bread. "Sudian, prepare my destrier!"

"At once, master." *As soon as I figure out what, in hell's confines, is a destrier.* Nightfall traced Edward's gaze to the grazing horses. *Ah.*

Quickly Nightfall set to work saddling and bridling the white and the bay, then lashing Edward's personal gear to the rump of his riding gelding. He tied the pack full of necessities to his own bay. Then he placed the remaining weighty trinkets onto the chestnut, binding them haphazardly in the hope that they would disappear during the ride. He tied the spade on the top of the chestnut's gear. *With all this equipment, we couldn't outrun a pregnant turtle.* Checking the spade's binding one more time, he loosened it and turned back to the prince.

"Ready, Master," he said.

Unwilling to trust the whims of the wind, Nightfall unobtrusively steered Prince Edward toward Nemix, the first large city in the area and one in which he had a strong chain of contacts. The maneuver proved easier than he ever expected. Caught up in the scenery and his own grandiose ideals, Edward did not seem to notice when they detoured past the villages of Quant and Rankelle nor when the spade slid from the top of the chestnut's stack and tumbled to the dirt. Quietly, Nightfall edged them from one set of trails to the other, traversing one of many familiar routes from Alyndar to Nemix. *At this rate, we may get to Nemix before dusk.*

At least, the bruises and stiffness from the previous day taught Edward something. He made frequent stops to eat and urinate, using each to work the kinks from his muscles or search the heavens for information about time and direction. At each stop, Nightfall unobtrusively jettisoned a few more objects from the unnecessary items packs, tossing them deep into the woods to keep from leaving a trail of gear and niceties for footpads to follow.

Late morning, a rustling in the tall brush by the roadside caught Nightfall's eye. Weed tops bowed and danced, revealing something's winding, awkward path. A muffled groan sifted through the grasses, nearly lost beneath the rattle of stalks and the clop of hooves on roadway. He reined back, then threaded behind Edward to interpose himself between prince and unidentified creature, hoping to a manage a close but unobtrusive look. He wanted to determine the best course of action, ignore or intervene, before Edward discovered the presence and made the decision for them.

Before Nightfall could swing his bay fully around, the white gelding jarred to a sudden stop. Its head jerked to the stirring weeds, and its ears swiveled forward into nervous triangles.

Edward tapped the gelding with his heels. When that failed, he kicked with the angry impatience of one accustomed to having orders obeyed swiftly. The horse paid no heed to the drumming on its sides, attention still riveted.

"A moment, Master." No longer able to avoid the situation, Nightfall dismounted and approached the roadside. Delicately, alert for ambush, he parted the weeds.

A man rolled in the ditch, wrists and ankles trussed and his cloak pulled over his head. He wore leather breeks and a well-fitting tunic with fringe. The needlework at the collar suggested wealth, and the supple skin of his palms and fingers made it clear he did not toil or fight for a living. Nightfall took his cues from other details. White striped the base of each fourth finger; apparently, he had worn rings until recently. A tunic pocket hung, torn and turned inside out. Starting bruises mottled the skin of his arms.

"Oh, dear," Edward said.

Nightfall hauled the cloak free, revealing an angular face fringed with tangled, honey-colored hair and a neatly trimmed beard. A grimy wad of cloth filled the stranger's mouth, and he stared at Nightfall with brown eyes that seemed relieved and angered at once. The man grunted.

Nightfall seized an edge of the gag, then hauled it from the stranger's mouth. It unwound into a sodden ribbon.

The man spat the remainder free. "Robbed and attacked. Five men. They took everything."

The gelding danced backward. Edward tugged at the reins to regain control. "When?"

The man sat, raising his arms for Nightfall to cut the bonds. "Moments ago. They rode that way." He inclined his head in the direction they had been traveling. "Overheard one of the dirty bastards say they were headed for Nemix." He gazed up at Edward. Apparently noticing the royal garb for the first time, he added, "Noble sir. They took—"

Prince Edward did not wait to hear more. He jerked the gelding's head about, then slapped the end of the reins across its rump. The horse surged forward, galloping in the direction the man had indicated.

Nightfall swore, dashing from the ditch to his horse in an instant. He ignored the shouts of the still-bound man behind him. *Surely, Edward wouldn't attack five highwaymen alone.* Nightfall flung himself into the saddle and urged the bay into a run as he settled in place. The horse lurched, delayed by the chestnut packhorse tied to its saddle. Then, both horses pitched forward, hooves chewing rents in the dirt. King Rikard's descriptions of his impulsive son returned to haunt Nightfall. *He* would *attack five highwaymen alone.* The realization turned the oath-bond into a shrill scream of pain. Nightfall stiffened, natural dexterity all that kept him from tumbling from the horse. The need seized him to charge ahead, hacking at bandits like a wild thing, interposing himself between the prince and any blow he might need to fend. He wrestled for common sense. Imitating the prince's noble but reckless stupidity would only see them both dead.

The rump of the white gelding bounced over the roadway. Topping a rise, it disappeared over the far side. Nightfall could hear Edward shouting challenges, his words indecipherable but his presence and beacon horse enough to catch the attention and spur the avarice of any thief.

Thought kicked in beneath the oath-bond's urging. Guile, not brute force, would rescue Prince Edward from his own rash yearning for fairness. The knots and cloak-binding had seemed the work of professionals. If they had let their victim overhear plans to run for Nemix, then they had no intention of actually doing so. *Which means they're probably holed up here.* Understanding accompanied idea. Impressions rerouted, he saw the territory in a different light. The perfect hiding place seemed to fill his vision, the forest on the rise. On the right side of the road, it fell away to a dry riverbed. The high ground would serve as a lookout perch, the low as a shelter from elements and prying eyes. Nightfall guessed they had chosen their robbery site deliberately.

The assessment flashed through Nightfall's mind in an instant. He pulled up his horse, and it danced to a stop, plowing furrows through leaf mold and mud. Likely, the sentinel would have his attention focused on Prince Edward, and Nightfall's antics farther down the path would go unnoticed. He would have to take a chance on that assumption. There was no time for more detailed strategy. Dismounting, he left the horses to graze and slipped into the right-hand forest area. Tied together, the horses would not stray.

Nightfall moved swiftly through the forest, nearly in silence, hoping Edward's calls would cover whatever few sounds he made. He kept his weight low to minimize noise. Sticks bent rather than cracked beneath his step, and stems brushed effortlessly aside. Within a few paces, he found smashed weeds, mulched leaves, and fragmented limbs. Strands of mane hair dangled from a jagged edge of bark. Someone had cut through the denseness of the forest, and no regular traveler would have need to break trail here. Encouraged, Nightfall pushed on. Shortly, he heard voices, soft and indecipherable through foliage rattled by wind and activity. Nightfall sucked in a deep breath. The nagging stab of the oath-bond reminded him that he had no room for failure; he had tethered life and soul to a royal, but suicidal, clod.

Nightfall gauged his motions, increasing his weight and dropping his usual caution, trying to sound like a small group of men slipping past. He spoke in a loud whisper. "Think Hira's being a bit *too* obvious what with that white horse, a pack that looks stuffed, and all that shouting?"

Nightfall altered his voice as much as the slight volume allowed. "Thieves got more greed than brains. Caught that group near Delfor with a soldier as loud as Hira." Nightfall referred to an incident in which a group of young amateurs was imprisoned. He doubted an organized setup was involved, but it seemed unlikely these men would know more details than the scant few he had at his disposal. "Quiet victims sometimes get missed, no matter how good a target."

Nightfall veered deeper into the forest. He could think of no better strategy for the thieves now than to lie low; but he rarely trusted others' judgment. If they saw him

alone, he knew of no easy way to save himself or Prince
Edward. That line of thinking raised the stress of the
oath-bond, sending its warning through him in crippling
waves. His hand slid naturally to the throwing daggers,
and memory bullied its way past magic. Since childhood,
Nightfall and Dyfrin had played a game they called "dagger catch" in which they flung knives at one another in
turn. Early on, they had used wooden blades and made
certain to grab each other's attention before striking.
Later, they had hurled live steel with lethal aim. Luck
and, later, skill had spared them any serious injuries.
Nightfall had even learned not just to dodge, but to snatch
the daggers from the air and return them instantly, a maneuver Dyfrin hatefully nicknamed "the razor rebound."
Now, Nightfall knew, his ability might serve him well,
but he dared not rely on it. Trees and Edward would foil
his aim, and it seemed far more intelligent for the thieves
to either avoid them completely or close in for a fight.

Nightfall continued his charade. "I presume there's
horses?" He answered his own nonspecific question in a
different voice. "The ranks up ahead have them, in case
the thieving bastards make a run for Nemix. But it
doesn't much matter. Soon's they hit the bait, we've got
them." He switched to a throaty bass, "Pretty embarrassing if they rob Hira clean and break away." Nightfall returned to the first voice. "At least we'll get a look at
them. And they won't get nothing. The most valuable
thing Hira's got is the clothes on him."

Nightfall doubled back, taking the first steps slowly
and quietly, then concentrating more on speed. He found
the horses grazing the roadside ditch and clambered onto
the bay. He kicked it into a lope, studying the forests with
an exaggerated scrutiny. Likely, the highwaymen would
not risk the trap Nightfall had detailed for a single purse.
If he stayed calm and followed Edward at a cautious distance, they would take him for a member of the hunt.

The ruse brought Nightfall safely past the hidden
thieves. He caught up with Edward by midday. Apparently, the prince had stopped his mount to wait for his
squire. Sweat sheened the prince's forehead, and foam
bubbled along his horse's coat. "Ah, there you are,

Sudian! Afraid I'd lost you." Edward glanced up the pathway, apparently planning to continue the chase.

Though eager to reach Nemix, Nightfall believed it wiser to cool his charge's ire first. A calm, leisurely journey, with no hope of catching criminals or dealing justice, seemed just the trick. "I'm sorry, Master. My horse came up lame." He reined to a full stop, though Edward frowned in irritation. "I pulled a sharp stone from the left forehoof. It's just a bruise, but it could turn into worse if we keep this pace."

Surely Edward had never cleaned a hoof in his life, yet he had, apparently, learned enough from books and tutors to understand the danger. A single unsound hoof rendered a horse useless. "Do we need to camp?" he asked with obvious reluctance.

"I don't believe so, Master. I think she'll do fine at a steady walk." *And that still ought to get us to beer and shelter by sunset.*

Prince Edward patted his gelding's withers, drawing back a hand sticky with foam. "They could all use a rest, I suppose. We'll never catch those thieves now. We'll just have to ride back and ask the stranger to describe them so we can turn in their descriptions to the constabulary in Nemix."

Turn back? Shocked, Nightfall did not have an immediate reply. The idea of repeating the same trip endlessly became a nagging frustration. The oath-bond had settled back into its regular buzz, and Nightfall dreaded that it might flare again when they rode past the thieves a second time. "Master, I can save us the trip. The stranger told me he didn't see his attackers. They pulled the cloak over his head too quickly." No such conversation had ensued, but Nightfall suspected he told the truth anyway. "Understandably, he was eager to be on his way. He's probably halfway home by now."

Edward frowned, glancing back the way they had come. "Perhaps he could describe some item they took from him, something we could watch for."

Nightfall considered the best means to save travel time and to get the matter dropped. Edward's heroic persistence had already become annoying. He could imagine the prince confronting and questioning every group of five he saw or spending months searching for a fictitious object. "Master, he told me they only took his purse. Three or four silver, he said." Nightfall invented an amount that would entice thieves but would not sound too significant to Edward. "Master, he said he wouldn't miss the money. He was just shaken by the ambush. They didn't hurt him."

Prince Edward's lower lip curled as Nightfall's "discoveries" strangled his options. "We can't just let these beasts keep attacking honest people on the road."

Nightfall made no reply. Edward had a cause to champion, and he clung to it the way a dog worries the last meat from a bone. The longer the discussion, the more the problem would grind at the young prince. Left alone to think, surely even he would realize no course remained to follow. Yet when it came to logical thought, Edward seemed the exception. Nightfall had originally believed much of the king's description of his son was exaggeration; now it seemed more like understatement. No doubt, Prince Edward would plunge them into trouble of a sort Nightfall was more accustomed to creating than solving. Worse, the best plans to rescue them from the situation might fail because Edward seemed inclined to dodge around his own protections and deliberately take on the danger again.

The prince sighed, reining his horse toward Nemix. For now, at least, he seemed to have dropped the affair.

Nightfall would see to it that state of mind became permanent.

Chapter 4

A demon cruel; a monster stark,
Grim moonlight, coldness, deepest dark.
Nightmares come to ones who doze—
In darkness where old Nightfall goes.
　　　　　　　　—"The Legend of Nightfall"
　　　　　　　　Nursery Rhyme, st. 4

Toward evening, clouds scudded across the sky, muting it to steely gray. Prince Edward studied his squire. "Where are you from, Sudian?"

"Alyndar," Nightfall replied easily.

Edward's brow crinkled. "That's odd."

Suddenly alert, Nightfall feigned calm. "Hmmm?"

"My father said you were from outside the country. That you knew some of the lands down south."

Thanks, Rikard, real subtle. Give me a history but don't bother to tell me. "He's right." Nightfall covered deftly, aside from forgetting the customary "master." "I was raised in Mitano, but I was born in Alyndar." It was a lie. Nightfall's mother had worked and borne him in Keevain, and he had lived his early childhood there. But he had enough knowledge of the other countries and cities to claim a youth in any of them.

"Oh." Prince Edward fingered the tightening scab on his face. Pinched creases appeared around his eyes. "That's slave land." His voice filled with accusation. "Did you ever keep slaves?"

Despite his composure, the question took Nightfall aback. "Me? Keep slaves? I was lucky not to be one." He regained his respectful demeanor. Not wanting to talk about a past he would rather forget, Nightfall channeled the questions back toward subjects he knew Edward could not resist. Restoring Edward's attention to vast and vague principles would also direct him away from chasing unidentified highwaymen. "Master, I understand that slavery is cruel. Forgive the question, but why do you hold this cause so important?" Nightfall watched trees glide past on either side of the dusty roadway, knowing the threatening rain would soon turn the path to mud. "Alyndar doesn't have slavery. And, surely, you've never been kept."

Prince Edward grimaced, pale eyes blazing. "Anyone can champion a cause that's hurt him in the past or one that makes his own life richer or easier." His gelding snagged a leafy branch, tearing it free. The wood swung from its mouth as it chewed. "Every time my father makes a law or proposal, every noble has to consider how it will help him, forgetting that the Father and the lesser gods want us to help one another the way He helps us all." Edward leaned across the horse's neck and untangled the limb from its bit. "Every life has equal value in the gods' eyes. There are no commoners on a baron's council. Who would speak for the slaves if I didn't?"

"I don't know, Master." Nightfall had to admit that Prince Edward had a point, albeit a childishly uninformed one. *Beaten and worked, yes. But, at least, the slaves get fed, clothed, and sheltered. Let free, they'd starve or die at the hands of stronger survivors on the streets.*

The clouds bunched tighter, blotting evening into shadow.

"Holy beard of the Father!" Edward drew up his gelding.

Nightfall had never heard Edward blaspheme before. Alarmed, he followed the prince's gaze to the chestnut packhorse. "What's wrong, Master?"

"The spade." Edward clambered down from his saddle and headed for the packhorse. "The spade is missing."

For the last ten leagues, at least. Respectfully, Nightfall dismounted also, trailing Prince Edward to the chestnut. For lack of anything better to say, he made a general noise of dismay.

Edward examined the packs and the ropes, then the place at the top where the spade should sit.

Nightfall held his breath, waiting for the prince to notice the numerous and sundry other missing items.

"Sudian, these knots are barely tight. We're lucky we didn't lose everything."

Lightning flashed a zigzag path across the sky, followed by the raw boom of thunder.

Luck, Nightfall thought, *is a matter of opinion.* "I'm sorry, Master. They must have worked loose while we rode." The first raindrops fell like cold pinpoints against Nightfall's scalp.

Prince Edward hauled down the chestnut's packs. "I don't believe this carelessness!" He whirled on Nightfall. "From now on, you're going to have to check the ties every time we stop. For now, there's only one thing to do."

Push on to Nemix before we get drenched. Nightfall nodded his agreement.

"You're going to go back and find that spade." Edward dragged the heaviest pack toward a clearing beneath intertwined branches that blocked undergrowth and light. It would shield him from the rain as well.

Go back? Nightfall's jaw sagged. For several moments he could not speak. This time, no clever lies could save him, and annoyance got the best of him. "Master, Nemix is just ahead. If we push on, we could reach it tonight. Surely they have spades. Don't you think it would be wiser to spend a dry night there?"

Prince Edward dropped the pack. "Sudian! I don't like your tone . . ."

And I don't like your person, but you don't see me sending you out in the rain to find a heavy tool we don't need. Wisely, Nightfall chose stony silence.

". . . and we already talked about questioning me. Don't. You got careless, and it cost us the spade." He placed his hands on his hips as rain dropped from the heavens in a sudden barrage, drumming onto the umbrella of leaves. "Accident or not, you need to learn from it. That's one of the reasons you're with me, you know; and I intend to be a good teacher."

Surprised, Nightfall found himself without a reply. *Is that what you were told? You're supposed to teach me? Teach me what? How to preach? How to infuriate my own relatives into sending me off on a fool's mission?*

How to build a camp for two using moats, palisades, and wooden stake defenses?

Apparently accepting Nightfall's silence as acquiescence, Prince Edward continued. "I'll set up the camp while you're gone."

Visions of a warm inn room and ale floated from Nightfall's mind, leaving an aching aggravation in its wake. Thinking it better in his current mood to leave Edward and spend some time alone, Nightfall unfastened the pack from his mare and lowered it to the ground. Springing into the saddle, he headed back the way they had come. *Even thieves are smart enough to stay in from the rain. Ned is safe from everyone but himself.* He kicked the bay toward the open pathway. The horse shied from the pelting rain then, at Nightfall's urging, lowered its head and braved the storm.

Once beyond Prince Edward's hearing, Nightfall muttered a string of frustrated obscenities. He hunched into himself, trying to protect his face and chest from the damp. The wind turned each patch of wet clothing into icy misery, and the horse snorted its dissatisfaction with every step. *I brought it on myself.* Nightfall saw neither means nor reason to place the blame elsewhere. *I knew he'd eventually notice some items missing, but I figured he'd learn we didn't need them, not send me back on this stupid errand.*

Quickly soaked, Nightfall ceased to care about the rain. Water trickled from his hair, down the neck of his tunic, the wetter areas now warmer than the damp ones that the wind could easily dry. It came to him that he had become angry beyond reason. *I'm losing the character of Sudian, and I should appreciate the chance to be free of that moron for a bit. Rankelle's only a few more strides down the side road, and I won't even need to pass the thieves' den again.*

Knowing himself well, Nightfall searched for the cause of his instability and discovered it near the surface of his thoughts. *Kelryn.* He knew he would find her in the dance hall in Nemix, and the idea of her twirling and capering as if nothing had changed stoked his irritation into fury. *Marak is dead, murdered by her betrayal. Yet, for her, life simply goes on.* He pictured her giggling in the arms of a young punk. The image would not come, and resentment faded with the failure. *Whether I like it or not, Kelryn's got better taste than that.* He sincerely believed that, despite the fact that she had been courted by the most notorious criminal in Nemix. Now, he envisioned her with a handsome, young courtier, anger freshly piqued by a picture that came easily. He recognized jealousy as the cause of the annoyance, and that flared his mood back to rage. *Maybe this time, she'll only take his money instead of his freedom and his life.*

Despite bitter thoughts, Nightfall could not help remembering small details: the way the dance hall lights sparked from hair white as an elder's, the time he had rasped the skin from his knuckles while sharpening a dagger and she had dabbed at and bandaged the wound with a caring that could not have been feigned, the way just looking at her had sparked the need to protect her from the world's ugliness and pain. *She betrayed me.* Rage died, replaced by a grief that hollowed him to the core. *I will kill her.* The pronouncement brought the familiar calm that accompanied a finished and irrevocable decision.

Nightfall headed toward Rankelle, aware the steward's stolen coins would buy him good food, beer, and a warm night of rest. *Thanks for the lesson, Ned. I feel wiser already.*

Nightfall returned late in the morning to find Prince Edward slumped over his pack. Alarmed, Nightfall crouched, gaze scanning the clearing for enemies or movement. A pile of partially burnt sticks lay heaped in the center, all that remained of a poorly fashioned campfire. A sagging lean-to graced the opposite side of the meadow. Near it, the horses grazed on leaves and vines.

The previous night, while surrounded by inn walls, spiced food, and ale, Nightfall had briefly considered staying in Rankelle. Then, the oath-bond had torn through his guts with a pain that doubled him, as if to split his physical body apart and scrape the soul from the deepest part of his being. He had stumbled from the tavern to vomit, vowing to return to Prince Edward, until the agony subsided. Now, the magic tingled, but he suffered none of the previous night's pain. *If Edward is dead, at least the bond doesn't hold me responsible.*

Seeing no signs of a struggle and hearing nothing to indicate nearby interlopers, Nightfall approached the prince. As he came closer, he could tell Edward was breathing deeply and regularly, and he saw no evidence of wounds. A book lay pinned beneath Edward's arm, its opened pages crinkled. Nightfall studied the words, upside-down and partially blocked by Edward's sleeve: ". . . for smaller camps, the great armies . . ."

Nightfall stopped reading. Quietly, he walked to the lean-to. Finding the other packs protected by the canvas roof, he set to work preparing breakfast and getting ready for another day of travel. *I wonder how long he stayed awake trying to build the fortress this time?* Nightfall shook his head. *Much as I hate to admit it, the young fool means well. And I have to give him credit for stamina. For a pampered prince, he handles pain and work better than I ever expected.* Finished with the food and packs, Nightfall rearranged the wood into an efficient pattern, placed the frog candle stolen from the steward amid the sticks, and lit it with the steward's tinderbox. As the wax melted, the fire roared to life.

Nightfall turned his attention to Prince Edward, sprawled over his pack, muscled limbs still and hair covering his face like a golden veil. *He sleeps like a dead man. And, in these parts, there's a fine gap between sleeping like one and becoming one.* "Master?" he called tentatively.

When Prince Edward did not respond, Nightfall came directly beside him. "Master!"

Edward did not stir.

Nightfall prodded Edward's belly with the toe of one boot. "Master, wake up."

Edward made a raucous noise, then dropped back to sleep.

Oh, for the sake of the gods. Exasperated, Nightfall

backed away. He hefted a rock, studied Edward, then wisely exchanged the stone for a pine cone. Lobbing it in a gentle arc, he let it fall onto the prince's face.

Prince Edward jerked, opened his eyes, and sat up. He scratched at the cheek where the pine cone had landed, then traced the route of the object from his face to where it lay in the grass. He looked up into the tree that must have dropped it, frowning.

Nightfall thought it best to distract Edward before his sleep-numbed mind worked through the realization that pine cones do not fall in the spring. "Master, breakfast is ready."

"Sudian." The prince rose with a swiftness that had to aggravate sinews cramped from his awkward position as well as the riding soreness. "How long have you been back?"

"Not long." Nightfall simulated the clumsiness that accompanies fatigue. "I retraced our steps as far as I could."

"And?" Prince Edward covered a yawn, his eyes bloodshot with exhaustion. His gaze found and locked on the crumpled book.

"I didn't find the spade."

Edward scooped the book into his lap, watching Nightfall grimly.

"I think a bear must have eaten it, Master."

"A bear?" Prince Edward studied Nightfall dubiously, as if to figure out whether he was being mocked. "Bears eat meat."

Nightfall kept a sincere expression on his face. "I've seen them chew branches and eat berries, Master. I thought they might eat spade handles, too."

Thoughtfully, Edward smoothed the wrinkled page, then leafed through, presumably seeking details about the eating habits of bears.

Nightfall turned back to the fire to hide his jaded grin. *I'll bet nobles can't shit without looking up how some great king or general used to do it.* Gathering the first of the packs, he headed for the horses, his thoughts shifting toward the coming journey. *Nemix by midday. And either Kelryn or I won't live to see the dawn.*

* * *

Prince Edward Nargol and Nightfall reached the city of Nemix in late morning. Mud sucked at the horses' hooves, and the white gelding pranced around puddles, spooking the packhorse behind it. Edward steadied it with weight shifts and tugs on the reins, but even he seemed to be wearying of the constant struggle with a poorly trained horse.

Cottages lined Nemix' earthen roadways, unevenly spaced and diversely built; obviously, homes had been squeezed between existing dwellings as the city grew. Stone walkways fringed the streets, and people whisked about their business on these, avoiding the rain-muddied paths. A few stopped to stare at the radiant, if tired, prince and his single escort in Alyndar's colors. Travelers came often to the city, bearing trade goods or wearing weapons and odd clothing; but royalty was scarce anywhere. And, though he displayed no sigil and rode with no armies, Ned's beauty and bearing proclaimed his nobility as surely as if he had announced it.

Nightfall traversed the familiar roadways with trepidation. Riding through Marak's city as Sudian felt wrong, like invading a rival's territory or committing a crime in the name of honest Balshaz instead of Nightfall. The feeling was compounded by Prince Edward's tendency to keep heading toward the scummier side of town, despite Nightfall's subtle attempts to change direction.

At length, tired of riding in zigzags, Prince Edward drew up before a cottage. A woman chased a pig from the doorway with a broom, and the squealing animal disrupted a flock of chickens pecking seeds between stones in the walkway. The birds erupted into a flapping, clucking disarray. Startled, Prince Edward's horse whipped into a rear, twisting in midair to bolt back the way it had come.

For an instant, Edward teetered. Then, his arms flailed the air, and he fell gracelessly into a puddle. Breath hissed between his teeth. Mud splattered his silks and turned the white horse into a spotted parody.

"Master, are you hurt?" Playing the dedicated squire, Nightfall leapt from his saddle and rushed to Edward's side.

The pattern of the pedestrians slowed as they paused to

stare at the grounded prince. Attention of any kind unsettled Nightfall, and he could not help feeling embarrassed for Ned.

"I'm fine." Edward lunged to his feet. "Catch Snow, Sudian."

Nightfall blinked, trying to figure out if the prince's phrase was some new form of dismissal. "Catch snow, Master?"

"Catch Snow!" Edward repeated, making an abrupt gesture toward the white gelding trotting toward the border. "Before he gets away."

The horse. He's named a damned horse. Nightfall sprang onto his bay and dug his heels into its ribs. The mare whipped into a gallop, charging after the fleeing gelding. Citizens drew up along both sides of the roadway, meticulously avoiding the street.

The gelding broke into a run as the mare pulled up alongside it, but not quickly enough. Nightfall inched ahead, then twisted the mare into a sudden turn that blocked the white's escape. The gelding pulled up suddenly, reversed direction toward Ned, then dropped to a walk.

By the time Nightfall returned, dismounted, and caught both riding horses by the bridles, he found a dripping Edward receiving the final directions to the one place in all Nemix from which he wanted to divert the prince: Grittmon's Inn and Tavern. Though the closest place to rest and clean, Grittmon's honest business was a front for a myriad of illegal rackets. In the locked back room, Nightfall had bought numerous pieces of information, received jobs and messages, and met a motley assortment of sociopaths and bodyguards. City guardsmen received their beer free at certain times, and were strangely absent at others. Once, paid directly by Grittmon, Nightfall had poisoned a rival criminal lord. The man had crumpled in plain sight of two dozen patrons. Yet the corpse had been disposed of without fuss; not even a whisper of the crime infiltrated the street gossip.

Prince Edward took the white gelding's bridle from Nightfall, leading the horse down the roadway. "Come on, Sudian."

Nightfall trotted after, leading the bay and the chestnut. "Master, there's a good inn down this way." He pointed in the opposite direction.

Edward did not break stride. "Thank you, Sudian, but there's a closer one over here."

"But it's not nearly as nice." Nightfall glared at the nearby spectators. With the action finished, they started to disperse. "And the food—"

"Food doesn't matter." Edward tugged at his clinging undergarments irritably, his walk awkward. "Right now, I just want to wash and sleep."

And live until tomorrow. That's important, too. "But, Master. Grittmon's isn't good enough for you."

"Sudian." Prince Edward swung around suddenly. "I'm covered with filth. I smell like a barn, and I saw the dawn before I fell asleep this morning. I couldn't sleep for worrying, when you didn't return, that I had sent my squire off to die." He turned back, continuing his march toward Grittmon's Inn. "I'm getting a bath as soon as possible if I have to use a cow trough."

Last night he worried about me? Nightfall fell into shocked silence, too familiar with Ned's sincerity to doubt the sentiment. *The babe in the woods alone at night worried about the demon. I don't believe this.* Only two people in Nightfall's life had ever seemed concerned for him. Kelryn's betrayal negated her affection; surely her concern for him had been as fake as her love. And Dyfrin was the kind of friend that came once in a lifetime, if ever, the sort who not only worried for him but seemed to read his every mood. Suspicions raised, Nightfall tried to guess what Prince Edward wanted from him. *I have little to offer except my service and loyalty. And he knows he already has those.*

Prince Edward turned a corner, entering the business district. Citizens paced the walkways, laden with baskets of fruit and vegetables, laundry, or personal crafts. A cart approached from the opposite direction. Edward and Nightfall drew the horses aside to let it pass before continuing onward.

Soon, Grittmon's stone and wood tavern came into sight, its green sign matching its cheerily painted trim.

Smoke fluttered from the chimney. The odor of hay and manure wafted from the attached stables, liberally mixed with the pleasant, distinctive smell of horses.

Prince Edward stopped, smiling his relief. "Sudian, I'll get the room. You take care of the horses, then head out to market and find a spade."

Gods! Not the damned spade thing again. Nightfall opened his mouth to protest, then changed his mind. Arguing would only irritate Ned. Grittmon's would not become dangerous until after sundown. In the meantime, he was free to handle his business with Kelryn while Edward tended to his personal hygiene.

Wanting to smooth Prince Edward's transition to a world where he had to pay for his comforts, Nightfall seized the horses' bridles and tugged them toward the stables. Drawn by the aroma of hay and water, the animals followed without much coaxing, trotting eagerly after Nightfall.

A stable boy in tattered, filthy homespun met him at the entrance. He wiped a runny nose on the back of his sleeve. "Can I help you, sir?"

"Here." Nightfall rummaged through the purse he had stolen from the steward, emerging with a silver coin. He offered it to the boy.

The child's gaze locked on the silver, but his hands reached for the bridles instead. "You pay inside, sir."

"No, this is for you." Nightfall pressed the coin into the boy's hand. "You'll get two more if the horses and tack are well cared for and here when it's time for us to leave."

The boy stared at the coin in his fist.

Nightfall unlashed his own pack as well as Prince Edward's, letting them slide gently to the ground. "Any gear I leave with the horses is welcome to disappear." With that, he shouldered up the prince's heavy pack and his lighter one, and chased after his master.

Nightfall caught sight of Prince Edward as he was entering Grittmon's. A lean, handsome pickpocket named Myar caught the door as Edward stepped to the threshold, holding the panel for the prince's entrance.

Always suspicious of politeness, especially from a

thief, Nightfall watched Myar's free hand dip into the prince's pocket and deftly flick the purse from Edward's possession to his own.

"Thank you," Edward said.

"My pleasure," Myar replied honestly.

Though crushed beneath the weight of Prince Edward's armor and effects, Nightfall rushed to the door before Myar could let it swing shut. "Master, wait!" Aware the pickpocket would be more attuned to cunning movements than gross effrontery, Nightfall crashed into Myar with enough force to drive him against the door.

Breath rushed from Myar's mouth in a startled cry. The packs teetered in Nightfall's grip, but he still managed to reappropriate Edward's purse, along with another in Myar's possession, and slip both into his own pocket. "I'm sorry. I'm so sorry." Nightfall fawned over the pickpocket, now dropping both packs in awkward apology. The heavy pack clanked onto Myar's toe.

Myar bellowed in pain, half-staggering, half-hopping out the door. Wedged in the door frame, the packs kept the panel from closing, and Nightfall tripped after Myar, wringing his hands and ceaselessly berating his clumsiness. "I really am sorry. I didn't mean—"

"Stupid!" Myar lashed a hand across Nightfall's face with a suddenness that surprised even the squire. Stumbling backward, he tripped over the pack. He caught his balance naturally, then thinking better of a blatant display of grace, sprawled to the barroom floor. His cheeks felt on fire, more from rising rage than the force of the blow. Not since his mother's death had anyone struck Nightfall, and it was all he could do to keep from leaping to his feet and jamming a dagger between the pickpocket's ribs. Instead, he pretended grogginess, rolling to his hands and knees. He gained a strange view of the common room, a sea of table, chair, and human legs.

"Witless servant." Myar pursued, aiming a kick at Nightfall's ribs. "Clumsy bastard."

Accustomed to acting, Nightfall kept his temper, cringing from the blow he knew must land. But Prince Edward stepped between them, seizing Myar's leg in mid-stroke with a quickness Nightfall would not have thought possible from one so inexperienced. "Don't hit my squire! No one hits my squire. Not even *I* hit my squire." He tossed down the captured leg.

Nightfall had never seen Edward angry before, and the prince's size and golden presence made him glad Edward chose not to hit his squire. It felt strange to let the prince protect him, yet it fit the act and he knew Edward was in little danger. Few thieves were killers and few killers thieves, and he knew Myar was no exception. Quietly, while all attention fixed on the exchange between Myar and Edward, Nightfall rose and slipped the purse back into the prince's pocket.

Myar retreated, glaring at Nightfall around his master. "Yeah. Well, maybe if you did hit him, he wouldn't be such an oaf." Spinning on his heel, Myar stormed off into the street.

Prince Edward turned, concern clearly etched on his features. "Are you hurt, Sudian?" He hefted his own pack, then took Nightfall's in the other hand.

"No, Master. Thank you, Master. You are, as the gods told me in my dreams, the most wonderful of all masters. And I am proud to serve you." Nightfall reached to take the gear, but Edward did not relinquish it.

"And I'm honored to have you, Sudian." He fumbled through his purse, passing Nightfall a silver coin, blithely unaware he had not had possession of his money just moments ago. "I'll take care of our things and the room. You get the spade."

I don't believe this. We just had a double robbery, an assault, and a shouting match in a barroom doorway, and he's still thinking about that damned spade. Nightfall accepted the silver, thinking it safer in his own pocket than Edward's. With it, he could buy a gross of spades.

The oath-bond buzzed through Nightfall, and he examined the inn's common room for evidence of danger. In broad daylight, few men patronized Grittmon's; and, at the present time, every customer watched Prince Edward. Four men sat in the far corner, the cards in their fists temporarily forgotten for the action in the doorway. Nearer, a pair of leather-clad city guardsmen exchanged relieved glances, apparently pleased that the conflict had not flared into a fight. A plump, aging barmaid sprawled at a table near the card players, chewing *kommi* and studying Edward with a look that expressed interest and an attitude that revealed doubt. Windows in the walls on either side of the door gave a view of surrounding streets. An elaborate stairway at the farther end of the room led to a catwalk. From previous experience, Nightfall knew that around the back side of the stairs, a door led into Grittmon's private room.

Looks safe enough. It occurred to Nightfall to worry about Edward's purse as well as his person, but he dismissed the thought. *I can't sew myself to his side. Maybe a robbery might give him a taste of reality.* The thought made him smile. Ned's innocence made life so simple for Nightfall, he hated the idea of corrupting it. *Besides, he's so cute when he's being childishly noble.* "I'll be back shortly, Master." Turning, he strode from the bar onto Nemix's streets.

The oath-bond quivered within Nightfall like a chill. He paused, moving slowly to see if it worsened, not wanting to lose his soul over a missing spade. But the feeling remained constant, apparently just a warning that he had left the prince alone and not in the safest place. *I'll be back before dusk. I can't be with him while he bathes, and no one who saw him work Myar will stand against him.*

The oath-bond eased, apparently satisfied with the rationalization. Nightfall headed toward the Nemixian dance hall. *Now, to take care of my own business.*

Nightfall negotiated the streets and alleyways from habit, too familiar with his route to pay it any heed. Fully adopting his persona as Sudian, he brushed between the pedestrians with the nervous curiosity of a young, foreign servant. The act came naturally, from years of practice at playing roles, and he trusted the quiet, brooding portion of his mind that functioned, even in sleep, to alert him to any threat. It left him free to plot.

In my real appearance, I'm established as a naive and fiercely loyal squire. A perfect disguise. Yet a thought that should have pleased Nightfall made him frown instead.

His own words rang false. *There's no costume more vulnerable and dangerous than one well-anchored and based on natural looks. If things go wrong, ditching Sudian would cost me my soul. And from now on, if caught, I always run the risk of being stripped down to the face too many people know as Sudian, Edward's squire.*

Nightfall wandered through the market square, his eyes seeing everything, but his mind filtering out the confused hubbub of merchants and patrons that bore him no threat. From recollection, he knew that the building that served as quarters for the dancers had no windows, only a pair of doors at either end of a long corridor. Two other means of entry came to mind. A chimney rose from the common room at one end of the hallway, but it would prove a tight and grimy portal; gaining access to it would require him to climb the building. *In broad daylight, no less. If I got caught, it would be impossible to explain.* The other entryway, the kitchen chute used for grocery deliveries seemed equally unsuitable. *Too many people around this time of day. And, again, there would be no sensible alibi.*

It was not the first time Nightfall had found a straightforward, simple plan the most practical. His agility, training and weight-shifting skill seemed to work best with unexpected contingencies or after his scouting revealed useful details less practiced spies might miss. *My best strategy, as Sudian, is to walk right in the front door and gather as much information about Kelryn's patterns and protections as I can. Then, if I see a way to kill her and make it look accidental, my job is finished. If not, I'll have to find a way to come back in the night.* A comfortable familiarity pervaded the thought.

Suddenly, pain bore through Nightfall's abdomen, sharp as embedded talons. Caught by surprise, he whirled before he realized that the agony came from within him. The movement splashed dizziness through his head, stealing his usual dexterity and pounding him to the walkway. Instinctively, he lowered his weight to minimize the fall. Then, feeling a hand on his arm, he restored his mass with a thought.

The oath-bond. Nightfall resisted the urge to concentrate on the benefactor who steadied him, aware he needed to appease the magic first. *I won't go out at night unless I'm certain Ned's safe.*

The pain eased only slightly. Vertigo still crippled Nightfall, and he let the stranger brace a solid proportion of his weight, fighting the urge to lessen it again.

"Are you well?" The unfamiliar male voice sounded distant through the buzzing in Nightfall's ears.

Still concentrating on the oath-bond, he tried to guess what other condition of the magics he might stand on the verge of violating. Only one possibility presented itself. *And if I go out to kill Kelryn at night, I won't take the guise of Nightfall.*

The oath-bond retreated further, and Nightfall ran with the thought. *Nightfall is officially dead, and I can't even raise the hint of a rumor that he's still alive. Even if it didn't violate my oath, it would be foolish.*

The pain fell away. And though he had done nothing to recuperate, just the absence of the pain made him feel restive and alert. He riveted his attention on the man beside him.

Keen, dark eyes studied Nightfall from a face a few years older than his own. Light brown curls and a manicured beard framed tanned cheeks and an expression of concern. "Boy, are you well?"

Nightfall could not recall the last time anyone had called him "boy." Even knowing he looked far younger than his age, he believed he should have enough years to avoid the slur. *It's the livery. It's the damned squire livery. And I'd better get used to it.* Nightfall's mind clicked naturally to the next step. *Perhaps even take advantage of it.* "I'm all right. Just a touch of vertigo." Logic told Nightfall that this man had simply happened along at the crucial moment, that if a youngster near himself had stumbled, he would have helped as well. Still, his mother's drastic personality changes had given him cause to learn to judge mood and intention from distant glimpses and to catch the slightest cues that warned of an approaching transition. He had come to know from her face and posture when running to her arms would earn him a hug and when it would earn him a slap. And when taking the blow was preferable to fueling her anger by hiding or dodging.

The skill had served Nightfall well in later years. Reading expressions had become as ingrained as a swordsman's riposte to a sparring mate's favorite attack. At a glance, he could tell which sources to trust and which to challenge. To an outsider, the skill might seem uncanny. Nightfall knew it was the cause of the rumors that stated he knew, without words, who wanted his services and that to lie to Nightfall was suicide. It had always pleased him that gentle threat had proved enough; he had not needed to actually kill to support the tales.

Now Nightfall's ability kicked in without need for concentration. And though his benefactor had a softness of features that encouraged trust, Nightfall saw through the facade. The man's eyes revealed the hard glimmer of one who has taken enough lives to no longer see the value in any single one. Several possibilities rose to Nightfall's mind. *A mercenary, perhaps. A soldier. A guard.* The occupation made no difference to Nightfall; the mind-set was all that mattered.

The man continued to hold Nightfall's arm, as if searching for something. "Are you sure you're well? Do you need me to take you to a healer?"

"No," Nightfall said politely, trying to think of an equally decorous means of freeing his arm. *This is odd. What does he want from me?* Nightfall considered quickly. His skill at reading emotion and intention helped little with deeper motivation, especially that of a stranger. "I'm fine now. Thank you." He glanced in the direction he had been headed, letting his gaze rove to the passing pedestrians as a hint.

Still, the man did not release Nightfall.

"Lord, thank you. I'm well." Nightfall made a sudden movement that freed him from the stranger's hold. "Excuse me, please. My master expects me back shortly."

The stranger fell into step with Nightfall. "Yes, of course. I'm headed this direction anyway. Let me just walk a little way with you to make sure you've got your equilibrium back."

Nightfall continued walking, cursing his need to play

the subordinate. "Whatever you wish, lord. But I assure you it's unnecessary," he said, hoping his tone conveyed discomfort. This stranger's concern for another man's squire seemed too peculiar to pass unchallenged. He combed his thoughts for some way to identify this man, some mistake he might have made to reveal his own alter ego. But Nightfall's experience made him certain no one could see through the change, except perhaps his old friend, Dyfrin, whose talent for reading people made Nightfall's look amateurish. *And this man is decidedly not Dyfrin.*

The stranger slipped into casual conversation. "Those are Alyndar's colors you're wearing aren't they? Who is your master?"

Nightfall could not help wondering why this stranger insisted on asking his questions in pairs, especially when Nightfall kept deigning to answer only the second. Still uncertain of the man's interest, Nightfall's first instinct was to avoid the query. But the need to keep his role as loyal squire intervened. He squared his shoulders, adopting a posture of visible pride. "I am the squire to Younger Prince Edward Nargol of Alyndar."

"Ah," the man said. "A position of honor." Something preoccupied in his tone made it clear that this was not the information he was seeking.

That fact and the quiet stillness of the oath-bond, eased Nightfall's mind, though not his guard. *It's not Ned. It's me he wants. But why?*

The two men approached a crossroad. Nightfall debated whether to turn left, toward the dance hall, or continue straight until he got a better feel for his unwelcome companion.

But before he could make a decision, the stranger stumbled over an irregularity in the stone walkway. He flailed, catching a sudden hold on Nightfall's forearm, as if to steady himself. But the motion seemed too clumsy to be anything but exaggerated, perhaps even staged.

Cued, Nightfall barely resisted the urge to triple his weight and save them both a fall. The stranger crashed to the walkway. Nightfall landed on his hands and knees, the stone tearing a flap from his britches, bruising his knee, and abrading his palms. The impact jarred him free of the other's grip. *He wanted me to fall. But why?* Nightfall's mind raced, racking his thoughts for some action of his that might have drawn the attention of a killer. *Is he a guard? A hired assassin?*

Neither idea seemed likely. *I haven't done anything illegal or suspicious, except rob Myar.* Nightfall rose, studying the stranger with an expression of veiled annoyance and surprise. *Myar would be a fool to report a crime that would implicate himself. Besides, it would take time. And, surely, a servant would not attract the attention of murderers and thieves. Sudian hasn't existed long enough to have made enemies.* Trusting his instincts, Nightfall knew the stranger had not been trailing him. *The first touch was coincidence. But something about it made him curious about me.* He forced his thoughts back to the original encounter.

The bearded man clambered to his feet, looking sheepish. "I'm so sorry." He took a step toward Nightfall as if to help him up, though the squire had risen first. Afternoon sunlight sparkled from eyes dark as the muddy roadway, enhancing the predatory glare that made Nightfall edgy. It went beyond the haunted look of one who has killed from necessity to a selfish disdain for lesser men's lives. Nightfall had seen the expression only once before, in the face of King Rikard's adviser.

Gilleran. Gilleran the sorcerer. The answer kicked in with shocking abruptness, bringing terror with it. *Could this man be a sorcerer?* Nightfall backed away in revulsion. He recalled the brief moment when he had dropped his weight, before he had recognized a stranger's hand upon his arm. *I used my talent for only an instant. He couldn't have possibly discovered it. Could he?* Surely, no normal man would have noticed such a thing. Yet, Nightfall had to guess that this sorcerer spent much of his time looking for excuses to touch and observe strangers, trying to spot that one out of every thousand people with a special, congenital ability. *If I can identify the contents of a man's purse with a touch, why do I doubt a sorcerer could recognize magic as quickly?* A more horrifying thought followed. *Can he sense the oath-bond? If so, I'm going to be running from every sorcerer in the world.*

"I'm really sorry," the man repeated, again shuffling toward Nightfall.

"Get away from me," Nightfall said, trying to sound indignant rather than frightened. He could still feel the place where the sorcerer had grabbed him, and it made him feel unclean in a way no plague-ridden beggar ever had. He fingered the tear in his linens with dismay, softening the demand. "Please. With all respect, lord, I think I was better balanced alone." *I have to presume he staged the fall to test me, because he wasn't certain of what he felt. So it probably wasn't the oath-bond.* The idea soothed his raw-edged nerves. *In that case, my allowing him to knock me down might well have convinced him he was mistaken.* Dodging around his benefactor, Nightfall continued down the street, attuned to sounds of pursuing footsteps beneath the stomp, click, and chatter of other passersby, headed from the market square. He heard nothing to suggest the man had followed. The wary prickle at his back disappeared.

With the immediate threat removed, Nightfall pushed the incident to the back of his mind. For now, he could do nothing but hope he had passed the sorcerer's test and stay alert for future experiments or confrontations. He turned a corner, stealing a glance in the direction from which he had come. The stranger had turned and was now retreating back toward the market square.

Relieved, Nightfall turned his concentration to the Nemixian dance hall. Just as quickly, doubts suffused him, wildly out of place in the mind of the night-stalking demon that had stolen the unstealable, swindled wise men, and shattered the sleep of the brave. Memory stole his composure, flinging him back to lazy summer Sundays spent meandering between stands, Kelryn's presence a warm constant beside him, her laughter like music in his ear.

Nightfall walked the last few blocks, haunted by images of that past, alternately mourning the potential eternity of love and happiness that Kelryn's betrayal had mangled to nightmare and despising the woman who had stolen everything he could give her: trinkets, his loyalty, his dignity, and his life. *For every act I did, I thought of how it might affect her. Everywhere I went, I looked for things that might please her. She meant everything to me, yet my love and myself meant nothing to her.* Turning the last corner, Nightfall approached the dancer's quarters.

The mid-afternoon sun sparkled from the polished brass hinges. Nightfall raised his fist to knock still with some trepidations, and that uncertainty bothered him. Since the first time, when he had raised a knife against his mother's murderer, he had never felt a qualm about those he chose to kill. In all cases, he had deemed a client's security or vengeance more sacred than the rights of the victim. Yet now that it came time to avenge his own life, reservations descended upon him.

It's the time of day, Nightfall guessed, at once aware that the need to work in broad daylight was only a contributing factor to his discomfort. Always before, he had performed his crimes at night and in the guise of Nightfall; but this would not be the first time he had used another persona for innocent, daytime scouting. He reviewed his rationalization for using a direct approach, but this failed to dispel his apprehension. The method was not what bothered him.

It's Kelryn. Nightfall shook with anger, missing the steadying composure that usually filled him before a kill. *Gods! What is it about that traitor bitch that cripples me?* He tossed the thought aside. Once he faced her, the strength would come. If it didn't, he was dead.

Nightfall rapped on the iron-bound wooden door.

Several seconds passed in silence. Then, the sound of approaching footsteps reached his ears, followed by the squeal of the door being opened. Cyriwan, the dance hall proprietor, studied Nightfall through the opening crack, his crusty, bearded face somber. "Can I help you?"

"I'm looking for a woman."

Cyriwan scratched at his beard, and dirt flaked to the floor. "Any woman in particular? Or just your general woman?"

"I'm looking," Nightfall said carefully, trying to see around Cyriwan without success, "for the most graceful dancer I've ever seen. She's got short, white hair like this." He combed his mahogany locks into feathers with his fingers. "Small, hazel eyes, a straight nose with a flat tip, and a gorgeous body."

"White hair?" Cyriwan squinted, glancing up and down Nightfall as if to identify his colors. All humor left him. "You mean Kelryn. And she don't work here no more."

Nightfall naturally fell into Cyriwan's speech pattern. "She don't?"

"Good day." Cyriwan backed to close the door.

"Wait." Nightfall edged forward, trying to look childishly eager, and scuffing a toe into the crack as if by accident. It had been decades since he had needed to do anything for his information except ask. "Why don't she work here no more?"

"There needs to be a reason?"

"No, I don't suppose so." Nightfall made contrived nervous gestures that placed his boot more solidly in the path of the door. "Is there one?"

"Not this time." Cyriwan tried to pull the panel closed, but it struck Nightfall's foot. The proprietor frowned.

Nightfall shifted his weight, making certain the coins in his pocket clinked. As Sudian, it would seem odd to suggest a bribe, but he knew Cyriwan well enough to suspect that the proprietor would request one. "Where is she working now?"

Cyriwan pressed his toe against Nightfall's, calmly edging it away. "Who are you? And why do want to know?"

"My name is Sudian. I saw her dance some time ago, and I can't get her out of my mind. Please, I have to see her."

Cyriwan shook his head. "I don't know where she's gone." Circumstance and the look on his face told Nightfall it was a blatant lie.

Hastily, Nightfall removed his foot from the door, feigning self-conscious apology. The maneuver had bought him some time, but to carry it too far would arouse Cyriwan's suspicions. Since the proprietor still had not brought up the topic of payment, Nightfall tried, aware Cyriwan could never resist a shiny coin. "Would it help if I gave you some money?" He pulled out a silver, displaying it in his palm in the manner of a man unused to buying his information.

Cyriwan licked his lips. Sweat beaded his forehead, but he did not reach for the coin. "You could give me your money, and I'd take it. But I still couldn't tell you where Kelryn's at. I don't know."

You know, you slob. But I haven't the faintest idea why you aren't telling. The Cyriwan that Nightfall had known would have sold anyone for a handful of copper. *It's not ethics. Cyriwan wouldn't know a moral if it danced a jig around him, pounded him dizzy, then throttled him dead. Even if Grittmon didn't approve of the incident in his doorway, there's no way word could have beaten me here. The only possibility is that someone who can keep tabs on this fool threatened his life or promised him huge sums of money for his silence. But why?*

Cyriwan continued to stare at the coin. "Perhaps I could interest you in another woman to take your mind off Kelryn? My girls are just dancers, but some of them do other things to earn a little spending money on the side." He winked. "If you know what I mean."

Nightfall knew. But playing the part of the innocent, young squire, he hesitated in consideration. "I think so."

"That silver will buy you the name of one who does." Cyriwan reached for the coin.

Though a silver should have bought him the name of every woman in Nemix who did, Nightfall allowed the proprietor to take it, then his arm, and lead him through the doorway. Cyriwan closed the panel behind him, taking Nightfall through his front office and into the familiar corridor lined with doors.

Needing facts, and finding them more difficult to obtain than expected, Nightfall took a chance. "Since I can't see Kelryn, do you think maybe I could . . ." He lowered his face abashedly. ". . . um . . . *have* . . ." He stumbled over the euphemism. ". . . the little redhead she kept talking to between performances." He alluded to Kelryn's roommate, Shiriel. *If anyone might know where Kelryn's gone, she would. And if I can get a look at the room, I should be able to tell if Kelryn's things are still there.*

Cyriwan caught the description. Again, he studied Nightfall.

Nightfall tried to look embarrassed by the scrutiny. He avoided the proprietor's piercing, dark gaze. His walk grew tight and awkward.

Cyriwan's lips twitched into the toothy, knowing grin of a man condescending to a child. "I can try. But it'll cost you an extra silver to ask for some girl, specific."

"Oh." Though he kept his head lowered, Nightfall memorized a hallway he already knew by heart. "Oh." He let thoughtful disappointment leech into his tone, followed by consideration.

Cyriwan stopped before the fourth door on the left, awaiting an answer.

Though he knew it was Kelryn's and Shiriel's room, Nightfall shuffled past it at the same speed so as not to broadcast his knowledge. Now a half step beyond Cyriwan, he halted and turned to face the proprietor. "Well, my master did say I could spend my money any way I wanted."

Cyriwan held out a hand laced with grime.

Nightfall plucked another silver from the dwindling horde he had taken from the Alyndarian steward. *Two silver for a copper's worth of information. If that doesn't convince him I'm an ignorant galley-clod, nothing will.* Concealing the callused palms that years of labor as Etan had gained him, he dropped the coin into Cyriwan's hovering fingers.

The silver disappeared into Cyriwan's fist like a meat scrap tossed to a starving dog. He knocked on the door.

"Who is it?" Shiriel's familiar alto drifted through the wood. Small and frail, she tended toward quiet shyness except when discussing a topic about which she held a strong opinion. Then, she could become passionately shrewd, strong-willed, and clever.

"It's me," Cyriwan answered gruffly. "I have someone with me."

Nightfall shifted from foot to foot.

A moment passed in silence. Then Shiriel opened the door. She wore a patched but flattering dress over her slight form, and her red hair fanned about her shoulders.

"Shiriel, this is Sudian. He wants to discuss a business proposition with you." Cyriwan nodded encouragingly, though whether at him or the woman, Nightfall could not tell.

Shiriel looked Nightfall over.

Nightfall held his breath. This would be Sudian's first inspection by someone who had known Marak well.

But Shiriel gave no sign of recognition. Apparently finding Nightfall adequate, she stepped back to let him enter.

The cubicle beyond lay in comfortable disarray. A single pallet covered a rectangle of floor, its head against the middle of the far wall. To Nightfall's left, a familiar night table and matching chair sported a jumble of cosmetics and clothing. All of the colors suited Shiriel. An open closet to his right held several outfits, including familiar dancing costumes, though none in Kelryn's larger size.

Shiriel closed the door. Turning to face the bed, she began unlacing her bodice.

"Don't do that." Nightfall placed a hand on Shiriel's shoulder, and she felt coiled beneath his touch.

Shiriel whirled, back-stepping until she stood against the pallet. The loosened fabric revealed the edge of each, tiny breast. "If you've got something sleazy in mind, you can leave now. I don't got to do this, you know. It's just a way to make extra money."

"How much do you charge?" Nightfall enjoyed a good session of sex as much as any man, but not when he was working. *And not with Kelryn's roommate.* The idea made him ill.

"Five coppers." Shiriel glared defiantly, her chest heaving and her demeanor stiff. The straight, red hair formed a cape about her shoulders, making her look more vulnerable.

"Here." Nightfall tossed her the last silver, leaving him only the one Prince Edward had given him and the coppers in Myar's purse.

Shiriel caught the coin in a small hand, bobbled it once, then studied it. Placing it into her cleavage, she gave her full attention to Nightfall. "What do you want? And I'm still not doing anything sleazy."

"Tie that thing back up." Nightfall tried to look flustered. "I just want to talk."

"Talk?" Brow crinkled, Shiriel retied her bodice. "Talk about what?"

Nightfall moved Shiriel's undergarments from the chair to the table. Turning the chair to face her, he sat. "Another woman who works here, name Kelryn." As he moved, he caught a glimpse of an object he had missed on previous inspection. Among the vials and jars sat a too familiar glass figurine of a swan. Its neck stretched delicately upward, ending in a finely-shaped head. The wings were spread in a feathered detail Nightfall had never seen on a trinket, before or since he'd set eyes on this one nearly a year ago. Marak had discovered it displayed in a glassblower's shop. It had cost him a week of dinners; but, at the time, it had seemed well worth the cost. *Apparently, it meant nothing more to Kelryn than the life of the man who gave it to her.* He had rehearsed the presentation, and the words returned to him now, ugly, empty, and hollow: "Finally, Kelryn, I've found a piece of art worthy of your beauty. But, even should this creature come alive, you would put its grace to shame."

Shiriel's eyes narrowed suddenly. "Kelryn don't work here no more."

Nightfall met Shiriel's gaze, careful not to rivet on the swan. "That's what the guy said." He pointed to the door to indicate Cyriwan. "Where does she work now?"

"That depends."

Now it was Nightfall's turn to look confused. "Depends on what?"

Shiriel shook her head, sending the fine locks into a shimmery dance. "Depends on why it's worth a silver to you."

Nightfall sighed. He stared at a water spot on the ceiling, and a slight smile curled about features more primed for a glower. Thoughts of Kelryn made him savagely angry. But for now he feigned infatuation. "I watched her dance once. She's the most beautiful woman I ever saw. Ever." He met Shiriel's green eyes earnestly. "Please. I have to find her."

Shiriel looked skeptical. Her drawn face took on a look of calculated doubt. "You don't know, do you?"

"Know what?" Nightfall added a note of concern to his curiosity. Idly, he fiddled with the disarray on Shiriel's table.

Shiriel leaned forward, lowering her voice. "I'm sorry to be the one to tell you. Kelryn has . . ." She dropped to a whisper. ". . . clap."

Nightfall suppressed a laugh, inhaled a lungful of saliva, and coughed violently. *Well, at least I spread that rumor thoroughly.* The hoarseness of his voice only added to his sincerity. "That doesn't matter. Shiriel, I love this woman. I have to see her."

Shiriel sat on the pallet with a sigh. She drew muscle-thick legs to her chest, staring at Nightfall. "You're from Alyndar, right?"

Nightfall nodded. Emblazoned with the country's colors and in the prince's service, he could hardly deny it. His hand drifted naturally toward the glass swan.

"So what do you people want with Kelryn?"

The question caught Nightfall off his guard. He blinked, his fingers closing over the figurine, his bewildered gaze diverting Shiriel's attention from the action. "Us people? What people? What are you talking about?"

"Look." Shiriel went straight to the point. "Kelryn never did anything wrong in her life. She's a damn good dancer and an honest one. She didn't know."

"I have no idea what you're talking about." The expression of confusion on Nightfall's face deepened. He slipped the swan into his pocket, drawing his whole person inward to mask the movement. "But you're starting to scare me. Is Kelryn in some kind of trouble?"

Shiriel seemed to take no notice of the theft. Her scrutiny of Nightfall's face intensified. Apparently, she was trying to read his expression and his sincerity. "That murderer they killed up there a few weeks ago."

"You mean Nightfall?" he supplied.

Shiriel nodded briskly. "She called him Marak, but they said he was the same person. It's no secret around here that she was his girlfriend."

Nightfall tried to look suitable agitated. "You're lying! You have to be lying."

"But she didn't know he was a killer." Shiriel defended Kelryn. "She didn't know she was seeing Nightfall. And, of course, she never committed any crimes." She wrung her hands, hugging her knees to her chest. "So, go away. Leave her alone."

Nightfall met Shiriel's intense expression with one of his own. "Have others from Alyndar come looking for her before me?"

"No," Shiriel admitted. "You're the first."

Nightfall rolled his eyes in exasperation. He relaxed a bit, idly drumming his fingers on the single, narrow drawer in the front of the desk. "Do I look like a king's executioner to you? A guard captain?" He spread his arms to emphasize his delicate frame.

Shiriel's scrutiny became intense. Suddenly, Nightfall regretted his bold plea for attention. *A close look might give me away. Then again, I suppose this is one of the safer places to test the new "disguise."*

After a few moments, Shiriel sat back, still without recognition. "No," she admitted. "But you could still be one. Or you could be working for one."

Nightfall snorted. He worked his fingers into the drawer, idly opening and closing it against his knuckles. He tried to sound like a youth in love. "Your loyalty is wonderful and makes sense to me. If I had the chance, I'd be just as protective of her. But Nightfall's dead." Spoken aloud, the words sounded strange in his ears. "King Rikard has no use or interest in the man's girlfriend. And even if he did, he's a king. He'd have just sent over a bunch of guards and taken her, not some stumbling squire who can't even keep his balance in the street." Removing one hand from the drawer, he fingered the hole in his britches.

Shiriel's features crinkled in thought, then relaxed at the obvious sense of his explanation. "He's the one who gave her the clap, you know."

Her words seemed like a complete non sequitur. Nightfall levered the drawer partway open to reveal a gem-studded pair of earrings and a scattering of cheap bracelets. A sheet of papyrus lay over an old brush with bent bristles wound through with strands of white and red hair. "What? The king gave someone the clap?"

"Not the king." Shiriel seemed to notice Nightfall's interest in her things for the first time. She watched his hands, as if to make certain he kept away from her jewelry, blithely unaware that the most expensive item in the room was already in his possession. "Marak. Nightfall. He gave Kelryn the clap."

Oh, great. Nightfall did not appreciate the slur, though he could not dismiss the irony. *Actually, though, she's right. I spread the rumor. So, in a manner of speaking, I did give Kelryn the clap.*

The conversation seemed to be going nowhere. Aware he could only safely leave Prince Edward alone at Grittmon's Tavern until evening, Nightfall tried to speed things along by returning to the point. "Look, I think it's clear that no one in Alyndar wants to hurt Kelryn. And, even if they did, why would they send a spy wearing their colors? I just think she's beautiful. I can't get her out of my mind." He adopted the nervous look of a youth forced to share his deepest secrets with his mother. "I just want a chance to meet her. Won't you give that to me?" He turned Shiriel the most desperate, sincere expression he could muster.

Shiriel stared back. Her face betrayed only thoughtfulness, but her hesitation revealed that she was considering the possibility.

Still playing his role, Nightfall let his gaze fall to his hands. Again, he saw the brush with as many of Kelryn's hairs as Shiriel's, and his glance slid naturally to the sheet of papyrus. Runes scrawled across the surface.

But before he could focus on them closely enough to make sense of the writing, Shiriel lurched to her feet. She cleared the distance between them in two running steps and slammed the drawer shut on Nightfall's fingers.

"Ow!" Nightfall leapt backward, clasping his throbbing knuckles. The drawer rebounded partway open. An earring bounced from the confines, skittering across the floor. "Why did you do that? Why in hell did you do that?" His pained indignation did not need to be feigned.

An answer came to him before she could say a word. *I saw something I wasn't supposed to. I have to assume it was the note.* He tried to reconstruct a picture of the letter in his mind.

"Get out of here." Shiriel stabbed a finger toward the door.

Nightfall backed away in defensive surprise, an image filling his mind's eyes. Now that he considered it, the letter had two sets of handwriting on it, not an unusual feature. Commonly, illiterates or those with less than perfect penmanship would hire a scribe, then authenticate or personalize the note with their own signature. "What did I do? Why are you mad at me?"

"Kelryn's like a sister to me." Shiriel made another abrupt, hostile gesture at the door. "I told her I wouldn't tell anyone where she went, and you damn near got me to break that promise."

In a cowering slouch, Nightfall moved toward the exit, still certain the letter, not a promise, was the source of Shiriel's rage. Now on track of the handwriting, he knew he had seen both sets sometime in the past. *Kelryn can't write. From Shiriel's reaction, I have to guess that the signature was Kelryn's. But the other hand seemed just as familiar. Why?* The answer remained maddeningly just beyond reach.

Shiriel opened the door.

Nightfall stepped up beside her, trying to look pained and innocently confused. "I'm sorry. I didn't mean any harm."

Shiriel's anger seemed to melt away. She started to say something, then quietly motioned him out instead.

Nightfall passed into the corridor, hearing the door whisk shut behind him, feeling the breeze of its movement. He headed for Cyriwan's office and the exit of the building, his mind still worrying the problem. *The parchment came from reeds, not bark. That means it's of southern origin.* He considered southern scribes. Three of his personae, Balshaz, Frihiat, and Marak, had been literate; and the first two lived in the south. Among them, he had sent or seen enough messages to know the local scribes. He tried to match the writing to a name.

But Nightfall had only caught a few glimpses of the parchment. The scribe's identity did not come to mind. Nightfall knocked on Cyriwan's office door, frustrated by a glimpse of writing that would not focus clearly in his thoughts.

Cyriwan opened the door. "Ah! Finished so soon?"

Nightfall nodded, gaze on the door to the outside, concerned that casual conversation might wipe the image completely from his memory.

Cyriwan ushered Nightfall to the opposite end of the room. "I trust Shiriel took good care of you."

Nightfall made a noncommittal noise. He grasped the doorknob, twisted, and opened the panel onto gathering grayness. He knew he still had a few hours before sundown, but Edward would have tended to his personal needs by now and was probably wondering what was keeping his squire. Nightfall stepped out into the street.

Cyriwan called after him, cheerily. "Come back again." Then the door clicked closed behind him.

Nightfall hurried back toward Grittmon's Tavern, taking a new tack with his scribe search. Rather than trying to remember details of writing he had barely seen, he ran through the list of individual scribes. And this strategy brought an answer where the other had not. *Sperra.* And yet the solution seemed only slightly less frustrating than the question. Nightfall recalled that the kind and elderly scribe had a habit of moving his quarters three or four times a year, to cities that needed his services most.

Nightfall probed his last silver. *I hope Edward doesn't ask me to return his money. I'll need the coin, plus the coppers I took from the pickpocket, to get the information I need.* The thought made him irritable. Decades had passed since Nightfall had needed to pay for his knowledge. *I know just where to find out what I need to know. And luckily, I have reason to be there.* Heading toward Grittmon's Tavern, Nightfall quickened his pace.

Chapter 5

Nightfall laughs, and death's ax falls;
Hell opens wide and swallows all.
He rules the depths where no light shows—
Darkness comes where Nightfall goes.
—The Legend of Nightfall
Nursery rhyme, st. 5

When Nightfall returned to Grittmon's Inn and Tavern, he found Prince Edward alone at one of the tables, chasing down a bite of bread with a final swallow of wine. He wore a fresh linen cloak over a blue silk tunic and breeks, and he had cleaned and oiled his traveling boots. The sword hung at his side, its tooled leather sheath and gem-studded hilt making it look more like decoration than weapon. The comb had left trails through his wet hair. He appeared bathed, comfortable, and well-rested. Engrossed in mopping up the last of the gravy on his plate with the end of the bread, he did not at once notice Nightfall's entrance.

Nightfall ducked inside, handing the door to a pair of exiting guardsmen. He took stock of the remaining patrons as he trotted toward Edward's table. Two men he recognized as swindling partners sat several tables away from the prince, toasting their latest victory. A prostitute perched on a stool before the bar, a slit in her dress revealing shapely thighs to a point just shy of indecency. She chewed a thumbnail, occasionally throwing encouraging looks toward the celebrants.

Nightfall knew the bartender, a giant of a man named Makai, strong and competent with a sword, who doubled as a bouncer when the need arose. Oddly, instead of one of the usual maids, the person delivering the drinks was a middle-aged man whom Nightfall recognized as Nemix's prime informer, a man who bragged that he could get a donkey to tell him its owner's life history. The incongruity of the scene put Nightfall on the alert, though he sensed no threat to Edward or himself. It was not uncommon for a criminal down on his luck or with city guards breathing down his neck to take a legitimate job at Grittmon's Inn to rebuild his store of cash. But Tadd the Mouth seemed to have the most secure job of all. There was nothing inherently illegal about gathering information, and everyone needed to know something at some time.

Finishing the last bite, Prince Edward looked up from his meal. "Sudian!" His voice boomed through the near-empty confines, drawing every eye.

"Master," Nightfall replied in a soft tone, still easily audible over the silence that followed Edward's call. Discomfited by the attention, Nightfall cleared the distance to Edward's table more quickly than propriety demanded. He stood beside the table while Prince Edward's gaze roved up and down his squire's person, his expression lapsing from happy welcome to perplexity.

"Sudian, where's the spade?"

The others in the tavern remained quiet, interested in the exchange, presumably from boredom or curiosity about what noblemen discussed with their squires.

Nightfall sat, selecting a chair that put his back to the wall and gave him the widest view of the common room as well as the staircase that hid Grittmon's secret meeting room. He hoped his repositioning to Edward's level would give him a chance to further lower his voice and turn the conversation private. "Master, I searched the entire town. Most merchants said they didn't make spades. The ones that did had sold their last." He opened his hands in a gesture of apology. "There's not a spade to be had in Nemix today."

Prince Edward frowned.

Nightfall let his head sag in submissive fatigue, his red-brown hair falling into bangs. He had tried to get Edward to realize that the spade was just excess baggage to weigh them down, but the time had come to admit defeat. *When I have to go to ridiculous extremes over something this insignificant, it's time to give up the battle.*

Tadd the Mouth approached, taking Edward's empty plate. "More wine, sir?"

"None for me," Edward replied. "But bring my squire's dinner."

Tadd took the prince's glass, then brushed back the long, sandy locks that fringed his bald spot. "I couldn't help overhearing . . ."

Nightfall suppressed a groan.

". . . you're looking for a spade, right?"

Edward nodded briskly, strong hands folded on the tabletop. "Yes, we are. But my squire says there are none to be found."

Tadd flicked a glance at Nightfall that suggested he found Edward's squire particularly incompetent. "Well, if the market has none, you might try a little smithy I know. It's just past the cooper's place on Meclarin Street." He traced directions Nightfall knew by heart, using a finger on the tabletop.

Why does the Mouth pick now to start giving his information away for free? The answer came to Nightfall instantly. *It's not free, really. He can tell Ned's got money, and he's working up his tip.*

Edward looked at Nightfall. "Did you try there?"

Nightfall surrendered. "No, Master, I didn't know." *Better to just buy the damned spade and get this over with once and for all. I can always ditch the thing again.* He started to rise. "I'll go there now."

"No." Edward gestured Nightfall back into his seat. "You stay. You need to eat and wash and get some rest." The tender concern on the prince's face surprised Nightfall. "I'll buy the spade."

I wish the young dupe would quit worrying about my comfort. I might actually start liking him. Nightfall drew breath to challenge Edward's decision, then realized it would be folly. *Ned would get mad because I'm questioning him. Besides, shortly, Meclarin Street will be safer than Grittmon's Inn, especially since, if I went after the spade, I'd be leaving him alone here.* Nightfall returned to his seat. "Master, you're too good to me." From the corner of his eye, he could see Tadd nodding in tacit agreement.

Prince Edward rose, clapping a meaty hand to Nightfall's shoulder. "Good servants are hard to find. Your loyalty and company are worth a lot to me." He headed for the door.

Tadd whisked off to get Nightfall's food, looking as if the sentimentality might make him ill.

Nightfall studied Edward's retreating back, uncertain whether to feel amused by the prince's naiveté or embarrassed that he had bared his soul in a public place. *Do I follow and keep watch on him or stay and eat?* The pervading odor of beer made his empty stomach queasy, reminding him he had not eaten since morning. He focused on the oath-bond, to see if it might suggest or sanction a course of action; but it buzzed its normal baseline, as if waiting for his own considerations for its input. *I'm supposed to obey his word except in instances where his welfare is endangered. So far, the magic hasn't considered the simple act of leaving him alone cause for alarm. There's no reason for me to expect trouble on a main street like Meclarin.* Having made the tentative concession to stay, Nightfall cringed, waiting for the oath-bond's response to his decision.

Its intensity did not change. Nightfall relaxed, guessing that, in this case, neither choice would have risked his soul. *Apparently, it judges my intentions rather than specific actions.* A thought followed naturally. *Presumably, so long as I did everything in my power and vision to protect Ned, his death would not necessarily result in my losing my soul.* He waited for confirmation or a painful reminder from the oath-bond, but neither came. Still, it hovered, like a live being within him, as vibrant as the day of its casting.

Whatever he thought of my honesty, King Rikard must have trusted my wisdom, at least. I can't believe he put his son's life, not just in my hands, but solely under the protection of my judgment. Nightfall barely suppressed a chuckle until another idea slammed him into silence. *Unless he wanted Ned killed. This way, he gets me to handle the murder and destroys my soul at the same time.* It seemed illogical. *Surely, he could have simply had Ned executed. And I was caught. Why didn't he just have Gilleran perform his ritual slaughter in the dungeon?*

The thought spiraled a shiver through Nightfall. He did not know exactly what the foul rite entailed, though he had to guess it was complicated. *I'd already escaped and killed some of his guards. Perhaps he feared I'd slay Gilleran, too.* It seemed like a logical concern. *This way, he got me to submit to an agreement that seemed believable but will probably cost me my soul. And he managed to deliver the young prince of nuisance, fanatic idealism, and embarrassment to an infamous butcher.*

Anger flooded Nightfall, though he knew his new track of thought was only a theory. He felt a sudden kinship with an innocent, blond prince little more than half his age. *Ned may be an idiot, but we have a common enemy, even if he doesn't know it.*

Tadd arrived with a plate of slivered lamb, gravy, and bread along with a glass of wine. He set them before Nightfall. "Good man, your master."

"The best." Nightfall smiled, glad to see the informer in a talkative mood. There were things he needed to know, including the location of a scribe named Sperra. *Better to follow that lead than to ask about Kelryn directly.* Cyriwan's silence had clued him to caution. "He's Prince Edward Nargol from Alyndar."

"So he told me." Tadd met Nightfall's gaze, and the squire glanced politely away. Too many times his piecing stare and an icy silence filled with threat had gained him information when conventional means had failed. "What's he doing out this way?"

Ah. An important question. Also a beautiful lead into one of my own. "He's King Rikard's younger son. He needs to get landed." Nightfall chuckled as if sharing an inside joke, then briefly met Tadd's gaze again. "Actually, neither my master nor I know much about landing. I don't suppose you happen to have some ideas?"

Tadd the Mouth stiffened almost imperceptibly. "None at all."

A confession of ignorance from Tadd nearly startled Nightfall into losing his own composure.

The Mouth laughed, the sound holding a note of tension. "What would an overgrown serving boy know of landing?"

Nightfall joined the laughter. "Apparently, nearly as much as a prince's squire. I figured he would know. He figured I would know." He laughed again. "It's almost embarrassing. I'm hoping we can find some books about it." The laughter seemed to loosen Tadd somewhat, so Nightfall took a chance. "And speaking of books, have you ever heard of a southern scribe called Sperra?"

"No," Tadd said.

"Would you happen to know where he would be . . .?" Nightfall trailed off, so certain of a positive response, it had taken the negative time to register.

"No," Tadd said again, a blatant lie. Nightfall cared little for the defiant hostility building in the informer's eyes. In the guise of Nightfall, he would already have had the Mouth on the floor with a knife at his throat. Although he had not yet fully established the character of Sudian, he felt certain the squire would not respond in a like fashion.

Nightfall reminded himself to remain calm. "What if I paid you for the answer?"

Tadd considered. "All right," he said, at length.

Nightfall reached into his pocket and retrieved three coppers from Myar's purse. It was not Nightfall's way to pay before receiving merchandise, but it fit Sudian. Nightfall handed the coins to Tadd.

The informer waited patiently for Nightfall to pose the question again.

Further annoyed by the formality, Nightfall repeated, "Where could I find a scribe called Sperra?"

Tadd pocketed the coppers. "Never heard of him."

"What!" Nightfall struggled to maintain character. "You said if I paid you . . ."

". . . I'd give you the answer," Tadd finished. "The answer is 'I don't know.' I didn't say you'd like it."

Nightfall glared, fighting to keep his anger in check. *Something strange is happening here. First Cyriwan and now the Mouth.* Many possibilities came to mind. *Some sort of legal pressure? A new guard captain perhaps?* The explanation did not fit. *The only thing I've had trou-*

*ble getting is information. Myar stole Ned's purse bla-
tantly enough, the guards left Grittmon's at their usual
time, and Cyriwan's dancers are still playing off-time
prostitute.* The realization narrowed the situation to one
possibility. *For some reason, they're guarding information, even basic, harmless news. That explains, too, why
Cyriwan wouldn't tell me where Kelryn had gone.*

Tadd wandered toward the bar, never fully turning his
back on the man he had just cheated.

But Nightfall found his own thoughts more interesting.
Shiriel wouldn't tell me about Kelryn either. He started in
on the food, feeling certain that the dancer's stated motivation for hiding Kelryn's whereabouts was true. Until
now, Cyriwan's had made less sense. *But why would
criminals declare a general halt to all information? Or, is
it a halt to all information given to me?* Nightfall realized
he had leapt from the too general to the too specific.
*More likely, it's a silence to all questions asked by strang-
ers. But why?*

Nightfall chewed thoughtfully on the overcooked lamb.
Grittmon's Inn had never become famous for its fare.
*Only an event of tremendous proportions would drive
them to such an extreme.* The answer eluded him. Nightfall took another bite of lamb, wrestling with the problem.

Tadd returned to his post, talking softly with the bartender. From the corner of his vision, Nightfall saw
Grittmon appear from behind the staircase and join the
discussion beyond the bar. Apparently cued to danger by
the appearance of the owner, the prostitute sidled from
the bar, short skirt flapping to her hips as she left.

Unable to solve the riddle, Nightfall turned his attention fully to his food. In the past, he had found his deeper
mind continued working on a problem long after his
thoughts had focused on other things.

Tadd refilled the mugs of the two swindlers, chatting
with them for a time, in a voice too low for Nightfall to
hear. Returning to the bar, he hefted a filled mug that the
bartender had left on the counter and headed for Nightfall.

As Tadd approached, Nightfall turned him a pouting
glare.

Tadd raised his free hand in a peace-making gesture. "Hey, *donner.*" He used a jocular street term just shy of meaning "friend." "Look, your master's been real good to me, and I feel kind of bad for what I did to you."

Nightfall grunted.

"Look, I really need the money, so you're not getting it back. What would you say if I gave you a beer to make up for it?"

Nightfall looked up, studying the man in front of him. "I'd say," he replied coldly, "that's an awfully expensive beer."

Tadd set the mug at Nightfall's elbow. "Aw, it was harmless. Don't be mad."

Nightfall sighed. "I guess I did learn something for my money."

Tadd assumed a bug-eyed look that begged forgiveness.

Amused by the exaggerated expression, Nightfall smiled grudgingly. "Fine. Two beers and all's forgiven."

"Deal." Tadd grinned, heading back toward the bar.

Guess the little pig-face wanted his tip after all. Nightfall continued eating. More accustomed to beer than wine, he hefted the mug. Just as he tipped it back, the answer struck him with a suddenness that made him feel like an idiot for not catching it sooner. *It's me, of course! They don't know who turned in Nightfall. Marak came from Nemix, so they have reason to worry that the traitor's right here among them.* He lowered the mug without taking a sip. Sensing abrupt tension from the area of the bar, Nightfall glanced that way. For an instant, he caught all three pairs of eyes upon him. Then each of the men behind the bar returned to work.

Cued to a personal threat by the oddity, Nightfall again raised the mug. This time, a faintly cloying odor reached him from beneath the familiar reek of bad beer. The underlying smell might have meant nothing to him had Grittmon not given him the same concoction to murder a rival crime lord in this tavern. *Poison.* Suddenly, the rules had changed, and Nightfall wished that he, not Prince Edward, had chosen the table. He would have taken one far closer to the door and farther from the catwalk.

They want me dead. Why? It occurred to Nightfall how suspicious he must look. *Two men from the city that executed Nightfall come into Nemix and head straight for the criminal's den. I rob a thief in the doorway, then head out to buy information, yet I can't find a normal implement in the market square. Finally, I top it off by questioning the informer.* Nightfall berated his clumsiness. *No wonder they're trying to kill me.*

Raising the mug again, Nightfall put it to his lips and pretended to take a long draught, buying time to think. The aura of tension grew tangible. *It's me they want. Surely, they won't risk hurting a prince.* Though logical, Nightfall knew the thought was fallacy. *There're men who come here only for the nightly entertainment of a brawl. Once violence starts, it's going to be awfully hard to stop. I have to get out of here in the calmest manner possible.* He set down the drink, wiping his mouth with the back of a silver-colored sleeve. Unhurriedly, he rose, headed beneath the catwalk and toward the back door.

Makai, the huge bartender, covered the distance more quickly. He placed himself between Nightfall and the exit. "Where are you going?"

Nightfall replied with innocent confusion. "To splash the grass."

"What?"

A creak behind Nightfall drew his attention. All too aware of the man in front of him, he twisted his head toward Grittmon, wearing a look intended to convey that he thought the bartender was an idiot. The maneuver also gave him a view of the pair of swindlers, both carrying full mugs and headed in his direction. Tadd had moved toward the back room, and Grittmon watched from behind the bar. Having gained his bearings, Nightfall turned back to Makai, following the swindlers' approach by sound. "To water the back alley. To empty the fountain." He dropped the euphemisms. "You know, piss."

Makai remained in place. "You haven't drank enough to have to piss. Go finish your beer."

Nightfall gave Makai a withering look. "Well, thank you for your concern." Glad for the assortment of daggers the king's men had supplied, he let his fingers close casually over one nestled in the folds of his tunic. "But I've been urinating since I was born. I think I've got a feel for how it's done now."

One of the swindlers moved in. Makai's glance cued Nightfall to the other's position behind him. He took a sudden side step, as if to walk around the bouncer. As he moved, he freed the dagger from its sheath, though still keeping it concealed. It was not his way to initiate violence, only to finish it.

The swindler whipped his hand, clutching the mug, through the space where Nightfall's head had been a moment before. Beer splashed Nightfall and Makai, puddling on the floorboards.

Nightfall whirled to face this new threat. As the swindler cast off the mug to reach for a weapon, Nightfall buried his dagger in the man's kidney. Blood ran down his hand, a warm contrast to the cold, sticky beer. Having lost the element of surprise, the second swindler dropped his mug and drew his sword. The tankard struck the floor, scudding across the planks, beer washing the wood beneath his feet.

Nightfall twisted his knife free, letting the corpse drop unceremoniously to the floor. The second swindler charged Nightfall. The squire tensed. Now that first blood had been drawn, it had become a straight fight. Against stronger men in greater numbers, Nightfall knew he had little chance to win. *But I don't have to win. I just have to make an opening to escape.*

The swindler thrust for Nightfall's abdomen. Nightfall sprang aside, trying to guess Makai's position even as he anticipated the swindler's next strike. The blade missed cleanly. A shout rang through the common room. The door to the back room swung open, and footsteps pounded on the catwalk overhead. *Reinforcements. Great. I can't even handle what I have.* Nightfall made a split second decision to turn the combat into an in-fight rather than draw his sword. The swindler swung high. Nightfall ducked beneath the strike, trying to render the longer weapon useless. As he moved, he jabbed at the other's thigh, more from habit then any hope that the blow might fall.

The swindler jerked back his leg, redirecting his strike. The abrupt, single foot movement on wet wood stole his balance. He fell, twisting to roll. In the all but nonexistent instant when the man's throat was bared, Nightfall struck with the speed and accuracy of a snake. *Two dead.*

Nightfall prepared to turn. But, before he could move, Makai's meaty arms enwrapped him from behind. The grip winched suddenly tight, slamming the air from Nightfall's lungs in a pained grunt. The agony from his previous injuries leapt back to focus, but this time his ribs held. He struggled, hoping the beer's slick wetness would make him harder to hold, but Makai clung effortlessly. The powerful embrace pinned his arms to his sides, and the dagger became useless in his hand.

Panic swam down on Nightfall. He tried to back-kick but found Makai's legs too close to allow momentum. The worst he could do was bruise the bouncer's shins. Twisting was gaining him nothing. Within moments, his arms had grown numb, and spots and squiggles scored his vision. Desperate, he swung his head. The back of his skull caught Makai squarely in the forehead, yet it was Nightfall who paid for the maneuver. A white flash like lightning blazed through his sight. Nausea racked him, and he felt his consciousness slipping, replaced by a constant, dull throb in his skull.

Makai's voice sounded distant and graveled. "And now, you little shit, I'm going to break you like a twig."

A gust of air over wet flesh revived Nightfall enough to think. He felt Makai begin to settle his weight backward to snap Nightfall's spine. In the instant Makai prepared, Nightfall hurled himself over backward, mentally trebling his weight as he did so.

Though he did not have far to fall, Nightfall came down hard, cushioned by Makai. Bone snapped, soft and sickening. Makai screamed. Twisting free, Nightfall lowered his weight to normal, pausing only to slam the dagger's hilt into the bouncer's throat before scrambling toward the back door. *I'm free.*

Nightfall had scarcely reached the knob, when the memory of the breeze of an opening door returned. Since the back exit was still closed, it could only have come from the front. The oath-bond screamed a warning, its language pain. Hating the moments it cost him, Nightfall glanced over his shoulder.

The front door stood open. Gray evening back-lit Edward Nargol in the doorway, clutching a spade. Between them, Nightfall counted seven men, an assortment of bodyguards, thrill-seekers, and butchers. To the prince's left, a man slunk off into the shadows, looking vaguely familiar, though Nightfall did not waste time searching memory for the man's identity. He seemed to mean the prince no harm. But a strong-arm man at Edward's back drew and cut for the prince's neck. And Edward seemed wholly oblivious.

"No!" Nightfall whirled, hurling his dagger. The blade spun past Edward's cheek and buried in the assassin's throat. Clawing at his neck, the man behind Edward collapsed.

The expression on Edward's features mixed horror with rage and betrayal. "Sudi—" he started. Then the thunk of the fallen corpse must have registered, and two men with swords sprang for Edward simultaneously.

Nightfall rushed to Edward's aid, far too aware of the five men between them and with little hope that either he or the prince would come through this alive. Even as he took the first step, Edward's spade cleaved air. It crashed against an attacker's skull, dropping him instantly. Edward reversed the direction of his strike, using the longer pole to ward off his other opponent. Despite certain death, Nightfall could not help feeling impressed. *I'll be twice damned. He did find a use for the spade.*

On the catwalk, the sound of bolts clicking into place jerked Nightfall's attention from the fight. He glanced up. Above him, three men rested crossbows against the catwalk's railing, every quarrel aimed for Edward.

The prince seemed to be holding his own against the swordsmen for now, so Nightfall turned his attention to the bowmen. Two running steps gained him the momentum to leap. He sprang for the catwalk, a sudden drop in weight sending him airborne. He caught the bars of the railing.

"What—?" one began.

Before the men on the catwalk could move, Nightfall used a thought to treble his mass again. A crack echoed through the confines. Nightfall's support disappeared, as the railing pulled free. Then, the certainty of death surged through him, and he plummeted, willing down his weight as he fell. A prolonged scream told him that at least one of the crossbowmen had fallen with him.

Nightfall hit the floor feet first, then dropped into a roll. Even as he moved, the boards shuddered twice as other men landed nearby. But, where Nightfall had tumbled feet first, the others had flipped over the rail. The screams changed to pained moans. All three crossbows clattered to the ground, and the railing shattered, driving a fist-sized stake of wood into Nightfall's thigh.

Nearly incapacitated by pain, Nightfall lurched to his feet. Ruthless and unceasing, the oath-bond stung like a hive of bees. Driven to action, Nightfall concentrated on the magic to help him bull through the agony in his leg. He looked toward the door, afraid of what he might see.

Edward had dropped the spade for his sword. He stood in the doorway, exchanging thrust and parry with a murderer and a gambler. Three corpses littered the barroom floor at his feet. The last crossbowman on the catwalk was staring down at the carnage, his eyes wide. Grittmon and Tadd the Mouth stood behind the bar. The informer seemed uncertain of his next action. Grittmon held a familiar brace of jeweled throwing knives.

Even as Nightfall recognized the danger, the first knife sailed toward him. He danced aside, and the steel struck the stone of the wall, raising sparks. One of Edward's opponents stumbled backward, clutching his abdomen.

Grittmon slung another dagger. Nightfall sidestepped toward the battle in the doorway, the abruptness of the movement slashing pain through his injured thigh. The knife embedded in the floor where he had stood. Grittmon's gaze whipped toward Prince Edward, and a slight smile played over his lips. He reached for the next knife.

He's going for Ned! The oath-bond speared through Nightfall, nearly crippling him even from its own duty. The agony of his leg seemed insignificant compared with

the need to place himself between the prince and
Grittmon's dagger. He wove between the flashing steel of
exchanged sword blows. A blade opened his sleeve to the
shoulder, though he did not stop to wonder whether the
killer's blade or Edward's had made the cut.

"Sudian! Watch out!" Edward pulled a stroke that
would have cleaved Nightfall in half, changing it to a
high sweep that whipped over his squire's head.

Grittmon pitched the blade for Edward. Still not quite
in position, Nightfall dove for the flying steel. His fingers
closed over the blade instead of the hilt, slamming it to
the ground. Razor-honed, the edge caused no pain at first.
Only the warm course of blood warned Nightfall he had
damaged his hand.

Prince Edward's sword hammered against his opponent's head. The murderer sprawled as Grittmon heaved
another dagger. The pain of Nightfall's wounds merged
into a red muddle of rage. As the knife sped toward him,
he caught the hilt in his uninjured hand, instantly turning
the attack back on its wielder in a razor rebound that
would have staggered even Dyfrin. The blade embedded
itself in Grittmon's left chest, above the rib cage. Nightfall doubted the wound would prove fatal, but impact and
shock stole consciousness from the proprietor. He fell
backward, sweeping a row of tankards and bottles to the
floor. Metal and glass clanged across the boards, spraying
shards and splashing wine the color of blood.

Nightfall glanced at his hand. Blood obscured the palm,
but tendons gaped through a gash across each finger. The
sight brought the pain in a rush. Nausea exploded through
him, and he dropped to his knees, half-blinded by pain
and dizziness. Only one thought remained intact. *We have
to get out of here. Fast.* He half-stumbled, half-crawled
through the doorway. Tearing his mangled sleeve free, he
wrapped it tightly around his hand to staunch the bleeding. "Master, to the horses. We have to go."

Edward paused to retrieve the spade before following
Nightfall into the growing darkness. "Sudian, wait.
There're men dead in there. We have to talk to their fam-
ilies. The town guard . . ."

Nightfall staggered to his aching leg, more concerned

with the men left alive in the tavern. It would not take long for Tadd to gather more criminals. Now that the immediate danger had passed, Nightfall's mind had brought forward a buried problem. When Prince Edward had arrived, Nightfall had seen another man in the doorway, one he had dismissed for more urgent matters. Now, he dredged the description from memory. *It was the man who helped me in the streets when I lost my balance, the one I think is a sorcerer. And he saw me use my talent against Makai.* Dread colored the raw mixture of emotion already coursing through him. "Master, the horses. We have to run."

"Run?" Prince Edward took Nightfall's arm, steadying his squire. "We've killed men. We can't just—"

"Master, I mean this with every drop of respect in my being. We are leaving. Now."

Edward studied his squire with pity in his glance. He ignored Nightfall's belligerence, apparently attributing it to his injuries. "Everything will be all right. I just need to get my things."

Thrown over the edge of hysteria, Nightfall made a lightning swift grab, catching Edward's cloak at the throat. Blood from his injured hand smeared the silk. "We'll be dead if we're not already. Now, go to the stable. Pay the boy the two silver I promised him. Then we're riding out of here until I fall off the damned horse. Then we sleep. Then, if you still think we need to talk to guards, we'll come the hell back!"

Edward stared blankly, horror on his features.

Weakness shuddered through Nightfall. His grip fell away, his injured hand plunging, useless, at his side. "Master." His voice emerged as a coarse whisper. "I'm only trying to do what's best for you. Trust me, this once, Master. Please." A buzzing noise descended over Nightfall, and consciousness receded before it. He went limp in Edward's arms, scarcely aware that the prince lowered him to the ground.

"You're going to be all right, Sudian." The prince's voice was soft, comforting, yet edged with tears. Edward hurried off alone.

"The horses," Nightfall managed. The effort flung him into oblivion. And he knew nothing more.

Chapter 6

Nightfall awakened to a dull background of aches that gradually settled into his right thigh and left hand. Someone stroked his hair with a tender concern almost as familiar as the accompanying pain. Memory told him what had to come next: his mother's flurry of teary apologies, the earnest promises that she would never strike her child again, the declarations of love and concern, vows that lasted only until her next frustration drove her to batter him again.

Nightfall curled his consciousness inward, gathering strength to fight the pain. He blundered toward understanding. *Someone's close enough to touch me.* The next thought followed naturally. *Someone's close enough to kill me.* It had become habit for Nightfall to awaken without fanfare. He had trained himself to lie as still upon waking as he did asleep, to breathe in slow, deep, regular patterns. He had studied awakenings until he had learned the most subtle cues, then he had practiced discarding them until the procedure had become ingrained. Now he had to assume he had awakened with his usual caution because the other's gentle fingers continued brushing strands of hair from his brow.

Under other circumstances, Nightfall might have taken the time he needed to orient himself, using feel and sound to determine time, place, and which persona he needed to play. But a person within striking distance was an immediate threat. The fact that the contact was sympathetic meant nothing to Nightfall; it was those who had touched him most tenderly in the past who had hurt him the worst.

Without so much as a warning tense, Nightfall sprang away and into a crouch, facing the place where he had lain. The abrupt movement flashed pain through his strained ribs and gashed thigh, spinning a collage of pinpoint lights across his vision.

"Sudian, you're all right now."

A buzzing in Nightfall's ears obscured the voice, and his sight faded to a uniform, gray curtain through which he could glimpse only a broad shadow. Still, only one person addressed him by that name and in that manner. "Master?" he tried, the word emerging in a croak. His mouth felt parched and sticky. "You're well?" The quiet vigil of the oath-bond confirmed the observation. Still, desperation tinged the question. With his soul linked to the prince's life, Nightfall could not afford to take such a thing for granted.

"Me? You're still worried about me?" Prince Edward approached cautiously, something dangling from his hand.

As Nightfall remained still, the haze obscuring his vision resolved slowly, revealing Edward in travel linens. Though not clean, they lacked holes and bloodstains. He held a waterskin. Behind him rose a wall of tall, thin-trunked evergreens, bare almost to their tops where a cluster of needles formed a green ceiling. Nearby, the horses grazed a copse of thistles and berries. A fire crackled within a circle of stones, the bright reflection of its flames dancing across the spade and a single, opened pack.

Realizing Edward had never actually answered his question, Nightfall pressed. "Are you well, Master?"

Prince Edward stood directly in front of Nightfall. He passed the waterskin. "Here, drink as much as you can. You lost a lot of blood before you got your hand bandaged. I'm afraid you lost a lot more when I pulled that piece of wood out of your leg."

Thirstier than ever before in his life, Nightfall took the waterskin and gulped down a swallow. His mouth had dried to the point where the water seemed to burn his throat, and it tasted thick and dirty. Still, his body craved liquids enough to overcome the discomfort. He drank for a long time.

Once he had his squire drinking, the prince addressed his question. "I'm fine, because of you. You saved my life, Sudian." He reached toward Nightfall's shoulder.

Instinctively, Nightfall flinched away, spilling water down his chin.

Apparently attributing Nightfall's caution to his recent injuries, Prince Edward returned his hand to his side and let the incident rest.

Nightfall felt the need to break the silence; but never having rescued another person from death before, he did not know what to say. To emphasize his own heroics seemed tasteless and unnecessary, but to downplay his accomplishment might belittle the prince's life. Then, aware he had hesitated too long in consideration, he ran with his own confusion. "Of course, Master. It's my job."

Edward mirrored Nightfall's bewilderment. "It's your job to die saving me?"

"If necessary." Nightfall sipped more slowly, the skin nearly emptied.

"Who told you that? My father?"

And his murdering bastard of a sorcerer, yes. Nightfall hesitated, weakness dulling his usually quick wit.

One of the horses snorted, flinging its tail in circles. A songbird flitted from a treetop, shaking free a shower of needles.

Edward did not wait for an answer. "I've had a long string of governesses, stewards, and guardians, not one of whom would have placed himself between me and an inchworm."

Nightfall put the waterskin aside, examining his bandages. Someone, presumably Edward, had replaced the hastily applied rag on his hand with a neatly wrapped and tied cloth. Another bandage wrapped his thigh, darkened by a patch of old blood. His fingers felt stiff and unresponsive. Fear nearly paralyzed him. Two of his personae, polio-stricken Frihiat and plow-injured Telwinar, had required him to feign being crippled; but the split-second timing of Nightfall's escapes already strained his abilities to their limits. Without the use of a hand, he felt as clumsy as a half-grown adolescent, and his survival had depended too many times on his reflexes for him to believe he would last long one-handed.

Oblivious to Nightfall's concerns, Edward continued on the same track. "You know, my father will pay you whether or not you risk yourself for me."

The prince's words pounded the last blow in a long string of annoyances and insults. Nightfall had always considered himself independent, yet the realization that he had lost the widespread and myriad contacts he had established through years of effort frustrated him. The oathbond trembled within him, a mockery of the pains that ached through him because of its presence. And he might well lose the use of his hand. Though the least of his problems, Nightfall lashed out at the thing that had thrown him over the edge. He twisted his face into a parody of deep, emotional hurt, a raw-edged expression approaching tears. "Master," he said almost inaudibly. "Your father is paying me nothing." Rising, Nightfall limped toward the fire and sat with his back to the prince, but not before he saw a wide-eyed look of sympathy and self-hatred form on the prince's features.

Guilt tingled at the edges of Nightfall's conscience. Unaccustomed to the emotion, he cast it aside; but the dismissal proved harder than he expected. For all the times he had dallied with men's lives, he had less experience with manipulating emotions other than hatred and fear. The image of the prince's face remained in his mind's eye.

"Sudian, I'm sorry." Prince Edward drew up beside his squire, his familiar, commanding tone gone.

Nightfall said nothing. He stared into the fire, fixating on mourning the destruction of his information net. He felt more alone than he had since the day his mother died, though that loss had filled him with the same mixture of grief and guilt. Only the day before, he had prayed to the sisters of the sunrise to take his mother's life; and, with the faith in magical thoughts that only a child could grasp, he held himself to blame as much as the client who had dealt the fatal blow. Grief and love had warred with shameful relief. He had cried, yet something deep within him had rejoiced, and that thing his mother would have called "the demon's influence" had become the center of his existence. His remorseless killings and thefts had proved him as evil as he believed himself to be, delved him into a cycle that ended with Kelryn, then began again with her betrayal.

Prince Edward shifted closer, glancing about as if afraid to be caught talking poignant issues with a servant. "Sudian, I, of all people, shouldn't have said that, I who also swore to champion a cause and hold it above life itself. I get so ill hearing people dream with their mouths instead of their hearts, listening to them talk about what should be done instead of acting to fix the problem. I've tried my best to act when the opportunity presented itself and to prod my father and brother to do the same." He lowered a hand to Nightfall's shoulder, and this time the squire managed not to pull away. "Sudian, your loyalty is not just appreciated, it's the most noble act I've ever seen. I guess I just couldn't fathom that kind of dedication to me."

The prince's grip felt warm and rock steady. Nightfall's annoyance slipped away, replaced by an almost unsuppressible urge to laugh. *His naive optimism is nearly as touching as it is amusing.* Seizing the opportunity to test his earlier theory about King Rikard wanting his younger son dead, as well as to lock in Edward's trust, Nightfall questioned while the prince's guard was down. "But, Master, you're so ideal. Surely, I'm not the first to see how much the world needs you. And your father must be proud of all you've championed."

Prince Edward's fingers flexed, indenting Nightfall's sleeve. "My father is a good man, but affairs of court keep him too busy to help the downtrodden."

"A pity, Master." Nightfall's pain had not dulled, but it had become familiar enough for him to think more clearly. He swerved with the prince's verbal dodge, restoring proper theme to the conversation. "All the more reason why he must cherish your struggle for causes he has no time to handle."

Again, Edward's grip tightened, gouging linen deeper into Nightfall's flesh.

The persistent weight of the prince's arm, as well as the tenseness of his hold, numbed Nightfall's wounded hand. He appreciated the lessening of the agony, but it frightened him as well. Pain, he understood. The fuzzy tingle fluttering through his fingers unnerved him, reminding him of the possible permanence of this injury. Nerve damage healed so slowly he might die of old age before his hand functioned properly again.

Apparently realizing the intensity of his grasp had gone way beyond comforting, Edward released his hold and turned away. "One day," he said, so softly Nightfall suspected he spoke to himself rather than his squire. "One day, human suffering will take precedence over politics." He whirled suddenly, confidence fully restored. "Sudian, we need to talk about strategy."

The abrupt change in topic and manner left Nightfall momentarily speechless. Clearly, the conversation had closed, and no nudges or twists would divert it back this time. "Strategy, Master?" Suddenly, the fog that accompanied blood loss and pain lifted enough to reveal memory of the moments before Nightfall had lost consciousness in Nemix. "Are we being followed?" He sprang to his feet, forgetting his injured leg until it seemed to suck all the sensation from his body and channel it into jabbing agony. He winced, waiting for the pain to fade back to baseline, along with the ringing void that temporarily shrouded his mind again.

"Careful, Sudian." Prince Edward flinched in sympathy, his warning senseless after the act. "And, no. I don't think anyone followed us. I ran, as you insisted, though I did leave ten silvers. I'm embarrassed that we had a hand in ruining that inn. The owner deserved restitution, and there's blood price to take care of for the dead."

The blood of that human crud was more valuable splattered on the roadway than in their worthless bodies. Nemix should have paid us. And restitution? For what? Grittmon's attempt to slaughter us? Nightfall stared. "Master, the owner was the man flinging daggers at us." It occurred to him then that pursuit was unlikely. Grittmon's bribes kept the constabulary out of the affairs of his tavern. He had paid for their blindness and deafness, not for their support. For all that the criminals had wanted Sudian dead, they had failed the job in numbers and on their own territory. There, they could claim accident. On international ground, the murder of a prince and his squire would not go unexplored nor unpunished, a price too high to pay for the life of a servant who had only sought information.

"And why was the owner throwing daggers?"

Nightfall continued to study the prince's face, as if to read the insanity nestled behind features that seemed as unrealistically beautiful and innocent as his nature. Even the fading whip mark scarcely marred the perfection of a countenance as rare and noble as his station. *Because he wanted to kill us, you blitheringly ignorant pretty-boy. And you gave our money to the first thief who notices it lying there.* Nightfall searched for a respectful reply, analyzing tone to decide whether the prince expected a specific response or demanded an answer because he could not guess the truth.

As time passed in silence, Edward's eyes widened. He flexed his hands impatiently.

Clearly, Prince Edward had not meant for the query to remain rhetorical, yet Nightfall could think of no comment that would not sound sarcastic or disrespectful. He searched for a simple lie.

"Sudian, why did we get attacked? Did you do or say something to instigate it?"

Nightfall adopted the most stricken look he could muster, which proved easy under the circumstances. "Certainly not, Master. I ate in silence. I got up to relieve myself, and I accidentally got caught in the middle of their fight. I had a choice: defend myself or die." He rolled his gaze to Edward, feigning desperation. "I'm no use to you dead from another man's argument."

"Nor dead from a dagger thrown at me. Nor dead from my own sword stroke."

"To die for you, Master, would be an honor. Nothing could please me, or the holy Father, more." Nightfall managed to meet Prince Edward's eyes and stomach the falseness of his own words. The oath-bond receded to a distant tingle, all but intangible for the first time since its casting.

Tears blurred Edward's eyes to blue puddles of joy. For once, he had won the devotion and pride his father had never given, the same that Nightfall had sought from the seven sisters as a child but found only in the gentle words of a friend named Dyfrin.

Though the magic went dormant, guilt hurt nearly as much as Nightfall's wounds.

As the day wore on, Prince Edward's sentiment gave way to a lecture that seemed endless. ". . . and you never hurl weapons in the direction of your allies. In the tavern, we both got lucky . . ."

I could have hit that thug in my sleep. You were never in any danger from me.

". . . A shouted warning would have alerted me to trouble without the risk of stabbing me instead of my enemy . . ."

And left you dead and my soul enslaved to your father's sorcerer.

". . . As to diving between my sword and an opponent . . ." From dawn until dusk, Prince Edward Nargol enlightened his squire with details and rules of strategy, frequently dismounting to sketch the battle techniques of past generals in the dirt.

Nightfall listened closely enough to nod or grunt in the appropriate places; but, as specifics gave way to history and universality, little made sense to him. The prince's voice became a drone that aided sleep and not much else. It occurred to Nightfall to question why, if these tacticians knew so much about battle, they were all dead; but he wisely held his tongue. The easy pace gave him the chance he needed to keep the healing wound in his leg well-stretched and free of binding scar. A recognizable limp, like a missing limb or permanent facial deformity, would steal all opportunity for competent disguises.

The ride to Delfor stretched into a two week crawl that kept the horses well-rested. The whetted edge of Grittmon's dagger had left a straight, clean injury. The edges approximated well, without jagged skin flaps, excessive healing tissue, or infection. Nightfall had hints that coordination and feeling might gradually return to his hand by the time he and the prince reached the familiar checkerboard of corn and hay that defined the outskirts of the village of Delfor. Each year, the farmers reversed which fields grew which crop, always staying with the fodder expected by its animal-raising neighbors. The two crops complemented one another perfectly, each restoring the nutrients that the other claimed from the soil. Nightfall had learned this tenet well as Telwinar, a gentle but reclusive Delforian farmer. In the spring, he tilled and planted. He plied his other personae and skills through the winter and the growing season. In the fall, he returned for harvest.

This year, Telwinar's fields would lie fallow as he disappeared, along with Nightfall's other identities. Within days, the other farmers would notice the lapse. The overlord would pronounce him dead, and his five fields would be distributed to neighbors or assigned to someone new. His few valuables would find their way into the overlord's coffers. Nearby farmers would claim his horses and equipment. Thieves would acquire the rest.

Nightfall smiled, certain he would miss none of it. He recalled the ceaseless beat of the sun, drying his skin to leather, the daily grind of hitching and driving horses, the tedium of scything hay and plucking corn ears, the ache of his muscles after a day of steadying the plow. Yet with the other memories came the crisp, earthy perfume of soil freshly tilled, a golden wave of wind-bowed stalks heavy with corn, and the sense of accomplishment that could not help blossoming into pride when the yield lay heaped in wagons for export. *Of which Telwinar got to keep only enough for the next year's seed and sustenance, alive in body, if not in soul, until the coming year.* The land, the crop, and the money from its sales belonged, as always, to the overlord.

The thought steered Nightfall's mind to the more pressing matter of the oath-bond. *The land belongs to the overlord. Or to the king.* He considered. Overlord Pritikis had inherited his holdings from his father, now dead. Other farmers toiled for different landowners: barons, knights, and princes. *So where did* they *get* their *land?* It seemed a simple question yet one Nightfall had never considered. He had worked only toward his own survival. Money and anonymity had pleased him well enough; and he had used his various personae to escape, rather than enhance, his notoriety. Only titled gentry, he knew, could own land at all, and the prospect of courting favor from the silk-swathed snobbery had never interested him. Now the question of process became all-consuming. *At least Ned comes with his own title. One less tedious detail I have to deal with.*

Prince Edward fell silent as the path left forest to become sandwiched between patches of moist earth speckled with the remains of the previous year's harvest, shredded by the plow. His horse balked at the change in terrain, shying with a suddenness that swung its rump into the packhorse. The chestnut's ears flattened in annoyance, and it threw its head to gain more rein for a fight. Nightfall veered his bay to give the packhorse more room. Hemmed between horses, it would surely turn warning into action and vent its frustration on Edward's gelding. The squire cut in front of the prancing white, using his mare's calm as a guide as well as boxing the gelding into stillness. *Next step*, Nightfall thought, *rid ourselves of the other pretty nuisance.* He glanced from white to chestnut. The spade lay secured above a single pack. The better part of their unnecessary gear had conveniently disappeared in Nemix, thanks to the well-paid stable boy. They no longer needed three horses, especially since his bay's "bruised hoof" had miraculously completely healed by the time they arrived in town.

Still, convincing Prince Edward of the fact seemed hopeless. At the least, the incidents with highwaymen and the spade demonstrated that the prince had a tenacity rarely seen in crusaders with vision tunneled by their own idealism. It gave Nightfall some hope that, once educated to the facts, Edward might effectively direct his actions toward attacking the foundation of the problems of the poor instead of preaching directionlessly or diving ignorantly into individual circumstances. Nightfall shook the idea from his mind. *By the Father's pissing crown, it's not my job to teach him reality. All I have to do is keep the poor, dumb fool oblivious until I get him some land.* Yet, the belief that King Rikard had sent son and squire out to die haunted Nightfall's thoughts. In some ways, the abuse Alyndar's king inflicted on his younger son seemed uglier than that of Nightfall's mother. At least Nightfall had learned what to expect from her, and she had not shrouded her cruelty behind false kindness.

As the white gelding quieted, Nightfall moved out of the way, trying to make his maneuver appear uncalculated. He never knew what simple act might impugn the manners of royalty; they seemed to memorize so many arbitrary details of behavior and draw offense from those who did not. But Prince Edward took no interest in Nightfall's actions. Instead, his gaze focused on the lopsided squares of farmland and the distant huddle of houses beyond. Like Telwinar, most of the farmers lived in cottages amid their fields while Delfor's other citizenry dwelt in the town proper, tending shops and plying trades. Children scattered across the croplands, preparing the ground for spring planting.

As they rode along the trail from forest to village, Edward remained in an uncharacteristic silence. Nightfall shifted, uneasy with the prince's quiet. Left to think too long, he would surely emerge with some marginally useful and wholly dangerous plan. Still, the hush gave Nightfall time for consideration as well. His instincts kicked in first, and it occurred to him that more hoof and foot tracks than usual scarred ground dried into ridges since the thaw. The horses rocked over hillocks surrounding the deepest of the prints, sliding into the impressions. They kept to a slow pace so as not to injure the horses' ankles, and even the white gelding ceased its dancing to lower its head and choose its steps.

Nightfall frowned at the implications of numerous visitors to a farm town. Traders and travelers, in groups of two to five, often stopped in Delfor. Though small, the village provided more comfort and security than another cold, damp night in the forest, a quiet haven between Nemix and the wild, trading city of Trillium. The latter sat just outside the jurisdictions of Kings Idinbal, Rikard, Gonrastin of Ivral, and Shisen's King Jolund. It kept trade free, allowing the merchanting of items and objects outlawed by individual countries. Thoughts of the crossroad city intensified Nightfall's discomfort. That open selling included slaves, and he shuddered to consider the chaos Prince Edward could instigate in such a place. Avoiding it seemed wisest, but Nightfall doubted they could. Edward's geography lessons surely mentioned the largest city on the continent, and Nightfall's best information sources lived there. One of his identities, Balshaz, the honest merchant, dwelt there on an irregular basis. *I'll just have to steer him away from the raunchier parts of town.* Taking a lesson from Nemix, Nightfall knew that plan would prove far more difficult than it seemed.

Prince Edward's voice broke Nightfall's contemplation. "What are those children doing? Playing some sort of game?"

Nightfall turned his attention to the seven youngest of a farmer named Pizah. The three largest tossed stones from the field into a rickety cart that jounced, shuddered, and threatened to break as each rock landed. The middle two gathered seeds and roots from the previous year's crop, dragging up the earliest volunteer shoots of new corn in a field now intended for hay. Two toddlers hammered at clumps of mud with sticks, breaking the biggest clods in preparation for the plow. "They're working, Master."

The horses' hooves made little noise on the soft ground. None of the children seemed to notice the newcomers.

Prince Edward made no comment, just a thoughtful noise. He drew the gelding to a halt, studying the tattered homespun and grimy faces.

Nightfall drew up beside his prince, not caring for the delay but seeing justice in Edward's discomfort.

The gelding stomped, snorting impatiently. Its hoof caught in the edge of an impression, and it flounced into a bucking dance, regaining its footing on the softer surface of field. A few of the children glanced over, and their comments drew the eyes of the others. Soon all seven stared at the well-nourished prince, resplendent even in his simple travel linens, and the attentive squire emblazoned in Alyndar's colors.

"Where are their parents?" Edward asked.

"Working, too, Master." Nightfall remained in place as the prince returned the gelding to the roadway. "Their mother's probably cleaning or cooking or sewing or sorting seed. Their father's off fixing the plow or mending horse fence or patching the roof. There's always a million things that need doing on a farm, Master; and usually six or seven of those are urgent." Nightfall knew the truth of his words only too well. Without the myriad hands and neighbors' children Telwinar paid, he could never have carried off the charade. As it was, Nightfall's escapades covered most of Telwinar's expenses. Luckily, helpers well and quickly paid rarely questioned, even to themselves; and Telwinar chose his assistants with care.

The white gelding launched into another of its stumbling romps, obviously goaded by impatience. This time, the awkward movements unbalanced Edward, and he jerked the reins in anger. The horse whipped into a half rear, twisting as spongy ground shifted beneath its hind legs. The beast panicked, flailing for footing, and Edward tumbled from its saddle again. "Damn!" The horse fell to its front knees. It continued to flounder until it fully regained its foundation, feet widely braced.

Perhaps the horse is worth keeping just for the humor of it. Nightfall choked back a laugh with heroic effort, though the children loosed a few giggles before propriety and fear hushed them. He leapt from the bay's saddle careful to favor his injured leg, and ran to Prince Edward's side. "Master! Are you hurt?" He extended his right hand to assist.

Prince Edward rose, ignoring the offering. He glared at the horse. "I'm fine." Clapping mud from his travel linens, he looked disapprovingly at the dirt clinging to the horse's forelegs. Steadying the gelding, he opened his pack and rummaged through it. He pulled out a stiff-bristled grooming brush that he handed to Nightfall. He then drew forth a silk riding cloak, donning it over his dirt-speckled shirt and britches. Closing the pack, he mounted, waiting.

Grumbling epithets beneath his breath, Nightfall took several swipes at the dirt on the horse's legs. The clumps fell free, smearing the mud beneath. As clearly fed up with the matter, the horse explored the back of Nightfall's neck with a muzzle sloppy from saliva and snot. Nightfall tensed but resisted the urge to give the animal a sharp slap across the questing nostrils, concerned it might dump the prince again if he did. His efforts with the brush seemed only to thin and spread the brown stain farther along the horse's legs in both directions. The white's coat attracted dirt like its manure drew flies.

The gelding took an experimental nip at Nightfall's ear. Cued by the hot breath, he sprang backward before the teeth closed. His head struck the beast a clouting blow across the mouth, for which he felt no remorse. The minor and temporary headache seemed small price to pay for vengeance. "Master, I'll need water to finish the job." Then, fearing that Edward might hand him a waterskin and picturing himself kneeling in filth on a well-traveled road with the hated horse sneezing mucus the length of his hair, he added, "A *lot* of water."

"Very well." Edward gestured Nightfall to his bay. The cloak hid dirt specks and travel stains well enough. Aside from a smear of mud across one cheek, the prince appeared fresh and ready for court.

Nightfall scurried onto his saddle, and they continued toward the village. The children disappeared into the distance, replaced by others equally young and busy. Field gave way to field, a long parade of squares discernible only by the remnants of their previous crops. Occasionally, a battered fence enclosed a section where a farmer allowed his workhorses to graze on stalks and stems left after the harvest. They passed three cottages, patched piecemeal after damage from wind, rain, and time. "Storage sheds," Prince Edward called them, until Nightfall corrected the misconception. Even then, the prince seemed unconvinced until they rode by a woman cradling an infant on the front porch of the tiniest of the dwellings. As the clustered buildings of Delfor drew closer,

Nightfall noticed a crowd at the junction of road with village. A few strides further, his sharp gaze discerned the group: all men and all dressed in the uniform of the overlord's guards. They wore dark blue breeks and tunics under the tabards of lavender and white that symbolized holdings under the King of Alyndar on the Yortenese Peninsula. *Members of the overlord's army on the edge of town? Why?* Nightfall's alertness clicked up a notch, and his thoughts sped. *Looking for someone. Us?* The oathbond buzzed within him, clearly taking its cue from his considerations. The idea seemed nonsense. He doubted the battle in Grittmon's Tavern would pique the interest of the overlord. If guards became involved in such a thing, they would be Nemixian or Alyndarian policing forces.

Prince Edward seemed not to notice the strange welcome, though whether because of lack of vigilance or unfamiliarity with Delfor's quiet norm, Nightfall did not know. A noble's survival did not depend upon physical alertness as Nightfall's had since infancy. His mind gave him no answer to the presence of the guardsmen, so he had little choice but to assume it had nothing to do with himself. Soon enough, he would know.

As the trio of horses drew to the town limits, a pair of guards sorted themselves from the other four and blocked the path. As they recognized Alyndar's royal colors on prince and squire, their manners went from bored to efficient. The two in front snapped to attention, hands low but away from sword hilts. The taller of the two, a curly-haired, lipless blond spoke. "Fine morning, lord. Have you come for—"

The blond's companion, a stout brunet with a neck as wide as Nightfall's thigh, nudged the other into silence. "Obviously they came to see the Healer." His gaze settled on the bandage encasing Nightfall's hand. He bowed. "Did you plan to stay the night as well, lord? . . ." He trailed off with deliberate caution, seeking a name and title.

Unaccustomed to formality, Nightfall missed his cue, especially with his mind worrying other concerns. *Healer?* He had spent longer than a month in travel or imprisoned in Alyndar. The previous month he had been shipbound as Marak. Prior to that, he had spent some time in the far south, on the Xaxonese Peninsula. He had heard nothing of a Healer in Delfor or elsewhere warranting a contingent of guards. As of the last harvest, no such person had existed in Delfor.

Suddenly, Nightfall became acutely aware that every eye, including Edward's, was centered on him. He guessed he was expected to say something, but he had no clue as to what that might be.

Prince Edward came to Nightfall's rescue. "Forgive my squire. He was badly injured protecting me, and pain seems to have addled his manners. The services of your Healer would be appreciated, and we will stay the night. Sudian, announce us, please."

Nightfall cursed himself mentally. Slipping back into his fawning squire act, he glanced at the soldiers sheepishly. "Prince Edward Nargol of Alyndar. The most magnificent master a squire could have. The gods—"

Edward silenced Nightfall with an embarrassed wave. "That's enough, Sudian."

The guards shifted restively, hiding smiles of amusement behind cupped hands or distracting gestures. The blond who had spoken first addressed the prince. "Delfor is honored by your presence, young Prince. We're a modest village. Our inn is small but at your service, the third building on the left down the main thoroughfare. Once you've settled, someone will come to escort your squire to the Healer. Will that accommodate, noble Sir?"

"Very well. Thank you," Edward said.

The guards stepped aside, and prince and squire rode into a farm hamlet that Nightfall scarcely recognized. Delfor had changed much since the last harvest. The shops, dwellings, and meeting hall seemed the same, but a new structure rose from the center of town near the community fountain. The once quiet streets held meandering beggars that Nightfall had come to associate only with richer cities and trading centers. The guards, usually completely absent, had become a constant and conspicuously obvious presence. He recognized an occasional citizen lost amidst the strangers.

As Edward and Nightfall entered the village, the beggars shifted toward them in a mass. As they moved, it became obvious that every one suffered from an injury or disease. Rheumy-eyed elders mingled with scraggly, limping youths. Several coughed globs of bloody phlegm on the packed roadway, and the odor of alcohol, filth, and disease stirred nausea even through Nightfall. The prince's face looked green.

Prince Edward, meet the downtrodden you champion. Nightfall took some amusement from the situation, though the oath-bond churned, intensifying the sickness raised by the reek of so many scrofulous and unwashed. Each had a sad tale to shout over the others, and Nightfall caught only snatches as each vied for their attention. ". . . six children starving . . . once a baron's adviser . . . lost my leg fighting for the king and the glory of . . . simple man in need . . ." The sad stories continued, every one ending with a desperate plea for money to pay for healing self or family. The white gelding quivered, nervousness stiffening its every movement.

Prince Edward's expression went from shocked to horrified to sympathetic. Though swaying with dizziness and obviously struggling against vomiting, he handed out six silver coins before Nightfall could think to stop him. Cries of "bless you, lord" rose above the laments, the success of a few only fueling the others. The crowd of beggars in the roadway seemed to triple in an instant. Hands pawed at prince, squire, and travel packs, smearing filth and disease. The oath-bond shrilled a warning, the pain becoming an agony that usurped all other wounds.

Brutally, Nightfall kicked and slapped at the nearest beggars, but his efforts only sent them all scurrying to Prince Edward instead. Cloth tore as the beggars clawed through the chestnut's pack, spilling foodstuffs and utensils to the roadway. Guards came at a run from all directions, their shouts lost beneath the pleading hubbub, dispersing the most peripheral of the beggars with violence. Nightfall drew a throwing knife, slapping the side of the blade across the rump of Edward's gelding hard enough to sting.

Pained and blind to its attacker, the white horse exploded into panicked frenzy. It reared and jumped, pink hooves cleaving the crowd. Several sprang out of the way, fatigue or injuries momentarily forgotten. Two stumbled, collapsing beneath the flailing hooves.

The oath-bond screamed through Nightfall, making new thought impossible and nearly crippling him from action. He concentrated on rescuing Edward, hauling him from the crazed steed and onto his own bay just as the gelding started a berserk bucking. Beggars dove for safety. The prince's bulk and momentum sent Nightfall careening from the saddle. Too late, he thought to increase his weight, landing hard on the roadway nearly beneath the mare's feet. He rolled aside, ducking to avoid the crazed gelding and the shying mare, vision filled with flying hooves, black and pink. From a corner of his eye, he also noticed that Edward's purse lay on the roadway; the scattered coins disappeared into scabby hands as they fell.

Instinct kept the knife in Nightfall's fist, and he lurched for the remnants of Prince Edward's money. A wild slash sent beggars scooting farther from his path. He snatched up the purse and its last four silvers with a speed that made the others look awkward. The oath-bond eased slightly, cuing Nightfall that Prince Edward had managed to keep his seat on the bay and the danger to him had lessened. Taking no chances, Nightfall cut a path to the horses, feeling the blade meet flesh three times before the remainder of the beggars learned to give him a wide berth. As the crowd thinned, the guards managed to regain control.

Pocketing the money, Nightfall sprang for the gelding's reeling head. As his fingers closed over a bridle strap, he tightened his arms and trebled his weight. The horse attempted to toss head and man without success. It jerked forward to bite. Enraged, Nightfall continued the horse's motion, using its own momentum to whip the head downward until their eyes rested at the same level. The horse stilled, red-flaring nostrils the only remaining sign of fear and rage.

As the oath-bond receded, the pain of hand and leg proportionately intensified, wounds jarred by the fall.

Fresh blood colored the bandage on his left hand, and all feeling short of agony left it. *Damn!* He searched for Prince Edward, finding him still perched upon the mare, now surrounded by a six man contingent of Delforian guards with drawn swords. The absolute absence of beggars seemed as peculiar as their masses had earlier. Venison jerky strips dangled from the chestnut's mangled pack like innards from a fatal wound. Other foodstuffs lay squashed in the dirt. Nightfall had eaten his share of discarded scraps, yet the idea of allowing Edward to touch anything left in that pack made him queasy. Releasing the now-calm gelding, Nightfall sorted through the chestnut's gear, discarding anything edible that stool- or germ-encrusted fingers might have touched.

While Nightfall worked, the overlord's men apologized to Prince Edward repeatedly; he counted fifteen times at least. The explanation followed, "Lord, since the Healer's come, their numbers have gotten out of hand. None of them's got enough money to pay for the cure, even if it'd work. Genevra only can handle injuries, not diseases or faults at birth or stuff missing or whatnot. But you can't tell them what expects miracles nothing."

Nightfall had packed the longest-keeping rations toward the back, and he discovered a couple week's worth of hard bread, cheese, and jerked pork still well-wrapped. The remainder of the food was a loss, and the vast majority of crockery lay shattered on the path. Shifting the hole closed, he retied the pack.

". . . didn't realize things had gone this far. Usually, they're spread all over town. They don't seem like quite so many then. They've never done this before."

Nightfall believed the guardsmen. If the beggars routinely caused damage like this, he suspected the overlord would have rounded them up and killed or expelled them by now. At the least, the sentries at the edge of town would have provided Prince Edward an escort. *Surely, they never expected him to indiscriminately hand silver to beggars.* Nightfall shook his head, blaming pain for his own incaution. *Even I didn't think him stupid enough to dangle steak in front of starving wolves.* His lapse bothered him. *A passion to champion those in need, a rabble of the Peninsula's scummiest, and a prince with no idea of the value of money or the desperation hunger breeds. What else should I have expected?*

The guards continued, now escorting Prince Edward toward the inn. "We're really very sorry, young Prince. Of course, your stay and food at the inn are on us. And your squire's healing is free. Are you sure you're not hurt, lord?"

Finally, the guards paused long enough to allow the prince to answer. "I'm fine," he said. "No harm done."

No harm done! Just two weeks of food left, four silver to our name, and a bleeding squire. Nightfall seized the tow rope of the packhorse and the white's reins, limping in the bay mare's wake.

Chapter 7

Razor claws and fiery eyes,
Leathern wings to cleave the skies.
His soul within stark midnight froze—
Darkness comes where Nightfall goes.
　　　　　　　　　　—The Legend of Nightfall
　　　　　　　　　　　Nursery rhyme, st. 7

The familiar coarse wood construction of Delfor's common room soothed Nightfall after the beggars' antics in the streets. The inn had become a staple in the farming village even long before Telwinar's arrival, and its rough-hewn beams, beer-stained tables, and blended aromas of alcohol, food, and honest perspiration seemed a haven after a hard day of labor. Edward sat amid a friendly ring of guardsmen, having bathed; and Nightfall felt secure leaving the prince in the hands of the overlord's men while he tended the horses, then cleaned and stowed their gear. The accommodations were simple but clean, the food fresh from the tiny personal gardens each farmer kept to supplement his family's income. The excess, such as it was, usually found its way here.

Nightfall had lingered over the basin and pitcher of water supplied by the innkeeper. Of his regular personae, only Balshaz the merchant concerned himself with cleanliness. Now, scrubbed skin and no need for paint, grease, and dyes made him feel strangely free despite his servitude. The gelding's foamy spit washed easily from his short-cut, mahogany locks, a welcome change from Marak's itchy tangle that had taken its color more from dirt and grime than dye. He gathered up their travel-dusty clothing for the washerwoman on the opposite side of town. He had some experience with laundering, but filth had become a familiar accessory to his masquerades and he knew nothing about the proper care of silk. He had left the tied bundle of clothing and one of Edward's silver coins in the hands of a local boy whose integrity he trusted, with explicit instructions to give money and garments to the washerwoman. The boy was told to report directly to him if the woman gave him less than four coppers for his trouble.

His work finished, Nightfall finally joined Prince Edward in the common room, scarcely managing to wolf down winter-stored turnips, peas, and squash before two more of the overlord's guards arrived. These bowed briefly, then one addressed the prince. "Prince Edward, the Healer can see your squire now."

Edward looked up from his food and company to reply. "Excellent, thank you." He glanced at Nightfall. "I'll be here or in the room, Sudian."

Nightfall rose reluctantly, dinner only half-finished. They had eaten well enough on the trip, but the work had left him hungry and cooked vegetables seemed far superior to the hard tack they had consumed for the past week. He glanced at Prince Edward, assessing the situation fully before leaving the prince's side. Delfor possessed nothing more dangerous than an occasional mean-spirited traveler in the worst of times. Poor farm villages rarely attracted thieves, even should Edward still have had money to steal. Nightfall believed the beggars would stay away. Though soft-hearted with the natives, the innkeeper brooked no nonsense from strangers, especially those who would not or could not pay for what they ate or harmed those who could. The rabble wanted Edward's money, not his life; and they surely knew they would earn no goodwill from him or other nobility if they mobbed him again. For the moment, Edward had a protective retinue of village guardsmen as well.

The two Delforian guards escorted Nightfall from the common room and back into the main street, their hovering presence an uncomfortable reminder of his arrest in Alyndar. Mired in exhaustion, worry, and pain, he floundered for the knife-edged clarity of mind he relied on in the most menacing situations. The Healer seemed godsent, appearing in the most unlikely place at a time when he needed the service. That stroke of luck concerned him far more than the presence of a pair of guards he could dispose of, if necessary, even one-handed. Anything convenient was a trap until proven coincidence.

As the three walked past shops and cottages, Nightfall sought information, keeping his queries and comments within the realm of normal curiosity. "The wound is deep. I appreciate your effort and generosity, but I doubt there's much this Healer can do for me."

The guards exchanged knowing smiles that unnerved Nightfall. "Genevra's good," the one to his right said. "She's fixed a lot of injuries people doubted she could help."

Nightfall studied the speaker's wide, friendly features. A brown mustache hid his upper lip. Coloring and the set of his face identified him as a Delforian native, and his accent fit the region. "Obviously she's someone important. I never saw a town so protective of a Healer, nor any Healer with such a following." Nightfall made a broad gesture that included the sparse beggars but also indicated the incident from earlier in the day. The guilt that came from the reminder might make the guards more talkative.

"She's a special Healer," the same man said. "Doesn't use herbs or stitches or nothing."

The other guard, also a native Delforian cut in, "She's got some sort of magical power, but she ain't like no sorcerer I ever heared tell of."

Just the pronouncement of "sorcerer" sent Nightfall's throat spasming closed. His step faltered for an instant, but he otherwise gave no sign of his distress. He searched for solace and guidance, finding it in the realization that Genevra far more likely belonged among the one out of every thousand with a natal ability than the one out of five thousand with a bent toward sorcery. The realization did little to allay anxiety, however. Hunting and slaying sorcerers probably kept the numbers of natally empowered and sorcerers even, and he had never heard of one of the congenitally gifted sharing her skill so flagrantly. Still, it made just as little sense for a sorcerer to do so. They could gain their spells by ritualistically slaughtering other sorcerers as well as from the innocently gifted. *Unless she's so competent she's trying to draw other sorcerers to her.* That brought another idea to the fore, one that might help him differentiate natal from captured skill. Dyfrin had a theory that the gifted could operate their powers by thought alone, perhaps accompanied by a simple point or touch when those abilities required directing. Sorcerers, however, needed to torment their stolen and bonded souls to activate their powers, a process that required gestures and/or words.

Nightfall's contemplations dropped him into a silence he knew he had to break to keep the conversation natural. "Magic? I don't know as I believe in it, but it can't hurt to let her try." For all his cheery confidence, Nightfall felt uncertain of his decision. The odds all seemed in his favor. If Genevra was a fraud, he lost nothing. If she turned out to have a congenital gift, she might have the competence to restore use to his hand, without which he had small chance for survival. If she were a sorcerer, she would still have to establish that he had a gift before she tried to take it from him. *Unless she obtained some spell that allows her to recognize powers in others.* The thought chilled him. The gifts took many and varied unpredictable forms, and he could not begin to guess the possibilities. If it existed, that particular gift, he felt certain, would become the coveted property of every sorcerer in existence.

The guards made wordless noises of agreement as they circled the fountain and approached the front of the central building. Nearby, the community hall seemed to have shrunk in the shadow of the Healer's structure, though both were constructed from the same Delforian oak. Nightfall made a mental note to stop in the hall before taking leave of Delfor. Few of the farmers and citizens could read, but they did keep up a pictorial and color-coded board to let others know who needed assistance or had jobs for hire. Using it, Nightfall might see to it that Telwinar's belongings, tools, and horses found their way to those most needy.

Catching himself falling naturally into Telwinar's character, Nightfall shook the thought from his mind. It belonged in the head of the withdrawn and plodding farmer, not starry-eyed Sudian or the demon who haunted men's nightmares in all corners of the continent. Instead, while the guards exchanged comments with four others standing alert before the Healer's door, his mind drafted the one most significant question.

The guards returned momentarily, and Nightfall spoke quickly. Once they gestured him through the doors, the time for chatter would end. "Does this Genevra have other magic besides healing?" He had never heard of anyone with more than one natal ability. Possessing two or more would affirm her as a sorcerer, though a single gift would tell him nothing. A sorcerer who had killed only once was still a sorcerer.

"Only the magic all pretty, young women have over men," the rightward guard said.

The other nodded agreement. "The magic of the nubile. This way, Squire." He gestured a path between the four sentries, who stepped aside to let the trio pass.

Though discomfited, Nightfall hid all signs from long practice. If she were a sorcerer, obvious anxiety would surely catch her attention.

The guards pulled open the thick panel. They ushered Nightfall through it and into an antechamber with a second door on the far side. "You'll have to leave any weapons here." The outer door clanged shut, locked from the outside. "You'll get them back."

The idea of disarming himself before a possible sorcerer rankled, and the injuries that hampered his usual agility only amplified his concern. Still, the precaution made sense. If not a sorcerer herself, the Healer had much to fear from a parade of armed strangers, any of whom could hide his bent for ritual murder and magic. Her skill seemed far more useful and precious than Nightfall's own. Mimicking Edward's guileless innocence, he handed over sword and belt and the remaining pair of his knives. He had left the six knives from Alyndar's armory in his gear and lost the third throwing knife in the battle in Nemix. He kept the one of Grittmon's jeweled blades he had recovered, hidden well enough that a standard search would not uncover it. The guards frisked him briefly; Nightfall guessed he underwent the abbreviated version as an emissary from Alyndar's king. Apparently satisfied, one pulled out a key and unlocked the second door. He pushed it open.

The room beyond smelled faintly of incense. Mats and pillows lay scattered around the floor, enough to sleep six or seven comfortably. A hearth lined one wall, swept clean; and shelves on the other held knickknacks in human and animal shapes, perfume, and toiletries. A niche in the wall supported a bar from which hung several cloaks and dresses, plain but well-sewn. A young woman sat cross-legged on a green cushion with corner tassels. Straight, blonde hair fell to her waist, shimmering in the light of several torches in sconces along the walls. Her fair features held the blush of youth; and Nightfall estimated her age between seventeen and twenty-one years. By her coloring, he guessed she was born of southern folk, from Noshtillan, Schiz, or Meclar. Once she spoke, her accent and the timbre of her speech would likely reveal her origin more specifically. A pair of guards stood nearby, their expressions grim and businesslike.

As Nightfall stepped into the room, his escort closed the door behind him, remaining inside to reinforce the woman's protections.

Nightfall executed a respectful bow, as he had learned in Alyndar. "Sudian, squire to Prince Edward Nargol of Alyndar."

The woman smiled, flushing with adolescent embarrassment at his formality. Her shy innocence, clearly no act, allayed Nightfall's fears. He doubted a woman this young could have concocted and executed such an elaborate scheme so near to the time of awakening of sorcerer's powers. "Yes, I know. According to these men . . ." She indicated the guards. "Your master told them you got wounded heroically defending his life."

Noshtillan. Nightfall identified her speech patterns from the first few words. Her expressions and voice revealed much. Though naive to decorum and politics, her easy talk and gentle gestures told him she had experience with men. "My master is kind and deserving of fierce loyalty." He approached with caution, gauging the guards as well as the woman. "You must be the one they call Genevra."

"I am." The Healer rose as he approached, and her movements revealed more about her past. She seemed nearly as nervous as he had felt en route. He attributed that to the same fear of hidden sorcerers and to relative inexperience with sharing her gift. However, she reached for him with a practiced tenderness that suggested knowledge of passion, probably with more than one man. She seemed noticeably graceful for a woman of her age, with muscled legs honed by some physical sport rather than standard labor: dancing or horse work, most likely. The callus-free palm that closed around his uninjured hand reinforced the image. "Sit." She sank back to her pillow and indicated the mat in front of her. "I presume the problem is your hand, though I can see you're limping, too."

Nightfall did as she bid, appreciating her powers of observation as well. While he had studied her, she had, apparently, studied him. Yet, her inspection clearly focused on his needs rather than his heritage or danger. He set to work unwinding the bandage from his fingers. It made sense to start there. Not only was it the more significant wound but attention to it would give her the chance to become more comfortable with him before having to minister to an injury in a personal location. As a prostitute's son, Nightfall had had little experience with modesty as a child; but learning others' embarrassments and weaknesses had served him well in the past, as a weapon as well as a tool for gaining trust. The last loop of cloth stuck to the slash, caked with blood. He pulled it free quickly, preferring a brief agony to a prolonged lesser pain, and the Healer winced in sympathy.

Genevra took Nightfall's hand. Green eyes met blue-black and held momentarily. Her beauty stemmed from more than youth, but he sensed a deeper pain and fear before she turned her gaze to his injury. No doubt, she knew the terror of the hunted, and all suggestion that she might be a sorcerer fled his mind. "I'll need to touch it. It takes some time to channel the energies properly, so find a comfortable position. It'll feel strange, probably like nothing you've felt before." She balanced his hand against her foot and the pillow, then looked at him for confirmation.

The position felt comfortable enough for now, but Nightfall took Genevra at her word, readjusting the location of palm and fingers until he found a relaxed and natural arrangement. The wound throbbed in a slow cadence. The fall from his horse had reopened the slash so it looked as if no healing had occurred, and he could still see yellow-white tendon gaping through muscle and skin. He nodded his readiness.

Unlike standard Healers, Genevra did not prod the wound. Without preamble, she clamped her grip to his. Nightfall scarcely felt the touch, though he did not know whether to attribute this to some specific of her gift or lack of sensation from the injury. The pressure did send a shock of pain through his arm that disappeared almost as quickly. The agony that had grown commonplace in the past weeks channeled away, leaving only the dull ache of his thigh and the persistent tingle of the oath-bond.

The Healer cringed, then shuddered. Her grip tightened, evidenced only by the shift of muscles through her forearm. Nightfall still could not perceive her hold.

Gradually, Genevra's expression softened and her teeth unclenched. "Does that feel better?" Her demeanor became generally more relaxed and the gaze she turned him brighter.

"Much, my lady." Nightfall smiled as their eyes met again, trying to mellow the piercing stare that had terrified so many. "Does this healing hurt *you?*"

"Only at first." Genevra's easy conversation made it clear she could talk throughout the process, though she tended to clip her words in the manner of Noshtillan's lower class. "I have to draw out the pain to get rid of it. The healing, though, is simple enough. I just channel energy to you, and your body does the work."

Nightfall considered how this fell into Dyfrin's speculation. A sorcerer's spell would torture the gifted soul, not the caster. Although the healing process took time, the summoning of the power did not seem to tax Genevra at all. He glanced around at the overlord's guards. The two stationed here watched the process with appropriate intentness, though their stances revealed boredom. His escorts chatted in low voices, their words too low to hear but their casual gestures revealing nothing menacing or of concern. Curiosity got the better of him then. He needed to understand why a young and pretty woman had trapped herself into the overlord's service, providing care that caused her pain several times a day. At the least, he might gain some useful information about local practicing sorcerers. First, however, he had to rid himself of snooping ears. "You're from the other peninsula, aren't you?"

Genevra stiffened slightly. "How do you know that?"

"Your accent." Nightfall kept his expression gentle. "I only ask because I was raised in Mitano." He clung to the lie he had told Prince Edward. "I also spent a lot of time on Noshtillan's streets. It's been a long time since I've had the pleasure of speaking Xaxonese. Would you mind?"

"Not at all." Excited by the prospect, Genevra bought right into the story. "Do you know *lavvey?*" She referred to the language of the streets, a version of Xaxonese so rapid, clipped, and colorful with slang that it seemed more like a second tongue.

Like I invented it. Nightfall grinned. "We-niff," he said in dialect, the standard shortened form of "well enough." Although none of his standard personae dwelt in Noshtillan, his malnourished figure and youngish features had allowed him to play a dozen grubby street urchins when the need arose. He glanced at the guards, noting their Delforian features. Those from upper class breeding might have learned Xaxonese, but the rapidity of *lavvey* would probably render that knowledge wholly useless.

Healer and patient chattered for several moments about buildings, merchants, and life on the city streets. At first, Nightfall believed she tested him, deliberately slipping into the deepest and quickest *lavvey* she could and making errors about Noshtillan to explore his knowledge. Nightfall parried each dodge with a deftness that came from long practice, correcting her mistakes without chiding or allowing her to lose face. It had too long been his job to know the ins and outs of every city on the con-

tinent, to evade his many enemies with a competence that
made him seem more demon than human.

Over time, Nightfall regained his sense of touch, and
the more normal pain that accompanied it seemed welcome. Gradually, that faded also, leaving the sensation of
impression from Genevra's hand and the clammy sweat
that arose from long contact.

Soon, caught up in reminiscences, Genevra's sham
openness became sincere, a change Nightfall noticed at
once and capitalized on with patient caution. He waited
for a lull in the conversation to ask the important question, "Why do you do this?"

"This?" Genevra indicated their hands with a shifting
of gaze. "I was born with the power." She released his
hand. "There. Try that."

Nightfall opened and closed his hand several times,
studying the location of the injury. His fingers moved
easily, only slightly stiff from disuse. A long scar marred
the palm. With time, he guessed, it would fade into the
creases. "Vrin," he said, a mild and innocent exclamation
of amazement.

"You just had the right kind of wound. Relatively
fresh, straight, and not life-threatening. I'm very limited
in what I can and can't do." She dismissed her talent as
quickly as Nightfall had passed over saving Edward's
life. "Now, let me see the other."

Nightfall stripped off his breeks, using a pillow to
cover the indiscretion to save her from embarrassment
rather than himself.

Unabashedly, Genevra studied the gash left from the
broken railing.

"Will I survive?" Nightfall settled into a comfortable
position.

Genevra swapped the sarcasm for some of her own.
"Not if you keep throwing yourself in front of knives."
She smoothed nonexistent wrinkles from her dress. "Your
master says you caught a blade in your bare hand."

Nightfall held up both hands, palms toward Genevra.
"Do these look like the hands of someone who caught a
dagger blade?"

The Healer laughed. "Is the younger prince really worth your life?"

I'm not sure he's worth his own *life.* Nightfall continued his act. "Three times over, at least."

Genevra delivered a more clever coup de grace than Nightfall expected. "Then why was someone pitching daggers at him?"

The conversation had shifted in the wrong direction, and discussion of details about himself bothered Nightfall. Still, it would risk the camaraderie he had worked so long to develop if he hesitated to answer. "We got caught in someone else's feud. Just in the wrong place at a bad time."

Genevra accepted the explanation. She pressed her palm flat to the wound. "It'll scar."

The concern seemed ludicrous. It would scar whether she assisted or not. Again, Nightfall chose gentle sarcasm. "Thanks for the warning. I'll cancel all my engagements to parade naked in public areas. Anyone who chooses to gawk at my unclothed thigh deserves whatever ugliness he sees." He stopped just short of double entendre. Time had taught him that even lowborn women cared little for flirting from older men. Personal innuendo would earn him no goodwill.

Genevra lowered her head. Her body tightened, and her face screwed into a knot of concentration. Again, pain seemed to flow from Nightfall's body, this time leaving only the buzzing itch of Gilleran's magic. After days of constant aches, with or without movement, the simple lack of pain was euphoric.

Nightfall waited until Genevra's features returned to normal, using the moments of silence to reclaim the conversation, still speaking in *lavvey.* "So why do you do this? I mean, why let others know what you can do? Why trap yourself into a small room with so many guards you can't even take a piss in private? Is Pritikis paying you that well?"

"He's not paying me at all." Genevra brushed blonde strands from her face with her free hand. "He feeds me and keeps me in clothes." She waved at the garments hanging in the wall niche. "He gives me a comfortable place to stay and anything I want, within reason."

"Except a life, to speak of."

"They keep me safe, and I heal whoever they tell me." She shrugged, managing to keep her healing hand still as she did. "There are worse existences than this."

"Working for no pay but sustenance. Sounds like slavery to me."

"No. This was my idea, and I chose it freely." A catch in her voice revealed details she had not disclosed that made the situation less of a decision than it seemed. "I gave the offer to the overlord. For the price of protection, I would heal his soldiers, or any others he asked, as I could."

"An agreement no sane man could refuse. My lady, you could have had much more. At the least, your freedom."

Genevra shuddered, and a bit of pain trickled back into the wound. "If you're offering me a job in Alyndar, the answer is no. I'm comfortable here."

"I'm only a squire, lowborn, and not authorized to make deals for the king, nor even for myself." Nightfall did not have to feign his earnestness now. "In fact, only between us, I would warn you never to join an alliance with Alyndar. The king's chancellor, Gilleran, is a sorcerer of the worst kind."

Genevra bit her lip, still coiled, and the twinge of pain that accompanied her lapse remained. "Thank you for the warning, Sudian. Sorcerers don't take well to tipsters. I understand your loyalty to your master, but why risk your life for me?"

Wriggling further into Genevra's confidence, Nightfall constructed a story. "Any lessening of a sorcerer's power makes the world better. My sister has a birth skill. It's to her benefit for me to identify the sorcerers and not to know her exact location at any time." The Healer's taut nervousness goaded Nightfall to search for its source. "I'm not a sorcerer, if that's what you're afraid of. I've no skills I didn't come by honestly and few enough of those. The guard can tell you I didn't question your movements . . . and I won't."

Genevra laughed stiffly, her manner loosening only slightly. "I'm not worried about you. First, a sorcerer your size would fall quick prey to others. Second, I like you, and no compassionless killer could make me feel comfortable in his presence. Third, if I believe the prince's story, and I do, no one could fake the devotion you've shown your master."

Nightfall wondered how Genevra would feel if she knew she was mistaken on all three counts. He put the clues together and believed he had found the answer. Fear had driven Genevra to exchange freedom for security, and that fear went deeper than vague possibility. "You're being hunted, aren't you? I mean specifically."

Genevra spasmed with such force the contact sent pain spearing through Nightfall's leg. Surprised, he jerked away, and the movement restored the Healer's composure quickly enough that the guards did not interfere.

"I'm sorry," she said, tears welling in her green eyes. "I didn't mean to hurt you."

"That's all right." Nightfall's words emerged more choked than he intended. He rubbed at the area around the wound. Despite the pain, it had partially healed, the muscle approximated and only the tear in the skin remaining.

Genevra gestured him back in place. "I'm sorry. I just can't help remembering . . ." She trailed off, the tears now rolling across her cheeks.

Nightfall reached for Genevra, memory of his youth strong within him. The difference between the nights he cried alone and those that Dyfrin held him seemed the size of continent and heavens together.

Blades rasped from sheaths. Nightfall froze, rolling his eyes to a circle of swords in the hands of alert Delforian sentries. From habit, he measured distances and competence, not liking his odds.

"I'm fine," Genevra said, voice weak from crying. "He's harmless."

"You're certain, Healer?" one pressed. "Don't lie under menace. We can run him through before he can carry out any threat against you."

Nightfall did not so much as breathe, convinced that

the guard had spoken truth. Here, it seemed, even guile would fail him.

"I'm certain. Leave him go."

The swords retreated, then returned to sheaths, to Nightfall's infinite relief. He recovered instantly, but stuck with the masquerade of young squire. He moved back to his place, withdrawing into himself and hoping his silence looked stunned.

Genevra returned to *lavvey.* "I'm really sorry. About the pain and the bared steel."

"Quite . . . all right." Nightfall balanced fear with gallantry. He quoted Prince Edward, "No harm was done."

"It's just, well, I saw a sorcerer tear a gift from a victim. That memory is agony that never dwindles."

The information attracted and repulsed at once, but the need for details of the sorcerers' ritual won out. Knowing the intricacies would make it far easier to escape, and the understanding might shed some insight into how to pluck the murderers from a crowd. "Tell me about it."

"No." Genevra replied so fast she nearly obscured the end of Nightfall's request.

"The knowledge might help my sister. And others like her and like you. Maybe I can even find a way to rid the world of whoever's stalking you. It's about time someone hunted the hunters." It was a hollow consideration, falling far short of a promise. Even as Nightfall, he had never dared to challenge sorcerers. Nearly every one kept his ghastly talent well-hidden and his powers unpredictable. It had seemed simpler and wiser to avoid them.

Nevertheless, Genevra found hope in Nightfall's words. "About a year ago, I got work dancing at a hall down in Noshtillan. Nothing to complain about. Old Uber treated us pretty good given Noshtill's just shy of slave country." Genevra did not continue her healing, obviously concerned that flip-flopping emotions might cause her to hurt him again. "When a show didn't go the best, he'd threaten to replace us all with bought girls, but he didn't mean it." The Healer smiled nervously, humor shaded by fear. "Uber'd travel a lot to dance halls in other towns. Whenever he'd see something he liked, he'd bring back girls to teach it to us." She glanced at Nightfall, apparently to ascertain his reaction to the story so far.

Nightfall gave his attention fully, clinging to every word. He nodded encouragement for Genevra to continue.

"'bout three months ago, he brought back this Nemixite. Good dancer. She taught us a mass of new moves, nice ones, too. Some of them Uber brings back get standoffish thinking they're so much better because someone brought them to teach. This one was real nice. We got to be friends." Genevra considered, chewing on her lower lip so persistently, Nightfall felt certain it would soon start to bleed. "So anyway, one day I go to see her to ask her about some moves. She didn't have no private signal out, so I just went in without knocking." She swallowed hard, suppressing major signs of distress that might attract the guards but unable to keep a tremor from her hands. "First thing I see is . . ." She closed her eyes.

Nightfall glanced between the sentries. Keeping his movement deliberate and without threat, he caught Genevra's hand and gave a comforting squeeze. The Delforians huddled and stared, their expressions hard, but they did not interfere.

"A man. A stranger." Genevra's fingers winched around Nightfall's tight enough to hurt even after the healing. He appreciated her decision not to try to use her natal ability and speak at once. She looked at him, eyes moist with distress. "He lay on the floor, his back arched, his face twisted in pain like nothing I had ever seen. He was bleeding." Her grip lessened slightly. "I don't know what I was thinking. Nothing, I guess. I reached to help him instinctively and touched his leg." She made an involuntary noise of anguish, soft as a whispered whine. "That pain, I can't describe it." Despite her denial, she attempted to do so. "It went deep, to the core. I felt as if I touched his very soul. He had a birth-gift of some sort, and agony had brought it to the surface. A force like a dull knife was hacking the talent from him, and the pain only brought the gift more fully to the front." Genevra made another wordless sound, this time more of a sob.

Nightfall gave Genevra's fingers a comforting squeeze,

though it served only to clinch her grip tighter in response.

"Then I saw *him*."

"The sorcerer?" Nightfall guessed.

Genevra continued, letting the story serve as answer. "He crouched over the man in pain, doing *something,* I never saw what. There was blood everywhere and . . . the pain and . . . and then he looked at me. Those eyes . . ." The Healer fell silent, attempting to gather enough composure to put words together in sequence. "The eyes seemed to flay me open, and he was smiling, like he enjoyed the agony he caused. And he knew . . . I know he knew. He touched my birth-gift, caressed it like a rapist, and I felt violated." Genevra started crying now, violent with anguish. She caught at Nightfall, and he held her despite the guards' glares.

Though young and beautiful, Genevra and her closeness brought Nightfall more discomfort than pleasure. Her description raised fear even in the hell-born demon he had come to believe himself to be. Her touch reminded him of Kelryn's false love and the tears of his mother's temporarily sincere apologies.

"I ran," Genevra managed to say at length. "I didn't stop till I reached the innocence of a farm town." She gestured at random. "And I made my deal with the overlord." Genevra pushed free of Nightfall's hold, her crying already lessening to sniffles. Though her dress had scarcely wrinkled, she brushed at it in grand gestures and placed her hands gently against Nightfall's wounded thigh. The healing process started again, but Genevra finished her story. "There was nothing I could have done for the man. If I'd stayed, I just would have given the sorcerer my power as well."

Nightfall nodded, hiding his own uneasiness behind concern for Genevra. "Sounds horrible. You poor thing."

"I was lucky." Genevra continued her work. "Whatever that man had must have been more important to the sorcerer than healing. He could have gone after me first. Or I might have blacked out instead of run."

Nightfall could not assess the truth of the comment. He knew nothing but rumors about how sorcerers claimed their victim's natal gifts. "Is it true what they say? Did he eat the man's beating heart?"

Genevra shuddered; this time, her healing did not falter. "I don't know. I didn't stay to see." She fell into a silence punctuated only by her own sighing breaths in the wake of her frenzy of grief over the memory.

Nightfall kept his head low, respecting her need for quiet. The guards relaxed a bit, clearly more comfortable with the hush than the conversation they could not fathom and gestures they could not fully read.

At length, Genevra took her hands away. "Finished," she said, but her manner betrayed a need.

"Thank you," Nightfall said, examining his leg. A jagged scar puckered the skin, and only movement would tell if it had left him with a limp. Still, though he wanted to stand and test the healing, he waited for Genevra to speak her request. When, after several moments, she did not, Nightfall prompted. "You want me to chase down this sorcerer, don't you?" Nightfall had no intention of complying, but it cost him nothing to claim that he would.

"Oh, no." Genevra still seemed paralyzed by the memory. "I wouldn't wish my worst enemy to face off with raw evil. I just thought . . . well . . . maybe if you're headed that way . . .?" She looked up, judging his reaction.

Nightfall returned her gaze with feigned affection and tenderness. "We're going south, yes."

Encouraged, Genevra finished. "Would you check on the dancer whose room I went to? Someone told me she never made it back to Nemix. I felt so guilty leaving her trapped with a sorcerer, but I was too panicked to try to save her, too. Now, I feel awful for my cowardice. I know she's probably dead, too; but I can't help hoping for her. If you find her, tell her I'm all right. And I wanted to help."

"I'll tell her." Nightfall agreed with sincerity. Delivering such a message could only gain more information and goodwill, though he doubted he could possibly find the Nemixian dancer alive. "What's her name?"

"Kelryn." Genevra launched into a description that Nightfall knew by rote.

Kelryn. Thoughts descended upon Nightfall in a storm. He would find her alive, he felt certain of it. The evil he had projected upon her intensified a hundredfold. She had not only betrayed him; apparently, she made a career of turning over the natally gifted to sorcerers. *She sold me and my love for a sorcerer's money.* He no longer doubted that Gilleran knew precisely what he was, and the realization sent a shiver of fury through him. For Kelryn's crime, she must pay with more than her life. He would find a way to inflict the pain that she had intended him and caused at least one other. "I'll find her," Nightfall promised, hiding his determination behind a practiced mask of candor. "You can depend on it."

Chapter 8

Those who brave the night will find
Horror, dread, and demon kind.
He slays them all and rends their souls—
Darkness comes where Nightfall goes.

—The Legend of Nightfall
Nursery rhyme, st. 8

An evening spent lauding the Healer slipped into a fitful night of plotting and rage. Kelryn's scheme appalled even Nightfall; beguiling innocents to an agony beyond death seemed leagues more evil than all his crimes together. He had stolen to survive and murdered from necessity, and every kingdom reviled him as a hellish and remorseless demon. Yet, Kelryn continued her dance, seducing young men as fodder for hunters who preyed on pain and souls. Women like Genevra appreciated her gentle sweetness and men her grace, never knowing that both hid a cruelty that revolted Nightfall himself. *And even I fell for her act.*

The latter thought intrigued as well as sickened. Nightfall had always prided himself on reading others' motivations and seeing through their chosen shrouds. Yet he could not deny that he had bought into Kelryn's tender concern for him as completely and easily as any of her lambish victims. He had approached the relationship as he did all others, with paranoid caution. She had won him over with a candor and intimate sincerity that had penetrated defenses more solid and sturdy than any fortress. Even now, knowing what he did, Nightfall could not shake memories of her smile and the glitter in her dark eyes that told him she truly loved him, without conditions, and that her devotion would outlast eternity. Now Nightfall wondered how many others that game of hers had snared.

Nightfall rolled silently, his caution more habit than necessity. Prince Edward's snores had continued uninterrupted even through the clatter of a stack of dinner dishes dropped in the common room below and a heated argument between a serving woman and a cleaning boy over a copper piece. Nightfall's anger degenerated into sorrow. *Me in love.* The idea seemed more ludicrous than the rumor that he heard all pleas for murder whispered on the wind. *That alone should have cued me to her deceit.* A few women had sought out Nightfall in the darkest, ugliest corners of the universe. These, he discovered, wanted notoriety after finding no glory of their own. Somehow, sleeping with the demon or, better, carrying his baby would bring them the attention they craved and change, if not raise, their station. He had never raped a woman, nor even slept with one in Nightfall's guise, yet at least three claimed their offspring as his. *But love? Never. How could any woman love what even my mother could not?*

Undoing the past had become an unproductive pastime that Nightfall believed he had long abandoned. He pushed away thoughts of his shortcomings as a child, the common sense that had failed him when it came to what his mother had called "following gods" instead of falling prey to the "demon's influence." In the end, the demon had done him better.

Nightfall stared at the Delforian wall, the wood scarred by gouges and dents from carelessly flung gear. He had worked with many thieves, informants, and killers without so much as a twinge of conscience; and he wondered why Kelryn's scam bothered him so much. A good swindler, when cheated by a better one, soon learned to turn his thoughts toward education rather than vengeance. He understood that women used flirtation as a weapon because few things disarmed a man more completely. But there were unwritten laws even among killers and thieves, ones that the sane fell into without need for understanding them or even knowing of their existence. A competent hoax relied on the greed of its victim. Thieves gravitated to the rich who could better afford their crime; it made little sense to risk freedom or life for a single worn copper. No assassin Nightfall knew chose victims indiscriminately. Usually, they found themselves hunting others of their ilk, slayers on either side of the law. And therein lay

the root of Nightfall's aversion. Kelryn sacrificed innocents to creatures more terrible than any mythical demon,
committing them to an eternal torment that made the
gods' hell seem benign.

On the inn room floor, Nightfall flopped into a new position, finding it no more comfortable than any of the
dozen others. This time, however, he found sleep.

The morning dawned in quiet glory, unusually cool for
spring. Nightfall awakened as the first sun rays crept past
the window, and he set to work at once. Anticipation of
the prince's wants reinforced the image of attentive squire
with a steadfast devotion to duty and also kept him from
the need to chatter mindlessly. By the time Prince Edward
joined him in the common room, he had reclaimed their
now-clean clothing and prepared the horses for travel.

Aside from the inn staff, only three other people had
appeared for breakfast, a trio of well-armed Ivralian men,
minor nobility who had arrived in Delfor the same night
as Edward and his squire. From conversation overheard,
Nightfall discovered they headed for Mezzin for some
sort of special martial training. They talked loudly, assuming rugged postures to impress the farmers, but
Nightfall doubted they posed the prince any threat. Beneath their need for peasants' adulation, they seemed reasonably mannered.

"Good morning, Sudian." Edward greeted his squire
with a broad grin.

Nightfall rose from his seat at a corner table, straight-
ening another chair for the prince. He waited for Edward
to take the proffered seat before returning to his own.
"Good morning, Master."

Prince Edward immediately raised the conversation
from the previous night, though they had already taken it
beyond its natural conclusion into the realm of extraneous
repetition. "Fine work that Healer does. I hope we never
have need of her services again, but it's good to know
she's here."

"Yes, Master. It is." Nightfall gave the expected response, though it seemed unnecessary as well as nonsensical. His casual discussion with the guards on his return

to the inn had revealed that, had the beggars not mobbed Edward, the prince probably could not have afforded the healing, even on the allowance his father had granted him. That idea triggered one more sobering. *We've got a total of four silvers, including the one he gave me for the spade in Nemix, along with six coppers remaining from what I took from Myar. That's supposed to last months.* The amount sounded huge to Nightfall. He and his mother had lived on far less for years, yet they had not needed inn rooms, washed silk, horses, or gratuities for information. *And neither of us treated money like spit.* Still, Nightfall took some solace from the fact that he carried backup wealth in the form of the sea captain's sapphire and the Alyndarian steward's wedding rings. If needed, he would have to find a way to use those that did not require an implausible or embarrassing explanation to Prince Edward.

A serving maid arrived, setting warm, buttered bread and bowls of cornmeal in front of Prince Edward and Nightfall. She also left them each a spoon and a cup of milk.

"Thank you," Nightfall said.

The woman smiled, then whisked back toward the kitchen.

Prince Edward stirred bread through the meal. "It's good to see the farmers getting something special to balance their hard work."

Nightfall had lost the thread of the conversation. "Something special, Master?"

"I mean the Healer."

Nightfall thought it best not to tell the prince that Genevra's services existed for the overlord, his men, and wealthy travelers. No farmer he knew could afford her services. Mouth full, he measured the expectation of a prompt answer against manners and decided to chew and swallow before responding. "Yes, Master. It's good."

"Today, we'll start looking around and talking to people." The prince explained between bites. "In order to help those people, we'll have to find out what they need."

Nightfall froze in place but not quickly enough to keep his eyes from flicking suddenly to Edward. "I've got the horses all loaded and ready to go." He added swiftly, "Master."

"Go?" Prince Edward fixed his squire with a harsh stare. "Go? We're not going anywhere. There's so much work that needs doing here." He made a broad gesture like a dancer at a grand recital.

The implications of that decision came in a wild rush. *We could stay here for months. Years. And not accomplish much more than assisting a farmer or two with spring planting and harvest.* The thought brought a reemergence of the oath-bond, a dull ache that seemed to span Nightfall's body. "But, Master, we've lost our money. How long can we impose on the innkeeper's hospitality?" Nightfall knew the overlord, not the owner of the inn, had paid for their stay so far; but he guessed it would grind on Edward's conscience more to believe he burdened a working man.

Edward continued his meal. "We'll work. We'll make our money the way the citizens do."

And won't it surprise you to learn that sitting around looking pretty and preaching morality to men with broken backs doesn't pay? Not to mention there's almost no coinage in a village this small. Nightfall had no patience for explaining apprenticeships or barter. "Master, forgive my ignorance, but I don't understand. How will working in Delfor get you landed?"

"Landed?" Prince Edward expelled a deep-throated laugh. "Of what significance is one man's landing when so many others live in poverty and sin? Landing is my father's goal. The divine Father has other plans for me. He wants me to elevate the downtrodden. He wants me to give every man and woman the life in freedom he intended. He wants me to rescue the enslaved and champion the meek." Caught up in his own grandeur, Prince Edward rose. "The Father lives within every man, a loving presence who guards his children and his flocks. By his sanction, I will see to it that everyone walks proud in the Father's shadow!" His last words echoed through the Delforian common room.

The innkeeper leaned over his counter, a smile of amusement breaking the contours of a face pocked by

weather and prior disease. The serving maid stared unabashedly. The three Ivralians applauded.

Apparently not recognizing the Ivralians' sarcasm,
Prince Edward executed a stiff head bow that acknowledged their "appreciation." Nightfall despised direct attention, and the Ivralians' performance embarrassed him
in the prince's stead. He kept his voice low but still managed to convey having become swept up in the fervor.
"Then away to the south we go!"

"South?" Edward paused, the glowing excitement of
his features gradually replaced by wrinkles of curiosity.
"Away to the south?"

"Slave country, Master."

"Slave country," Edward repeated with such concentration Nightfall half expected him to tack on the "master"
as well. "We can always come back here, but there're
grander matters to hand. Sudian, prepare the horses."

Grabbing the last of his bread, Nightfall scurried to
obey a command he had fulfilled an hour previously. He
did not dare to smile. For now, he had achieved his goal,
but it had only opened the potential for a million more
massive problems in the south. *How do I land a noble
who doesn't care to be landed?* Nightfall scoured his
mind for sources between Delfor and Trillium who might
give him the answer.

Nightfall suffered the consequences of whipping Prince
Edward to a moralistic frenzy on the southward ride from
Delfor. From the moment city limits turned to alternating
squares of farm field, Edward ranted philosophy until
Nightfall thought his ears would take flight of his head to
escape the repetition. Soon, fertile crop lands gave way to
the more familiar forest, and Nightfall welcomed the
change. The trees provided cover that even the prince's
loud voice could not fully ruin. The trunks scattered
sound, and most bandits had only scant experience with
following bouncing echoes. Once they left the main road
to camp, Nightfall doubted anyone would bother them,
even should they have anything besides horses, tack, and
clothing worth stealing.

Gradually, litany gave way to more normal discussions

about weather and supplies. Prince Edward did not mention his missing money, though whether from ignorance, bland indifference to its loss, or because he did not see it as his squire's concern, Nightfall could not guess. Nobles' relationships with servants seemed distant and rampant with strange customs and manners he had no interest in trying to understand. At least the oath-bond-inspired need to fling his person between Edward and danger had kindled some loyalty in return. The prince forgave or explained away many of Nightfall's improprieties.

They set up camp in a clearing strewn with a damp carpet of leaves. Mushrooms poked their caps through the mulch, some like wrinkled umbrellas, some like plates, and others orange and white domes towering over tiny stalks. From long habit, Nightfall visually sorted edible from poisonous, smashing a patch of toadstools with the chestnut's pack. With the horses set to graze and bedding spread, the prince and his squire enjoyed a sparse meal of jerky and mushrooms. The silence seemed heavy after Edward's cheerful, if tedious, lecturing. Nightfall concentrated on the crackle of the flames and the distant noises of animals in the brush. An occasional fox call whirred through the night, and the polecats screeched at intervals, sounding much like human babies.

Nightfall needed information. Soon enough, he would find a source he trusted. In the meantime, he had little choice but to use what he had. He sat up straight in front of the fire, shadow striping the ground behind him. "Master, how do you get landed?"

Edward turned his head, expression open, obviously surprised. Clearly, it was one of those things gentry seemed to know at birth and assumed others did as well. "I'll have to perform some grand and heroic deed so noble that a king chooses to knight me and grant land."

Nightfall considered, trying to sort his confusion as much as possible before interrogating Edward again. It made no sense for a prince to become knighted. *Why trade a higher title for one lower?* The answer dawned slowly. *Because he's a prince of Alyndar, and he's certainly not getting his property from King Rikard. He'll need a title in the kingdom where he's landed.* Nightfall knew boundaries well; awareness of where one man's jurisdiction began and another's ended had helped him evade pursuit on more than one occasion. Alyndar's kingdom borders had remained relatively stable for centuries. The rulers in Shisen and Ivral waffled between war and peace. Kings Jolund and Idinbal seemed constantly in dispute over the southern triple cities, and Trillium had been occupied by Shisen, Hartrin, and Ivral on various occasions. Still, Edward's claim did not gibe with Nightfall's observations. Many who seemed to have no grasp of heroism owned territory; several bore titles other than knight and some had been born to their nobility in other kingdoms than their land.

After a brief pause, Prince Edward clarified his statement, though he still addressed none of Nightfall's doubts and questions. "I could oust a threat: a crazed wolf mangling citizens, a plague of rats, an army . . ."

. . . an assassin terrorizing the king and his family. The idea, and its subsequent arrangement, entered Nightfall's mind for only a moment before inciting agony from the oath-bond. Pain doubled him over, and he gasped desperately for air. His thoughts scurried for the cure. *No terror. No assassin. Nightfall is dead.* The magic receded, the abrupt change from torture to ache so sudden he had to fight down the contents of his stomach.

"Sudian? Sudian!" Edward knelt at Nightfall's side, steadying him with broad, strong hands. "Are you well?"

"Fine, Master," Nightfall wheezed, seized by a mixture of frustration and anger. He felt like a helpless prisoner, as kept as any slave by a magic that would, in time, claim his soul as well. He wondered if that same incapacitating pain would always accompany the shreds of spirit Gilleran claimed from him or only when the sorcerer chose to use Nightfall's natal gift. The consideration threw him over the edge. He rose, pulling free of Edward, and staggered past the clearing to vomit as far from the camp as possible. Fear raged to fury. The oath-bond constrained him too tightly to create a situation that might get Edward his land. That, he guessed, had been the intention. *The king gets his son killed without doing the deed himself and rids the world of a demon. The sorcerer gets my soul. The perfect arrangement.* And yet, Nightfall still saw flaws in the plan. Again, simpler arrangements could have achieved the same results. *They could have executed me and sent Ned out with some bumbling squire. Left on his own on foreign soil, the prince would surely enrage the wrong person and wind up dead.*

Nightfall considered the possibilities again as the oathbond waned to its normal tingle. It occurred to him that King Rikard might prove his better when it came to clever strategy. Alone, Prince Edward would have lost all his money in Grittmon's Inn, but his life would not have become endangered. He probably would have returned home for money or given up his quest. Perhaps the king realized that his innocent younger son needed an experienced traveler to get him even beyond the borders of Alyndar. Perhaps he trusted Nightfall to drag the boy to the nasty and dangerous haunts that the prince could never have found alone. *Perhaps he just figured I'd get so frustrated with the colt's abrasive innocence I'd just kill him quickly and have done with it all.* These thoughts charged Nightfall to determined rage. *I'll get him landed, all right. And once I do, I'm free. Then the demon will exact his own payment.*

An image of Dyfrin came to Nightfall's pain-dulled defenses like a fever dream. His mouth pressed to a grim line beneath a small nose and a shock of sandy hair. "Vengeance serves no master. Its rage steals even the most ingrained judgment, and it consumes the one it claims to serve." But, for now at least, the promise of revenge seemed more attractive than giving in to despair.

Prince Edward crashed through the brush to stop at Nightfall's side. "Do I need to take you back to the Healer?"

Nightfall shook his head, dispelling the fierce reverie, the idea of returning to Delfor intolerable. "No, thank you, Master. She only heals wounds. She couldn't help with this."

"What is *this?* What can I do?"

Edward's sincere concern seemed nonsensical. *Why does he care? Damn it, why does he have to care so much?* "I must have gotten a bad mushroom in with the others." He tried to turn the devotion back in the proper direction. "Oh, Master, what if I poisoned you, too?"

"Poisoned? Don't be ridiculous, Sudian. I feel fine." Prince Edward assisted his squire to stand, though he no longer needed the help. He led Nightfall back to the clearing and pressed him down onto the thicker pile of blankets.

The prince's strength surprised Nightfall. He did not resist physically, continuing to pretend to feel the weak shakiness that he had suffered only too honestly before. "Master, this is your bed."

"Mine, yours, what does it matter?" Edward's eyes glistened with welling tears. "Get some sleep."

Nightfall closed his eyes, but sleep would not come. He had wanted the prince to trust him implicitly, yet he had never anticipated the protective concern that accompanied that trust. As much as he hated the idea, he could not help liking Alyndar's prince.

Prince Edward and Nightfall followed the woodland path just off the Klaimer shoreline. Two weeks' journey along the coastal bend brought them within a half day's ride of the city of Trillium. This time, they straggled off the path westward to camp in a ragged cove well-hidden from wind, wave, and bandits. Nightfall knew the haven well. He had used it as a bolt hole as well as a temporary shelter. It gave him access to city, ocean, and forest near a grove of walnut trees and berry copses that attracted prey of many kinds. A cabin in this area of plentiful food housed a hermit named Finndmer whom Nightfall knew well. The grizzled loner logged for construction lumber and firewood that he sold in Trillium. He also hauled in loads of walnuts and berries, or hunted depending on the season. These pursuits paid for his necessities; but his other escapades covered the women and the niceties that made a two-story cottage, plain from the outside, a veritable palace within. Many times, Nightfall had pitted his glare against the older man's bulk and experience; and the other had always cracked first.

Finndmer served as the area fence for merchandise, his location just beyond the continent's largest city enviable.

Whatever a man's need, Finndmer knew where to find the goods or information, if he could not supply them himself. However, caution kept him mostly silent around those he did not know and trust. Sudian did not seem the best character for breaching a hard-headed thug's defenses, but Nightfall knew better than to even consider using a disguise. Just the vague thought churned the oathbond to a pain that reminded him vividly of its danger.

Nightfall waited until Prince Edward settled for the night, his snores forming a duet with their own echoes. Bellies filled with grass, two of the horses lay on the cove stone, forelegs tucked beneath their chests. The packhorse remained standing, head contentedly bowed. The prince's safety seemed sure. In Nightfall's years of using the cove, he had never once seen evidence that anyone else knew of its existence. Any major threat would cause the horses to panic, and their banging and cries would carry through the woodland hush.

Nightfall slipped from the camp. Waves slammed the cliffs with a whooshing sound that turned to a gulping suck as water siphoned back from between the rocks. Moonlight drew glittering crests on every ripple, and stars speckled the night sky. Nightfall took the looping path back to the main road. It was easy enough to access the cove; the zigzagging back-tracks had proven no difficulty even for the horses. Nightfall attributed the success of his hiding place more to people's natural tendency to choose woodlands over rocks for camping and to spiral in the other direction when coming to look upon the sea. Most people timed their travels to arrive in Trillium rather than camp so near its borders, and Nightfall suspected that same feature as the reason for the location of Finndmer's cottage.

Nightfall pushed through a press of spring growth to the main road, using natural landmarks to orient. A few strides toward Trillium, he found the crude path of ruts from Finndmer's wood-laden cart. He approached with caution, aware that anyone might come to see Finndmer. Nighttime only made it more likely that a visitor might choose to slaughter a small stranger to keep his whereabouts a secret. Though Nightfall had few doubts he could hold his own against such an attack, it seemed wiser to avoid confrontation. As much as possible, he wanted to play the selflessly faithful squire and avoid the need to justify his wandering to Prince Edward or to anyone else.

The crushed stems smelled of new growth and dampness. Nightfall followed a curve in the trail, and Finndmer's cottage suddenly became visible through the trees, a hulking shadow etched against leafy branches. Nightfall paused, scanning the surrounding clearing for movement. A pyramid of logs filled a corner of the yard, the cart beside it stacked to overflowing. A few logs had spilled to the ground near its wheels. A horse rested in a split rail corral, sprawled like a dog on its side. Night stole color vision, and Nightfall could tell only that it bore a dark color from ears to tail, interrupted by white patterns on the nose and feet. It seemed strange to see a horse in its position, but he knew from experience that secure livestock often slept in such a fashion.

Nightfall smiled at a memory that came unbidden. He recalled Dyfrin's first horse, given to him by a grateful friend rescued from slavery years earlier. Dyfrin had proudly taken Nightfall to see his new possession, only to find it lying still on its side, its eyes closed and no part of it moving. Nightfall remembered Dyfrin's gasp of horror, apparently the horse's first warning of their approach. It had scrambled to its feet, ungainly as a new foal, clearly startled. The withering look it had given Dyfrin remained indelibly etched in Nightfall's mind.

The moments Nightfall wasted on reflection brought a misplaced sound to his ears. Instantly, his mind refocused on it, sorting direction before bothering to try to identify it. Apparently, someone was headed up the pathway toward Finndmer's home, approaching from behind him. Methodically, Nightfall ducked below the level of the creeping vines, careful not to rustle leaves with his movement. He crouched, utterly still.

Shortly, a man approached and passed, his unfaltering footsteps suggesting he had noticed nothing amiss. Nightfall waited until the other had fully passed, alert for signs of pursuit or sounds of an accomplice or bodyguard. He heard nothing to imply that the passerby had a companion. Only then did Nightfall sneak a look. By tread and dress, the other was a man; and his demeanor identified him, at once, as a predator. *A killer,* Nightfall suspected, though whether guard or assassin he could not guess. His dress seemed nonspecific, and it did not reveal his origin. Nightfall discovered a familiarity that suggested he had met this man before, though he could not quite figure out whether appearance or movement had tipped the recognition. Quietly, he followed.

The man marched directly to Finndmer's door. He glanced to the right and left with a nervousness that suggested a first visit. Though no stranger to murder by Nightfall's accounting, the man lost the calm self-assurance he had displayed during his walk, which told Nightfall that he did not seek informants often. This killer preferred to work alone. The man raised his hand, moonlight glinting off a pair of golden rings, and he knocked in cadence to the first two lines of a well-known tavern song. That code told Finndmer and Nightfall that the bartender in the Thirsty Dolphin had sent him.

A light appeared in the upstairs room that Nightfall knew as Finndmer's sleeping quarters. Shortly, it disappeared, and Nightfall followed the woodcutter's route by the shift of lantern glaze past windows. At length, the door opened on silent hinges. Light bathed the area around the door, giving Nightfall a clear view of Finndmer and his customer. The glow revealed features Nightfall recognized at once as belonging to the man who had assisted him when he stumbled in Nemix, the one he believed to be a sorcerer. The men exchanged a few words, then Finndmer gestured the other inside. The door swung shut, plunging the forest back into darkness.

Sorcerer. Nightfall crawled from brush into shadow, crossing the clearing with an animal silence. Experience told him Finndmer would take his client to the back room to chat. He also knew a crack in the mud chinking would reveal most of the conversation. A hole in planking beneath roof-thatch would allow him vision if he chose it over hearing. For now, understanding the sorcerer's intentions took precedence, and he slipped into listening position.

The familiar, mellow voice of the sorcerer wafted to him, its softness rendering some words incomprehensible. ". . . can't mistake him. Large, blond as a whore . . . silks and tailored linens and . . . royal lineage. He rides a white . . . or gelding, I think. His squire wears Alyndar's colors." Leather scuffed against wood as the sorcerer apparently turned away from the wall, and his volume and clarity decreased. "A small . . . young . . . hair. Built like . . ." The rest trailed into obscurity, to Nightfall's annoyance. The ability of this sorcerer to describe would tell much about him. In his experience, few people went beyond estimated age, hair color, deformities, and general body type, all of which could be easily altered when the necessity arose.

Finndmer's response seemed booming in contrast. "I won't assist in or sanction harm to a prince. I'm an honest man. I won't become accessory to assassination."

"Assassination?" The word remained muffled, but the sudden whisk of foot on floorboards cued Nightfall that the sorcerer had turned again. The loud distinctness of his words confirmed the thought. "Dear me, no. I mean the prince no harm. Ever. The squire, Sudian." A choked quality entered the sorcerer's voice, a good approximation of grief. "He slaughtered my brother in a tavern in Nemix."

Nightfall felt certain none of the hoodlums in Grittmon's Inn bore any relationship to the regal and dignified sorcerer. He continued to listen, enraged that one man might turn personal desires into a manhunt that would require all of Nightfall's skill and guile to avoid.

"I have a right to blood price, if not vengeance; but the prince will come to no harm." A pause followed, then Nightfall heard the muffled clink of coins through the fabric of a purse. "Have you seen them?"

"No."

"There's three times more if you do and word gets to me. Assuming I catch up to them, of course."

"Of course."

"I mean no harm to the squire either. I want to talk to him; he's worth nothing to me dead."

"Detainment?"

"Worth double if he's delivered to me."

A prolonged pause followed, eventually broken by Finndmer. "Anything more?"

"No," the other replied. "Just that. Nothing more."

Footsteps clomped, gradually receding. Nightfall faded into the brush. On occasion, Finndmer became suspicious enough to patrol the area around his cottage. This time, however, the sorcerer left alone. The door slammed shut, and Nightfall watched the progression of the lantern up the stairs and back into Finndmer's bedroom. The light winked out.

Nightfall crouched in the silent darkness considering options. Cold night remained a familiar friend that kept loneliness at bay. He had never considered his contacts anything more than business associations, yet now the chains and communication nets he had discovered and, at times, enriched and developed would likely prove his undoing. The people of his new world saw him as a witless servant, those of his old as a security threat. Even Dyfrin would not trust his connections to Alyndar's law, and the oath-bond would prevent revealing his true self to his oldest friend. *Dyfrin might recognize me, though. He's the only one who knew me as a child.*

Nightfall considered his options as the night progressed. To do nothing assured that his description became the business of every silver-grubbing beggar and street thief in Trillium. He had no choice but to confront either sorcerer or woodcutter before they spread the word. When it came to spreading news, at least, the sorcerer seemed the lesser danger. People who elicited information from bartenders usually did so because they had no specific contacts, and Nightfall doubted the man knew other ways than Finndmer to infuse his offer through darker channels. Anyone offering large sums of money to enough people on the streets might penetrate the underground eventually, if not killed for his proclaimed wealth first; but Nightfall doubted the sorcerer would dare to draw that much attention to himself. His proposition would reach guards, other sorcerers, and wizard-haters as quickly as criminals; and few working for the law in any country would allow designs against a prince or his squire.

Nightfall sighed. His usual methods of silencing threats would fail here. In "demon" guise, he would have bullied Finndmer into a hush he would not have the courage to break. If the need seemed enough, he might have resorted to murder, though it would not have gone wholly unavenged. Finndmer had long ago proven himself a vital link in the illegal communication and fencing chain.

As the buzz of the oath-bond intensified, Nightfall shifted his contemplation, trying to think like Dyfrin, a personality that suited Sudian better than any of Nightfall's own. No doubt, Dyfrin would recommend gentle discussion first; but Nightfall suspected he could not win Finndmer's trust fast enough and the sorcerer was a hopeless cause. *So what would Dyfrin do next?*

Only one answer came. *Money.* Finndmer had remained in power because the thieves and murderers he serviced could trust him, at least to a point. Outlaw honor ran high when the price for disloyalty usually meant a gruesome death that would provide an example to others who considered using contacts and the net to serve their own causes alone. Still, the sorcerer was as much an outsider as Sudian. Finndmer had made no specific promise to do as the other bid, only listened to his proposition. In this case, allegiance might shift to the highest bidder without concern for reaction from Trillium's nastiest.

Nightfall left his hiding place with caution, though all his senses assured him the sorcerer had taken leave without doubling back. His consideration continued as he approached the door. Nightfall had his own personal knock that he would not use here. To do so, he believed, would violate the oath-bond as surely as introducing himself as the demon for which the populace had named him. He saw advantage to using a different code, one that suggested a dangerous colleague of Finndmer's had sent him; but the strategy would surely backfire. Finndmer would likely check on the source and discover the lie. He would naturally conclude Alyndar's royalty had beaten the pattern of knocks from Nightfall. Prince Edward and his squire would become the target of an organized mob far larger and more competent than the one in Nemix, and Nightfall would look like a weak-willed traitor.

Nightfall simply chose to tap out the triple beat that most people routinely used. When no answer came after several seconds, he repeated the sequence louder.

Finndmer's voice wafted through the window. "Who is it?" He sounded appropriately annoyed for a man awakened from sleep.

Nightfall glanced about, trying to look nervous. He kept his voice low, just in case he had misjudged the sorcerer's ability for ruse. "My name is Sudian, sir. I came—"

"Your name is what?" Finndmer bellowed. "Speak up, child. I can't hear you."

Child? Nightfall let the comment go unchallenged. His discomfort might make him sound younger, and the cut of his squire's livery seemed more suitable to a boy. "Sudian, sir. I came—"

"Just a moment. I still can't hear you. I'll come down."

Nightfall listened intently beneath the stomp of Finndmer's feet on the staircase. Wind ruffled the pliant, spring leaves, the noise higher-pitched and lighter than in the other seasons. He heard nothing that sounded like deliberate movement and felt none of the wary prickling sensation he invariably knew when unseen eyes studied him. Nightfall mentally traced Finndmer's route, and the door swung open on-time with his speculation. The fence had not delayed long enough to gather devices for detainment or capture; apparently he would give Nightfall a chance to tell his side.

Finndmer stood in the doorway, clutching his lantern and squinting in the sparse light it shed. "Well, come in, young man. What brings you to an old woodcutter's home in the middle of the night?" He did not wait for Nightfall to answer but backed away to give him space to enter. When he obliged, Finndmer closed the door and headed from the entry hall into a sitting room filled with padded benches. Linen covers tacked to the wood concealed pillows cut to fit the bench tops, and embroidered forest scenes paraded across the fabric. Shelves held bric-a-brac from every corner of the continent, mostly small craftworks like painted thimbles, mugs, and statuettes. Though many bore the shapes of animals, none rivaled the glass swan Nightfall had given to Kelryn, taken from her roommate and now carried always in a box on his person. Finndmer gestured at one of the benches then sat on another, within comfortable speaking distance. He waited.

"Well, sir," Nightfall started, not needing to feign difficulty finding his words. "I'm not sure how to explain this."

Finndmer made a vague, yet benign, gesture to continue. He yawned, hiding it behind a hand, but the message came through clearly to Nightfall. He had not yet given the fence a reason to listen.

Nightfall rose and paced. The position of the benches kept him too far from Finndmer to discover how much the sorcerer had paid, and movement would better mask any thieving he might need to do to find the answer. With only four silver coins and a handful of copper, Nightfall dared not misjudge the sorcerer's resources. He suspected he would need the captain's sapphire ring now. Though he hated the thought of sacrificing his last ditch security wealth so soon, gaining Finndmer's goodwill would mean the difference between freedom and a constant need to dodge and hide, exactly the sort of situation for which he had saved it. Given Prince Edward's regal presence and open outspokenness, and his own need to wear Alyndar's colors, Nightfall felt certain violence would become a daily occurrence if he did not settle the matter now.

"There's a man." Nightfall turned and headed toward Finndmer, gauging reaction by facial features. "He's followed me and my master, Prince Edward Nargol, since we left Alyndar. He keeps promising people money to hold us for him. Then, when he catches up with us, he tries to kill my master." Nightfall spun again, assessing Finndmer. The woodcutter sat in silent contemplation, his expression revealing nothing. "He started a big fight in a Nemixian bar that got a whole bunch of people killed. We wound up paying restitution and blood price, and the man who instigated it all never even paid the money he promised."

"Is that so?" Finndmer said conversationally, his thoughts surely deeper than his look would indicate. Only a hand in a pocket of his sleeping gown betrayed him. His fingers flipped a coin repeatedly, its circular form imprinting the fabric.

Nightfall listened for the click of metal against metal, guessing from the sound that the pocket held three coins, copper or silver. It made little sense for Finndmer to carry his assets to bed, so Nightfall guessed he toyed with the presumed-sorcerer's front fee. Having ascertained that without the need to steal and return the money, Nightfall took his seat.

"Why are you telling me this?"

Nightfall met Finndmer's gaze directly, then glanced away as quickly, trying to look suitably discomfited. "I saw him come here. The man trying to kill my master, I mean. I thought maybe he'd offered you money, too. Usually, he picks grimy, evil-looking people, ones he thinks might have a link with killers and ruffians. I don't know why he picked you." Nightfall chose his words with care. The sorcerer's apparent sloppiness, as well as his inadvertent steering of royalty toward Finndmer's ties to the underground, would bother the woodcutter as few other things could. "Did he come here?"

Finndmer frowned, keeping his answer vague. "A man visited. I don't know if he's your man."

"Did he ask about us?" Nightfall knew he walked a thin boundary now. If he pressed too hard without payment, he might alienate his informant. However, he had to play his character as well as his knowledge. A squire too streetwise and bribe-competent would draw suspicion.

Finndmer considered longer than either a direct positive or negative response required. Finally, he slipped into an act of his own. "Please, sir. I'm just a poor woodcutter trying to eke out a living in a harsh and lonely place. Treason? Assassination? I would have no hand in those things, I swear it."

Nightfall believed him, at least in a general sense. However, simply providing information to the sorcerer in ignorance did not make him an accessory. "I'm sure he promised payment, perhaps even offered some money right away. That's how he does it."

Finndmer opened his mouth, presumably to deny the remuneration. Self-consciously, he pulled his hand from his pocket and the coins he had glibly jangled moments before. "Why's this man after your master? What can he gain from killing a prince, other than a painful execution?"

"I'm not sure, exactly. My master doesn't tell me everything." Nightfall leaned closer, as if sharing camaraderie and a secret. "From what I can gather, this man's some sort of nobility. His family wanted his sister to marry my master, but my master refused. From what I've heard, she's not the kind of woman you'd like to wake up to in your bed."

Finndmer chose a local euphemism. "If she were a cow, you wouldn't know which end to milk?"

"More like the bucket you put the milk in. In shape and complexion."

Finndmer assumed an exaggerated expression of revulsion, mouth puckered and eyes crumpled. It brought out every wrinkle on his aging face, crow's-feet prominent at the corners of his eyes and lips.

"Anyway, the family handled it well enough, except for the vengeful brother. That's why I'm prepared to give you this." He pulled the ring from an inner pocket of his cloak. Gold gleamed in the lantern light, and blue fire seemed to wink from every facet of the sapphire. Nightfall kept his hand moving slightly from the moment he displayed the ring to keep the highlights glittering in a ceaseless dance.

Finndmer stared, fascinated.

"All you have to do is convince that man my master and I headed east, toward Tylantis or Shisen, or north back to Alyndar." Nightfall resisted the urge to tack a threat onto the end of his request, a vague vow of retribution should Finndmer go back on his word. The warning would break character, and it also seemed unnecessary. Directing the sorcerer, whether honestly or falsely, might still gain Finndmer the other nine to twelve silver pieces the sorcerer promised, and he would not have to share with Trillium's network.

"Done," Finndmer said.

Nightfall tossed the ring.

The woodsman's deeply etched, callused hand flicked out suddenly, catching the offering. He cupped it into his palm, studying it in the lantern light while blue reflections shivered across the walls and ceiling. "Shisen should seem logical enough, what with the tournament there. The event's still months away, and already droves of royal-born have headed there to get a 'feel' for the battlegrounds." Finndmer shrugged, "Dirt's dirt to us commoners, you know, but high-bred seem to think it'll give them an advantage. Of course, *I* might look for a miniscule edge, too, if I had a chance at a duchy."

Duchy? Land! Excitement rose in Nightfall, and he praised the sense of obligation that made Finndmer eager to talk after feeling overpaid. "Some duke's giving away his land?"

Finndmer laughed. "Of course not. About a year ago, the duke and his wife got killed in a carriage accident. Whole family of bleeders. No heirs. Not even a cousin. King Jolund took back the land for a while, but he's got enough to deal with. So he set up this tournament to find a strong and competent leader. I think he figured a famous warrior as a duke would attract soldiers to help him fight the border wars." His eyes narrowed. "I'm surprised you haven't heard of it. Surely, your Prince Edward was invited."

Nightfall shrugged. "Not that I'm aware of. Not that he would necessarily tell me." *Even when I deliberately asked about ways to get him landed.* "How else does a man get landed?" He explained the motive behind his question, finding truth the most appropriate. "We're on a mission to get my master landed, but neither of us has a real clear idea of what we need to do. Any information you could give us would help." He plucked the stolen wedding ring from his pocket. "I can pay."

This time, Finndmer took the ring directly from Nightfall's hand. He seemed eager to carry on the conversation, and that was uncharacteristic enough to set Nightfall's nerves on edge. He attributed it to the amount of wealth he had flashed so far, though greed did not usually motivate Finndmer to recklessness. He liked his money, but he made a comfortable living already. "The fastest way would be to marry bucket-head."

"What do you mean?"

"The sister. If she's got any holdings, and your master marries her—immediate landing."

Nightfall considered what should have seemed obvious. *A handsome, young prince who's gentle and innocent. What woman wouldn't marry him?*

"It's not just owning land that makes a man landed. There's got to be holdings of some sort, a keep or castle, at least a huge home. And, of course, you have to be of the nobility to have holdings."

Long-trained, Nightfall found the loophole at once. He smoothed wrinkles from his pants with a palm. "To have holdings. But not to have land?"

"Anyone can buy land. A title is more difficult."

"Anyone can buy land?"

Finndmer shrugged, smiling. "Even I own land."

Nightfall doubted the claim. He knew the same baron who lorded over Trillium had possession of a vast area around the city that included Finndmer's clearing. "You own this?" He opened his arms to indicate the forest.

"This?" Finndmer laughed. "No, my land is farther south, past Noshtillan."

"How much do you own?"

"Enough to place a castle and some pastures. Of course, I can't, though. I'm not nobility." Apparently, Nightfall still wore his skeptical look, because Finndmer rose and said, "Stay here. I'll show you." He headed through the doorway to the kitchen, then disappeared from sight.

Nightfall yawned, head aching from the need for sleep. His mind remained clear, however, alert for a trap. If Finndmer chose to confine Nightfall for the sorcerer, he would need locks as complex as those in Alyndar's prison. His mind ticked off one other means of landing that he had heard and forgotten. *War.* One noble who killed another could usurp his holdings. If Nightfall located a particularly oppressive ruler, he might manage to talk Prince Edward into such a course. *Two men against an army. Brilliant.* For now, he discarded the possibility, glad, at least, that hearing more options had set his own thoughts in motion.

Shortly, Finndmer returned clutching a tube made from a hollowed bone and corked at one end. Pulling out the stopper, he shook a piece of paper into his hands, unrolled it, and passed it to Nightfall. "You read, I presume? It's in the southern language."

Nightfall nodded his head absently, taking the paper. "Well enough." He perused the flowery hand and pompous wording, reading for intention rather than specific. It described a chunk of land at the southernmost aspect of the world, directly south of Noshtillan. To Nightfall's surprise, it seemed like a sizable piece. The name on the deed was Finndmer Smeirnksson, and the signature read King Jolund Kryskan. It seemed authentic, though Nightfall knew too little about deeds to feel wholly convinced. "So how would a man go about buying land such as this?"

"First . . ." Finndmer reclaimed the deed, rolling it and stuffing it back into its tube. ". . . he'd have to find someone willing to sell. Then, you'd need money. That's all it takes."

"And you might know someone willing to sell?" Nightfall studied Finndmer.

Finndmer smiled. "We're playing a game now, aren't we? If you're asking if I'd sell, the answer is maybe. The land's not doing me any good since I can't build there. As old as I am, I'm not likely to get knighted for heroism. But land is land, and there's status that goes with it. It'd cost three hundred silver, and I don't bargain."

Nightfall suppressed his surprise, though his nostrils flared slightly in response. Three hundred silver exceeded what every craftsman made in Trillium pooled together for a year. He could imagine trying to gather the sum, copper by reluctant copper. After the longest string of Nightfall's heists, he could never recall having more than fifty silver at once. *If I can't gather three hundred silver, no man can.* Nightfall considered, the situation becoming nearly as much challenge as need. Put in other terms, three hundred silver seemed a small enough price for his soul, especially since he had already lost the first of his five months to travel. *But how am I going to come by three hundred silver honestly?* Nightfall squirmed out of the necessity. *I don't have to be honest. I just have to give the appearance of such, especially to Ned.* "I'll get the money somehow. If a scribe hired by me can vouch for the authenticity of that document, you have a deal."

Finndmer grinned.

Chapter 9

Birthed within the black abyss,
His silent gift, a deadly kiss.
Gone before the rooster crows—
Darkness comes where Nightfall goes.
> —The Legend of Nightfall
> Nursery rhyme, st. 9

Spring warmth returned and, with it, a dreary fog that intensified Nightfall's drowsiness. He rode at Prince Edward's side, for once glad that the prince loved to talk and did not require much response from his audience. This time, he rambled about releasing slaves to help construct the ideal world that existed only in the minds of the naive, a world where people did not exploit one another and all mankind was inherently good. It only convinced Nightfall that he needed to keep Edward from the smaller market in the southwest corner of Trillium, though that did not seem too difficult. The other quarters would surely prove large enough to hold his interest; likely, he would never realize that a piece of the border city had gone unexplored. Instead, the problems would arise when Prince Edward insisted on moving westward, toward Brigg, Hartrin, and Mitano.

Nightfall would worry about that when the time came. For now, the need for three hundred silver pieces took first priority. Theft seemed a hopeless possibility. Robbing pockets, it would take months or years to acquire the necessary capital; and the sheer volume of victims would almost guarantee at least one arrest. Trouble with the law in Trillium was a matter even Nightfall did not take lightly. Because the constabulary allowed any sale or activity legal in any of the continent's kingdoms, the universal laws, such as those prohibiting theft, required strict enforcement and extreme punishment. Otherwise, the town could degenerate into rampant chaos. Stealing a small number of expensive objects would require more of Nightfall's expertise than he believed the oath-bond would allow, and it would set a city-wide search in motion. Somehow, he would have to earn the money in a legitimate fashion that would not upset Prince Edward. At least, Trillium's broad definition of legality left him leeway.

As Edward and Nightfall rode over the crest of a hill, they discovered an overturned wagon on the road. Winter melons lay scattered over the packed earth and into the ditches, their orange-red rinds clearly visible against the greenery. Some had cracked open, revealing pink fruit speckled with seeds. Nearby, a man stomped and lashed his arms through the air, movements jerky with rage. He howled a string of obscenities that carried through the dreary dankness, amplified by humidity.

"Oh, dear," Edward said simply, continuing toward Trillium, a route that would take them directly to the fallen wagon.

Nightfall sighed, certain of his fate for the next half an hour, at least. The prince would never let a needy stranger go unhelped, no matter how inconvenient for his squire.

The stranger turned and looked up as they approached, mud-streaked cheeks flaring crimson. He fixed dark eyes on the prince apologetically and executed a brief but respectful bow. "I'm sorry for the sharpy-words. Didn't know you was there, noble sir."

The farmer's voice startled the white gelding, and it took several, sudden backward steps. "No offense taken," Prince Edward answered, as if it mattered, pulling his horse back under control. "What happened here?" He gestured at the toppled cart and its scattered cargo.

Nightfall tried to figure out the answer before it came. The skid marks were not deep enough for a miring in mud to explain the circumstances. The length of the drawing tongues suggested that a horse rather than a human usually hauled the load, consistent with the estimated weight of cart and melons. The sideways twist to the front wheels and bent metal swivel ring confirmed the probability of a horse-related problem.

The farmer's response only affirmed what Nightfall

had already deduced. "Horse shied at a snake. Took the whole damned wagon over." He made a wordless sound of disgust, accompanied by a wave of dismissal that made Edward's gelding stiffen and jerk its head. "Damn nervous Suka. Ain't worth the fur the Father gave her, but she's all I got." He glanced up the path, empty to its disappearance around a bend. "Or had. Probably to Trillium by now." He looked longingly at Edward's trio of horses. Nightfall took note of how he gazed most briefly at the high-strung white.

Nothing like a farmer to spot a good horse by manners instead of breeding. Nightfall suspected he could talk Edward into giving a horse to the farmer, but he doubted the prince would choose his own steed. It seemed far preferable to keep all three than to lose the chestnut or bay. "Master, may I try to catch her?"

The prince smiled, clearly pleased with his squire's decision to lend aid. "Certainly."

Nightfall dug his heels into the bay's ribs as quickly as the confirmation was spoken. "Yah!" The bay sprang forward, clearing two horse-lengths in an instant, then it shot down the pathway at a drawn-out gallop. Nightfall leaned against its neck, balancing his weight on the withers and holding the reins nearly at the level of its eyes. The speed of its charge and the wind caressing his face made him feel detached from reality and truly free for the first time since the captain's confrontation on *Raven*. There was something he could not explain about the raw power beneath him and speed so impressive it created the winds that made even a race for his life seem wondrous. He had stolen and run horses for as long as he could remember, and the sensation of flight never dulled, comparable only to the lurch and roll of a ship in a gale. To control such energy, whether through sail or rein, made him feel invincible.

Once around the curve, Nightfall discovered a dark brown mare grazing the ditch grass on the more densely forested side of the road. Cued by the sound of pounding hoofbeats, it whipped up its head, trailing harness leathers from nose, withers, and rump. Nightfall drew rein, slowing his mount to a trot, then a walk. If he continued run-

ning, herd instinct might send the mare skittering at
random, perhaps injuring a leg in the brush. The idea of
chasing her down the path at an open gallop seemed a
joy, but he had Edward to tend. At least, the ride had reawakened the stream of consciousness that too little time
sleeping had blunted. A series of bets seemed the best
way to get money fast, and he only needed to turn the
odds a bit into his own favor.

The darker mare whinnied a cautious welcome that
Nightfall's bay did not bother to answer. Suka approached, neck stretched to meet the newcomer without
need to stand too close. The two horses whuffled nostrils
for several seconds. Apparently tiring of the game, Nightfall's mare made a high-pitched snort of challenge, and
the dark brown half-reared. It came back down circling;
and Nightfall managed, at the length of his reach, to catch
the reins. Turning, he ponied the cart horse back to its
owner. It followed docilely.

When Nightfall arrived, he found the farmer replacing
melons in the now upright cart. Prince Edward had dismounted, tethering pack and riding horses together to prevent either from frolicking away. He clutched the top of
the swivel bolt in one hand, the axle in the other. Eyes
closed, muscles straining, he was gradually restoring the
shape of the pin. Nightfall could not help feeling impressed, certain his meager strength would have failed
him in such an endeavor. At least the royal tutors seemed
to have taught some useful skills, and nutritious food
from birth had only helped to hone his strength. The bolt
would still need replacing, but the cart would carry the
farmer to Trillium's market and home.

Nightfall dismounted, attaching both horses to the others. If any of the animals tried to escape now, it would
have to drag all of the others, some backward or sideways. The dark brown tossed its head, unsettled by the
closeness of strangers. Gradually, hunger took over, and
all four settled into a grazing pattern. Nightfall assisted
the farmer with gathering melons, silently counting as
each piece of fruit found its place on the cart. Prince
Edward finished his task, then perched upon one of the
drawing tongues while the others finished their work. As

the last of the undamaged winter melons fell into place, Nightfall tallied forty-eight. The farmer picked up one of the broken melons that had fallen with its open side up. He pulled off a chunk for himself and handed the remainder to Nightfall. "How can I possibly thank you?"

"No need." Prince Edward separated his horse from the others. He left the bay and chestnut together and held out the cart horse's reins for Nightfall to take. "I'm glad we could help."

Nightfall set aside the melon, accepted the reins of cart horse and gelding, and steadied the white while Edward mounted. Once the prince found his place in the saddle, Nightfall walked the cart horse to its owner. He lowered his voice so Edward could not hear. "Are you taking these to market today?" He indicated the melons.

The farmer shook his head. "By the time I get there, it won't be worth the unpacking time. There's a little inn on the edge of town. It's not well-known, so it's a lot homier than the Thirsty Dolphin that most folks go to. I'll stay there and recommend you do, too. It's cheaper, quieter. Food's better, and they're real good at taking care of people's things." He bit melon from rind.

Nightfall nodded absently, well-familiar with both of the mentioned inns, as well as a third on the farther side of town near the smaller market he needed to avoid. "Any chance you'll take the road past the Dolphin on the way to market tomorrow?"

The farmer chewed and swallowed. "Could arrange it. Why?"

Nightfall avoided glancing toward Prince Edward, concerned the prince might gesture him away before he finished. "My master and I would consider ourselves repaid if you pretended you never met us before."

"That's it?" The farmer studied him curiously, clearly hoping for an explanation, though he probably guessed he would not receive it.

"That's it." Nightfall confirmed, mind clicking through the possibilities. When odd jobs had proven scarce, Dyfrin had earned his sustenance by entertaining with sleights of hand, bets, or minor scams that preyed always upon the greedy. From his fatherly friend, Nightfall had learned to cultivate opportunities where he found them. The more frequently the same con got used, the more likely the victim would recognize it, and Dyfrin had a way of turning every situation into a creative boon. Unfortunately, he also had a soft spot for those in need that Nightfall had never understood. Well-liked for his generosity, Dyfrin could have lived as a secure member of almost any city had he not so often become the quarry of those who took without appreciation or repayment. It had long occurred to Nightfall that he had proven one of Dyfrin's latter projects, a child in need who had given little back, in verbal gratitude or wealth. Familiar guilt twinged through him at the thought, and he discovered a longing to see his old friend. The last he knew, Dyfrin had returned to their birth city, Keevain. The oath-bond would keep Nightfall from identifying himself, but he could still thank his partner anonymously. He owed the man that much and more.

"I'll head for market first thing sunup." The farmer smiled, adding facetiously, "stranger." He took several more bites of winter melon, tossed the rind, and headed for his cart.

Nightfall picked up the broken melon the farmer had given him. He snapped off chunks, handing the best two to Prince Edward. Keeping two for himself, he mounted one-handed. They headed toward Trillium, Edward chatting about the farmer, Nightfall forcing himself to think like Dyfrin. He needed to earn his fortune quickly, before the prince explored too far. And, for all the times Nightfall had cursed Dyfrin's impetuous and obsessive eye for nicety and detail, he wished he possessed it. No one could pick a victim or a friend like Dyfrin.

The road widened as Trillium came into sight, a massive cramping of buildings that stretched as far as Nightfall's vision. Tents crowded the border, belonging to those who could not afford an inn room; and Nightfall knew that night would find many more sleeping on the unprotected ground. Five roads came together at the eastern edge of town, from the southern cities, from Keevain, Shisen and Tylantis, from Ivral and Grifnal, from the north, and from the city itself. Wagons jounced over well-worn pathways, most carrying early spring or perennial crops from local farmers. Merchants from the southern cities brought citrus fruits and hardier vegetables. From the Yortenese Peninsula came meat and fur, and the central countries imported milk, cheese, and woven cloth.

Nightfall knew the slave countries would import to the western side of town, bringing Hartrinian herbs, spices, and crafts in addition to their living wares. The sellers of mood-altering drugs and sexual perversion mostly based themselves directly out of Trillium, though a few sneaked their wares from other places beneath the guise of more legitimate goods. Cure-alls and beautifiers found a brisk market in Trillium as well. Desperation or impatience would lead the sickest and vainest to trust the miracle medicines of swindlers over the slower practicalities of Healers. Most of the panacea salesmen whom Nightfall knew made random, harmless concoctions, occasionally mixing in alcohol or hazing herbs for effect. He still remembered the justification one man had given Dyfrin: "That rash'll go away anyway. By the Father, why shouldn't my treatment take the credit?"

Despite the heavy penalties for illegality, the poison trade flourished in the black market; and Nightfall knew all the best places to purchase knives with reservoirs, arrows with painful barbs that did not pull free, and belts and boots with compartments or sheaths for blades. All trades thrived here, and visitors caught up in the glitter and searching for instant wealth fell easy victim to sucker bets and schemers. So long as he kept his tricks reasonably honest, Nightfall suspected he could win or lose big. *But three hundred silvers?* He shook his head at the enormity of the sum.

The rattle and bounce of the wagons they passed, as well as the shouted greetings between friends meeting at the town edge, sent the white gelding skittering so often its excitement merged into a constant dance. Prince Edward dismounted, which seemed just as well. If he got thrown in the cart traffic, he might suffer injury much more serious than a simple fall. "Sudian, we'll have to build camp here."

Nightfall sprang from his bay, suspecting that towering over his master looked disrespectful. His mood sank at the prince's words. No place would serve as a better central point than the Thirsty Dolphin when it came to finding bets and challenges as well as information. The word "build" applied to camp only worsened the situation. He pictured moats, palisades and wooden stake defenses hovering amidst the simple tents and bed rolls, and the image might have seemed humorous had the realization of a night of painstaking labor not accompanied it. "Master, there's a wonderful inn in town."

"Sudian." Prince Edward glared at his squire. "I didn't ask for a travelogue. I said we set camp here." A cart jostled by, metal chains in the bed clanking. The gelding lurched, all but tearing free of Edward's grip.

Nightfall guessed at the reason for Edward's insistence, and the prince's pride annoyed as much as it impressed him. "Master, I apologize deeply for my boldness, but I am aware that we're short of money."

Edward's glower deepened enough to almost make the young, friendly innocent look angered. How much of it was inspired by the horse and how much by his squire did not matter. The risk of his master's disapproval and a tongue-lashing seemed little price to pay for a chance to spend his nights in an inn. And Nightfall already trusted the prince not to harm him physically, at least not without cause far more significant than this.

"I've been meaning to return this to you, Master." Nightfall pulled one of the silvers from his pocket. "You gave it to me in Nemix to buy the spade I never found." He met Edward's displeasure with an expression of hopeful trust. "Master, I can't stand the thought of you sleeping on hard ground with beds so near. At least you go to the inn. I'll spare our money by staying here."

The sacrifice, though insincere, softened Prince Edward at once. He accepted the coin, rubbing it between thumb and forefinger. "Of course I'll stay at the inn and you'll stay by my side. This should buy us a week's lodging for both or a half week with three meals included."

Nightfall hesitated, uncertain how far necessity demanded he carry his shallow humility.

The prince saved Nightfall the need. "If I go alone, who'll taste my food for poison?" He grinned, clearly joking.

Nightfall smiled back, pleased to discover the solemn visionary had a sense of humor. He did not know whether to feel glad or endangered that ignorance and lack of experience counted more for the prince's foolishness than the inherent stupidity he had credited. Eventually, he believed, Edward could learn sarcasm. *Then, watch out King Rikard and Alyndar.* The idea of even this cunning vengeance seemed sweet, but Nightfall found the thought of educating Prince Edward intriguing as well. Time was telling that, once he gained some insight and abandoned the arbitrary traditions hammered into royalty from birth, Edward might prove a competent leader after all.

"Let's go." Prince Edward gave an abrupt jerk on the gelding's lead rope that brooked no nonsense. The animal followed docilely, though its ears remained pricked like sentinels and it rolled its eyes to the whites.

Nightfall handled chestnut and bay together, both alert but compliant. He took the lead as swiftly as propriety allowed, choosing a route to the Thirsty Dolphin that would not reveal the nearer and cheaper inn the farmer had mentioned. He kept to the main streets, dodging foot, cart, and horseback traffic, focusing on detail and letting his natural wariness absorb the familiar background bustle of Trillium. Edward trailed without question or complaint, his eyes flickering from sight to sight.

Upon arrival at the stone and mortar inn, Prince Edward headed inside to tend to the room and payment while Nightfall took care of animals and packs. Juggling three horses became a nuisance even for Nightfall. Every slight movement of one caused an excessive opposite reaction of the others, and their pulls unbalanced him twice before he mentally doubled his weight to anchor. At the stable door, he took all three ropes into one hand. Precariously balanced, he raised a fist to knock.

Without warning, the wooden door whipped open from the inside with swift, unnecessary force. A heavy-set, bearded Mitanoan in merchant silks huffed through the entrance, apparently oblivious to squire and horses standing directly in his path. He bashed into Nightfall, the sudden obstacle and all its extra mass staggering him. The gelding reared, ripped free, and charged for the barn entrance, churning road dirt over both men.

The merchant roared at the insult.

Nightfall dropped his weight to normal. "I'm so sorry, sir." *You big, clumsy ass.* "I didn't see you."

"Didn't see me?" The merchant rose, and Nightfall read violence in his stance and expression. "Didn't *see* me?"

Anticipating a warning slap, Nightfall did not dodge. Better to let the man defuse his anger with a simple act of brutality than enrage him further.

The Mitanoan's fist crashed against Nightfall's cheek hard enough to send him sprawling. "Stupid, snotty slave." A boot toe slammed into Nightfall's ribs. A second kick rushed for his gut. Nightfall twisted from its path, then curled back to catch the leg. Instinct took over. He wrenched at the captured limb, yanking the man to the ground. An instant later, Nightfall had a knife blade at the other's windpipe. The control he had harnessed through years of playing various commoners was all that rescued the merchant from death.

Outrage formed a tense mask on the man's face. "The penalty for murder is stiff. You'll die in slow agony."

"Probably," Nightfall returned, not bothering to inform the merchant that, had Nightfall wanted to kill him, he would already be dead. "But think where *you*'ll be." Unobtrusively, he slipped the merchant's purse from its pocket and into his own.

A trickle of fear in the merchant's eyes betrayed some false bluster.

Nightfall sheathed the knife and rose. Bared steel would attract attention he did not need or want, and it would make him seem the aggressor. The white gelding stood just inside the barn, under the control of a stable boy who feigned disinterest in the proceedings outside. The bay and the chestnut dropped their heads to search for strands of grass between roadside and dwellings.

The man scurried beyond reach, but he did not let the

matter drop. "You'll be beaten soundly for this, maybe killed. I'll see to that. Who's your master, slave?"

Through the open doorway, Nightfall saw the stable boy curl his fists impotently. He had gained an ally more, he guessed, from a common enemy than any bond of friendship. "First, *sir* . . ." He gave the title the same disdainful pronunciation as the man had given slave, ". . . do you see a collar here?" He flicked his fingers across his own neck in an unmistakable throat-slitting gesture. There is no slavery in the north. It'd do you well to remember that. Second, my master is Prince Edward Nargol of Alyndar. Call me slave to him, and you might face worse than what you got." He flashed a toothy smile. "He's bigger. Third, *sir,* you can tell him what you wish, but the bruise on my face will prove far more telling than the one to your damned pride." He snatched up the bay's lead rope, then the chestnut's, and headed for the stable.

The merchant stammered, but he did not try to interfere physically again. He stormed toward the Thirsty Dolphin.

By the time Nightfall hauled his charges inside, the stable boy had already stripped the tack from the errant gelding and shut the horse into a stall. Taking the bay's lead rope, the youngster hauled off saddle and bridle, then led it to the next stall. He gestured for Nightfall to place the chestnut in the one beyond it. After adding pack, saddle, and leading halter to the pile, Nightfall did so. Only then, he examined his helpmate. He looked to be twelve or thirteen, reasonably well-proportioned and sized for his age. Black hair hung in a straight curtain down his neck, and uncombed bangs fell into his eyes. Beneath the left cheek, an angry area of redness and swelling indicated that he had taken a recent blow.

Nightfall guessed its source at once. "Did he hit you, too?"

The boy turned away, tugging open a small door built into the white's stall. He nodded, without meeting Nightfall's gaze. "Some of the ones from west is like that. They think 'cause slavery's legal here they can treat everyone what works for board instead of money like they's owned." He hefted Edward's saddle, dragging it to the compartment. He lugged it inside, then closed and locked the door. Finally, he met Nightfall's gaze with pale green eyes. "Thanks." He explained. "For what you done out there." He waved toward where the confrontation had occurred. "I know you didn't do it for me, but it sure guv me some joy."

Nightfall moved the other two saddles near their respective stalls.

"You don't gotta help, sir. Your horse'll get special treatment just for what you done already."

"I insist." Nightfall paused, one hand on the compartment built into the bay's stall. The work seemed simple enough and the time away from Edward a pleasure. It gave him something to do while his anger faded. Besides, he was beginning to understand Dyfrin's obsessive insistence on helping others and the favors that attitude garnered in return. Many treated stable boys as nonexistent, though they saw and heard much of significance. At the least, it would ascertain good care for the horses and assistance should a fast escape become necessary. Placing a hand in his pocket, he counted the merchant's coins through the fabric of his purse. Money and its relative value remained consistent throughout the kingdoms. Only the pictures inscribed on the surfaces varied. He identified two silvers and seven coppers. "Here." At first, Nightfall thought to hand over the coppers, but he would need smaller change to get the betting started. Instead, he offered a silver.

The boy stared at the coin, wide-eyed. Then, apparently concerned Nightfall might take it back, he snatched it from the squire's fingers. "Thank you, sir. Thank you so much."

Hardly pays for the dignity the bastard stole from either of us, but it'll have to do. Nightfall responded to the gratitude with a nod and helped the boy stow saddles and bridles. "My name's Sudian. Right now, the title 'sir' doesn't seem like much of a compliment."

"Mine's Benner Morik. Let me know what I can do for you and your master." He rummaged beneath a pile of rags and pulled out a handful of leafy, translucent stems. Taking one, he crushed it, rubbing the pulp onto the bay's neck.

Nightfall recognized the boy's surname. It tied him into a network of cousins splashed through the town as menial laborers, tavern waitresses and merchant's helpers. The boy's abstraction interested him more. "What are you doing?"

The boy beamed, clearly glad to finally earn the favor Nightfall had shown him. "This is for special customers only. Keeps flies away."

"Really?" Nightfall had never heard of such a thing before. He reached out for a stem, and Benner obliged him. It felt tough and stringy, though the stem held plenty of juice. He sniffed at it. It had no odor. "How's it work?"

"Don't know," the boy admitted. "But it works real good." He lowered his voice conspiratorially. "Thought about rubbing rotten melons all over that sir's horse to *bring* flies, 'ceptin' it'd be cruel to torture the animal for its owner's nastiness."

Nightfall agreed, though he gave the conversation only half his attention. "Its lot's probably bad enough." He glanced at the stem in his hand. "Do you mind if I keep this?"

"Go 'head. Just don't go showin' it to ever'one, if you don't mind. Otherwise, I's gonna be spending ever' moment of my life rubbin' horses, and I ain't gonna get nothin' else done."

"Our secret," Nightfall consented happily. The fewer people who knew about the fly repellent, the more useful it became to him. He lifted the packs.

Benner gave him a pained look. "Luck with your master. Hope you don't git in too much trouble for what happened."

"My master's fair." Nightfall had only a vague idea how Edward would react when propriety clashed with morality and loyalty. He believed King Rikard's assessment that Edward would not hit him, at least not without just cause; the prince's actions so far had assured him of that. Yet, he wondered how the prince, being ignorant of the oath-bond, expected to keep Nightfall obedient and tractable without some show of dominance. As Nightfall, he had gotten his way on most occasions by the threat of danger alone; his reputation precluded the need for violence.

Nightfall considered his early years, before he had a reputation or even a name. Then, he had proven his prowess well enough, not by random beatings but by demonstrating his agility or his skill with knives. He recalled a day, years ago, when he, as Marak the sailor, served as a crew member of a merchant ship that pirates commandeered halfway across its route. An image of the sea filled his mind, a rickety, flagless ship low in the water from the weight of catapults and stolen cargo. His nose wrinkled from the remembered odors of salt, unwashed flesh, and blood. He had watched the pirates slaughter his crewmates gleefully, one by one; and, by the time they came to him, he had already unknotted his bonds. He recalled ducking beneath the ax stroke meant to decapitate him, the moans of the dying, planks washed red and slick with blood. He had made it to the railing, stealing three daggers from pirates en route. "Kill me and lose the best man you ever had." From the upper deck, he had pointed to the captain below. "That knothole beside your captain has drawn its last breath." It had seemed a desperate bet, an impossible throw that required perfect judgment of gravity, angle, and backspin. A miss would have assured humiliation as well as death. Had he accidentally struck captain or crewman, he would have met a prolonged agony of torture. But the stolen knife had flown true, and he alone survived the pirate's capture.

Nightfall recalled his own reaction to his mother's ferocity, the love/hate relationship she had inspired. A stranger who inflicted her sessions on him would meet a swift death, but the ties of blood had crippled him from any consideration of vengeance. He wondered why slaves did not revolt and kill masters like this merchant, and many answers came without need for consideration. *Fear of punishment. Fear of starvation. Fear, perhaps, of freedom itself. The unknown.* Still, Prince Edward's compassion did not seem the answer either. Without the oath-bond, Nightfall would never have served him, and even the younger prince's family seemed little pleased by the need to associate with him at all.

"Maybe Amadan'll let the whole thing go. Maybe he won't tell your master."

Nightfall doubted the merchant would allow the matter to drop, even for a few moments. It did seem better to allow the stranger to present his version of the story without interruption and give Edward at least a few moments to consider it before Nightfall defended his actions. "Good eve."

"Good eve," Benner returned, though the afternoon sun still hovered halfway between midday and sundown. Despite Nightfall's bold dismissal, the boy cringed before turning to continue his work. Clearly, his master would not prove as gentle under the same circumstances.

Nightfall stepped back out into Trillium's streets, immediately lost amid the broad mixture of racial dress and features. Dumping the coins loose into his pocket, he ditched the merchant's purse in an empty alleyway, grinding the fabric into the dirt. An attack he could explain away as self-defense, a theft he could not. Hugging the packs more tightly, he took a deep breath and headed back toward the Thirsty Dolphin.

Prince Edward Nargol drank a mediocre-tasting beer at a table in the common room, watching the Thirsty Dolphin fill with patrons that spanned a wide variety of features and dress. Males outnumbered females by a vast majority, and the latter seemed mostly to take the secondary roles: barmaids and servants. A few young ones slunk from table to table, gyrating hips and jiggling breasts as they walked. These would speak with men in soft tones until one rose and accompanied her through the back doorway that led to the inn rooms. Edward wondered about the purpose of these meetings, though the demeanor of those involved suggested something clandestine or sexual. The seductive dress and sinuous movements of the women excited Edward, despite his best attempts to keep his mind elsewhere, and made him long for a girlfriend of his own. For a fleeting moment, he envied his brother, wishing he could drop his crusade, stay home, and find a woman to mutually please. He stifled the idea, appalled and embarrassed at once. The Father had given him a mission, a gift and an honor too few men received. If he remained a virgin until he completed the god's bidding, heroes had made greater sacrifices.

An adolescent girl a few years younger than himself shimmied by, clothing so tight he could see the outline of her nipples, distinct against the fabric. He sipped his beer, trying politely not to stare. Yet, against his will, his mind undressed her, flashing him an image of naked flesh that stimulated him to erection.

Eyes locked on the passing beauty, Edward did not notice the stranger standing over him until the other made a cautious noise of greeting.

Mortified, the prince tore his gaze from the girl and placed it squarely on the man before him, a stout, middle-aged stranger. Edward blushed, feeling as if he had broadcast all of his unholy thoughts to every person in the common room. Yet, only the man studied him.

"May I buy your drink, good Prince?" the man said, his dress revealing high station short of nobility.

Prince Edward found his thoughts difficult to focus. "Excuse me?"

"May I buy your drink?" he repeated.

The request confused Edward. "Well, I suppose so. If you wish." He set down the mug. "But wouldn't you rather have one of your own?"

The man stared, as taken aback as the prince. "Are you Prince Edward Nargol from Alyndar?"

"I am."

"Noble sir, my name is Amadan Vanardin's son. I'm a merchant. Is it all right if I join you?" He gestured at a chair.

"Certainly."

Amadan sat. "And I'd like to pay for your drink for you, sir. Would you mind?"

"Mind? Certainly not." Edward found the request odd, but he appreciated it. No one had ever offered to finance his beer before. "What a nice thing to do. Thank you."

Amadan gestured at a barmaid, then returned to the conversation. "How's the beer, sir?"

"Lousy," the prince admitted. "But it did take the edge from my hunger while I'm waiting for dinner."

"Then it served some purpose, at least." The merchant smiled to indicate a joke, but his hands moved constantly from flat on the tabletop to clasped to his lap, as if he could not figure out where to place them.

Prince Edward could not fathom a man so nervous in his presence. He grinned back, trying to place the other at ease.

A barmaid hastened over, dress fluttering, long dark hair in disarray. Though harried, she still managed a smile for the attractive, young prince. "Is this the gentleman you were waiting for, noble sir?"

Edward thought he sensed disappointment or displeasure in her tone; but, as that made no sense, he dismissed it. "No. He'll be along soon."

She turned her attention to Amadan, and all of the breezy friendliness left her. "What can I get for you, sir?"

"Beer," Amadan said, then glanced at Edward. "Do you need another?"

Edward shook his head without bothering to assess how much of his drink remained. It would be impolite to impose on this stranger's generosity.

The barmaid spun on her heel, striding back into the crowd.

Amadan replaced his hands on the table, tapping them. He wore two silver rings on one finger, the inner one loose, and these rang together with every movement. "I need to talk about a sl . . ." He caught himself, ". . . a servant of yours."

"A servant of mine? Sudian?"

"He's a servant, lord. I didn't ask his name."

"I have only one servant here." Edward sipped his beer. "Go on."

Amadan's gaze dodged Edward's. "I don't know how to tell you this, except to just tell you." Now, he met the prince's soft, blue eyes. "Lord, your servant threw me down on the ground, held a knife to my throat, and threatened my life."

Edward could not have been more surprised had the merchant told him his squire had sprouted wings and flown to the moon. Confusion kept emotion at bay. "Sudian?"

The merchant stared, mouth a grim line. Clearly, he had expected more reaction. "He named you as his master. And he wore your colors."

Prince Edward needed confirmation of what he believed he had misheard. "Sudian threw you on the ground, held a knife to your throat, and threatened to kill you?"

"Yes, lord."

The next question followed naturally. "What did *you* do to *him?*"

Amadan blinked, now looking as bewildered as Edward felt. Then, apparently believing he had misunderstood the intention of the question, he twisted it to cover consequences rather than motivation. "I hit him, of course, lord. As I would punish any impertinent slave. But certainly not hard enough to make up for—"

Rage boiled up in Edward. "You *hit* him?" He slammed his mug to the tabletop. Beer sloshed over his fist. "You hit *my* squire! How dare you hit my squire!"

"I don't believe this!" Amadan leapt to his feet. "Your slave tries to murder gentry, and you're yelling at me?"

Edward kept his head low, trying to control his temper, the memory of the dead slaver still as fresh a reminder as the scar the whip had left on his face. "That is the second and last time you refer to my squire, or any servant of Alyndar, as a slave." He flicked his gaze up to the merchant without moving his head. "Sudian's been with me a long time." Even as he said the words, the prince realized that he had misspoken. Little longer than a month had passed since the squire had joined him in the courtyard. It only seemed long because of Sudian's fierce loyalty and all that had happened since leaving Alyndar. "He wouldn't harm anyone unless he saw them as a threat to me."

Amadan seized the back of his chair and leaned toward Edward. "Lord, if he thinks I'm such a threat to you, why isn't he here now defending you?"

"Then he saw you as a threat to *him*. It's one and the same to his thinking." He quoted Nightfall. "You see, if he's dead, he can't protect me."

"A threat to him?" The merchant resumed shouting.

"He's a servant, by the great Father's beard! Of course I'm a threat to him. If one of my slaves did what he did, I'd have them publicly flogged to death."

The idea shuddered horror through Edward, and he cringed at the image of every lash. He despised the thought of any person owning another, but the idea of one so brutal doing so enraged him to the edge of violence. His hand blanched on the mug. He had vowed to free the slaves, and this seemed as good a place as any to start. "Are these slaves of yours here?"

Amadan made a vague gesture into the crowded barroom. "All three, lord."

"How much would it cost to buy them from you?"

Amadan stared, clearly surprised and ruffled by the diversion. "I didn't bring them to sell, Lord. It's easy enough to buy some of your own. What I want to know is . . ." He leaned closer, gray eyes boring into Edward's blue, ". . . how are you going to punish that snotty, little bastard who doesn't know his place?"

The insults shoved Edward over the edge. Control lost, he rose, his massive shadow spanning the table. "I'm going to tell the 'snotty, little bastard' that the next time a merchant brutalizes him, he shouldn't threaten to kill him." His voice deepened, gaze unwavering. "He should just kill him."

"You're joking."

"Hit my squire again and find out if I'm joking." Having spoken his piece, Edward retook his seat, seeking the self-control he had lost in the Hartrinian camp in Alyndar . . . and now once again. As much as he wanted to free the man's slaves, he had no intention of murdering anyone to do so. The god-given right to dignity extended to slavers as well as to slaves, to evil as well as to good. Edward wished slaves and masters could trade places one day each week, to see the world from the other side every time they raised a whip. Then, he guessed, every man would feel as strongly about freedom and self-respect as he did. "Now, how much would it cost to purchase your slaves?"

Amadan curled his lower lip, his face a study in hostility. "More than you'll ever have." He whirled, storming deeper into the common room.

As Prince Edward watched Amadan go, he noticed for the first time that the conversations at every nearby table had ceased. The eyes that did not follow the blustering merchant fixed directly on Edward. He smiled politely, noticing that each patron glanced away when their gazes met, embarrassed to be caught staring. Gradually, the dull hum of conversation resumed at its normal background volume. Nevertheless, Edward noticed when Amadan returned to his table and his slaves. In a bold display obviously intended for the prince, he grabbed the one female of the three by the hair and a breast, jerked back her head, and planted a sloppy kiss directly on her mouth. She quivered but did not resist.

The sight left Edward cold even to the cultivated allure of the barflies and prostitutes for the rest of the night. Tears filled his eyes, and he cried for the pain of those three and so many others.

Chapter 10

Counting years like grains of sand.
Countless fall beneath his hand.
Time, his minion; night, his clothes—
Darkness comes where Nightfall goes.

—The Legend of Nightfall
Nursery rhyme, st. 10

The inn room in the Thirsty Dolphin seemed sparse but adequate. Little space separated the two sleeping pallets, though they seemed far preferable to the scattered hay on the floor that served as beds in smaller towns. A table in the opposite corner, near the door, stood firmly on squat legs. A tub across from it held all the basins and pitchers necessary to draw water and bathe, an uncommon luxury; and a drain hole opened onto conduits that carried the dirty water into the sewage gutters lining the larger streets. A chest of drawers, scarred with nicks and dents, lined the wall near the table. One drawer sagged open while Nightfall crouched on the floor, transferring garments from Prince Edward's pack.

The door latch clicked.

Nightfall paused, a folded tunic in his hands, taking note of the sound. Whoever had come, presumably Edward, had made no attempt to do so quietly.

The door swung open, the hinges squeaking mildly. Prince Edward stepped through, closing the panel behind him. The bolt slammed into place.

The small, windowless room made Nightfall feel suffocated as tight places never had before Alyndar's guards locked him in their dungeon. Fear flashed through him, suppressed only by the rationalization that he still had control. From the inside, opening the now-locked door required just one more movement. "Master, hello. Did you need something?"

"We have to talk, Sudian."

Nightfall lowered the garment to his lap, certain the topic involved a certain incident outside the Thirsty Dolphin's stable. He fixed his gaze attentively on Edward.

"There's a man here named Amadan Vanardin's son. He says you held a knife to his throat and threatened to kill him."

Nightfall said nothing, awaiting a direct question, though he knew an explanation was expected.

"Did you?" Edward pressed.

"Yes, Master. I did." Nightfall refolded the tunic and placed it atop the others in the drawer. He kept his manner and his tone matter-of-fact.

Prince Edward sighed. He sat on the edge of his pallet beneath the room's only lantern. Light splashed white lines and golden glitters through his hair. His hands slid into his lap, and he stared at his fingers for several moments.

Nightfall drew a shirt from the pack, more uncomfortable with Edward's silence than his lectures. The others had amused him. This quiet seemed abnormal.

Finally, Edward looked up. Nightfall thought he had gathered the necessary words; but, when the prince spoke, he used only one. "Why?"

Nightfall set his work aside. Though it seemed unnatural, he stepped into the semicircle of light. He plucked off his purple and silver shirt so Edward could clearly see the darkening bruise the merchant's boot had gouged against his chest and the abrasions the road had slivered from his arm and side. In the light, he believed the prince could also tell where Amadan had struck him in the face.

Prince Edward winced, and Nightfall replaced his clothing. "Is that why?" the prince asked.

Though Nightfall knew the reason would probably suffice, he found a better one. "No. He also pounded on the stable boy. Master, I only did what you would have done. I know you believe in defending the downtrodden. You wouldn't have let him hurt that boy."

"I wouldn't," Prince Edward admitted. He studied Nightfall for some time before finishing. "But I'm a prince. I can do that. I can't let my servant threatening a highborn's life go unpunished."

Nightfall froze, believing he had finally found a transgression that would earn him Edward's wrath. Magic or none, he would not stand still for any man to batter him. The defiance raised a pounding wave of nausea and agony from the oath-bond that told him he would. Survival took precedence over any need to dodge pain or humiliation. Vengeance, if necessary, could come later. What he could not avoid, Nightfall would take bravely, but he would see to it that the prince suffered as much for the pain. From experience, Nightfall knew that, for Edward, that meant a direct attack to the conscience. "I understand. Beat me however for as long as you feel it's necessary." Kneeling, he lowered his head, fighting down every instinct that told him to close his defenses.

"Beat you?" Edward's missing strength returned and flared to annoyance. "I'm not going to beat you." He shivered distastefully at the thought. "What's that going to teach you except more violence?"

Nightfall had to concede that Prince Edward had a point, although he had already received all the lessons he ever needed about brutality. And learned them well.

Edward pointed at Nightfall's pallet. "Sit."

Obediently, Nightfall rose and did so.

"We're going to discuss and memorize the seventeen rules of etiquette. The long version." Edward heaved a sigh. Apparently, he had found a topic tedious even to himself. "By the time I got through talking to Amadan Vanardin's son, I almost put a knife to his throat myself. The lesson might teach us both some restraint." He launched into the session. "When addressed by a man of superior station . . ."

Nightfall almost wished he had gotten beaten instead.

Nightfall slept through Prince Edward's dinner in the common room of the Thirsty Dolphin. His conversation with Finndmer had kept him awake much of the previous night, and he knew he would need the wee morning hours to begin the many gambles and schemes taking shape in his mind. A multitude of possibilities paraded through his thoughts, but he concentrated hardest on the situations chance and consideration had given him opportunity to set up in advance. Dyfrin had often claimed that serendipity came to everyone daily; a wise man learned to turn small details to his advantage. And Nightfall knew organizing all of that would prove easier while the gentle and honest prince lay safely asleep.

Prince Edward returned around midnight, changing into his sleeping gown in the dark, and crept quietly into his bed. Awakened as always by movement, Nightfall lay in silence and feigned sleep, guessing the time by feel alone. The lack of a window made cues from the sky and moon impossible, but Nightfall had become a reasonably good judge of interval, even asleep. He fell into a shallow half-drowse, allowing himself some extra rest and the prince to sink into unbreakable slumber. Then, as solid snores filled the room with echoes, he slipped out, padded down the hallway, and glided through the entryway into the common room.

Nightfall assessed the patrons at once. Five local youths flung darts and daggers at gashed and battered cork targets painted in concentric circles. They based their game at a nearby table, mugs and bowls of beer lined up for an easy sip between turns. Their sport intrigued Nightfall, though the stakes seemed too low to bother with. Eventually, he might find need to pit his dagger-throwing abilities against others for significant winnings. Until then, it made no sense to reveal, or even give clues to, his skill.

Three merchants sat at a table near the bar, their simple but well-tailored dress revealing them as wealthy Grifnalians or Ivralians. These seemed more interesting, though Nightfall knew they would probably prove slow to warm to a stranger and shrewd with their money. Still, their decision to attend a rowdy tavern this late suggested some daring and curiosity about the wilder side of Trillium. Two tables from them sat a pair of local hoodlums eying the sparse crowd with the same attention as Nightfall. The remainder of the patrons consisted of fifteen middle-aged Trillian men in groups of two to four.

The appraisal took moments, and Nightfall hesitated only casually before choosing an empty table between four locals, who appeared alert and involved, and the merchants.

A barmaid scooted from behind the bar, threaded between the tables, and approached Nightfall. Dark hair swirled to her waist, and her brown eyes probed his. "Are you Sudian, Prince Edward's squire?"

"Yes."

"Your master said you'd probably come along. He paid for your dinner. Would you like it now, sir?"

Nightfall smiled at Edward's thoughtfulness. He suspected the prince had probably ordered the meal early in the evening, while Nightfall stabled the horses, and it had become forgotten in the wake of Amadan's accusation. Nervous energy had kept hunger at bay, but now Nightfall realized he had not eaten since the broken melon. "Yes, thank you."

The barmaid headed back toward the kitchen.

Nightfall glanced over at his neighbors, made eye contact with a chunky redhead, and smiled. The man nodded in return, grinned, and muttered an incomprehensible greeting before returning his attention to his friends. Nightfall did not press. Things needed to unfold in a natural manner that made it seem as if beer, rather than desperate need for money, drove his actions.

Shortly, the woman returned, placing a mug of beer and a plate of food in front of Nightfall. He studied the contents, looking for something he could use. Steam twined from a mound of whipped squash speckled with shreds of meat. Beside it, a quarter of winter melon rocked in the wake of the server's movement, bowed like a smile; a fly buzzed in spirals around it waiting for it to still. Square cut chunks of cheese filled the final corner of the plate, and their shape inspired the last details of an idea. He shoveled squash and meat into his rumbling belly, concentrating on the warm food while it remained so. Then, using one of his throwing knives, he shaved the melon from its skin, cutting the pinkish fruit into rectangles. He alternated eating cheese and fruit, waving away the occasional fly that alighted on the melon. At intervals, he met various gazes, encouraging any stranger with interest in Alyndar to feel free to approach him.

Three cheese and four melon bits still decorated his plate when a young woman in rags and a collar slunk through the doorway to the inn rooms. She glanced about the common room through a shoulder-length mass of sandy hair, her fear evident. Her gaze fell on Nightfall, and she shuffled toward him hesitantly.

Nightfall watched her approach, wondering why the slave had singled him out of all the men in the tavern and suspecting he would soon find out. In silence, he waited, certain he was not the only one curious about her intentions.

The slave stopped a polite distance from Nightfall and knelt before him.

Nightfall hesitated, unaccustomed to such respect. The rules Edward had pounded into his head the previous evening left him free to do as he pleased with the situation, so long as he did not displease her owner. "Come here," he said, patting a chair beside him.

She rose and obeyed, keeping her head and gaze low, hands clasped in her lap. She seemed tense enough to break.

"What's your name?"

"Mally, lord."

"I'm no lord, Mally. My name is Sudian. I'm a servant, the squire to Prince Edward Nargol of Alyndar."

The woman stared at her fingers, saying nothing.

Nightfall shifted, seeking a means to turn an interruption into a boon. He hated the time wasted but also recognized the complication as a means to draw the attention of other men in the tavern. Played right, it might open the way for gaining confidences. Few would suspect a man unnecessarily gentle with a slave of conning them of money. "You came to me for a reason. I'm not good at guessing people's thoughts. You're going to have to tell me."

"Well, sir," she mumbled quickly. "I—"

"Call me Sudian." Nightfall reached out slowly and without threat, touching her clenched hands.

She winced but did not pull away, obviously unused to taking solace from physical contact.

"And look at me when you talk," he added, keeping his voice soothing. "My boots can't answer you."

Hazel eyes rolled cautiously upward, alighting on his momentarily, then skittering away.

Nightfall smiled.

Again, she met his gaze, then glanced away. Gradually, she focused her attention on his nose, not quite ready to meet his eyes directly for any significant length of time.

Nightfall settled for the compromise. "What can I do for you?"

Mally had a face that Nightfall suspected had once been pretty. Now, her cheekbones stuck out sharply. Her crooked nose sported a lump where it had once broken, and he could not tell how much of the patchy discoloration of her face came from grime instead of bruises. Straight, knotted hair obscured her features. "Your master, the prince. A good man?"

"Most definitely."

"Doesn't hit you too much?"

"Never."

"Never?" Mally finally met and held his gaze. Her manner hardened, and purpose lit her eyes. "Get him to buy me."

"What?"

"Get him to buy me, and I'll do anything for you."

"I can't—" Nightfall started.

Mally interrupted. "Anything. Please!" She grabbed his hand in both of hers, squeezing. Her grip trembled with fierce desperation. "Please?"

Nightfall freed himself from her hold. "There's nothing I can do. I'm just a servant."

"Your master protects you. He'll listen to you. I know he will." Now that the barriers of shyness had broken, she became relentless. "He offered Master money for me and the other two. Master said 'no,' but he was angry. He'll sell. I'm sure he'll sell."

Nightfall shook his head. "Prince Edward can't keep you. There's no slavery in Alyndar."

"You're not in Alyndar."

"Now," Nightfall admitted. "But we plan to go back

eventually. And no matter where, it wouldn't do for the prince of a free country to own slaves."

Mally went indignant. "Then why did he offer to buy us?"

"I would never presume to judge my master." Nevertheless, Nightfall speculated. "Perhaps it fit the conversation. Or he may have wanted to set you free."

"Free?" Mally repeated, hunching into herself, eyes wide and childlike. "I'm not looking for freedom, just a kinder master." She plucked at her collar.

Mally's words disgusted Nightfall, and all interest in helping vanished. He recalled his own struggle for freedom, not from slavery but from the many forces, human and natural, that had sought to crush him on the streets. Life came easy only to the highborn. "What's wrong with freedom?"

"Nothing." Mally's voice became a frightened squeak. "If you're born into it. I've seen hunted slaves return, tortured to death in the public square. Those that stay free starve or fall victim to any gang of street-raised monsters who wants to use them."

The words raised an ancient memory, long suppressed. At eleven, Nightfall had been weathering the cold, dark alleyways of Keevain for three years. He recalled gulping down a stolen muffin so quickly he choked on the crumbs, hunger usurping caution. He had heard the two men too late, boxed between them in a night-dark throughway. He had run, but not fast enough. He remembered the ankle snatch and twist that had sprawled him, the huge, scarred hands clamped to his privates, and the sickening tear of his already tattered britches. Their threats rang through his ears: claims of ownership, a vicious rape, and a slow death. One had trapped his head between clothed thighs, the odor driving up the first food he had eaten in days. The stranger had recoiled from Nightfall's sickness, inadvertently leaving the boy an opening. Spiraling loose with wild kicks, he had stolen the man's knife, thrusting the blade into the man's groin with a gashing twist that severed the artery. Instinct had goaded him to escape then, but rage had taken over.

Nightfall had slashed the other's throat and left them both bleeding in the alley.

The remembrance clipped through Nightfall's mind in an instant, accompanied by bitterness. He kept his voice low so those nearby could not hear. "My master has the only servant he needs. If you can protect him better than me, prove it. I'll gladly step aside and let you have the job."

Every piece of Mally's exposed flesh turned white. "No, sir. No. I'm not trying to take your place. I'm just—"

"You're just looking for the easiest life possible." Nightfall considered the implication of his own words. "And that's only natural. But everyone else's too busy making things easier for himself. Things won't change for you unless you make them."

"Make them?" Mally's gaze returned to her lap. "That's what I'm trying to do."

She had a point Nightfall could not deny. "You've taken the first step, but you're working on the wrong problem. Your problem isn't getting a new master, it's getting rid of the old one."

Mally glanced up, clearly confused; but Nightfall did not give her time to question.

"Think about it. But I can tell you one thing: if Prince Edward bought you, he would set you free. If that's not what you want, don't come to me for help." Nightfall ate another cheese cube, indicating that the conversation had ended, in his mind.

Taking the cue, Mally rose from the chair, though she remained hunched in deference. "Thank you, sir, for your advice and consideration."

Nightfall nodded acknowledgment, but he said nothing more. He watched the slave skitter, head low, across the room to the doorway and disappear through it. It had required daring for her to slip away at the risk of punishment to discuss her lot with one her master hated. Nightfall wondered whether she would find the courage to carry through on his suggestion or even to consider a life without shackles. Yet, to her and so many, chains and collars seemed a small price to pay for regular meals, protection, and shelter.

The red-haired Trillian moved to Nightfall's table, accompanied by a slender brunet. Their two friends remained in place, watching the dart match and whispering between themselves. The heavy-set one spoke first. "Another begging the employ of Prince Edward Nargol of Alyndar?"

Nightfall blinked, surprised. "There've been others?"

"Two serving girls, the stable boy, and a merchant's stock man. That's the first slave I know of."

"Good man, my master."

"Obviously," the other Trillian said. "And he allows his squire in the common room alone?"

Nightfall shrugged. "If he's in a safe place and under certain circumstances. It has little to do with what he allows. I wouldn't leave him if I believed anything might harm him." He smiled. "Good man, as I said."

The dark-haired Trillian buried a hand in his stiff beard, gaze locked on the dart game. The redhead accepted the burden of amenities. "I'm Tekesh, and my friend's name is Ifinska." He indicated his two remaining companions at the table, a bearded brunet with recessed eyes and a tall, thin man with gray-speckled black hair, in turn. "Porlenn and Limalzy."

Nightfall acknowledged the more distant pair with nods. "Sudian," he said, not bothering to tack on title. These men already knew his master.

Ifinska continued to watch the dart-playing youths.

Nightfall had assessed each competitor's ability naturally upon entering the common room, his judgments based mostly on build, movement, and arrangement of muscle groups. He had off-handedly watched enough of their play to get a reasonable feel for ability. "Hey, Ifinska."

The brunet turned his head with obvious reluctance.

"Do you know those boys?" Nightfall gestured at the dart and dagger games.

"The one up now's my cousin."

Nightfall glanced to the game where a lanky youth

stepped up to the targeting line brandishing a dart. Nightfall looked back at Ifinska. "He any good?"

Ifinska returned his attention to the game. "I'll bet he sticks it in the target."

"Faint faith." Nightfall figured the odds at two to three in Ifinska's favor, a wager not worth taking. However, he saw a means to quickly skew those chances, though not as far as he would have liked. More importantly, the betting would begin and, he hoped, grow into a fever that left no time or interest in computation. "Three coppers says he doesn't land it in the yellow, red, or green areas." He chose the central rings, their area covering nearly half the board. Quick consideration made the bet seem even or slightly biased toward Ifinska; the zones were about the same size; and the boy would, undoubtedly, aim for the middle. Yet Nightfall held a less obvious edge. There remained a one in three chance that the youth missed the target completely or the dart did not stick.

"Three coppers," Ifinska agreed.

Unaware of the second wager upon his success, the youth hurled the dart. It flew true, embedding in the second ring from the center.

Nightfall calmly tossed three copper pieces to the tabletop, but Ifinska let them lie.

"These against another three on this next boy. Same bet."

Nightfall glanced over. He knew the youth currently up to the line, a soldier-in-training whose preferred weapon was dagger. Nightfall's merchant persona, Balshaz, had flung against him on occasion, and the boy had held his own better than most. He had fared well over the course of this evening, as well. However, that success might prove its own ruin as he had won enough five-for-a-copper beers to impair his aim. Already, Nightfall could see that he had stepped too close for his usual spin. Nightfall clung to the role of ignorant foreigner. "All right, it's a bet."

The dagger thumped against the central area, then clattered to the floor. Ifinska flicked the three coppers back to Nightfall, frowning as if the boy had betrayed him.

The next to challenge the cork was a scrawny, homely

youth who had lost largest that night. The configuration of his muscles gave him a natural clumsiness that would probably lessen as age added growth to his torso and it came more into proportion with his arms and legs. Nightfall had watched his aim improve steadily through the evening just from the practice. "Same bet?" he asked, certain Ifinska would refuse.

As expected the brunet shook his head.

"I'll make the opposite wager." The redhead who had called himself Tekesh slapped down three coppers.

Nightfall disliked the flip-flop of odds he had deliberately created in his favor. "All right, but only if I get the central five rings." That brought the odds to even, slightly in his favor if the improvement that had come with practice was considered.

Tekesh hesitated, then nodded acceptance.

Apparently not wanting to get closed out of the betting, Ifinska jumped back into the game. "I'll take the two outer rings if you spot me a copper." Removing his purse, he worked the coins to the mouth and let them drop to the table. They bounced, winding about an edge, then fell flat to the wood.

The boy stepped up to the line, studying the target.

Tekesh objected. "If I lose the two outer rings, I get to take out a copper." He placed a finger on one of the three coins in front of him.

Nightfall shrugged, secretly pleased with the maneuvering. His chances of winning had not changed, but his potential profit had grown to four coppers for three.

The dart flew, striking and holding in the fourth ring from the center. Another win for Nightfall.

The betting in the Thirsty Dolphin's common room dragged far into the night, spreading from table to table like a fire. Though the goal and bets changed and reversed, Nightfall always kept the odds only slightly in his favor so that the others won often enough to maintain interest. Within a dozen bets, Nightfall had drawn in the merchants, Ivralians both, though the natives came and went as their money allowed. Nightfall kept the nature of the bets varied and interesting, mostly to distract others from computing odds that Dyfrin had taught him to estimate in an instant. On occasion, he slipped some of his winnings into his pockets, keeping an attractive amount on the table without making it obvious that he had taken in more than his share. The fluctuating participants and their sheer numbers helped to hide the fact. He won often, but no more than his calculated odds suggested he would. When interest flagged, he would purchase a round of drinks for the more recent participants from his winnings, keeping many there long past intelligent propriety.

As night progressed toward day, the number of local Trillians diminished, including the dart-playing youths. Those remaining had drank far more than the three beers Nightfall had nursed through the night. A camaraderie had grown between the remaining bettors, one Nightfall had every intention of exploiting. During the thick of a heated debate over whether the last person entering the tavern had sandy-brown or dirty blond hair, no doubt in order to determine the winner of a silly bet, Nightfall unobtrusively swiped the bug-repelling weed the stable boy had given him against a side of each of his two remaining melon cubes. He waited until the argument subsided, then placed the food in the center of the table, one repellent side up and the other down. He studied the smallest of the Ivralian merchants, a handsomely featured man named Kwybin. Slurring his speech as if from too much drink, he pointed at the melon cubes. "I'll bet you a silver the next fly that lands picks this one." He pointed at the cube placed repellent-side down.

Kwybin laughed. "You'll bet on anything, won't you?"

Nightfall seized the opening. "Lost my wife and children in a card game." He met the Ivralian's gaze directly, giving no clues to indicate he was joking. "And I wasn't even playing." He gestured the melon cubes briskly to keep the flies from alighting while the merchant decided. "You in or not?"

Kwybin considered, glancing from cube to cube as if to find some subtle difference in form that would make one more attractive to insects than the other. While he debated, his taller companion, Hyrowith, placed a silver coin on the table. "I'll take the bet."

Nightfall sat back, hands clasped in his lap and well away from the melons. The size of the wager, as well as its strangeness kept most of the patrons in place, gawking. Before long, a fly hovered over the fruit, circled twice, then landed on Nightfall's cube.

A spattering of applause and sympathetic noises swept through the group. Though he had lost, Hyrowith laughed. "I guess the bugs like you better. I'm not sure that should bother me." The others in the common room laughed.

Nightfall smiled. He reached for the cubes, rolling them casually as if to return them to his plate. Despite the seeming patternlessness of his gestures, he kept track of the repellent-marked sides at all times. His caution paid off. Kwybin could not resist his part of the action. "My turn." He smacked a silver piece to the tabletop. "I'll bet on the winning piece." He pointed to the cube on which Nightfall had placed his last wager.

It proved easy enough to leave the chosen melon repellent-side up this time. Nightfall shrugged. "One's as good as another." He moved away from the fruit, pushing his newly won silver toward the other. Several moments passed in silence as patrons glanced from melon to air, seeking flies in the quiet stillness of The Thirsty Dolphin. Then, a sweet-fly wove through the onlookers. Delayed by those who tried to bat it toward one cube or another, it gave Nightfall his second win.

Dawn light touched the windows, the thick glass warping it into a glaze that could not compete against the myriad candles in brackets on the walls. Nightfall finished his cheese, took a last swallow of warm beer, and stretched. "One more," he said cryptically, then explained. "I need one more bet to complete the night, something that everyone who wants to can join." He glanced about the tavern, pretending to seek something on which to pin his money, for dramatic effect alone. He knew precisely where his best bet lay, and he only needed to delay until it came to him.

Several patrons shouted suggestions, from a personal round with the dart to contests that involved drinking to the point of vomiting. Nightfall dismissed them all as not exciting or chancy enough. Then, he opened the common room door and glanced up and down the city streets. Far in the distance, he saw an approaching wagon, little more than a dot on the roadway. The direction fit perfectly, and the distant, barely audible, clop of hoof on cobble clinched the identity to just short of certainty. He whirled suddenly, as if the almighty Father had tossed the perfect idea from the heavens. "I'll guess something about whoever next passes this doorway."

Several patrons crowded to join Nightfall in the entryway, inadvertently becoming his witnesses that the streets stood empty. "What'll you guess?" several asked in various fashions.

Nightfall pretended to consider for some time. "Depends on what comes."

The last remaining teen from the knife and dart contest spoke next. "I'll check ahead and let you know." Clearly beer had clouded his judgment enough that he did not worry what his parents would think of his spending the entire night in a tavern. He trotted into the street, glanced up and down the block, then headed toward the dot on the horizon.

Nightfall tried to elicit interest beyond that already raised by speculation about the grand finale of a servant who had laid money down on everything from strangers' skill to the preferences of flies. "We'll make this interesting. A number. Age? Weight?" He discarded the obvious and headed toward the ridiculous. "Number of hairs on his head—"

The youth returned shortly. "Wagon coming. Melons headed for market."

The obvious came to several minds at once, even alcohol-fuddled. One Trillian, a relatively recent comer to the proceedings, started things moving, "I'll bet three coppers to one you can't guess the number of melons on that cart at a glance."

Nightfall pulled at his chin, rough with morning stubble.

"You wanted a challenge," one reminded.

"A challenge, yes," Nightfall repeated thoughtfully. He smiled wanly. "All right. What are winnings for but to lose. The thrill of the game and all that." He turned back to the crowd as more patrons filed to the entrance to watch for the coming merchant. "I'll match every coin placed on that table one for one." He pointed to the table nearest the door. "I win if I guess the number of melons on the cart within two."

There followed a sudden mad scramble for the table, every man wanting his share of action skewed so far against a gambler who had, apparently, had way too much to drink. A shabbily dressed, young man who had placed no wagers himself, but had rooted for Nightfall from the start, spoke up. "Have you thought about those odds, Sudian? Even three to one wouldn't hardly seem fair."

Several patrons glared at the speaker, clearly worried that a shock of common sense might lose them the sure win this bet appeared to be.

Nightfall again looked out the door, stance light and balanced against the frame. "I either guess right or I guess wrong." He glanced back at the speaker. "Right or wrong. Two possible outcomes. Fifty:fifty." He shrugged. "Even money. Sounds right to me."

The warped logic brought even the most reticent bettor to the fore. By the time the wagon came up on the Thirsty Dolphin, twelve silvers worth of copper littered the barroom table. Nightfall recognized the dark brown mare hauling the cart as the one he had returned to its owner the previous day. The farmer clutched his horse's reins, looking startled by the crowd. His gaze fished Nightfall from the others, and he smiled slightly. True to his word, he gave no other gesture or greeting to indicate he had met Edward's squire before.

Nightfall fixed his gaze on the cart, bobbing his head as if counting. His scrutiny allowed him to ascertain that few, if any, of the melons had been stolen or bartered since he reloaded the cart. Still, it made sense for him to guess low rather than high. Melons could only diminish, not multiply, in the night. As the cart rattled past, he moved into the road behind it as if to complete his tally. When he turned back toward the tavern, he discovered every eye fixed on him.

Building tension, he crossed back to the doorway in silence. The patrons moved aside to let him enter, backing away as he took a seat at the money-ladened table. A few more coppers had joined the others while he stood in the roadway.

Dramatically, Nightfall looked up. "Forty-six," he said, at last.

"Forty-six. Forty-six. Forty-six?" The number made its rounds through the crowd, and anticipation turned to confusion as the realization sank in fully that there seemed no instantaneous way to determine the victor. After a few moments of discussion, the group chose six men from their midst to help the farmer unload and tally his product, none of whom had any money at stake nor bore more than a passing relationship to anyone who did. Having recognized two whose honesty Balshaz had trusted as well as the one youth who had cheered him since the start, Nightfall did not protest. He sat quietly, nodding with polite abstraction as the others made comments about his stupidity or luck, depending on their proclivities and confidence.

The wager itself did not concern Nightfall; he already knew the outcome. He only hoped the counters at the market would hurry, before Prince Edward awakened for his breakfast. Soon enough he would know that his squire had spent much of the night making wagers. Nightfall could soothe and explain easier, if need be, without three quarters of his take displayed across a barroom table.

Nightfall managed a haggard smile. Once the count came through, he would own a copper total of forty-four silver coins, with a few copper to spare. It seemed a fortune and a pittance at once, more than most men saw in a decade yet less than a sixth of what he needed to buy Edward his land. He doubted he could pass another five nights as successfully at the Thirsty Dolphin, not without placing his honesty too far in doubt or earning the wrath of a victim certain he had been cheated. *Even if I could stay awake that long.* Already Nightfall felt fatigue gnawing at the edges of his constant and necessary alertness. By the following day, schemers would come, either to quietly study his techniques or to relieve him of his newfound riches. To confront others of his ilk, some of whom specialized in scams while he only dabbled, he would need all his wits about him.

Nightfall lowered his head and let his thoughts run.

Chapter 11

Where Nightfall walks, all virtue dies.
He weaves a trail of pain and lies.
On mankind heaps his vilest woes—
Darkness comes where Nightfall goes.

—The Legend of Nightfall
Nursery rhyme, st. 11

By the time Nightfall collected his money and rushed back to the inn room, Prince Edward had only just awakened. The prince lay on his back, eyes repeatedly whipping open then drooping shut as he attempted to come fully awake and start the day. He seemed to take no notice of Nightfall's silent entrance. Playing dutiful squire, Nightfall levered through the drawers, choosing clean silks for his master and unrumpled silver and purple for himself. In Trillium, they would have no trouble finding a washerwoman to clean and press their clothing, though Nightfall would see to it that the process of hiring took time. Focusing the prince on the mundane would leave less chance for idealistic, inciting lectures to slavers and their charges.

As Edward finally won the battle against his sagging eyelids, he spoke. "Good morning, Sudian."

"Good morning, Master." Nightfall turned to sorting wrinkled and dirty from passable, the day's wear already chosen.

Edward sat, and the blankets fell into a jumble across his legs. "Are you ready for a productive day?"

Nightfall did not like the sound of that. He looked over, a pair of breeks dangling from his hand. "Productive, Master," he asked, careful to phrase the words like a statement rather than a question.

"Slaves to liberate. People to educate." Edward shoved aside the blankets. "The Almighty Father's word to spread. He has given us this day, and we will use it for him."

Nightfall tossed the breeks onto the dirty pile, mind racing for a distraction. He would need several more days of betting to accumulate the necessary capital to buy land. If Edward insisted on preaching at slavers, they would need luck just to survive until the evening. He failed to find a long enough list of occupying tasks to keep Alyndar's youngest prince reined, but he did manage to put together words from his lessons on war. He quoted Sharfrindaro, one of Edward's favorite generals: "The battle doesn't start until first scouting is done. Strategy without knowledge is doomed to failure."

Edward corrected the inaccuracies: "The war does not begin until advanced surveillance is completed." He considered. "Why bring that up now?"

"Well, Master." Nightfall twisted his words to build points rather than questions. The need to concentrate on presentation had the additional effect of making him sound more eloquent than usual. "It seems wise to consider the words of those we admire before taking on a battle no one else has dared to fight."

Prince Edward reached for the clothing Nightfall had chosen for him, dragging it up beside him on the pallet. "You mean we should study the ways and patterns of slaves and those who keep them before executing the Father's will."

Nightfall shrugged, returning to his sorting. "I'm not suggesting anything. I'm just guessing at your plans."

Apparently, Nightfall had found a positive combination of proposition and modesty, because Edward considered longer as he shed his sleeping gown and flipped his breeks over his feet. "I hadn't thought of the matter exactly as a war," he admitted. "It's not as if there's killing involved." He winced, apparently reconsidering the incident Nightfall had heard about in Alyndar in which Edward had accidentally taken a Hartrinian slave master's life. "And there are no sides. Once they understand the pain and wrongness of their actions, men who keep slaves will gladly free them."

And kings will gladly give their castles to the homeless.

Nightfall hoped the events of the last few days had given Edward an inkling of reality. *At least, I should try to educate the romantic, guileless dizzard while I have him thinking for a change.* "If we could gather every man who has owned or thought of owning slaves, I'm certain your silver tongue could carry the truth to them as it has to me. But to bring the message to each, one by one, seems a task that will outlast our lifetime."

Prince Edward rose, breeks only halfway in place. The binding cloth spoiled his regal pose, and his partial nakedness stole dignity from his bearing. "I would consider it an honor to live and die serving the Father in this manner."

"And I would consider it an honor to live and die serving you." Nightfall exchanged his own tunic from the previous night for the cleaner one he had selected. Alyndar's purple and silver had grown tediously familiar. "But I've done only part of my job if I deflect a knife from killing you that then stabs your foot. Each slave freed may be a victory. But can we really claim success for rescuing three if we could have used the same time and effort for ninety-five?" Nightfall mulled a strategy he had raised and discarded some time ago. Once, he had thought of slaying a king's enemies one by one, crediting the purge to Prince Edward and, thus, earning his master title and land. He had dismissed the possibility because the sequential murders might require him to become too much Nightfall. He had also abandoned the tactic of encouraging the prince to go on a similar spree based on honorable dueling. First, no matter how competent the prince—or Nightfall's unobtrusive cheating—the odds would catch up to him in time. Nightfall spoke the second reason aloud. "It would take an eternity to defeat an army, or a cause, man by man."

Edward adjusted his breeks. He pulled on his tunic, belted it, then added the calf-length overtunic, its neck and hem decorated with threaded patterns in silver and gold. "Sudian, I'm the scholar of war. You're coming dangerously close to questioning my judgment."

Finished dressing, Nightfall met Edward's gaze directly, seized with a sudden urge to grab the naive prince by the throat and shake him until sense jarred loose from the cobwebbed corners of his brain. Instead, he funneled his frustration and belligerence into words. "Master, I would question directly if I thought it would serve your cause and lessen the harm to you. I would rather die for the impropriety than let any hurt befall you." Nightfall kept his hands free and his attention alert, hoping Edward would translate this to the significance of his point. "Even good people, like your father and brother, do not see the Father's light when the best of all men presents it to them. People like Amadan care only about making their own lives easier. Do you think you can convince him, and others like him, to give up their slaves?"

"There is good in everyone. With the right words, may the Father give them to me, I will convince him."

Nightfall cursed Prince Edward's boundless innocence and faith.

Then the prince added another point that made Nightfall wonder if experience had not begun to crack the shell of idealistic ignorance. "If I cannot convince him, then I will buy and free his slaves myself."

Nightfall had already found the flaw. Paying Amadan for his slaves would only grant the Hartrinian the money to purchase more. In the name of right, the prince would pay an exorbitant sum, and Amadan would wind up with more slaves to brutalize than before the sale. Nightfall swerved with the argument. "There's another thing to consider." He continued to hold Edward's gaze. "I mentioned the possibility of freedom to one of his slaves last night. She refused it."

Edward's eyes crunched closed, and his jaw wilted. Though he clearly trusted his squire, he found the incident too impossible not to question. "A misunderstanding, surely."

Nightfall shrugged and returned to sorting. "You've heard the story of the Hartrinian twins and the tiger." He knew the honest prince would deny the assumption, having no way of knowing Nightfall had made up the title and the story on the spur of the moment.

"No," Edward admitted. "Which book is it in?"

Having little knowledge of books of any kind, Nightfall

covered neatly. "It's not in any book as far as I know. It's the story of how Hartrin became slave territory, and people down this way have been telling it to their children since the whole thing happened." He glanced at Edward again. "Would you like me to tell it?"

The prince nodded absently, obviously still puzzling over how he could have missed hearing such an important tale.

Nightfall created an answer to the unspoken query. "It's not the sort of story I think nobility likes much. It's about a set of twin princes, the first royal offspring of a king, whose name I never knew, though the boys were called Ursid and Brionfra. A slight woman, narrow in the hips, the queen seemed incapable of birthing her children. She labored longer than a day, until it appeared certain she would die along with her offspring. Then, at last, a Healer came who believed he could take the children another way. He sliced open her womb from above and hauled the babies from their exhausted mother."

Edward listened raptly.

Nightfall had never considered himself much of a storyteller, but he continued, not wholly decided on the course of the tale. "Yet, though he saved all three lives, the Healer had done one thing wrong. In his haste, he had pulled Ursid out first, though Brionfra, with his little head jammed in the birth canal, was nature's choice for elder prince. Ursid became the heir, Brionfra cheated of his birthright."

"Not cheated." Edward cut in. "Not really."

Nightfall shrugged. "It seemed that way to him, and that's really all that matters here. Brionfra spent most of his life trying to regain the authority he had lost through accident of birth. He surrounded himself with servants, gradually increasing their dependence on and debt to him until they became the slaves we know now."

Prince Edward shuddered, as if the words, by themselves, caused him pain.

"The king and other nobles saw the following Brionfra had gained, the work it saved him, and the authority he possessed. Impressed, they gathered slaves of their own. Most, as Brionfra's, began as servants. Others, particularly women, came as debts collected. More than one father sold his daughter for money he either could not gather or could not part with. Still more came as war spoils; those who could not be cowed used to fight one another as entertainment."

Prince Edward's eyes sparkled with the driving need that had become too familiar to Nightfall. He rose and paced, working off the energy injustice inspired.

Nightfall eased up on the detail, afraid to lose his point by firing up the prince too much. "Ursid hated what his twin had started. Believing slavery evil, he set out one day to free them all. So, while his family slept, he gathered the kept-ones. Those chained were unbound. Those imprisoned were freed. Ursid rallied them all together and spoke of creating a new city of free men and women. He released the most vicious of the fighting slaves last . . ." Nightfall paused dramatically. "The wild man's last act was to kill Ursid, elder prince of Hartrin."

Edward stopped in mid-pace, whirling to face his squire. "This is a true story?"

Nightfall nodded. "Details become obscured or embellished as tales get passed. But this event is recorded in history." Nightfall hoped Edward's books contained some tidbit that could be interpreted to substantiate his claim. "Like the animal they named him, the slave enjoyed the slaughter that had been his lot."

"What happened to the others?" Edward asked the obvious question.

"They scattered, of course. Out of fear the fighting slave might kill them, too. Or that they might get in trouble for escaping."

"Or to keep their freedom."

"Of course. But that seemed less likely. Within one moon cycle, three quarters of the slaves returned, begging forgiveness."

Edward continued to stare. "They came back? Why?"

Nightfall plucked at his sleeve, feeling disloyal for the lie. He tried to quell his discomfort with the knowledge that his story might bring some enlightenment to the prince, might save them both from wasted time, ridicule, and violence. "Guaranteed food and reasonable shelter. A place to call home and a daily routine that did not rely on becoming the toughest person on the streets." He met Edward's soft, blue eyes. "Loyalty. That, *I* understand."

A pink tinge further softened Edward's young features. He mulled the words in silence.

"Master." Nightfall delivered a blow he doubted Edward could fend. "Even if the law came down from Alyndar that all servants who did not go would officially become slaves, I would not leave you." *Not without having my soul ripped from my body and tortured through eternity.*

The prince's lips pinched, and he seemed torn between tears and rage. "That could never happen. My father would never make such a decree."

Nightfall said nothing. The unlikelihood of the proclamation did not dilute the sentiment much.

"You're paid for your work."

"I've already told you I'm not."

"You will be when we return to Alyndar."

"I will not accept it if you offer."

Prince Edward again took a seat on his pallet, all fire draining from him. "Why are doing this to me?"

Nightfall wished he could take pleasure from the prince's discomfort, but he could not help thinking of his master as a fellow victim. Now that Edward showed some signs of acting with his head instead of his heart, Nightfall found a new respect. "Because you're good and noble. Because the Father believes in you, and I can do no less."

"That's not what I meant." Prince Edward leaned an elbow on his knee, burying his chin in his cupped palm. "Why are you comparing your lot to slavery? Do I treat you so badly?"

"Badly?" Nightfall adopted a stricken look. "Master, no servant has ever been happier. All servants and slaves should have a master as kind as you." He smiled. "And some probably do. As you say, there is good in every man."

"Good in every man," Edward repeated aloud as he considered the deeper implications. "Yes." At length, he shook his head. "I need to think a while. I'm just not ready to believe that people owning others is anything but evil. I don't think I ever will be."

Nightfall seized on Edward's introspection. "You've attended court. How do nobles react when they lose large amounts of something: power, money, land?"

"Not well," Edward admitted. "They always argue. More than one war has started that way."

"And if those same things get phased away slowly, one compromise at a time?"

"It's happened. That's how the peninsula came together under one king. Took longer than a century. No bloodshed."

Nightfall played his card. "So, if a leader gradually empowered the slaves ... say, gave them a few rights or alternatives to slavery besides theft or fighting over crumbs in the streets. If slaves could choose their masters, that might encourage slavers to treat their charges better. Or make some minimal standards for slave care: fewer hours, shelter, and reasonable amounts of food ..." Nightfall rambled with little coherency, never having needed to find solutions. Always before, he had simply survived, yet the knowledge he had inadvertently gathered along the way gave him a solid foundation for change. Though he told himself he was merely finding a way to cool Edward's dangerous ardor, he could not help getting swept up in the excitement now that reasonable alternatives fell into consideration.

Edward sat quietly for several moments, staring at the ceiling, his only movement the drumming of his fingers against the pallet. "Sudian, thank you."

Nightfall cocked his head, trying to look suitably modest. "Thank me, Master?"

"For showing me how to translate book knowledge into strategy. For reminding me that words on a page mean little without reality, and that the tactics of war have application to conflict of every type."

The series of larger words at the end of Edward's explanation confused Nightfall, but he caught the gist well enough. Before he could think of a humble reply, the prince swept him into an embrace.

Shocked nearly to panic by the contact, Nightfall struggled against the need to bully free. The sincere warmth of Edward's embrace was unmistakable, as telling as the most tender of his mother's moments, those occasional times when she convinced him she would never batter him again despite past promises and pain. Nightfall suppressed the natural feelings of caring and trust that always rose in the wake of another's honest vulnerability and kinship, hating himself for what he saw as a weakness. He had opened himself once and might still pay with his soul. Every instinct told him to seize the moment, to find some use for the newfound depth of loyalty the prince felt toward him. Yet, the effort of keeping his own emotions in check occupied him fully. And it seemed so outside his nature, too like the frailty that had gotten him into trouble with Kelryn, that it maddened him.

Edward released Nightfall, but the same innocent fondness filled his expression and his eyes. He smiled. "There are customs and rules to the relationship between noble and squire that I won't violate. But, when we're alone, you may call me Ned."

Few things would have pleased Nightfall more than calling the prince "Ned" in the presence of King Rikard and his court. The oath-bond churned in warning, growing stronger in the moments it took him to formulate a reply that would rescue him from physical distress without hurting the prince's feelings. The king had made it a part of the magical vow to always address Edward in this fashion. "Master, I could not."

Edward's grin wilted.

As the oath-bond receded to its familiar baseline, Nightfall found his explanation. "I promised your father to help you get landed. Until that time, my job is not finished; and it would feel wrong to call you anything but Master."

The light returned to Prince Edward's eyes, and a half-smile again bowed his lips. He shook his head wordlessly, clearly impressed by his faithful and, apparently, unpretentious squire. He rose and headed for the door. "Come, Sudian. We have an enemy to assess and plans to formulate." One hand on the door latch, he turned. "You've come to this city before?"

"A few times, Master." *A few meaning about nine thousand.* Nightfall trailed Prince Edward, cursing himself for not finding an opening to mention the previous night of gambling before someone beat him to it. One way or another, it would come out over breakfast. "I can find areas more likely to have slavers." *Though I won't take you to any of them.* An unpressured tour of the city might do them both good, and Nightfall had no intention of allowing Edward to get within city blocks of the slavers' markets.

Prince and squire headed for the common room.

The day went well for Nightfall. He managed to keep Prince Edward from the seedier parts of Trillium and distract him with the glitter and bustle of the myriad markets. Edward delighted in educating Nightfall about Grifnalian goats, Tylantian hump-backed horses, Hartrinian courier doves, and southern plains' lizards. The knowledge that came from books caught the bulk of the descriptions, but missed the odors, temperament, and general feel that reality had brought to Nightfall long ago. Though odd-looking and relatively slow, the hump-backed horses had endurance and an ability to travel far without sustenance. An ancient tale with obscure origins described a hump-back returning to Tylantis with a rider that had long before succumbed to thirst. Nightfall had seen Hartrinian sea doves, rare long-winged birds with a penchant for locating ships and returning to established roosts. Unlike pigeons, these birds would fly out with a message before returning with a reply. King Idinbal regularly used them to identify approaching vessels; and, given the circumstances of Marak's arrest, King Rikard apparently had some of his own.

Every foreign fruit or vegetable caught Edward's eye. Nightfall used the prince's curiosity as an opening to explain his winnings. He admitted to only a fraction of his true profit, using most of what he mentioned to purchase samples of foods Edward had never before tasted. Apparently certain of his squire's honesty, a concept Nightfall found amusing to the point of absurdity, Edward accepted gambling as innocent enough. Nightfall felt sure it would prove beneath the prince's dignity to engage in such activity himself, but he would not begrudge Nightfall his simple pleasures so long as they did not interfere with his work or cost from Edward's pocket. He made it ominously clear that Nightfall would pay, and pay well, if his debts fell beyond his means or harmed his master's reputation. Nevertheless, Edward could not help but appreciate the time, food, and security having money regained them. He seemed disappointed when a sudden thunderstorm brought their sightseeing to a premature end at midday.

The morning's camaraderie stretched well into the afternoon. Edward chose to study the book he had lugged with them since the start of their journey, leaving Nightfall the opportunity to catch up on sleep without having to worry about the safety of his master. He awakened in time for a late dinner. Then Edward slept, aware that Nightfall would spend the earliest morning hours with wagers, contests, and speculations.

The rain pounded the roof and shuttered windows of the Thirsty Dolphin until nearly midnight, when Nightfall made his appearance in the common room. A few of the native Trillians had returned, accompanied by several newcomers, including two Nightfall knew too well. They sat on opposite sides of the tavern and never gave one another more than a casual glance. Fat Johastus had chosen a corner table where he sipped beer and soaked up the last bit of gravy from his dinner with a chunk of bread. His round, dimpled cheeks tinged red gave him a false aura of jolliness. The other man, Rivehn, could not have looked more different. His wan features seemed scrawny to the edge of illness, and his straw blond hair only added to the image of unhealthy pallor. Nightfall saw through their stranger act. As Balshaz, he had quietly watched them pull enough scams to know they were a team. As Nightfall, he had followed them to the alley behind the jeweler's shop where they divided their spoils.

Nightfall recognized no other schemers, pleased that his winnings the previous night had seemed innocent enough not to draw too much attention. He would need to perform well tonight before his luck became too suspect or his nightly outings interfered with his charge. He knew he could never win the two hundred sixty silver he needed in a single night, but he would make a few strides in that direction. Hopefully, another money-making strategy would come to him, one that did not place himself or Edward at significant risk.

In addition to the Trillians, Nightfall discovered a few travelers. Most of these he recognized, at least in a general way, from his time in their countries or as merchants in this or other markets. He intentionally geared his wagers toward the ones he knew carried money, choosing trivia or actions at which they felt confident of their expertise. Where he could, he "divined" information about others whom he knew when in other personae, details of which a stranger from Alyndar could not possibly have knowledge. He explained this talent with a trail of deductions based on mannerisms, characteristics, or movement that fascinated his victims. He tossed darts or target daggers against a few who fancied themselves competent, careful to keep his maneuvers simple and to lose occasionally enough not to scare away his marks. Side wagers sprang up, for and against him, keeping the money flowing from hand to hand and the excitement for the games high. Nightfall took careful note of the partners, noting that Johastus bet contrary to him rarely, but always made a production of it when he did. Consistently, Rivehn wagered with him, winning well along the way.

Nightfall found it difficult not to approve of the strategy. He would not condemn a man for recognizing and riding with a winner, but he knew them both too well to relax. They had something more in the works, he felt certain. Greed would not allow them to remain satisfied with gradual wealth. Eventually, they would try something massive and ugly, and Nightfall hoped he would not get caught off-guard by the attempt.

At length, Nightfall took his first break from the game, flopping into a seat around an empty table and waving the bartender to supply a round of beers to the participants. Johastus squeezed his bulk into a nearby chair that could scarcely contain him, scooting it up to the table. "Toss you for the tab."

The comment seemed nonsensical. Nightfall pulled himself up to a position more befitting conversation. "Excuse me, sir?"

Johastus opened a meaty hand, and a standard copper coin of the Xaxonese Peninsula rolled from his fist. Moist from his grip, it reflected the torchlight in patches. It rocked along its edges, then fell flat, revealing the side with the country name, Hartrin, and the origin of the engraving, baron's mint. "I pitch my coin. You pitch yours. The first one who gets Idinbal's face up buys the round." He levered a fingernail under one side of the coin, flipping it to the image of the Hartrinian king.

Nightfall studied the coin, scarcely daring to believe Johastus and Rivehn appeared to have chosen one of the oldest and most artless scams in existence. He had not only seen it performed many times, he had watched these two carry it out without a hitch. Still, though his mind told him the sequence of events to come, no method of foiling the scheme accompanied it. Scams that persisted did so because they worked, and Nightfall had never seen this one fail. He opened his mouth to decline, and a new idea awakened. Behind every successful swindle lay a victim whose greed exceeded his intelligence, and overconfidence only sweetened the pot. If he could find some way to turn the scam back on its operators, he doubted he could find a more ideal target. So far, he risked nothing. The two would see to it the first coin toss fell in his favor. "So I can either pay for this round, like I planned; or I can take a fair chance on you paying for me."

Johastus nodded. "Right."

From the corner of his eye, Nightfall noticed Rivehn casually threading through the patrons toward them.

Nightfall showed the appropriate amount of suspicion. "What do you get out of this?"

Johastus raised and lowered his massive shoulders. "I've lost a fortune betting against you already. I might as well play one directly. At least, if I lose this time, I feel like my money's going to a good cause." He made a grand gesture to indicate every man in the bar.

Though a meaningless gesture, Nightfall followed the movement with his gaze. Since he had already agreed to pay for the round, Johastus' money would, essentially, go into his own pocket. However, no good pigeon would ever point out such an advantage. "How could I refuse?" Nightfall fished in his pocket for a copper coin. By the time he pulled it free, Rivehn had arrived at the table.

The slender swindler chose the seat directly opposite Nightfall, thrusting the chair backward between his legs and draping his arms, with cool indifference, over its back. "Couldn't help overhearing. Can I get in?"

The barmaid set three mugs of beer on the table then hurried off to serve the others.

Nightfall glanced to Johastus, who shrugged. "Why not? Every stranger who joins the game makes my chances of paying less."

In response to the statement, Nightfall nodded, noting how Johastus had taken the need to fake unfamiliarity with his partner to a transparent extreme. *Stranger, indeed.*

Rivehn freed a coin of his own. "Why don't we play it odd side pays? We all toss and catch, call out what we got, and the one that don't match takes the tab."

Nightfall pretended to consider, as if he had never heard of such a game. Outside of a barroom, he had not. "All right." He worked his coin between his first two fingers and thumb.

Rivehn and Johastus also positioned. The skinny man counted. "One, two, three—toss!"

The three men flipped up their coins together, caught them, and glanced into their own hands.

"King's head," Johastus announced.

Nightfall also had Idinbal showing, but he knew their scam would work more quickly and efficiently if he gave the opposite response. "I have the reverse."

"Reverse," Rivehn echoed.

"Damn." Johastus thrust a fist into his pocket and headed toward the bar to pay the tab.

Rivehn seized the moment. "Listen, the big fellow," he inclined his head toward Johastus, "he's a merchant with more money than sense. I think we can relieve him of some of his ... um ... burden. You in?"

"In?" Nightfall repeated, feigning ignorance of the street slang.

"There's a fortune in it if we work together." Rivehn kept his attention riveted on his companion at the bar, as if fearing he might return too soon.

"A fortune?"

"A fortune," Rivehn repeated. He tore his gaze away with apparent effort. "You in?"

"In. I guess so. What do I have to do?"

"Whatever side of the coin comes up for me, you say the opposite. I'll do the same. I'll collect the money. When it's over, we meet at the main market gates and split the take."

Nightfall geared his responses to other suckers he had seen caught up in this scam. He took note of the fact that the location Rivehn chose to meet him was on the opposite side of the city from the money-sharing place he usually went to reunite with Johastus. That seemed to confirm his suspicion that they still used the same site, though he could always follow to make certain. "What money?"

Rivehn waved him silent. "Just follow my lead." He raised his voice to the normal conversational level as Johastus returned. ". . . always tastes sweeter when someone else buys it." He took a long gulp from the mug.

Nightfall cradled his own drink.

Johastus made a disgruntled noise, though in a good-natured fashion. He flung himself back into his seat and sipped at his beer.

Rivehn laughed. "So long as we got something going here, why not try to win your money back?"

Johastus lowered his mug, wiping foam from his lips with the back of his hand. "Depends. What are you suggesting?"

Rivehn glanced casually at Nightfall. "We toss coins. This time, odd side wins, and we'll play for the three tossed coins."

Nightfall shrugged, followed by a nod to indicate that, although he found it an unusual gamble, he would play.

"I've obviously got some talent for being the odd side." Johastus smiled. "Let's bet."

And they did. With Rivehn and Nightfall always claiming opposite tosses, Johastus could not help but match one of them every time. Occasionally, Rivehn allowed Johastus a win or a draw; but, as night faded into predawn, the money had landed in three unequal piles. The smallest lay before Johastus, the largest at Rivehn's hand.

Nightfall kept count of the coins, especially as the stakes turned from copper to silver. He estimated a one hundred thirty-five silver total when Johastus finally hurled his "last" coin to Rivehn. "Obviously, I should have said my prayers this morning. I'm out of some god's favor." He rose, snatched a fur wrap from a hook near the door, scooped up his meager pile, and headed out into the night without bothering with parting amenities.

Rivehn kept his expression blank, giving Nightfall a conspiratorial wink. He gathered his own winnings into a bag, then unobtrusively started on Nightfall's stack.

"Hey," Nightfall whispered, reaching to protect his money.

Rivehn shook his head stiffly, the gesture scarcely noticeable. "I need it all to split even. Remember where we meet. We'll both take a long, slow route so no one follows." With a single gesture, he swept the last of the coins into the bag. "You can leave first and wait for me. It'll seem suspicious if we go at the same time."

The swindler counted on Nightfall's greed and fear of the law proving stronger than his doubts about Rivehn's honesty. To create a scene here would surely reveal the scam to all present and earn hostility from every man who had lost a copper to Nightfall since his arrival in Trillium. Nightfall could not quell all of his concerns, however. The scheme had all the classic features needed for success: simplicity, duplicity, and a sharing of blame such that he could not report the crime to authorities without admitting his own guilt. Soon, Rivehn and Johastus would gather to split their take from him, little knowing their pigeon had plans to rob them of their cash and his own. He would have to trail Rivehn to make certain the swindlers' dividing site had not changed. Now that Rivehn had nearly all of his money, he could not afford to make a mistake.

Nightfall headed out the door, trying to appear a bit too casual, for Rivehn's benefit. Once outside, he sauntered into a nearby throughway then around to the back, where the exit from the inn rooms opened onto a cobbled road. Once there and alone, he scuttled toward an alley that would give him a reasonable view of both doors. He had taken only a few steps when the front panel swung open. Mally, the slave girl, scampered out. She froze for a moment in the doorway, moonlight plastering her shadow against the Thirsty Dolphin and fusing it with so many others.

Nightfall watched her, curious.

Mally glanced about furtively, pulling her thin, tattered dress close against the wind. "Sudian?" she called.

Nightfall cursed silently.

"Sudian, please. I need to talk. Please. I know you're not far." She spun with the strange combination of grace and awkwardness that reminded him of Kelryn after too many shows and practices. Irritated by his new train of thought, he put it from his mind. Mally headed into the same throughway he had taken. "Sudian!" she shouted. "Sudian!"

Nightfall weighed the benefits of his hiding place against the risk of her alerting guards, Rivehn, Johastus, and Prince Edward. He reversed direction, headed past the back exit, and caught her arm just in front of the rear doorway.

Mally spun with a gasp. Up close, he could see that one eye had swollen shut and bruises marked her cheek and jaw in a line. Dried blood caked her nostrils. As she recognized him, relief softened her battered features. She hurled herself into his arms. "Oh, Sudian. Sudian, please. You have to get your master to buy me. You have to. Please."

Nightfall felt dampness through his tunic and hoped it came from tears, not blood. "Look, Mally. I'll talk to you later. As long as you want. I have to do something important now."

Mally's grip tightened. Apparently, she had watched

him from the back of the tavern for some time, waiting for her chance to catch him alone. Now that she had him, she would not let go so easily. "Please, Sudian. You're my only hope. You have to help."

"Later, Mally." Nightfall broke free of her grasp.

"No!" She seized his legs, twining herself around him. "Don't leave me. Please, don't leave me." She sobbed, irrational with pain and fear. One of her hands glided up to stroke his thigh.

Revolted as well as driven by urgency, Nightfall could not have responded to her caresses if he had wanted to do so. "Mally, let go. I'll do what you asked. But if you don't let go, my master won't even have enough money to buy breakfast."

The back exit slammed open, and Amadan stood framed in the archway. Face buried against Nightfall's leg, Mally took no notice. Nightfall went still, realizing he had no words to explain the situation in which he found himself, even should Amadan give him the opportunity. The merchant shuffled toward them, eyes narrowed, mouth locked in a grim line.

Nightfall had found himself in difficult situations before, but this was not a familiar one. As the demon, he would have ditched the slave in any way possible, even if it meant dumping her corpse to the cobbles. He would have run, a shadow quicker and more streetwise than any highborn man. Now, he froze, knowing whatever he did or said would reflect on the prince he had enslaved his soul to protect. No matter where or how fast he escaped, Amadan would know precisely where to find him. He doubted politeness would gain him much, but surely far more than insolent silence. And he needed Mally to realize the danger as well if he ever hoped to regain his freedom of movement. "Good eve, lord." He gave the most respectful bow possible with a woman latched onto his legs.

Mally looked up, and her face went bloodless. Even the bruises seemed to lose all color. Sobbing, she crawled back toward her master across cobbles that had to hammer and tear her knees. She groveled at Amadan's feet, and he ignored her, his attention fully on Nightfall.

"What were you doing with my slave?"

Nightfall considered the answer long and hard, finding no response that would not sound snide. Edward's endless lessons on etiquette had taught him that silence would not meet the merchant's approval either, so Nightfall chose humility rather than a direct answer. He lowered his head. "My deepest apologies, lord. I meant no harm." He rolled his eyes in time to see Amadan's hand speeding toward him.

The idea of allowing the merchant to hit him again rankled, but Nightfall knew etiquette demanded it. He could weather a slap if it ended the conflict quickly. As an added bonus, it might win Edward's approval for himself and trouble for Amadan.

Nightfall tilted his head to spare his face. The warning glint of metal in Amadan's hand came too late. The merchant's fingers slammed against the side of Nightfall's head, weighted by solid steel. The hilt of a dagger, Nightfall guessed, before light exploded in his head. He never felt the fall, only found himself sprawled and dizzy on the cobbles, Mally's scream ringing through his ears. He caught a spinning glimpse of Rivehn leaving the tavern, and need forced him to bull through the vertigo. He managed to stagger to his feet.

Amadan's kick cut Mally's scream short, and the woman tumbled, whimpering, to the ground. The cruelty charged Nightfall to hatred. He would never take another blow from Amadan, and neither would any other. Though weak on his feet, he charged.

Suddenly menaced, Amadan flung the dagger at Nightfall.

The response came as little more than instinct. From the ease of long practice, Nightfall snatched the hilt from the air and rebounded it with deadly accuracy. The blade found its mark in the merchant's throat, and combined momentum buried it deep. He collapsed, gurgling, unable to scream. His eyes remained widened, even in death.

The back door opened.

Nightfall faded into the shadows, prepared to kill or escape as it became necessary.

Amadan's other two slaves came partway through and

stopped, gaping. Rooted in place, they kept the door wedged with their bodies.

Nightfall knew Mally's scream might soon bring more, and none of them could afford witnesses. "Move! Quickly. No one needs to know more than that he and you left before sunup." Nightfall directed, a bodiless voice from the darkness. He doubted slaves gathering their master's possessions, no matter how hurriedly, would attract suspicion. Any who knew their master would see nothing amiss in the nervousness of these slaves at any time. Without another word, he scrambled after Rivehn, doubting he could find the swindler in the twisting maze of Trillium's streets. He would have to hope Rivehn and Johastus had not changed their haunts. And that Amadan's property would cling to their new freedom.

Chapter 12

Wolves and bats and beasts of night,
Spirits black that flee the light,
Cringed in fear when he arose—
Darkness comes where Nightfall goes.
                              —The Legend of Nightfall
                                Nursery rhyme, st. 12

Once located, laughing in their den, Rivehn and Johastus lost their easy fortune to Nightfall's silent talent. Nightfall crept away unseen, richer by not only his own money but theirs as well; and his theft did not disrupt their mirth nor their mocking comments about his naiveté. Nightfall did not dally, gloat, or allow greed to drive him to foolishness. He simply took the two purses, equally full of the money they had won from him and one another in play, and headed surreptitiously back toward the Thirsty Dolphin.

Sunrise lit the sky a dull orange and pewter, and a steady glow suffused Trillium's many roadways. The oath-bond buzzed a steady, dizzying cadence, a warning either that Nightfall had slipped too close to forbidden persona or that he had left Edward alone too long. In defense, Nightfall funneled his mind and goal fully on returning to the inn, an action that should appease the magic whatever its particular source. Shadows and alleys kept him well-hidden from the few folk about at first light. He found them simple to avoid. Most concentrated on tasks they needed to complete before the city came fully to life: loading carts for market, organizing shops for business, or hauling buckets of water for morning rituals or cooking.

By the time Nightfall arrived back at the stone and mortar building that served as Trillium's rowdiest inn and tavern, he discovered a common room filled with travelers eating breakfast, including Prince Edward Nargol of

Alyndar who chatted with a small group of Trillians as he ate. The oath-bond abated enough to allow Nightfall other thought. Concern came first, that Edward would become too intrusive about his activities or punish him for not attending every need prior to his awakening. Nightfall knew he deserved the tongue-lashing, but he worried that another long, droning lesson might lull him to sleep, that lapse earning him two others. By its weight and his direct knowledge of the scam, he estimated that he now carried approximately two hundred silver. It seemed an unbelievable fortune, one he could not have attained on his own, at least not without falling fully into the demon guise. Still, he doubted Finndmer would accept the lesser amount as payment for the land as much as he felt certain Edward would not allow him another night of gambling. Somehow, he would need to make up the difference.

Nightfall headed directly for Prince Edward's table, trying to look suitably agitated and repentant. He made a show of directing his attention fully on his master, though he studied the others from the corner of his eye. He knew the best dressed of the men at a glance, a horse trader by the name of Gerbrant. Though aggressive when it came to sales, the merchant had always seemed reasonably honest. He enjoyed taking chances as much as any man, though Nightfall had never known him to rig the odds or cheat a customer he liked. He did, however, tend to overlook the flaws in his own animals. The other two worked for him, and both had placed a few small bets the previous night in the tavern.

Nightfall bowed, head low, looking appropriately humble. "Master, I'm sorry. I went out to . . . well, to . . . relieve myself. And I got to looking around and took a walk and lost track of time . . ."

Edward waved his squire silent, then gestured at the only empty chair at the table. "No harm done, Sudian. Sit."

Nightfall obeyed, still keeping his head down and attentive only to his master. A plate of fried eggs and bread lay in front of the prince, steam carrying its fragrance to Nightfall's nose. Though hungry, he did not know whether his stomach could stand food after a night of excitement and beer, though he had practiced caution and moderation. The implications of the evening maddened him. If anyone with authority connected him with Amadan's death, they would undoubtedly hang him. Should Rivehn and Johastus have underground connections, Nightfall would again find himself endangered by the myriad connections that had once served as the closest things to friends. Even should he survive the oath-bond, his new freedom might buy him a life worse than the one he had had: a lowborn hunted by authorities and criminals alike. But this time, he could not hide behind disguises and aliases, his true appearance no longer a haven.

Edward signaled one of the barmaids to bring Nightfall breakfast. "This is my squire, Sudian."

Gerbrant acknowledged Nightfall with a preoccupied nod. His companions smiled, and one spoke before his employer. "I know Sudian well. And so does my copper." They both laughed.

Nightfall glanced up, keeping his grin sheepish and avoiding Edward's eyes. He hardly thought sharing a round of beer translated to "knowing well," but it fit the gibe.

"Are you going to drop some money on the race?" the other asked. "You were quick enough for everything else."

Nightfall crinkled his brow, confused by the question. "Race?"

The prince looked from workers to squire, still obviously uncertain about their connection. He explained. "Gerbrant has a fast horse. A longtime competitor challenged him to a race, and it's happening this afternoon."

The first worker spoke again. "Other fellow's so underconfident, he beat up our jockey." He laughed inappropriately, adding quickly, "Didn't work, though. Samma's small, but he punches all right for a little one."

"Got away with a few scrapes and bruises," the other finished. "We've kept him locked up safe since then. Got guards on Dash—that's the horse—too."

Nightfall could almost hear Dyfrin's voice screaming in his head. *Listen to all and listen well. Given chance and a little ingenuity, most men will hand you their money. Make it seem their own idea, and return what you*

*don't need. Greed pays in moments; kindness and fairness
for a lifetime.* Living always from instant to instant and
situation to situation, Nightfall had found small use for
Dyfrin's long-term advice. Now, as always, he tried to
find a means to use the men's volunteered information to
gain the last of the needed money. He doubted pitting
horse against horse would earn enough attention from
Trillium's populace to make a bet worth his while. However, when a horse dealer got behind an animal, he tended
to do so with serious, almost blind, prejudice. The more
interesting stakes would lie in the bet between horse owners.

Nightfall attempted to hide his interest in joining the
contest behind loyalty. "My master lets me ride a horse
that's faster than any. I've run down lots of other horses
with it." He finally looked directly at Edward again, trying to keep his demeanor proud. The bay he rode had
much to recommend it for speed, stamina, and health, a
true prince's beast, better than Edward's own in Nightfall's mind. Though surely not the quickest in the world,
and probably not even of the three, it should hold its own
well enough. And Nightfall had already computed a way
to more than even the odds.

Gerbrant laughed, finding Nightfall's bragging ludicrous. "We're not talking about horses with a bit of the
quickness to them. Homrihn's been talking up this running horse of his forever. Says it can cover the distance
between Brigg and Trillium in the time it takes to think
out the sights from here to there." A smug expression
crossed his features. "You're welcome enough to add
your animal to the field if you got fifty silver to back up
your claim about its speed."

Prince Edward visibly stiffened, though he gave no
verbal warning. Gerbrant's workers snickered.

"What's the fifty silver for?" Nightfall feigned ignorance, though his speculation had, thus far, proven correct.

"That's the stake." Gerbrant finally settled his gaze on
Nightfall, though he stole a glance at Edward, presumably
to read the prince's reaction to his squire's bold challenge, made freely without pause for permission. When

the prince gave no indication that Nightfall's words or actions had angered him, Gerbrant continued. "Homrihn and I each put up fifty against the other. You add fifty and get yourself a rider, you can compete."

Cued by Gerbrant's behavior, Nightfall assumed the manner and tone of an excited child. "May I, Master? Please."

Prince Edward shifted uncomfortably in his seat, obviously torn between common sense and his squire's fanatical faith in a horse. He lowered his voice so even Nightfall could scarcely hear. "Do you have the money?"

"And enough to cover meals and lodgings for a long time," Nightfall whispered in reply.

The prince pursed his lips, obviously impressed. "These men told me you had done well in the betting. I hadn't realized how well."

Only Nightfall recognized the understatement.

Edward shrugged, making his disapproval clear with gesture and tone, though his words did not match. "You may use the horse." Though he said nothing more, Nightfall read intention easily. The prince had grown concerned that success would give his squire an inflated and false confidence when it came to gambling. More than one good man had become a slave to the chance for fast money, even long after he lost all of his own and what he could steal, beg, or borrow. Nightfall felt certain that, once in private with his charge, he would receive a long lesson on the evils of gambling. He had played his last card. The horse race, like the swindler's scam, had fallen into his lap; but careful planning, not serendipity would turn it from rout to profit. He had no choice except to win this race, one way or another. Edward would not knowingly allow him to wager again, and any attempt to bypass the prince would risk the trust he had gained as well as the consequences of the oath-bond.

The last thought stirred a buzz of quiescent magic, and Nightfall could not suppress a shiver. He was skirting its edges too often for comfort. "Thank you, Master. Thank you so much." Rattled, he nearly lost his act, and he forced his concentration back to the role of a squire eager to prove the worth of his master's property.

Gerbrant watched the exchange in silence, apparently catching enough to assume Edward's consent for, if not approval of, his squire's participation in the race. He addressed his comments to the superior. "Lord, the horses will run on Adeseele's oat field, just south of town. Weigh-in for riders is midday." He smiled. "You're welcome to make side bets with me or anyone else, Prince Edward."

"Thank you," Edward said.

Gerbrant shifted methodically, obviously waiting for more from the prince, presumably a wager made in the heat of the challenging moment. When none came, he pushed back his chair, stretched, and nodded a parting amenity. "Good day, lord and squire. You'll understand if I don't wish you luck."

"Good day," Edward returned.

Gerbrant headed from the common room, flanked by his helpers. As they retreated, the serving maid arrived with Nightfall's breakfast. She set it before him and whisked back to her station.

Prince Edward kept his voice below the regular ebb and flow of conversation. His features crinkled with honest concern, and his pale eyes echoed the sentiment. "Sudian, I appreciate you finding a way to get money when we needed it. I confess I encouraged you when I probably shouldn't have. Luck is a fickle mistress. It will become unfaithful too soon. When it does, I don't want it to leave you so accustomed to winning that your mind sees nothing else."

Though painfully hungry, Nightfall gave Edward his full attention to indicate he viewed the situation as gravely as his master. "Master, thank you. Once the race is won, I'll have enough silver to buy you what I've gambled for; and I won't need any more wagers or games of chance."

Edward's expression lapsed into one of surprise, and a strand of yellow hair fell across his forehead. The careless beauty of Prince Edward of Alyndar struck Nightfall; he seemed exactly the man women conjured in their fantasies. Though Nightfall held no interest in the looks of other men, he knew a sense of pride he could not quite explain for serving the epitome of female dreams. For the first time, he noticed the absence of the usual bitterness he had known in the presence of nobles born to wealth who flaunted their privileges like badges of honor and courage. He had scratched the surface of the prince's ignorant naiveté and found a potential wellspring of goodness beneath that matched the handsomeness of his external features. Unfortunately, it appeared that it might take a thousand men with a thousand spades to dig through the shell of guileless innocence he had built around himself since infancy. Should he become a ruler, he would prove kind to his people at the expense of his own safety and welfare. Soon enough, someone stronger and meaner would wrest authority from him unless he could find some person or group to advise and defend him.

Understanding came to Nightfall in a sudden rush. For now, he held that position, and the oath-bond bound him to perform it well. *Could that have been King Rikard's intention from the start? Could a king known as "the hammer-handed" foresee that even a cold-blooded killer's false loyalty would become real in time? Did he send us out together in the hope that adversity would draw us closer, believing his headstrong and simple-hearted son would gain an ally nasty enough to keep even him out of trouble?* The genius of such a strategy impressed Nightfall, but his heart would not allow him to believe that a father would waste time plotting such intricate strategies for the welfare of a son. No parent could give so much. Surely, his original thought, that Rikard had sent out his embarrassment to die, would prove the truth.

"You've worked this hard to buy something for me?" Edward's voice shattered Nightfall's train of thought, and it took unreasonably long to return to a conversation his mind had far outstripped. "I have everything I need. Why would you risk all and exhaust yourself for me?"

Nightfall lowered his head, seeking to reorient himself and find the proper words to answer at once. "I believe in you, Master, and all your good works. I'm buying something that can help you carry out all your Father-blessed plans." He looked up slightly, as if ashamed of the paltriness of his gift. "It's only a small start, but it will grow."

"What is it, Sudian?"

Nightfall dropped his gaze again and shook his head vigorously. "Master, I'd rather not say yet. I would feel like I failed you if I didn't get the money I needed. If I do get it, I'd like to surprise you. May I do that, Master?"

"Surprise me?" Edward considered the possibility, obviously unaccustomed to the idea. "Very well, surprise me then. But I don't need gifts from you. In fact, I still owe you the wages my father didn't pay."

"Master, you've handled my food, supplies, lodgings, and other needs. The pleasure of serving you is more than payment enough." The sweetness of their exchange made Nightfall want to vomit, though the secret knowledge of his own deceit placed it all into perspective . . . at least for him. Sensing that even Prince Edward might have finally gotten an overdose of sappiness, he turned his attention to his breakfast, but not before he noticed tears of joy in his master's eyes. And felt guilty for them.

A film of clouds muted the sun, bringing the smell of damp though no raindrops fell. The first green sprouts of the oats poked through a dark mulch speckled with ground stems from the previous year's crop. The track consisted of a straight plow path along one edge of the growing plants, hemmed on one side by village shops and cottages and on the other by an ankle-high mound separating road from crop, newly constructed for the race. Six villagers sat in judgment at an end line cut into the ground, and a small, mixed crowd of locals and visitors leaned against buildings or sat in the alleyways to watch. Nightfall saw only a handful of the odds makers and bet takers. An impromptu horse competition drew only a modicum of interest, and they could make better money in the gambling houses at night.

Although malnutrition had kept Nightfall relatively slight, the other two riders stood significantly shorter and thinner than himself. They weighed in, allowing servants to prepare their horses. Nightfall handled his own mount. He gauged the competition, equine and human.

Gerbrant's Dash was a well-muscled gray gelding with an enormous rump. Homrihn's Mr. Quick, a chestnut stallion, had long, lean legs and a massive chest. The latter pranced and blew until foam coated its neck and flanks. Nightfall guessed the nervous energy it expended now would cost it dearly in the race. The riders seemed more intent on the weigh-in than their mounts, with the nonchalance of men who have spent a lifetime around horses.

Nightfall judged his options carefully as his turn to weigh arrived. He looped the bay mare's lead rope around a sapling, trusting the surrounding grass to occupy her attention. His plan required that he weigh in as heavy as possible, but common sense deemed that he do so without drawing attention to his talent. By the time he reached the flat balancing platform and sat in the middle as the others had done, he concentrated on adding another quarter to his mass. The men placed measuring weights on the stack in the opposite pan until both sides hovered the breadth of a fist from the ground, equally balanced. Nightfall glanced over, calculating the total. His weight-shifting ability was a gross process that did not allow for specific or minor modifications. The boulders on the opposite side indicated that he weighed half again as much as the lightest of the riders, reasonable for a man Nightfall's height. He hoped that his tailored linens hid his lack of bulk well enough.

Both relatively well-fleshed men, Homrihn and Gerbrant accepted Nightfall's weight without comment. The riders groused about the extra loads their mounts would have to carry to even the race, but not for long. Their balanced distribution in the saddlebags would prove easier for the horses to carry than Nightfall's excess bulk, under ordinary circumstances. With a few last grumbles, they performed their individual rituals of prayer, limbering exercises, and whatever sequences of movement and phrase had brought them luck in the past. Dropping his weight back to normal, Nightfall saddled and bridled his nameless mount and sprang into position first. While the others shifted weights and legs into the most comfortable or presumed "winning" positions, Nightfall used ropes to bind himself to the saddle, seeing danger as well as necessity in the action. If the horse fell, he could not leap clear of danger; but he would need the security once the race began. He kept a stick in hand to coax the mare to greater speed.

Farmhands led each of the horses to the track while another strung a rope across it. Accustomed to running, the stallion and gelding danced to the rope line, then backpedaled repeatedly. The musky odor of horse sweat became a reassuring constant. Familiar with Snow's nervousness, Nightfall's mare took little notice of the antsiness of her rivals. She remained alert, head raised, one ear forward and the other cocked back for Nightfall's commands.

Gerbrant stepped into the middle of the track and raised his hands. The conversations stilled to silence. "Friends, we have gathered to watch a competition between the fastest of the fast." A brief flurry of betting ensued, men placing their final wagers now that they could compare all three of the horses close together. "The rules are simple. The first nose to cross the line at the far end . . ." He gestured the six judges at the finish. ". . . belongs to the winning horse. Any rider who touches or strikes another rider or horse, guarantees third place for his mount, regardless of when he crosses the line. The race begins when the rope is dropped. First, I'd like to introduce you to horses and riders . . ."

Gerbrant droned on, and Nightfall turned his attention to Prince Edward. The young blond perched on an overturned crate in the alleyway, watching with interest though he took no hand in the proceedings. When Nightfall's gaze found him, he smiled.

Nightfall bowed his head respectfully. The more time Gerbrant wasted with his preamble, the larger Nightfall's advantage become. The other two horses were gradually wearing themselves down with excitement. He turned his attention back to his mare. Experience had taught him that much ground could be gained and maintained by a fast and far-reaching start, especially on a short course. The mare had shown that ability when she chased down Edward's gelding and the farmer's cart horse when each had run riderless and with a headstart. The first moment could well determine the victor. He sat in a comfortable position, worrying more for stability than air resistance. Weight distribution and balance meant far less to him than to the others. He noticed that they sat well-forward in their saddles, keeping the majority of their mass centered on the horses' withers and their chests and heads low. Nightfall caught a solid grip on the reins and on his stick.

At a gesture, the rope fell. Before it hit the ground, Nightfall kicked the bay. As the mare's forehooves left the ground, he dropped his weight instantly to as near nothing as his capability allowed. Suddenly without need to counter a rider's weight, the mare turned her usual massive initial leap to a long glide that approached flight. Nightfall had little chance to enjoy the sensation as wind flung his near-weightless body backward, threatening to rip him from his seat. Only the thongs he had had the foresight to tie kept him in position, and those chewed into his thighs, calves, and ankles. The reins left bloodless lines against his palms.

All three horses strained forward, necks outstretched, legs pounding, driven as much by the crowd's shouts and cheering as by the sticks slapping repeatedly against their muscled flanks. Though faster, the other horses had little chance of catching the mare whose flying bound had vaulted her a quarter of the way down the track in an instant and who could gallop unfettered by a passenger's bulk yet still charged by the faint sting of a striking stick. The bay crossed the line first and cleanly, without need for the judges to deliberate. Nightfall restored his weight gradually on the backstretch as he pulled the horse to a snorting stop and the others whipped past him. A grin lit his face, and he laughed, happy for the first time in as long as he could remember. He had his money. Soon enough, he believed, would come freedom.

Nightfall spent most of the southward journey from Trillium convincing Prince Edward of the propriety and necessity of buying land. Obtaining the deed, in and of itself, had not appeased the oath-bond. Apparently, it required some acceptance from Edward or plans to build the appropriate structures to meet the criteria for becoming landed. Nightfall did not understand the petty details involved in fulfilling his part of the magics, but he felt certain he had finally come close to his goal. *Freedom.* The excitement that accompanied the thought had become a constant companion over the two weeks of travel around Meclar, Schiz, and Noshtillan. Anticipation formed a baseline thrill as strong as the receding buzz of Gilleran's sorcery, tempered only by doubts Nightfall could not quite shake: What if King Rikard or Gilleran had lied about the workings of the oath-bond? What if he had become permanently trapped into Edward's service? What if, once he realized his part of the bargain, the magic killed him regardless of outcome? What if it worked as promised, but he had misunderstood his role? Those questions haunted Nightfall well into every night, and pleasant dreams and ugly nightmares alternately followed him into sleep.

By Nightfall's calculations, he and Edward would arrive at their destination that day. Fused into a single, shapeless mass, clouds blanketed the sky, blotting the sun and leaving the general atmosphere a damp, dreary gray. Nightfall considered taking a different route, one that would add a day or longer to their journey to allow the full effect of the new acquisition to strike them both, grass pastures and rolling hills lit to emerald beauty by the golden rays of sun. Yet eagerness and desperate need would not allow the delay. Soon enough, they would come upon Edward's new property; and it would have to look impressive enough through the weather nature provided.

Just past midday, Prince Edward and Nightfall crested a hill, and flatlands loomed ahead. The horizon filled with ocean, and a salt smell mingled intermittently with the closer fragrances of wetness and greenery. Nightfall could not recall the last time he had felt so twitchy. He found himself seeking the light flutter of the oath-bond, uncertain whether to feel distress or comfort in its mild presence. Excitement drove him to an uncharacteristic, nervous prattle meant to fully convince Edward of the value of his squire's gift. "It's less important how a man gets his land and far more important what he does with what he has. There . . ." He pointed vaguely ahead, having taken to referring to the land in this fashion. ". . . no slavery will ever exist and servants will know their master's actions will fall always under the watchful eye of Prince Edward." A muddy, vaguely sulfurous odor joined the other scents of the flatlands.

As they approached the edge of the described land purchase, Nightfall went quiet along with his master. Trees grew in random patterns, as the wind had blown their seeds decades previously. A welcoming carpet of bluish grass paved their way, spreading over the stretch of ground as far as Nightfall could see. To him it seemed the most beautiful place in the world.

Nightfall whooped, driving his horse suddenly into a canter. It balked, then, apparently trusting its rider, sprang forward at his urgings.

"Sudian, stop! Wait!" Edward shouted, too late.

The bay mare glided for a few strides, driven more by collective momentum than individual strides. Then, its hooves struck more solidly, and the ground seemed to fold beneath it. Its legs sank into a watery muck; and it floundered, twisting and flailing in a panicked frenzy. Though equally surprised, Nightfall recovered his senses instantly, trying to calm the wild lurches of his mount. The mud sucked them both deeper burying the horse to its chest and Nightfall's legs to the thighs. He swore, using the reins to regain control. The horse stilled, clearly stuck, yet not miring any further.

Now, Nightfall recognized the trees as high-rooted, broad-leafed *crenyons;* and it amazed him that he had not noticed these before. The blue-green covering he had mistaken for grass now seemed obviously slime-slicked mud and water. He stared, stricken to silence as much from shock as the realization that swampland could never serve his master's purposes. By Finndmer's definition, Edward would need to build a keep and outbuildings to become truly landed, and this moor could never hold a building. A paralyzing swirl of emotion struck Nightfall at once; general rage mingled with disappointment and self-directed anger. His ignorance about land had allowed him to become as much a victim of this scam as the horse owners had been of his. More so, because they had no way to guess his weight-shifting talent. As if to add insult, the oath-bond plunged back into full force, driving a pain through him that only added to the irritation and confusion.

Prince Edward dismounted, staring at his squire as if he had performed the stupidest act in existence. Under the circumstances, Nightfall had to agree with his master's unspoken assessment. "Are you hurt?" the prince asked.

"No." Nightfall tried to extricate a foot from the mud and met more resistance than he expected. He guessed that he might work his way free by leaving his boot in place, but he would have to fight his way back through muck that might close over his head. "Just stuck, Master."

"Why, in the Father's good name, did you ride into a swamp?" Prince Edward asked the obvious, though irritating, question.

The horse remained still, its struggles futile. Both ears lay flat backward in fear or agitation. Nightfall turned his attention from trying to concoct a plan of escape to answer Edward's query. "I didn't realize it was swamp."

"Wasn't it obvious?"

"Not to me, Master." Nightfall glanced around, incredulous at his own stupidity. Though aware that excitement could blind a man to danger, he found himself unable to believe that his mind had drawn such an elaborate illusion. "At least not before."

"It's obvious now."

Nightfall quelled rising sarcasm. This did not seem like a good time for inane conversation. "Yes, Master. It's obvious now."

Prince Edward sat back on his haunches. Nightfall and the horse lay well beyond his reach. "What can I do to help?"

Nightfall shook his head, uncertain, assessing the situation cautiously. If Edward got a rope from the pack horse's burden, they could probably work it around the bay's neck. In the subsequent bout of thrashing and squirming, they might manage to pull it free, if it did not throttle itself first or break a leg in its frenzy. One thing seemed certain. Nightfall had no intention of remaining on the animal's back while it lashed about in wild panic. And, for now, it served as a base and an island. Nightfall reached down and scooped up a handful of rich, brown mud, ripe with the odors of detritus and sulfur. The idea of swimming through that muck disgusted him, yet the best plan of action seemed obvious. If he wrapped the rope around himself first, Edward could pull him free and they might rescue the horse together. Still, he knew nothing about swamp sludge and its properties, and it only made sense to ascertain that it would not drown or poison him before attempting to fight his way through it. "Master, do you know about this stuff?" He flung the mud he had scooped back to where it had come from. "Will it suck us under like a whirlpool? Does it harm flesh?" He added quickly, responding to the oath-bond, "Just don't come any closer, please, Master. I don't want you hurt."

The mare gave a mighty heave that raised horse and rider over the swamp for a moment, then she fell back with a watery splash that sprayed mud over Nightfall from head to waist. She fought madly for several moments, legs churning mud in futility. When she settled, and Nightfall managed to turn his attention back to shore, he found Edward reading the book he had packed. Nightfall stared in surprise, scarcely daring to believe Edward had chosen this moment to entertain himself. "Master?"

Edward looked up. "What color is the mud?"

What color is the mud! Incredulity made Nightfall bitter, and he quelled the instinct to become flippant. "Mud-colored, I guess, Master. A brown-green color. With a bit of blue in swirls."

"Blue." Edward returned to his book, flipped a few pages, and read. "Charseusan."

"What?"

"Charseusan blue-green swamp mud. That's the name of what you're stuck in."

Oh, well, thanks. It makes things a lot easier now that I'm on a name basis with filth. The irony penetrated despite his predicament. Associations with slime were nothing new to Nightfall.

"It's called for the charseus plant, a blue-green grass/ algae that can live over or under water. The mud's mostly made up of dying plants and other dead things. The blue-green comes from the live charseus plant." He turned another page. "Oh, interesting. The live plant makes lots of air. That's why there're so many bubbles just under the surface of the mud."

I don't believe this. I don't, may the Father damn my soul, believe he's giving a nature lesson while I'm stuck ass deep in swamp mud. Nightfall corrected himself. *That's Charseusan blue-green swamp mud.* "Master, this is all very interesting. But my horse and I can't get out."

Edward did not bother to look up from his book. "Don't worry. It's just regular mud. It's not going to pull you deeper so long as you don't struggle at random. You do know how to swim, I presume?"

Oh, yes. My governess, steward, and handmaiden taught me while they bathed me. Nightfall had learned the basics of keeping afloat from the paranoia that someone might someday try to drown him. He had perfected his stroke as Marak, frolicking with his sailor buddies when the ship lay in irons. "Well enough, Master. But I worry for my horse. She's afraid, so she's fighting crazed and aimless. She's a lot heavier than I am, too."

"Only by your choice." The vaguely familiar voice came from the solid ground to Prince Edward's right. A figure emerged from the sparse *crenyon* forest. Curly hair and a well-groomed beard offset soft features betrayed only by the dark, predatory eyes Nightfall knew well enough. Once before, he had studied the face, when this man had steadied him in the town of Nemix and, apparently, learned about his natal talent. The sorcerer wore linens appropriate for travel, though tailored to a rich man's fancy; and Nightfall cursed the thieving instincts that forced him to notice the two silver rings on his fingers. Looking away from the man's gaze now would demonstrate fear and feed the murderer's confidence. At this distance, the hands could not harm him, unless they hurled some magic he had no means of fathoming. "You could weigh more than she if you wished."

Prince Edward returned to his mount and replaced the

book in his pack, ignorant of the danger posed by the newcomer.

Nightfall played innocent. "Weigh more than a horse?" He laughed, trying not to let it sound too strained, while his eyes measured the distance to shore. "I'd have to devour a hundred feasts and quickly."

The sorcerer was unamused. Although a slight smile curved onto his features, all gentleness disappeared from his manner.

Edward leaned against his gelding. "Since my squire is indisposed, I will make the introductions. I am Prince Edward Nargol of Alyndar, and this . . ." He gestured politely at Nightfall. ". . . is Sudian." He turned his full attention to the newcomer, brows raised for the appropriate response.

Though appalled by his master's obliviousness, Nightfall appreciated it. The prince's frivolous conversation might keep the sorcerer distracted long enough for Nightfall to formulate an escape. Cautiously, he eased his leg over the saddle, the movement slow and deliberate, designed not to draw attention. He tried to slip gently from the animal's back but managed only to bury his own body, chest-deep, in mud sticky as glue and heavy as scale weights. One hand plunged deep into the muck for balance. He managed to save the other by clinging to the cantle. The horse floundered into another bucking attempt at freedom, and a hoof slammed Nightfall's knee hard enough to incapacitate him. Without the cushion of mud, it would have shattered the bone for certain. He gritted his teeth and waited for the pain to diminish.

The sorcerer's gaze followed Nightfall's course. His stance displayed assurance, and his features twisted in obvious amusement. For now, he played along with Edward. "You may call me Ritworth the Iceman. I've come for your squire."

"My squire?" Edward glanced briefly at Nightfall, then back at their guest. "My squire has enough to do tending me. His services aren't for hire."

"It's not his services I'm after." His grin became more like a rictus. "It's his soul."

The words struck Edward dumb, and he frowned in

consideration. A chill swept Nightfall, as crisp and painful as the coldest winter night. It made little sense for the sorcerer to reveal himself this way, and he seemed too smart to make such an obvious mistake. Accustomed to reading motives, Nightfall put the pieces together quickly. He recalled the Healer's description of the sorcerer's ceremony in Delfor, how pain had driven a dying man's natal ability to the surface. It seemed a small jump to guess that not just physical agony, but intense emotional trauma, could affect one of the talented in the same fashion. Clearly, Ritworth planned to send Nightfall into a panic, thereby drawing his gift to the surface. The torture would come later, amid the final tearing of soul from body.

The idea brought a rush of the very terror Nightfall knew he had to suppress. Even as he struggled to drive it down, the oath-bond fluttered to noisy, painful life within him, an ear-splitting alarm that made action all but impossible. Nightfall gasped, the agony in his head scarcely bearable. For an instant he wondered if the sorcerer had used a spell to create the pain, but his heart told him otherwise. It came of other, more familiar magic; and he traced the thought that had reawakened Gilleran's handiwork. It came in an instant. There could be only one reason Ritworth had so casually revealed himself to Edward. The sorcerer planned to kill the prince.

Irony only intensified the excruciating mixture of headache and hysteria. One magic must drive him to chase away the only man who might rescue him from the other. Either way would cost his soul eternal torment, yet one could spare the life of a man he was growing to like. He gathered breath to shout, mud yielding to the expansion of his rib cage. "Master, run! Run! Save yourself!"

The oath-bond receded, allowing thought to trickle in, accompanied by an uncontrollable fear. As his vision cleared, he saw Ritworth shout something uninterpretable, finger pointed at Edward.

"Run!" Nightfall shouted again, flopping into the swamp mud for a desperate run to shore. The muck closed around him, swallowing him into its depths, and he managed to move less than an arm's length from the horse in the time it took Ritworth to cast his spell.

Prince Edward drew his sword and ducked at once, using the gelding as a shield. Something radiant struck the side of the white's head, back-splashing in sparks and droplets like iridescent liquid. The horse went still, his eyes locked wide with raw terror and shock. Frost formed on ear hairs and whiskers, then the magically frozen head shattered into fragments on the ground, and blood pooled from a neck that seemed more glass than flesh.

For an instant, time stood still. "Holy Father," Prince Edward said in awe, and his voice seemed loud in the sudden hush. Nightfall grabbed desperately for any object of substance, groping through the thick, unyielding mud. The daggers in his leg and boot sheaths had become buried beyond hope, and he fished for tunic pockets washed askew. The sorcerer's head lowered, and he mumbled, apparently tapping captured souls for another spell. The oath-bond became a constant scream that bounced agony through Nightfall's brain. He touched some object in the sludge, and his fingers winched desperately around it. It gave, nothing more than a fragile stem. Through a fog of disappointment, Nightfall kept his hand tight around the ball of mud. It would not kill, but it might distract. He hurled it at the sorcerer. "Damn it!" he screamed. "Run! Save yourself, or he'll kill us both. Just run!"

More from habit than effort, Nightfall's aim was true. The mudball slopped onto Ritworth's chest, and glowing strands in multiple colors rocked like a rainbow from his fist, sputtering randomly to the ground. A few strands brushed their creator, and he flinched from their touch, barking curses that bore little relation to the grating language that called his magic. He glanced at Nightfall, anger only making him appear larger and more savage.

Prince Edward bolted for the shelter of the forest.

At the movement, Ritworth spun. He shaped more sorcery, his words a dull growl. Nightfall blessed the delay that came of using power stolen by murder rather than chance of birth. He hoped Dyfrin's other theory also proved true, that each use of the spell loosened a sorcerer's tie to his victim until the soul broke free and the talent with it. It would make Ritworth more sparing of his abilities. Nightfall hurled another mudball. Again, he hit his target, this time in the back; but Ritworth anticipated the missile, managing to finish and launch his magic at Edward's retreating form. Skewed by the force of the blow, or some diversion from the prince, the ice attack crashed into a tree. A white explosion of light spread from the impact, and the tree groaned and swayed, a chunk of its form nearly opaque. Edward disappeared into the brush.

The oath-bond washed back to baseline, leaving Nightfall mercifully clear-headed. Likely, the sorcerer had only a small repertoire of spells, those he had managed to discover and wrest from their innocent owners. Most of those would prove useless for attack or defense. Still, he only needed the ice magics to kill; and, from the Healer's description, the pain he inflicted could come of more mundane means. Nightfall thrashed at the mud with coordinated movements, managing to eel toward shore only slightly before the sorcerer's dark gaze pinned him and the death-mask smile returned. Ritworth laughed, the sound rich with evil.

Despite his best efforts, terror flashed through Nightfall. He clung to stability and practicality; he knew fear and had never allowed it to rule or paralyze him before. Needing a grounding point, he wondered how much practice it had taken the sorcerer to perfect such an ugly sound. Still feigning ignorance, he ceased struggling and met the sorcerer's icy glare with the blue-black eyes that had demoralized so many. "What do you want with us?"

"I want your talent, Sudian Edward's-squire." Ritworth strode to the edge of the swamp, careful not to step too close to the banks. "It's no use pretending. I know it's there. I can *feel* it."

A force colder than metal in a blizzard brushed Nightfall's consciousness. Though it scarcely touched him, it spiraled a chill through his entire body. He forced consideration, afraid to sacrifice directed thought for the emotion that would make the sorcerer's task simpler. He knew that users of magic could not sweep minds contin-

uously; too many of the natally talented successfully hid
their abilities for that to be the case. Apparently, such action required an imprisoned or otherwise stationary target
and/or a high degree of suspicion. Or, perhaps, it first ne-
cessitated fear, pain, or serious mental agitation. Nightfall
suspected that the agony caused by the oath-bond had
proven his undoing. Now, he fought down the rage and
horror inspired by Ritworth and the carelessness that had
sent him plunging into a swamp. He would need to act
solely from logic and react only in a dispassionate manner to all that happened next. He would have to learn
quickly to disconnect pain from the emotions it inspired.

Sidetracked into feeling only with his intellect, Nightfall took a moment to consider the mistakes he had already made. Clearly, he should have interrupted Prince
Edward sooner and begun the extraction of self and horse
from the swamp. Incredulity at Edward's use of a book in
such a situation and ignorance of the full extent of danger
had played a hand in the delay. He also suspected that
Ritworth had not simply come along at the precise moment he showed himself. Finndmer had sold them out; no
one else knew their destination. The old fence had collected his money in every possible way: Ritworth's information fee, then Nightfall's payment for diversion, the
sale of land suitable only for stonejaw turtles and snakes,
and finally the finder's fee to the Iceman upon his return.
Replaying his plunge into swamp mud, Nightfall only felt
more certain of the solid ground his eyes had seen; and he
guessed Ritworth had used some kind of sight magic on
him that had spared Edward. The prince had seen the
swamp quite plainly. Lastly, Nightfall cursed himself for
leaping into the swamp mud without freeing his daggers
first. That, he could blame on no one but himself.

Ritworth pointed a finger at the stretch of swamp between himself and Nightfall. He mumbled the same ar-
cane syllables as previously, and the part closest to the
bank froze into a solid clump. "Your master won't get far
on foot. Once I'm finished with you, I'll kill him before
he can reach Noshtillan." He stepped onto the newly created bridge and aimed the finger to craft an extension of

his frozen path. "You know that, don't you?" The nasty grin seemed to have become permanent.

"I know you're a murdering, conscienceless bastard." Nightfall returned the smile, as detached as possible from emotion. "Is that the same thing?" Apparently Ritworth had bought Nightfall's fawning, selfless squire act as had everyone else and expected threats against Edward's life to rile him more than those against his own. That boded well for attempts to catch the sorcerer off-guard, assuming strategy mattered at all. Locked in mud, Nightfall sought a means to escape. He lowered his weight, hoping it would keep him from sinking any deeper.

The next block of ground froze, leaving only one more area before Ritworth came close enough to easily fling spells or objects at Nightfall. "Life is what it is. If the Father intended us to respect other's lives, he wouldn't have made them so simple to take nor some of us so much more powerful than others." He bridged the final gap.

Nightfall waited, coiled. Many options paraded before him, most dependent upon the sorcerer's course of action. It would prove easy enough to freeze Nightfall's head, as he had the horse's; but that would kill instantly and lose him the soul he had stalked. Freezing the mud around Nightfall would almost certainly cut him in half, again bringing shock and death too quickly. Anything short of magic that Ritworth chose to throw Nightfall believed he could rebound even from his awkward position. He had no way to guess what other powers the wizard might possess and, thus, no means to prepare to counter them. His lighter form gave him more mobility, and he searched diligently for the pockets and lining of his tunic and the daggers secreted within. He doubted he could throw well enough to kill the wizard without dying himself, but a regular death seemed far preferable to the permanent hell promised by the sorcerer's ceremony.

Ritworth stepped closer, gaze locked on Nightfall. He knelt, scooping blue-green swamp mud into his palm, then shaping the mass into a crude figure of a man. He mumbled as he worked. He glanced at Nightfall every few seconds, keeping track of every movement though it took time and accuracy from his molding. He rose, holding his creation before him. With his free hand, he fumbled a dagger from his pocket, nearly dropping it before catching a firm hold on the hilt.

Nightfall steadied himself, prepared. Blades, at least, he understood.

But Ritworth had witnessed most of the battle in Grittmon's Tavern, and he did not hurl the weapon. Instead, he scratched the tip of the blade along the figure. Apparently, some magic had gone into its crafting because it remained whole in the sorcerer's hand and did not crumble as drying mud usually did. He gauged Nightfall's lack of reaction, then stepped to the edge of his safely frozen ground.

Nightfall tensed, guessing the mudman somehow represented himself. Apparently, it required construction from ground he was touching and also a proper proximity. Otherwise, he felt certain Ritworth would have used the technique on him previously. He wriggled backward in retreat, the movement maddeningly slow, adjusting his weight to find a balance between hampering and propulsion.

The next sequence of blade through mud also tore his chest like fire. He screamed without intention, and agony forced him to catch his breath. For an instant, he felt the wizard's presence within him, reaching for a talent driven by pain from the core. Nightfall heaved his concentration aside, focusing on whatever other issues he could dredge to mind. For no reason he could fathom, Edward's lesson filled his thoughts, cycling endlessly. *Charseusan blue-green swamp mud. That's the name of what you're stuck in.* A glimpse down his tunic showed him flesh unaffected by the magic. No blood had actually been drawn, only the pain that accompanied such a wound. He inched backward as fast as the mud allowed.

Ritworth laughed again, the sound pitched to inspire terror. He jabbed the knife blade deep into the mudman's gut.

Pain skewered Nightfall, and the memories cycled, still present but no longer under his control. *It's called for the charseus plant, a blue-green grass/algae that can live over or under water. The mud's mostly made up of dying plants and other dead things.* Nightfall clutched at his gut, scarcely daring to believe his intestines still hung safely in his body. *DEAD THINGS.* He writhed, scuttling farther backward, and the suffering disappeared. Apparently, he had managed to work himself beyond range of the spell. Seizing the sudden reprieve, he gave another heave. His spine crashed against something solid, jarring him to the teeth. Surprised more than hurt, he glanced at the object he had hit, the bay mare half-submerged in swamp mud. *The blue-green comes from the live charseus plant.*

Ritworth swore, then laughed again. He cast another of his freezing spells, gaining him several steps closer to Nightfall, now trapped against his beast. "Too easy." He drove the dagger deep into the mud figure's groin, twisting as if to sever every organ.

Spasms racked Nightfall, the pain beyond any he had known. Had the damage been real, he would have surrendered to oblivion. Now he knew only the agony, his single need a quick death. He felt Ritworth's presence join his own, felt the other tug and pull at a mind-set flying for the surface, trebling pain that already seemed long beyond his ability to bear. He screamed again, doubling over so suddenly his face slopped into the goo. His thoughts ran without him. *The live plant makes lots of air. That's why there're so many bubbles just under the surface of the mud.* The words meant nothing now, but the desperate, gasping breaths he took to fill his lungs with mud and end his life did. Air funneled in, accompanied only by a thin stream of choking dirt. *You do know how to swim, I presume?*

Somehow, Nightfall managed to suck in bubbles without choking too violently on the slime that accompanied them. His legs felt liquid, but he pressed them against the horse's side. The torture became an all-encompassing universe, the flaying of soul and talent from body an agony so fierce it would not dull. Yet, his mind clung to the realization that distancing himself from the sorcerer would stop the pain. Using the horse as a springboard, he launched himself at an angle toward the bank. His hands and legs flailed and bunched like a frog's. Beneath the

surface of the swamp mud, he held his breath and swam,
finally gasping in a lungful of bubbles when the need for
air became too desperate.

The body pain vanished first, and Nightfall felt the sorcerer's grip slipping as his weight-shifting talent receded
back toward the core. Still bound with Ritworth, he felt
the sorcerer's enormous rage and frustration as his own.
The magical grip clenched tighter, clinging to the gift it
almost had. Then, abruptly, the hold disappeared, and surprise replaced the anger.

Nightfall clawed his way to the surface, gagging and
sputtering on the mud he had forced his lungs to bear. He
smeared stinging muck from his eyes in time to see
Prince Edward's follow-through sword stroke, an attack
that had, apparently, missed its target. Nightfall had come
within a long arm's reach of the bank. Ritworth gathered
power, presumably for his ice spell while the prince
tensed for another attack.

Nightfall scarcely noticed the jangle of the oath-bond,
the once-excruciating pain seeming minuscule in the
wake of so much more. He scrambled to shore, fighting
legs that seemed too weak to carry him. His muscles did
not properly obey. He tripped, falling flat on his face.
Spell and sword leapt forth at once. Though surely intended for Edward, the Iceman's sorceries struck his
blade instead. Edward dropped a weapon suddenly too
cold to handle. It struck the ground, exploding into splinters. Nightfall scrabbled to his feet, now seizing one of
the daggers he had not managed to locate while encased
in swamp. He hurled it for the back of the sorcerer's
neck.

But mud weighted the blade, making its flight unpredictable. It struck Ritworth's arm, dull edge leading, just
as Edward bore in with bare fists. The wizard spoke a
harsh word and flapped his hands. His body rose from the
ground, and he flew over Edward's head toward the
safety of the forest. The prince sprang back. Nightfall
threw his last two throwing knives. The first pierced the
air a split second behind the soaring sorcerer, the blade
plummeting into the swamp. The second missed cleanly
as Ritworth swept from sight.

The goading throb of the oath-bond lessened to its usual tingle, and the near absence of pain seemed a joy and comfort beyond anything Nightfall had known. He headed for the pack horse, digging rope from the bundle and ignoring the flopped body of Snow. He had wanted to rid them of the gelding's nervous presence forever, it seemed, yet never in this fashion. He could not help feeling guilty for the thoughts he had held against it in much the same way he felt his own wishes had caused his mother's death. For now, he needed to concentrate on freeing his mount.

Prince Edward headed back down the frozen pathway. "Are you badly hurt?"

"No, Master. Just shaken. I'll be fine." Nightfall continued freeing the rope as feeling returned to his body.

Edward drew closer, glancing around for Ritworth's return.

Nightfall did not trouble himself to do the same, trusting the trained perception that came from years of living on the street to alert him to danger. Never again would he allow illusion, excitement, and frustration to blunt that necessary sixth sense he needed for survival.

The prince drew up beside his squire. "Why does a sorcerer want your soul?"

Nightfall coiled the rope, forming a loop to catch the bay mare. He glanced at Edward, knowing the prince had grown up with a sorcerer as his father's adviser and certain even this sheltered youth had heard rumors. Denial would gain him nothing, only distance him from the trust he had sought to gain and mostly succeeded. The sorcerer's claims had already revealed too much. "Master, I didn't mean to hide anything from you. The fewer who know about my ability, the better. A word in the wrong place ... if a sorcerer overheard ... or one who would sell information to sorcerers ..." He rolled a sad gaze to Edward, continuing his work with the rope but letting the thought trail. "I've never told anyone before." *Except a vicious, back-stabbing whore who sold me to your father.*

Prince Edward fell silent for several moments, absently looping the extra rope, assisting his squire unconsciously. "I understand." He frowned. "So who told this sorcerer?"

"No one," Nightfall admitted. "He watched me closely enough to figure it out on his own." He tossed the loop, missing the horse by a hand's breadth. In response, the mare resumed her struggles, battering at the mud with hooves exhausted from the fight. He wound the rope back for another try.

"It doesn't matter, you know." Edward continued his search for the returning sorcerer. "Servant or equal, I'm not going to abandon you when the next sorcerer comes either."

"Thank you, Master; but your life has to come first. If I thought others would come, I'd leave you." Nightfall threw the lasso again. It landed just in front of the animal's ears and around the back of her head, and he coaxed it to slide along her nose. His own loyalty made sense. He little understood Edward's, however. Any other noble would have sacrificed his squire to preserve himself without need for a moment's consideration. *Why did he come back? What does he hope to gain from me?* "At the least, sorcerers have to compete too much to discuss their quarry with one another. We may see the Iceman again, but I don't think others will attack."

The rope jerked into place around the horse's neck.

Edward considered. "Now that I know, what is this talent of yours?"

Nightfall concentrated on the rope, believing the prince had earned the right to know but hedged by the memory of Kelryn's betrayal. "It helps me ride horses," he said, not quite lying. He tugged at the rope, aware he did not have the strength to pull the beast free himself yet knowing better than to request the aid of his master.

Prince Edward came over to help anyway.

Chapter 13

He feeds on elders and children,
On soldiers, kings, and beggarmen.
He never stops and never slows—
Darkness comes where Nightfall goes.
                    —The Legend of Nightfall
                    Nursery rhyme, st. 13

A multicolored wash of dancers frolicked through the muted lantern light of Noshtillan's stage, their many and varied steps weaving into beautiful patterns of flash and movement. Prince Edward and Nightfall sat on one of the scattered benches, a crate just taller than knee-height supporting their drinks, its weathered wood still tainted by the mixture of spices it once held. It was not the best of the furniture in the performance room of Noshtillan's dance hall. The central, more populous area contained some real tables and larger crates, but concern drove Nightfall to keep their backs against the wall and away from windows. He doubted the self-proclaimed Iceman would attack them in a crowd, even in a place where propriety and law deemed they remain unarmed; but paranoia would not allow him to drop his guard for a second.

Prince Edward and Nightfall had traveled as swiftly as the pack horse and the mud-caked mare could carry them, Nightfall surrendering the superior mount and his sword to his master. Ritworth had not bothered them on the journey, perhaps as shaken as his victim by the failed assassination. More likely, Nightfall suspected, the sorcerer was biding his time, waiting to catch his quarry in another indefensible position.

Nightfall had no intention of allowing himself to become vulnerable ever again. This excessive alertness had wrested sleep from him when they arrived in Noshtillan in the wee morning hours. Sheer exhaustion had eventually stolen consciousness from him, a dream-gorged slumber filled with chases, threats, and embarrassments. Even then, every sound had jarred him awake, and he harbored vague recollections of some dank corner of his mind processing and dismissing each normal city noise. He had sneaked his daggers, well-hidden, into the dance hall, preferring to risk arrest over being cornered without defenses.

Nightfall had mentioned the dance hall in the hope of discovering whether or not Kelryn still lived and, if so, where she had gone. He had not expected Edward to jump so enthusiastically on the idea, his verbalized intention to find an activity to soothe both of their jitters. The attention Edward lavished on the show revealed another motive, unconscious or just unspoken. Edward's manners made him appear older and his innocence far younger. Yet, when it came to women, he seemed every bit the eighteen-year-old male he was.

Nightfall remained still, hiding nervousness behind a casual aloofness broken only by an unconscious fondling of the glass swan through the folds of his pocket. Though irrational, he could not wholly suppress a superstitious belief that its presence might draw the woman who had previously owned it. Once a token of his love, it had become a symbol of his hatred and need for vengeance.

The current show ended, and male and female dancers exited the stage. Prince Edward sipped his beer. "Wonderful, wasn't it?"

Nightfall could not recall the last time his master had remained quietly awake so long. "Yes, wonderful." He watched as the serving girls rearranged the stage lanterns, bunching them toward the center. Experience told him the more erotic dancing would start now, progressing from suggestive to pornographic by evening's end. He smiled, suspecting Edward would now see a display unfamiliar to him, one he would likely enjoy if he did not become too flustered to watch. He savored the opportunity to see his sometimes tyrannical master transformed into a squirming teen. Nightfall vowed to observe closely for more reason than entertainment. If anyone would know of Kelryn's whereabouts, these girls would prove the best informants.

The music began, a sultry and original song performed by a three-man band at the far side of the stage. Four girls clad in silky dresses slunk onto the stage from the sidelines, their movements sinuous. Prince Edward stared, the beer in his hand forgotten, his gaze leaping from one to the next in a dazzled circle. Nightfall froze, his eyes riveted on only one, the last to enter. He recognized the body first, outlined in perfect detail against the shimmering, clinging fabric. He knew every muscle and curve too well not to recognize Kelryn. The short white locks and plain features only clinched her identity. *Kelryn.* Nightfall might have remained stuck in Charseusan blue-green swamp mud for all he managed to move. Emotion came next, in a frenzied rush that left him breathless. Attraction rose, unbidden, beaten down by a rush of rage and hatred that made his entire body feel on fire. The beer churned in his gut, and he was glad that they had not yet eaten dinner. As it was, the last remnants of their morning meal sat like lead.

Nightfall found himself aimlessly rubbing the swan through the fabric of his pocket and forced his hand still. He stood. "Excuse me for a few moments, please, Master."

Without taking his eyes from the performance, Edward nodded.

Nightfall hurried from the room, not bothering to detail his intentions further, glad for the distraction that made no explanation necessary. Probably, Edward would assume he'd left to relieve himself.

Once through the double doors of the performance chamber, Nightfall entered the main corridor, glancing right and left to judge the location of the dancers' rooms as well as get a general feel for the layout. Dance hall workers wore red shirts and pantaloons or dresses with black trim, making them easy to spot amid the rabble. Most of the milling folk in the corridor consisted of men who knew when the style of showmanship changed, now headed into the hall. The others seemed mostly family groups, leaving for the same reason. Nightfall blended into the latter, his sharp gaze discerning a guard stopping people who meandered down either hallway rather than directly outside or into the spectators' area.

Perhaps because Nightfall believed Prince Edward wholly secure in a crowded public place, the oath-bond remained passive at its tingling routine. Afraid to stir it, Nightfall reminded himself repeatedly that he intended no specific, Nightfall-like action, only minor spying and climbing. As much as he wished to reveal himself before slaughtering the woman who had betrayed him, to let her fear and understand her mistake, he knew he could not do so. Never before had he wanted to draw attention to his work in any way. The straightforward simplicity of Nightfall's crimes had made them easy to copy, thus causing many more than he committed to become attributed to him and making him seem to be in many places at once. Those things had much to do with the demon's name with which the masses had burdened him. Yet, this once, he wanted the satisfaction of a victim's understanding. He wanted revenge.

Nightfall circled the dance hall, an oblong building with several rectangular wings that held the quarters of dancers, workers, and overseers. A few well-timed glimpses through windows led him to the performers' area; he found it last of the four wings. The time used to avert the suspicions of passersby on the evening roads had dragged, and he guessed Kelryn's session on stage had probably finished during his search. It bothered him that she might reach her quarters before him; he wanted to lie in wait. Yet, this would have to work as well. Quite likely, he would not have recognized her room anyway without her presence. Choosing wrongly would delay his mission and his return to his master.

Nightfall discovered Kelryn's voice first, the familiar alto lilting through a shuttered window. She chanted words to the tune of the dancing song, occasionally humming phrases she could not recall. He drifted to the correct room, only to find the window shuttered and the wood painted closed. Frustration gripped him. For a moment, he stood rooted, thwarted, annoyance adding to the fires of his rage. He could crash his way through the barrier but not without alerting Kelryn, and every neighbor, to the danger. Turning, he trotted back to the dance hall entrance.

Once inside, he chose the left hallway. An enormous man in dance hall clothing stepped into his way. "Did you need something, sir?"

Nightfall tipped the man six copper, generous enough to get his way without becoming too memorable. "One of the girls invited me back."

The guard brightened, standing aside, and Nightfall continued his walk. He had expected it to prove that easy. Once the seductive dancing began, many of the girls would earn extra money by making arrangements on the side. He had balked at using the hallway previously because it required working his way past a guard who might remember him after the crime. Now, that could not be avoided. He would simply have to hope the man had not looked too closely or that he would become lost amid a sea of suspects. Kelryn had escaped his wrath so far by keeping on the run. This time, he had her cornered; and that opportunity might not present itself again.

The corridor seemed endless, and Nightfall counted doors as he went. Yet, though it had seemed to take forever to get there, too soon he stood before the door to Kelryn's chamber. He fingered the dagger in his sleeve, well aware of the location of the other three blades on his person. His heart pounded, and his thoughts raced. He attributed a blossoming tickle in his chest to the excitement of finally slaughtering the one who had stolen his love, then betrayed him, of putting to rest the one woman to whom he had dared fully expose himself and all that he was. Ready, he drew a deep breath and eased open the door.

Nightfall took in the scene in an instant. The room contained a dresser/table with a matching stiff wooden chair, an inset closet, and a bed. Kelryn stood in the open center of the room, her costume clutched in her hands. She wore only two pieces of lacy undergarments, the top covering breasts and upper torso and the bottom spanning from waist to halfway down her thighs. The sheer fabric hid nothing, enhancing rather than hiding the delicate nipples and impressing a perfect triangle in the lower regions. His entrance surprised them both; his memory had not fully captured the grace of her form, thinner than in the past. An awkward silence ensued during which Nightfall managed to step inside and lever the door closed behind him.

Kelryn dropped the dress and back-stepped. Cosmetics flaked beneath her eyes, hiding dark circles poorly. Beneath a web of sleepless, red lines, he found a fear in her eyes that seemed older than the shock of a strange intruder in her room. "I'm—I'm sorry. I'm not taking clients."

"I'm not a client." Nightfall drifted closer, sexually aroused despite himself. It occurred to him that nothing would stop him from ravishing her first, and she deserved the humiliation and pain that would come with a rape prior to murder. But some emotion he tried to deny held him back. Just the brief idea of such cruelty instantly sapped him of desire, and a battered pocket of caring colored his thoughts even as he ignored and reviled it. He would have to fight his heart and spirit just to find the courage to kill her.

Apparently recognizing something violent in his stance, Kelryn took another backward step. Her gaze flicked to his blue-black eyes and held there momentarily, as if reading something in their depths. Her blank stare bunched into a mask of surprise, then a smile lit the corners of her features. "Marak," she whispered.

The recognition caught Nightfall completely by surprise. He cringed, waiting for the oath-bond to sever body from soul; but it remained quiescent. Clearly, her unassisted identification did not count as him revealing himself. "What?" was all he squeezed from vocal cords that would not function.

"Marak. You're alive." The tight smile became a huge and open grin. "You're alive!" Joy colored Kelryn's tone and a happy blush tinged her cheeks. She ran toward him.

Before Kelryn took her second stride, Nightfall seized the glass swan and hurled it to the floor at her feet. It shattered, slivers of colored glass skittering across stone. A glaze of light trickling through a crack in the shutter glittered from every shard.

Kelryn checked her rush, back-pedaling. Only her well-practiced grace saved her bare feet from the largest fragments. The smile wilted into open-mouthed bewilderment. "Wha—why? Marak?"

Nightfall had hoped the destruction would trigger a release for his anger and charge him to the necessary violence. Though he had brooded over the reunion, he had never rehearsed the words he would speak before the murder. Always before, the proper threats and warnings had come as naturally as breathing. Now, he seemed to have forgotten even the language of his childhood. Rage rose, directed fully inward. He could not recall feeling this awkward or disarmed since his mother's beatings had become routine. Only action mattered. If he needed to slaughter the traitor in silence, he would do so. Killing, at least, he knew well. He poised for attack.

A sudden pounding on the door startled Nightfall. Prince Edward's unmistakable voice boomed through the panel. "Sudian?"

Nightfall tensed and froze, the need for decision breaking him free from his trance. He strung together the scenario of how Edward had tracked him. Apparently concerned for the length of time his sorcerer-hunted squire had taken to perform a simple function, the prince had gone searching. Probably, the guard had steered him to the proper corner of the dance hall. Whether or not the prince or someone else had witnessed his entry into this particular room remained to be seen.

Kelryn's tired, hazel eyes fixed on Nightfall's face. She remained still, taking her cues from him.

Nightfall waved Kelryn to stay silent and in place.

Edward hammered at the door again. "Sudian. I know you're there. Answer me at once."

A string of words flooded Nightfall's mind then, every one profane. It occurred to him first to slay Kelryn swiftly and claim he had found her corpse on the floor. His shock at discovering a bleeding body should suffice as reason for delaying his response to his master's call. In demon guise, no other plan would have proven necessary. He guessed that, most likely, the prince had caught a glimpse of him disappearing through this door; but, as Sudian, he dared not risk the possibility that someone else had spotted him,

a person who had watched the door since Kelryn's return.
If Prince Edward opened the door before he finished the
slaying, or if the dancer managed a scream, his story
would fail. Under other circumstances, he would murder
the witness, too. This time, however, such action would
cost him his soul and, though he hated to admit it, his conscience. Even without Gilleran's magic to restrain him, he
would not harm Alyndar's younger prince.

These considerations flew through Nightfall's mind in
an instant. He glared into Kelryn's face with a menace he
believed she would not dare to challenge. "Play along.
Make a mistake and my torture will make the Father's
hell you find afterward seem merciful." Without awaiting
a reply, or even a change of expression, he partially
turned to open the door. Any attempt by Kelryn to feign
innocence or surprise might drive him to the very violence he had sought and failed to dredge forth moments
earlier. She lived now only by the grace of two things: a
sorcerer's magic and Nightfall's growing devotion to his
master. He tried to convince himself the first reason remained the more important of the two.

Nightfall pulled the door open, and Prince Edward
stood outlined in its frame. Though he hated the need,
Nightfall resumed his proper role, taking care to keep his
attention and his warning stare on Kelryn. "Prince
Edward Nargol of Alyndar." His arm traced the appropriate flourish, though with hurried awkwardness. "Master,
this is Kelryn. We grew up in the same town."

Kelryn curtsied, still graceful despite her obvious bewilderment.

From the edge of his vision, Nightfall could tell Prince
Edward had not moved. His silence seemed so uncharacteristic it became worrisome. Nightfall routed more of his
direct attention on his master.

The prince gawked at what was, apparently, the first
near-naked woman he had seen. He squirmed, trying valiantly to tear his gaze away, propriety battling pleasure
with a frenzy that seemed unwinnable. "Oh," he managed, averting his eyes with impressive self-control. "I'm
sorry. I didn't know you needed . . . I mean . . ." He

stepped inside, closed the door, and politely kept his back to Kelryn.

Nightfall flicked his gaze deliberately to the dress on the floor. Kelryn raised her brows in question but picked up her clothing and shook glass fragments from the fabric. She pulled it over her head, adjusting the seams. She broke the silence. "I apologize for my dress, noble sir. I wasn't expecting company. I hope I didn't offend."

"Offend?" Prince Edward took a surreptitious peek to ascertain that Kelryn had used the moment to make herself decent before he turned around fully. "Dear me, no. I'm sorry we barged in on you. I had no idea." He looked at Nightfall for an explanation, but his eyes betrayed him, slipping back to examine Kelryn's firm and slender figure through the close-fitting material.

Nightfall knew a twinge of what felt maddeningly like jealousy. "Master, I'm sorry for my long absence. I saw Kelryn for the first time in years and thought I should greet her."

"You would have been remiss to do otherwise, Sudian." Although he addressed his squire, Edward's attention locked on Kelryn's eyes. He shuffled toward her, heavy boots crunching glass shards to powder. "I'm so sorry about disturbing you, and I'd like to make amends. Would you have dinner with Sudian and me tonight?"

No! Nightfall shook his head, gesturing briskly for Kelryn to decline.

The dancer hesitated momentarily. Then a smile curled onto her face, and she shrugged slightly for Nightfall's benefit. "Noble sir," Kelryn said softly. "I would be honored."

Nightfall perched on the broad window sill of their inn room, staring through the wavy glass. It overlooked an alleyway, and the wall of the opposite shop had become tediously familiar while Prince Edward bathed, dressed, and groomed. Nightfall believed he could picture every weathered mortar chip and splotch of dirt on building stone with his eyes closed. His mind worried the situation no matter how hard he tried to thrust it from his thoughts, and the same conclusion rose repeatedly. An association between a betrayer and the man whose safety determined the lot of Nightfall's soul could only lead to disaster. He needed to halt the dinner before it began. Barring that, he would make it an experience neither wished to repeat. Once they separated, he could find a way to slaughter Kelryn without Edward's knowledge or interest.

The prince's voice jarred Nightfall from his inescapable contemplation. "Sudian, what do you think of this?"

Nightfall swiveled his head to study his master. Edward wore a blue silk shirt beneath a supple leather tunic, and his breeks matched the shirt so perfectly in shade they had obviously been dyed, if not tailored, together. In lieu of his usual travel boots, he had donned lacing doeskin dress wear colored to match his clothing. He had combed his wet locks back, and they now fell in rakish, blond feathers around the straight and sturdy features. Nightfall had to admit his master looked appropriately princely, and it only added to his annoyance. "What do I think about what, Master?"

"This." Prince Edward made a gesture that spanned from his neck to his feet. The movement sent the spicy scent of perfume wafting to Nightfall.

Nightfall scowled, determined to place the dinner back into proper perspective. "I think it's wonderful, Master, if you're attending a court feast. For guzzling ale and spoiled meat in a dirty, southern tavern with a whore, it seems a bit formal."

"Whore?" Edward blinked, expression bewildered. Then, his eyes narrowed, and a red flush of irritation arose. "Sudian! That's a horrible thing to call a lady."

"A lady, yes. A prostitute, no."

"Stop it, Sudian! What happened to the manners I taught you?"

Nightfall spun around on the sill, drawing one leg to his chest and allowing the other to dangle. "Master, Kelryn accepts money from men to have sex with them. I believe that's the definition of whore."

Edward smoothed back stray hairs. "When did you last see your lady friend?"

Nightfall weighed the answer, trying to guess the intention of the question in order to give the best response. "A few years ago, Master."

"People change, Sudian."

"With all the proper respect, Master, Kelryn seemed awfully comfortable nearly naked in front of two men."

"She's a dancer." Prince Edward pushed his sundries aside and sat on the desk beside them. The room also contained a wash basin, a crate, and straw on the floor that served as beds. Their supplies lay propped in a corner. "And we surprised her. She probably worried more for her safety than her garb." He smiled, his expression whimsical. "When a woman has a body like hers, there's little need to hide it."

Nightfall bit his lip. In response to the prince's defense, annoyance flared, though Nightfall did not wholly understand the intensity of his own reaction. "Being a prostitute doesn't keep her from being my friend. But it's not a proper association for a prince."

Prince Edward smoothed nonexistent wrinkles from his clothing. "I appreciate your concern, Sudian. But I'm in a better position to judge my asssociations than you." He studied Nightfall who still wore the same fading livery he had donned for the dance show. "Did you want to freshen up, too?"

"Master, I just think . . ." Nightfall trailed off, realizing he should answer the question before making his point. "I mean no, Master. I'm ready enough for dinner with Kelryn." The words brought memories of the foolish lengths to which love had once driven him. Then, he had dressed in his cleanest and best to entertain this woman, carefully combing out the dirty tangles that defined the character of Marak. "I mean she . . . well . . ." He wanted to speak cautiously but wound up blurting instead. "She has the clap, Master."

"The clap?"

"You know, Master. Bad blood. The delicate disease."

"I know what the clap is, Sudian." Annoyance tainted Edward's voice. "And I also know how it's spread. Having dinner is not the way." His eyes narrowed. "And how do you know what she has?"

I gave it to her. At least if you ask her old roommate in Nemix. "She told me, Master. I know."

Edward made a pensive noise.

"Master?" Nightfall encouraged Edward to share his thoughts.

The prince obliged. "Perhaps she only feared she had it. Or perhaps she felt other need to claim such a thing."

"Other need, Master?" Nightfall spun completely around to face Edward, letting both legs hang from the sill. Valiantly, he kept challenge from his tone. From any other man, the suggestion that Kelryn might have lied to keep him from her bedroom would have driven him to violence.

This time, Prince Edward dodged a reply. "Or perhaps she has the clap. What matter? Does that make her any less a person?" He leapt from the table and headed for the door.

Though discomfited by the entire situation, Nightfall followed quietly.

Prince Edward and Nightfall met Kelryn in Heffrilen's Tavern in eastern Noshtillan, a pricey dining and drinking facility without an affiliated tavern or gambling hall. Servant-powered fans swirled pipe and cooking smoke into lazy circles, and violinists turned over the central stage to jugglers, acrobats, sleight-of-hand magicians, and solo lutists in turn. From past experience, Nightfall knew the food was mediocre; their gold would pay for ambiance and entertainment. He had given most of his leftover silver to Prince Edward, leaving only six for himself; and the realization that his master would spend much of that money on the woman who had betrayed him only fueled annoyance that already felt like a bonfire within him. Even the oath-bond seemed to recede beneath the wild blaze of emotion.

Kelryn had worn her sleekest, most elegant dress, a flattering green linen that fell in sweeps to her ankles. Marak had purchased it for her, and it had once been his favorite. Though he hated it now, he could not deny that it complimented her figure, and Edward's long stare only affirmed his impression. The prince drew back her chair, waving her to sit with a dignified flourish that bordered on a bow.

Kelryn sat, flushing at the royal treatment. Her lowered eyes flitted a glance past Nightfall's questioningly. Then, as she read the smoldering anger there, her embarrassed modesty became more of a restless concern. "Thank you," she said.

Edward took his seat. "You're very welcome, lady."

Nightfall's jaw tightened. He seriously wondered if he could stomach food while Kelryn played his master for the innocent fool he was. He wondered what she wanted from Alyndar's younger prince. His money might win her dinners and trinkets, but not much more; and she would soon find that his status here gained him little in the way of privileges. Eventually, she would tire of him. Sooner rather than later, if Nightfall had his way.

Edward started the conversation. "So you and Sudian grew up together. When did you first meet?"

Kelryn glanced at Nightfall for clues. In truth, they had come together for the first time a scant five years ago.

Nightfall gave her nothing, testing. She had heard his vague comment to Edward in her room, and he had added nothing to the details. Whatever she said would serve well enough so long as she did not revert to truth. Her reply would show how seriously she had taken his threat.

Kelryn hesitated to the edge of impropriety. Then, when Nightfall gave her no hints, she improvised. "Birth. Mine, at least. He's older."

"Alyndar or Mitano?" Edward asked.

"What?" Kelryn looked nervous.

"Sudian told me about how his family moved from Alyndar to Mitano when he was young. I just wondered whether you met before or after the travel."

Nightfall raised his brows, surprised Edward had recalled an offhand detail born of Nightfall's need to cover for King Rikard's claim that he came from the south. He hated having to create Sudian's history piecemeal, but he had never expected to be recognized. Never before had anyone identified him across disguises.

"Before," Kelryn said, apparently concentrating more on the need to sound casual than on keeping the story as plausible as possible. Then, seeing a need to explain the oddity, she added, "Our families moved together. Our mothers were distant relatives and close friends. I have a brother Sudian's age. . . ."

A serving maid approached, a plump teenager with long, dark hair tied away from her face. Kelryn broke off and became suddenly intent on the newcomer, using the interruption to escape the need to create a lifetime of history from air. "Good evening."

"Good evening, lady," the youngster returned. She took a position between Kelryn and Edward, then curtsied. "Good evening, noble sir." She ignored Nightfall. Servant livery tended to make a man invisible, a benefit in Nightfall's mind. "Today we have mutton cakes, venison stew, roast pheasant in gravy, and shark steaks. What can I get for you?"

Edward and Nightfall had eaten in so many inns where storage and hunting determined the fare, the choice caught them without opinion. Kelryn, too, remained silent longer than mannerly. The cook in the dance hall surely made a single dish, each meal depending upon available supplies. Likely, however, she had had rare occasion to dine here. Nightfall had also done so, in "demon" guise and as Balshaz the merchant. From experience and gossip, he knew that seafood carted up from the south tended to age more before preparation than the hunted or farmed animals in Noshtillan. He had also learned that Heffrilen's cook's talents fell short when it came to spicing fish.

Nightfall broke the silence. "Kelryn, I know your likes and dislikes. Might I suggest the shark steak?"

Kelryn glanced at Nightfall, obviously surprised to find him talking to her. "Thank you, Sudian, but I've had my heart set on fowl. I'd love to try some of yours, though." She rescued herself from bad food, placing the onus back on Nightfall at the same time.

Nightfall gave her the win, having little at stake in the verbal spar. Though he knew Edward's order should come next, he responded to the attention of companions and serving maid, now directed toward him by her comment. "Kelryn, my dear. After our fishing trips on the Lixdar

River, how could you forget that eating shark makes me ill? I'll have the mutton, if my master will forgive my selecting before him."

Prince Edward made a gracious gesture of dismissal. "If you recommend the fish so highly, Sudian, I guess I'll have it."

Nightfall stiffened. Rescuing his own taste buds had proven easy. Saving the prince would likely become more difficult. "Please, Master. Don't go by my advice." He tried to look stricken, keeping his voice low. "If your taster gets sick, how will you know . . . ?"

Edward returned his squire's gaze, brows raised in question. Nightfall had not insisted on testing his food for poison for some time.

Nightfall kept his return stare earnest, hoping Edward would attribute his resurgence of paranoia to the sorcerer rather than Kelryn.

A light dawned in the prince's eyes, and he smiled at the serving maid. "I'll have the pheasant, too, please. And a glass of your best wine for each of us."

The server gave Kelryn an envious look that spoke volumes. Her sigh told Nightfall that she wondered how a dance hall girl snagged a prince as handsome and polite as any storyteller's hero. She trotted off to fill the order, and conversation fell once more to Prince Edward.

"Families so close they move together." The prince returned to the previous conversation, to Kelryn's obvious chagrin. "Sudian must have seemed like another brother."

Kelryn glanced at Nightfall who returned a glare in sullen silence. Everything about the current situation irritated him, from the need to guess Kelryn's motivations, to the prince's dutiful kindness to one he believed his squire's friend. Trapped into breaking bread with an enemy, he felt as restless as a child getting lectured, and the serving maid's assumption that Edward and Kelryn formed a couple raised an anger that seemed dangerous and sourceless. Apparently taking its cue from Nightfall's consideration of Kelryn as a threat, the oath-bond maintained a steady, head-jarring ring.

Kelryn gave the only safe answer. "Oh, very much so. Like a brother, but without the competition for my parents' attention. In some ways, he seemed more brother than my brother."

Edward folded his napkin onto his lap and tried to draw Nightfall into the conversation. "And you only said you grew up with her. Was she like a sister to you?"

Nightfall replied dutifully. "Yes, Master. A sister." He copied Edward's table manners since he had never been trained to have any of his own. Few places wasted cloth on linens, and it never occurred to him to place one on his lap.

When Nightfall did not go on, Edward pressed. "Tell me what it was like. Growing up together, I mean."

Kelryn also directed her attention to Nightfall, letting him play featured speaker this time.

Nightfall shrugged, in no mood for chatter, especially happy lies. "Master, there's nothing to tell. Really."

Prince Edward shook his head, grinning even as he dismissed his squire's detachment. "Has he always been like this? Modest, I mean. He didn't even mention to anyone that he saved my life."

"Yours, too?" Kelryn joined the conversation with all the eagerness Nightfall lacked. "He killed a snake that tried to bite me once. A poisonous type. Grabbed it with his bare hands, killed it, and continued a story he was telling without missing a word."

Edward gave Nightfall a pleasant look that both admired and condemned his squire's humility.

Nightfall shrugged. That incident had happened, though only a few years ago. And, to his recollection, the topic of conversation had remained the snake for quite some time afterward.

The prince turned back to Kelryn. "I got caught in the middle of a bar fight. Sudian grabbed a dagger intended for me in midair. Nearly lost his fingers." He nudged his squire. "Show her, Sudian."

Obedient to his master's command, Nightfall gave Kelryn a quick glimpse of the scar. She cringed in sympathy, though whether unconscious or feigned, Nightfall did not try to guess.

"If he makes you his friend, you never need to doubt his loyalty," Kelryn said, the statement sounding ludicrous to Nightfall from the mouth of a traitor. Forming bonds had always proven difficult or impossible for him, and only his friendship with Dyfrin had lasted.

Prince Edward agreed heartily. "Loyal to me before himself. A rare and special squire, indeed."

Nightfall glanced around the tables at the other patrons, uncomfortable with Edward's heartfelt but ignorant praise and Kelryn's fake allegiance.

Kelryn smiled, her plain features alight and almost beautiful in the lantern glow. Even the sunken eyes and bloodshot whites that evinced fretful nights seemed to disappear. "Then you must be very remarkable yourself to earn such treatment."

"Thank you."

Nightfall believed he saw a reddish tinge to Edward's cheeks. He hoped but doubted conscience was the thing disturbing Kelryn's sleep.

Having found a familiar topic of conversation, Kelryn stuck with it. "Sudian always protected me. For instance, he hated that I used to sometimes have to sleep with strangers for money. He'd spread rumors that I had the clap so men would stay away."

"Really." Edward's tone went thoughtful, and he glanced at Nightfall.

Caught in a lie, Nightfall avoided the prince's gaze and wished the night would swiftly end.

But it did not. Late evening chased into night, and the conversation scarcely seemed to change. Each of Nightfall's companions extolled his virtues while he sat in a bitter silence interrupted only by the occasional need to address a direct question. He kept his replies clipped, monosyllabic when possible, and avoided lengthy explanations or descriptions. The food arrived. Nightfall ate quickly, hoping to set the pattern for the meal and the night. But Kelryn dined with her usual slow elegance, and the prince appeared more interested in conversation than food. It seemed an eternity before Prince Edward left to tend to payment in private, leaving Nightfall and Kelryn alone.

Kelryn scarcely waited until Edward passed beyond

earshot, whispering to keep other diners from over-hearing. "Marak, how . . . ?" She reached for his hands.

Nightfall moved first, catching her fingers in a grip that appeared tender but was tight enough to cause pain. "No acts or explanations. You'll only enrage me." He met her hazel eyes with an icy glare. "You're alive because of the prince and only because of the prince. If you harm him, I'll feed you to the wolves piece by screaming, bloody piece." He threw her hands away and returned his own to the tabletop.

Kelryn paled, obediently silent.

The urge seized him to storm from Heffrilen's Tavern, leaving his rage bunched and tangible at the table while he escaped into the night. But he knew the anger would only accompany him, and he would not leave Prince Edward alone and vulnerable in a deceiver's grip.

Kelryn's eyes blurred, filled suddenly with moisture. "Marak, listen. Please."

Her farce dragged pain and fury to the surface. Before he could think, his half-closed fist slammed against her cheek, throwing her head sideways and sending tears splashing to the unoccupied table beside them. With unconscious grace, she managed to catch her balance and keep the chair, or herself, from falling.

Nightfall stared at his hand, outrage against Kelryn and himself welling in concentric waves. Not since he had avenged his mother's murder had he lashed out in anger and never in any guise other than that of Nightfall, especially in a public tavern. He knew fury at himself for loss of self-control, against Kelryn for driving him to that loss, and against the mother who had taught him to respond to unhappiness with violence. That he had hurt Kelryn did not matter. Hours before, he would have slain her; given the opportunity, he would do so now. Something deep inside drove him to apologize until his soul emptied of guilt and sorrow, to beg for the forgiveness of the only woman he had ever loved. Yet, he dismissed the seed as something ingrained from his childhood and forced away the image of his mother pouring forth promises of devotion and tranquillity while he still ached from the blows she beseeched him to excuse. He believed no leftover vestige of caring made him feel guilt and drove him to seek absolution, just a haunting memory from his youth.

Kelryn's head sagged to the table, and her shoulders shook rhythmically as she wept in silence. Nightfall looked away in time to notice Prince Edward returning. A new discomfort swept him, one that took consequence into consideration. He could not explain Kelryn's tears to his master, and he would not bully her into a lie now even should he have the time to do so.

Prince Edward returned to his seat talking. "It's dark outside already. I hadn't realized . . ." He trailed off, apparently noticing Kelryn's state of mind. "Are you all right?"

Kelryn wiped her eyes, then raised her head, tossing back her short, white locks in a gesture that she probably intended to look casual. "I'm fine. Just a bit queasy. The food tasted wonderful, and I thank you for it. I just think maybe something in the gravy isn't sitting well in my stomach." She started to rise.

Edward stood and caught Kelryn's arm. "Here, let me help you up." He steadied her as she gained her feet. "Do you need a Healer?"

"No." Kelryn rubbed the remainder of the tears from her eyes, using the gesture to brush aside strands of hair clinging to her forehead. "I'll be fine. I just need some rest."

Edward continued to clutch Kelryn's arm. "Here. Let me walk you home." Finally, his attention shifted to Nightfall. "Sudian, why don't you go back to the room and get things settled for the night? I'll take Kelryn home."

The idea of leaving those two alone pulsed dread through Nightfall. The oath-bond's warning tingle worsened. "Master, I can escort her." He tried to gear his tone to imply "my friend, my responsibility" rather than concerns about the decision.

The prince's reply was firm, making it clear that he would brook no further suggestions. "I appreciate your offer, Sudian, but I'd rather handle this exactly as I instructed."

Nightfall's next recommendation, that he accompany them, died on his tongue. Edward's manner suggested it would not be well-received. "Yes, Master. I'll see you back at the room." He headed for the exit, the oath-bond becoming stronger with each step he took. He quelled it with the understanding that he would not leave Edward alone with Kelryn. Even if not for the risk of her association with sorcerers, he had no wish for the two to discuss him without knowing what got said. Although he felt certain Edward would trust his word over hers, he could prepare better if he knew what he needed to defend against. Likely, she would tell Edward things she would not dare to have mentioned in Nightfall's presence, at least about how he had struck her that evening. Surely, she knew she could not dissolve the relationship between prince and squire in a night. She might insidiously infuse Edward with information, winning his trust until she delivered the blow that destroyed them both: Nightfall for being the demon of legend and Edward for associating with him.

Nightfall backed into the shadows outside of the tavern and waited.

Shortly, Prince Edward and Kelryn exited into the warm, summer air. He kept her arm in his own, worrying for her every step like a mother with a toddler. Nightfall waited until they passed, then followed at a distance that kept him well-hidden but revealed nearly every word of their conversation.

"Feeling better, lady?"

"Much, thank you, Ned. I think I just needed the night air."

Prince Edward seemed noticeably relieved. "I'm sorry about the food. I wanted to nourish, not poison, you."

"No, please, don't apologize." Kelryn touched the prince's upper arm with her free hand. "It was the best meal I've had in a long time. And I really do feel fine now."

"Do you still want to go straight home?"

"A walk might be nice."

Kelryn's words and gentle tone brought back vivid remembrances of Nightfall's own times with her. With them

came a raw jealousy he could not deny. Bad enough
Kelryn seemed to be striking up a friendship with the one
he needed to protect. The thought that she might sleep
with him drove Nightfall back to the wrath the shock of
hitting her had dispelled. Worse, he could not quite figure
out why the idea bothered him so much. It might do for
the prince to lose his sexual innocence. He just wished it
could be with anyone but her. Wished, not only for the
prince, but for himself. For all that he hated her, the love
and esteem he had once held for her could not be fully
banished; and that realization only fueled the anger.

Prince Edward and Kelryn strolled through the darkened streets, oblivious to the shadow that trailed them in
practiced silence. Although they seemed to walk together,
stride for stride, only Kelryn knew the town well enough
to lead the way. They chatted about the sights, such as the
night allowed, and the meal, gradually wandering further
from the streets and alleyways to a grassy knoll just north
of the town's edge. There, they sat beneath a spry, young
oak; and the conversation ceased as they settled into
place.

Nightfall found a hiding place, low and shadowed by a
copse of prickly bushes. He kept his need focused. Every
movement, of Kelryn or a surreptitious stranger, might
mean danger to Prince Edward. Every word might place
Nightfall in a compromising position that risked anything
from simple punishment to the loss of his soul to magic.
Yet, he could not help but notice how the moonlight
striped highlights through Kelryn's silver hair and the
dress outlined a figure that had come to define female
perfection, at least in Nightfall's mind. Even her face
seemed to gain a beauty in the glow. The moon complimented the prince as well, adding life to golden features
that needed no enhancement.

"So how did you and Sudian come together?" Kelryn
started the conversation, turning it back toward the topic
that most bothered Nightfall. The tactic surprised him. He
had expected her to snuggle up to Edward first, winning
him over with sex before turning him against his squire.
Yet, Nightfall could also see the strategy in defining his
relationship with Edward before attempting whatever evil

she planned. Perhaps she was still in the fishing stage, gathering information, checking Edward for a natal talent or for wealth, and seeking the best means to sell out Nightfall and his gift/curse once again.

Prince Edward studied Kelryn, obviously liking what he saw. "He came to the palace and pledged himself into my services with a vibrant loyalty to me and my causes that I appreciate every day we're together." He looked away into the distance, a transparent attempt to balance his staring. "Does he do that often? Pledge himself, soul and mind, to people and their principles?"

Kelryn shook her head. "Never before that I know of. You must be as special as you seem." She pulled her legs to her chest and stared at the stars. "In fact, Sudian tends not to trust anyone."

"I've noticed that." Prince Edward glanced back to Kelryn, excited by his observation. "Why is that?" His words disappeared into an uncomfortably long hush. The song of night insects seemed to grow impossibly loud.

"I don't know that he would want anyone to know this . . ."

Nightfall crouched deeper into the darkness, attentive, locked into one strategy. If he retaliated for Kelryn's revelations, he would add credence to them. The only sensible response would be to remain in place, listening for the details so he could consider ways to counter her lies and truths.

Kelryn continued. "I told you our families were close, but I didn't say why. Sudian never knew his father, and his mother had no interest in or experience with raising children. She was an only child, too, I think."

Nightfall listened intently. He had avoided talking about his childhood, even with Kelryn, and had told her only that he had no father and his relationship with his mother was less than ideal. His love for Kelryn had made him want to discuss happier details and confess the deepest, darkest secrets about himself; but he had avoided the sore specifics.

The insect chorus rose and fell in cycles. Prince Edward stretched into a more comfortable position, attention fully focused on Kelryn. "He had a bad mother? That makes him not trust?" Edward struggled for the connection.

Kelryn tried to supply it. "Many times, he'd come to our cottage limping or too bruised to play or sit. Once, I remember, he couldn't use an arm for months. Lots of nights, he'd sleep with us or out in the streets or in a field somewhere. He never said so, but I'm sure his mother would send him away or beat him when she got upset. And we were all poor, even with a Papa to earn money, so there was lots to get upset about."

The story disturbed Nightfall, hitting too close to the truth. Kelryn's intentions still eluded him. It made little sense for her to talk about him rather than flirt with her victim, and she had so far managed only to evoke pity. Perhaps she did not realize that Edward's drive to help the downtrodden would only make him more sympathetic to the plight she had described.

"Oh, poor Sudian." Edward lowered his head, clearly sorry. "I didn't know."

"And that's probably for the best." Kelryn shifted, but Nightfall could not quite tell if she had touched the prince's hand or only made a soothing gesture. "I don't usually like lying, but I wouldn't tell him that you know. I think compassion and understanding make him uncomfortable, for the same reason as trust." She returned to the original question. "Whenever I saw her with him, his mother was always loving and merciful. It seemed like she was constantly apologizing for something, and she probably was. So, anyway, I think Sudian associates comforting with hitting. And caring with betrayal. So he doesn't trust anyone." She added quickly, "Except you, apparently. You must be really special."

Nightfall let the words wash over him, wondering how she had come so close. Not since Dyfrin had taken young Nightfall under his tutelage had anyone managed to guess so many details about his past. He could not help considering her explanation for his behavior, though he discarded it. He hated pity because it did not suit the strong and private person he had become, and he associated caring with betrayal because the two went hand in hand. It seemed eerie to hear the words in the voice of one who had reinforced the truth of the concept, she who had pretended to love then turned him over to a sorcerer instead. It only proved that she had known and fully understood the cruelties she inflicted upon him, and she had no shame or conscience.

Kelryn's explanation seemed to lose Edward, like a poorly crafted story with roots so outlandish even a child could not believe. "I couldn't imagine hitting *anyone*. How could a mother batter her own son?"

Kelryn shrugged. "Don't expect me to defend her. But I know from others that, when you're trying to feed and fend for self and family with no means to raise money except to sell yourself to strangers in front of children you hope will fare better than yourself but probably won't, a woman can get terribly mad and frustrated. Hit a stranger, and he hits back. Hit your own child, and he still has to love and depend on you."

"This happens often?"

"I doubt it. But I don't think Sudian is completely alone in this either."

Nightfall could imagine the light shining in Edward's innocent, blue eyes at the thought of a new cause to champion. To one who saw evil in slavery and striking of servants by masters, the thought of adults beating children had to burn like a brand. He waited for the prince's rallying call, the endless stream of committed words he could never translate into action. For the first time since he had seen Kelryn again, he smiled. Though hardly the worst he could wish on her, he appreciated that she would suffer through one of Edward's long, rambling tirades.

But the prince did not speak. Instead, he sat in a pensive silence, apparently considering all aspects of the problem for the first time. Despite the darkness, position and attitude told Nightfall that consideration, not shock, kept the prince uncharacteristically quiet. The disruption of the relationship between mother and child put the slave and servant beatings into a new perspective. Surely, Nightfall's story about slaves shunning freedom only added to the frenzy of thought taking form in Edward's head. No easy resolution here, at least not to a prince dedicated to goodness, right, and fairness to all.

To Nightfall, however, the solution came in a rush. In the past, he had tried to deal with, deny, or forget the ugliness that was a theory to Edward but an existence to him. Never before had he pressed forward to find an answer for other children in a similar quandary. Now it seemed obvious. The moment she chose to hit him, his mother had lost the privilege of raising a child. He should have run; or, better yet, some adult should have spirited him away to a farm where the hardship of more mouths to feed became balanced by more hands to tend the chores. He would have missed his mother's love, but he would have traded it for that of another who did not temper her affection with pain. As a bonus, he would have had a father and siblings and responsibilities that gained him praise as well as punishment. To consider the needs or feelings of the battering mother made no sense to him. Her intermittent love for him was no justification for the thing she had made him into, for the innocent lives he had taken with little remorse.

Nightfall pushed his own ideas aside, wondering how much had come from his speculation about Edward's thoughts. He could no longer blame his spree of murder on his mother; his own hand had wielded every weapon.

Kelryn changed the direction of the conversation, if not its subject. "Whatever he suffered as a child, Sudian's a good man. I only ever needed to mention a problem to him, and he handled it for me every time. Those he cares for, he cares for well."

Only Nightfall understood the understatement. The few men who dared to manhandle Kelryn had quietly disappeared, never known to be victims of the demon. Over time, Kelryn had become cautious about her complaints, making certain to hastily add, "But he's a nice person. I like him," when she feared he might take action with a punishment beyond the scope of the crime.

"He's certainly done well by me," Edward returned absently, thoughts still apparently on the previous topic.

Kelryn rose. "I need to head home. I've got practice in the morning. Thank you for a pleasant evening."

Prince Edward leapt to his feet, youth lending him a grace that nearly matched Kelryn's. "I'll walk you back.

The streets aren't safe for a beautiful, young lady out alone at night."

"Beautiful?" Kelryn took the first few steps, the agile movement adding to her loveliness. "Thank you. That means so much coming from a handsome man used to women of high breeding."

"All the cosmetics and perfumes in the world can't give a woman the natural radiance you possess."

Kelryn lowered her head modestly, her smile visible even through the night.

The maudlin, stilted line nauseated Nightfall, but the image even more so. As much as he hated the thought, the prince and the dancer looked good together.

Chapter 14

Three kings and their armies rode
To hunt the demon in the cold;
But where they've gone, no mortal knows.
Darkness comes where Nightfall goes.
                    —The Legend of Nightfall
                      Nursery rhyme, alternative verse

The dance hall looked familiar in the moonlight, its many
wings jutting like insect legs into the night. Nightfall
watched Prince Edward and Kelryn amble toward the
main doorway, still discussing him, though the theme had
changed from his history to his personality. They talked
about his loyalty, generosity, and the honesty that bordered on brutality. The description seemed so opposite
the usual hatred and grudging respect applied to him, he
repeatedly suspected they had switched topics. But always, just as he became certain he had missed a reference, he recognized the name "Sudian" or a specific that
could only apply to himself. All of the examples they
used were true, the motivations they ascribed to him far
less so. Prince Edward always found the best in anyone,
and it bothered Nightfall that Kelryn seemed sometimes
to know him better than he knew himself.

Despite his discomfort and the rage that waned only
slightly with time, Nightfall remained aware of all sound
and movement around him. As they passed the dancers'
quarters, something seemed amiss or, at least, different
from his inspection earlier that evening. A brief study
from a distance brought him the early details he sought.
The painted-closed shutters to Kelryn's window seemed
changed in contour, and he caught a glimpse of fragments
of a shiny substance on the ground beneath it. While the
prince and dancer headed for the entrance, Nightfall crept
up for a closer inspection.

As Nightfall drew nearer, he recognized glass shards

sparkling like dew amid the grass spears. He frowned at the oddity. Even castle glass was rarely thin enough to allow a clear view, and the thicker, more poorly made the pane, the more difficult to break. The dance hall windows had seemed particularly shoddy on first scrutiny. Also, the pieces seemed oddly shaped for glass: tiny droplets that clung to the greenery, long dribbles that dangled through the shutters, and flat oblong chunks that seemed more to have coalesced than to have shattered. Alert, he slunk to the window and picked up a particle. It felt slick and dry, just as he expected from glass, though colder to the touch than the late spring air could explain. Now, too, he saw the shutter. The bottom right corner had broken, and chunks of wood interspersed with the glass in similar patterns. Dribbles of glass striped his vision, closing off a hole large enough to admit a person.

Dread began as a gnawing in Nightfall's gut, growing into a pain fed by his own concern as well as the oathbond. The image of the horse's head splintering near the swamp filled his mind's eye and could not be suppressed. Ritworth's spell had left gore in patterns no mortal weapon could have reaped. Patterns like the shutter and the window.

Agony swept over Nightfall, nearly paralyzing him. He glanced at Prince Edward and Kelryn, just in time to watch the main door swing closed. *Too late.* Nightfall knew that by the time he caught up, raced inside, and fought his way past the guards, anything could have happened. If the Iceman had squeezed through, Nightfall could do so as well. He might more easily assess the danger from the window than the door; surely whatever trap Ritworth might have set would spring so as to catch someone entering in a normal fashion. He just had to hope he could appraise the situation and remedy or warn in time. His fear washed cold at the realization that neither he nor Edward had carried obvious weaponry to dinner. The two remaining throwing daggers he had secreted on his person would have to suffice.

Nightfall crouched, gradually rising until he could just peer through the window. Across the room, the door remained closed. The dresser/table filled the corner nearest it. The largest pieces of the swan lay piled on its center, the splinters and shards around them. Beside it perched a glass decanter of a grayish, translucent liquid that he guessed might be a watery glue. The matching chair rested slightly askew, a dress folded neatly over its back. The bed lay flush with the wall to Nightfall's right. To his left, he caught a poorly angled view of the inset closet, barely able to make out the edges of fabric from garments set within it. Nightfall frowned. Nothing seemed specifically out of place, which only made him more uncomfortable. Magical ambushes he would not necessarily see; and, if Ritworth wove his danger in the hallway, Nightfall might already be too late. He raised his head fully for a more direct view. At that moment, the door lock clicked open. Something inside the closet moved.

Standing outside the door to Kelryn's chambers, Prince Edward could not recall having enjoyed a night more. Their conversation did not matter. Her attentiveness to his words and genuine interest had spurred his emotions as few other things could. Since his mother's death, his every conversation seemed to elicit only servant-loyal boredom or disdain from his brother or father. Kelryn had attended his words with a brightness that revealed fascination, and he clung to her words just as tightly. And, always, the image of Kelryn's smoothly rounded curves remained burned in his memory. He had never seen a woman naked before, except in art, and the painters and weavers had never captured the perfect reality of breasts and thighs. The mental picture drove Edward to the need to chisel the female form from marble, to capture the beauty no previous artisan had managed.

Kelryn jerked the key from the lock, pocketed it, and shoved the bolt aside. She turned to face Edward before opening the panel. "Thank you so much for the dinner and the company. Please tell Sudian good night for me, too."

"The company was my pleasure as well." Prince Edward pushed open the door to allow Kelryn access. It admitted a bar of light from candles in sconces in the hallway. Movement caught Edward's attention at once. A man unfolded a long, lean frame from the closet inset, the sorcerer's face sparking instant recognition.

"You're dead, boy!" Ritworth's arm arched, and he grumbled the familiar, sour syllables of his ice spell.

Prince Edward shoved Kelryn aside and grabbed for the chair, moving from the hips first as his fight instructor taught. In situations requiring instant evasion, that part of the body tended to lag. Still, he doubted he could outmaneuver magic. As quickly, Kelryn pulled a tie at her throat. Her dress dropped to the floor in a rumpled heap, revealing flimsy undergarments that somehow made her seem more naked than flesh alone.

Her maneuver obviously surprised Ritworth, who hesitated just long enough for Edward to seize and hurl the chair.

The sorcerer dodged and swore as he finished the casting. Magic swept the desktop, an unfocused slash of light that flung swan shards to the floor. The chair grazed Ritworth's shoulder, staggering him, then crashed against the window with enough force to shatter both. Splinters and chunks rained, thunking to the floor amid the higher pitched slam and rattle of glass. From outside, a dagger whizzed by Ritworth's chin. The hilt bounced from Kelryn's arm, then it clattered to the hallway floor. Suddenly filled with ice, the decanter exploded, flinging slivers and triangles of glass. Kelryn screamed. A guard's answering shout floated from down the hallway, and feet pounded the wooden floor, headed in their direction.

Kelryn shrieked again and again, exploding into a mindless, berserk panic that seemed all the more crazed for her calm diversion a moment earlier.

Though he noticed the change, Prince Edward did not waste time assessing damage. The sorcerer had come for him, and any attempt to console or aid Kelryn would only place her in the line of fire. The sooner he dispatched Ritworth, the safer they all became. He charged the Iceman, fragments of swan, decanter, and window crunching beneath his boots.

The sorcerer caught his balance just in time to notice the danger rushing down on him. He twisted, casting, the need to dodge stealing accuracy. Ice sprayed from his fingertips and sparkled like dust motes in the room's center, a clean miss. Hoping to prevent the harsh vocalizations that seemed necessary for the spell, Edward drove a punch into the sorcerer's throat that doubled him over. Seizing Ritworth's neck in one hand and a leg in the other, he hurled the sorcerer toward the wall.

Ritworth sailed through the air, grunting guttural noises that were not quite words. He flapped. A hand's breadth from the wall, he swerved abruptly, flying toward the broken window at a speed that sent him crashing through the last clinging shards of glass and wood. Just outside, he collided with a man, and both collapsed in a heap to the dirt. Edward ran to the window. As he peered through, blood splashed his face from the battle outside. He recoiled, wiping it from his eyes. By the time he looked again, Ritworth was soaring for the sky. Nightfall crouched amid a puddle of broken glass and ruptured shutters, shards sparkling in his red-brown hair. He clutched a dagger flecked with the sorcerer's blood.

"Sudian?" Surprised by the presence of his squire, Prince Edward reached through the opening to give assistance.

A man spoke from the doorway. "What's going on?"

Edward turned his head, arm still extended. A hefty guard waited just outside, wearing dance hall red and black livery, hand tensed on the hilt of his short sword.

Kelryn cowered in a corner, using her dress as a shield and sobbing uncontrollably. Blood trickled from her leg.

"Did this man hurt you?" The guard indicated the prince by inclining his head.

Widened eyes locked on the window through which Ritworth had disappeared, Kelryn shook her head. Relaxing slightly, she managed speech. "Prince Edward of Alyndar? Dear Father, no. He saved my life." She managed a smile for Edward that made him feel warm from chin to knees, though the obvious pain in her tone bothered him. "A stranger attacked us. A sorcerer. He fled through the window."

Nightfall chose that moment to crawl into the room, ignoring Edward's proffered hand.

The guard stiffened, drawing his sword. "Is this the one?"

Kelryn stiffened, swiveling to look. At the sight of Nightfall, she breathed a relieved sigh. "Oh, no. That's the prince's squire. The sorcerer is gone, I hope." Her own assessment helped compose her. She donned her dress methodically. Limping to the desk, she studied the chaos of glass on its surface, then leaned against it without daring to sit.

The guard sheathed his weapon, looking nonplussed. Apparently, it bothered him that so much damage could occur before he responded to screaming. "Oh. Well. We'll search around outside. See if we can find him. What'd he look like?"

Kelryn gave a passable description; and, having seen the man twice now, Edward filled in the details. The guard exited, leaving Kelryn, Edward, and Nightfall alone.

Nightfall shook out his cloak, and a shower of glass fragments tumbled to the floor to join the others. He brushed more from his hair with flicks of his hand.

"There's a broom in the closet," Kelryn said. "Let me get it."

"No." Edward went to Kelryn's side. "You're wounded. Sudian can take care of sweeping." He glanced at Nightfall to indicate that, although he had spoken casually, he meant the words as a direct order. Leaving his squire to tend to the glass, Edward hefted Kelryn, laying her gently on the bed. "Where does it hurt?"

Kelryn gathered the fabric of her dress to reveal her right thigh. The sight of the silk sliding along the fair skin gave Edward a pleasure that instantly channeled to guilt. He felt immoral enjoying the beauty of one in pain, especially when that injury came about because of an attack by his enemy. Soon, the dress lifted enough to reveal a blood-smeared, jagged gash in Kelryn's flesh, surely caused by the destruction of the decanter by magic. Edward used a handkerchief to clean and tend the wound.

Nightfall busied himself sweeping up every crumb and flake, pausing only to retrieve his thrown dagger.

"I guess I won't be dancing for a bit." Kelryn mused as Edward worked. "Did you know that man?"

"I'm afraid I did," Edward replied honestly as he probed the injury for remaining pieces of glass. He did not miss his squire's sudden, warning glance. As promised, he would not reveal Nightfall's natal talent. "You're right about him being a sorcerer, and he wants to kill us for some reason. I'm sorry I got you involved."

"I'm involved?" All of Kelryn's rabid terror returned in an instant. She curled into herself, eyes suddenly moist again.

Edward blamed his ministrations for her discomfort and suffered as much for inflicting it. "I'm afraid we can't chance that you are." He met Kelryn's hazel eyes, deep and dark in the half-light. "I want you to stay with us. We can protect you until we've got him safely in the hands of guardsmen."

Kelryn glanced at Nightfall, and a strange expression crossed her features briefly. She caught Edward's hand, eyes skittish as a cornered deer's. "I'd like that very much."

Though her grip felt cold and clammy with sweat, Prince Edward enjoyed the contact.

That night, Prince Edward arranged for them to sleep in shifts, but Nightfall did not bother to awaken the prince when his had ended. He could not sleep. In fact, the restlessness grew into an endless, driving need he could not identify to satisfy. He felt possessed by a thousand contrasting desires. Unidentifiable things in his core goaded him to slaughter Kelryn while the prince slept; others nearly as strong directed him to curl against her for comfort and warmth. Another part of him wanted to surrender to it all, to kill or abandon woman and prince and allow the oath-bond to have him. The same survival instinct that had kept him alive this long kicked in to fight the latter, but the others swirled through his mind in a dizzying chant. His mind told him to follow the course of necessity and patience, to work through the oath-bond and wait for the opportunity to serve his hatred without compromising Alyndar's prince. Yet, Nightfall's heart supported the opposite choice, the same that, as a child, had driven him to butcher the man who had killed his mother. The image of Kelryn blood-covered and screaming would not leave his thoughts, and the demon-force told him to dominate and torture, to let the death she deserved become the ultimate mercy.

Nightfall recoiled from his thoughts, finding them as ugly as those that had made him despise Kelryn in the first place. Dyfrin had taught him to control that villainous rage that went beyond justice. "Kill enemies when you have to," the Keevainian had once said. "But do so with calm dispatch. Uncontrolled violence is doomed to failure, in its consequences as well as its actions. Emotion is the enemy of rationality and logic. When it becomes strong enough to guide your conduct, your life is no longer your own."

Edward slept soundly through Nightfall's considerations. Kelryn, however, grew fretful as night slipped toward its darkest hours. She rolled and whimpered in her sleep, apparently pursued by nightmares as disquieting as Nightfall's thoughts. Occasionally, she cried out, wordless noises of fear that miraculously did not awaken Prince Edward. Distracted by her movement and vocalizations, Nightfall felt drowned beneath a sea of conflicting emotions; and the path of control and personal right seemed blurry as a distant mountain peak in fog. He had no idea what course of action would serve him best, and that loss of direction whipped him nearly to panic. He found himself contemplating how his actions would affect others as well, and the foreignness of this consideration only added to the turmoil.

At length, Kelryn's thrashing ceased. She cringed into a corner, like an infant in a womb; and her strangled sobs became comprehensible words. "No, no, no. No. Sorcerer. Blood. Pain." Her fists tightened, fingers blanching; and her tone changed from fearful to desperately angry. The intensity of emotion made him certain she was reliving trauma, not just dreaming. "He's a vicious murderer. Kill him. Kill him. Oh, just kill him." She flopped to her other side, entreaties lapsing into silence.

Nightfall's heart quickened, all concentration driven

from him. He could only guess at the reference and meaning, could only surmise that she wrestled with a past reality that filled her head when sleep emptied it of the mundane. His own name fit perfectly into the scene. He could imagine her battling scruples, first denying the sorcerer his identity from conscience, then recalling that the man she protected was an assassin who deserved to die. He wondered at what price she had finally sold him.

That concept reawakened the uncertainties that had, so far, kept sleep at bay. One thing seemed certain. He needed to sort through the boil of idea and emotion assaulting him without Kelryn's internal strife to disturb him. He needed to be alone.

Pulling a cloak over his sleeping gown, Nightfall slipped across the room and out the inn room door. He had no specific idea where to go, though he maintained enough presence of mind to realize it could not be far. He suspected Ritworth would need time to ponder his failure as well as the gash Nightfall's dagger had torn through his side and hip as he sailed through the window. Still, Nightfall would remain within watching distance of all entrances to the inn or Edward's room.

Nightfall padded down the empty corridor and the exit stairs. Many things about the previous night seemed as maddeningly illogical as his thoughts, and he tried to draw it all into one coherent explanation. Kelryn had honestly seemed happily surprised to see and recognize him, yet he had once believed in her love for him also. She could fool him as no one else had managed. He would have to draw his conclusions based on other things than the woman's reactions. Her sleep-talk, at least, seemed more revealing.

Nightfall pushed open the outer door. The late spring air, filled with the scents of flowers and new greenery, helped to clear his head. As the fog lifted, his senses became more attuned and he recognized the soft patter of irregular, trailing footsteps. He slunk into the shadows.

Shortly, the door edged open. Apparently awakened by her own night-demons, Kelryn peered through, eyes scanning the stretches of pasture, trees, and roads between surrounding buildings. Nightfall waited only until she limped outside and closed the door quietly behind her. Then he seized one of her forearms, wrenching it against the small of her back, and wrapped his arm around her throat. He pressed a dagger to her cheek. "Don't make a sound."

Kelryn choked off a scream with the help of pressure from Nightfall's arm.

"Haven't you done me enough harm? What more do you want from me?" he demanded.

Given their current position, the question seemed absurd. Kelryn rolled her gaze to Nightfall. "Marak, please. The last thing I would do is harm you. I love you."

Unconsciously, Nightfall tightened his grip. Red rage washed his vision, and he waited for it to pass.

Kelryn gasped. "You're hurting me."

"Consider it payback." Despite his words, Nightfall loosened his grip slightly as the world came back into focus. "In the morning, you're going to tell Edward you appreciate his protection, but you'd rather stay with relatives. Then you leave and call off your sorcerer."

Kelryn cringed at the words. "*My* sorcerer?" The incredulity in her tone seemed impossible to feign. "*My* sorcerer? You can't possibly believe I would choose the company of vicious killers."

The words sounded ludicrous from one who had once had a serious relationship with the primary criminal of the continent. "You chose *my* company."

Kelryn defended. "Before I knew who you were, I fell in love with you. Love defies logic. Besides, you never killed the innocent or killed without conscience the way sorcerers do. You liked to believe you were the demon everyone called you, but you never were. You never could be. That's how I knew you wouldn't carry through on your threat to butcher me."

Kelryn's assertion enraged Nightfall, placing in question even the persona he believed to be his own. The demon seed. The godless murderer. He had little choice but to prove her wrong. To do otherwise would deny his very existence. Nightfall jerked Kelryn's arm, spinning her to the ground. He crouched over her, one knee planted against her chest and the dagger hovering at her windpipe. "I have no mercy for traitors. Don't mention love again. You betrayed me. You sold me to a sorcerer for what? Gold? Power? A trinket?" Nightfall's own words gave him pause. Wars of conscience did not end cheaply, and surely trapping the most hunted and hated criminal on the continent should have bought her something more than another dancing job and a dingy room in a Noshtillian hall. Nothing in her quarters had suggested a hidden fortune. Yet, it would not be the first time Nightfall had met a person whose wealth had come too easily, who had spent every copper within months.

"What?" Kelryn stiffened beneath him, favoring her injured leg. "Marak, listen to me. I know how it looks—"

Nightfall increased his weight so the pressure on her chest cut off her protestations. "Nothing more. I'm not going to listen to any more of your lies. If you won't tell Edward you're leaving, I'll just kill you and tell him you slipped away in the night."

Kelryn gasped for breath, squirming to free her lungs from his weight.

Nightfall dropped his mass back to normal, still feeling torn by the maelstrom of emotions and possible tactics. He could no longer suppress the reality he had tried so hard to deny when circumstances had finally brought him face to face again with Kelryn. Through all the hardships, the promise of revenge had propelled him long after other reasons for struggle had failed. It had proven stronger even than the fiery instinct for survival that had kept him alive on the streets. Yet, when his chance had finally come, he had frozen like a child caught stealing his first copper. It seemed as if Dyfrin's teachings had chosen that moment to come together at once, fully coherent from the surface to the core of their morality. As much as he tried to convince himself otherwise, he could not have killed Kelryn at that time. Nor, he doubted, could he do so now. The thing that had paralyzed him in her quarters was love. The hatred for her had grown and flourished, yet the love he now despised as much would not leave him.

Kelryn inhaled and exhaled several times before speaking. She kept her eyes fixed on his, measuring the effect of each word. "I would rather die by your hand than a sorcerer's. I once saw a sorcerer at work. For all the rumors about you and despite your threats, I don't think you could inflict worse."

The recollection of Ritworth's magical torture remained powerful enough to send a shudder through Nightfall. She had a point he could not deny. Though legend stated otherwise, he had kept his few killings, whether planned or in sudden self-defense, as quick and painless as possible. Still, it was not his way to reveal weakness either. "Don't dare me to hurt you. You won't like what you get." In spite of his words, he made no move toward violence.

Kelryn did not flinch, her gaze remaining rock steady. "Do what you feel you must. I've always been direct with you, and I won't stop now. The truth: I'm scared to death of that sorcerer. I was ready to fight at Ned's side until I figured out what Ritworth was, then I froze like a helpless child. I can't face him alone. I *am* going to accept Ned's hospitality and guardianship. I swear to you, to the holy Father, to any thing or deity you choose that I mean him and you no harm."

Nightfall pursed his lips, trapped, uncertain of his next course of action. The oath-bond began a mild buzz that steadily grew. Feeling certain of Edward's current security, Nightfall tried to analyze the reasons for the magic's awakening. The problem, he believed, came of his vow to follow Edward's word only except where it conflicted with his safety. Clearly, Edward wanted Kelryn present, and Nightfall no longer felt certain she posed a danger, at least not to the prince.

Kelryn raised her brows, still sprawled on the ground. "Would you like that explanation now?" Though she offered, she seemed reluctant to give it, as if it might prove nearly as ugly as the truth Nightfall believed he already knew.

"No." All of Nightfall's resentment returned instantly. Torn in a thousand different directions, he did not want more to consider now. Kelryn had betrayed him. There could be no other answer. She had had months to concoct a story, enough time to make it believable. He would not give her the tools to destroy him again; the love that unmanned him might also force him to believe. And that would give her the opportunity to betray him again. He had suffered that agony once and never more.

"I'll wait till you're ready, then." Kelryn fidgeted, still seeking a comfortable position pinned beneath knee and dagger. Though she did not speak the words, her inflection implied: *I'll wait until we're both ready.*

Grudgingly, Nightfall backed away, freeing Kelryn. "These are the ground rules. First, you don't hurt Edward, talk, or direct him into any action that might make him harm himself, or allow or arrange for others to do so. Second, you do not address me unless absolutely necessary." He paused, trying to anticipate loopholes and other possible needs. "Third, keep your damn clothes on."

Kelryn sat up carefully, rubbing at her neck. "I agree to all terms, so long as you allow me to change and bathe, at least in private. May the Father suffocate me in the deepest part of his underworld should I do anything against those rules."

Nightfall did not wait for Kelryn to finish but slipped quietly into the night. At first, he just wanted to escape, to let the summer breezes clear his mind of a tangled lump of idea he had no patience to sort. A thought managed to trickle forward from the back of his mind, a memory of his discussion with Finndmer the Fence. He had already written off the money he had spent for swampland. As Nightfall, he could not have tolerated the deception, but Sudian had no reputation to protect. Petty vengeance had to give way before greater and more pressing needs. He had learned much from his discussion in the woodsman's cottage, including that a man could become landed through marriage. Buying property had failed, and this new consideration moved in to take its place. Two of his five months had already passed, leaving him no closer to fulfilling the oath-bond than at the day of its casting.

Nightfall recalled a night when the wind howled, flinging hail hard enough to sting welts across exposed flesh. He had huddled amid stored hay in a farmer's loft, the warmth of animal presences rescuing him from a storm that had taken less experienced children and beggars permanently from the streets. He ate well, having stolen his meal from one of the many feasts in honor of the first-born child of the aging baron of Schiz. He remembered contemplating the irony beneath the sounds of hail hammering the roof and the soft conversations of other homeless who chose the barn as their refuge. He did not seek their company. Had those below discovered him, they would have attempted to take his food and found him far more competent at defending it than his age implied. The rich celebrated the birth of a child by gorging on and wasting food while the poor desperately hunted for scraps to sustain one more.

Nightfall knew that serving Edward's best interests meant more than just clinging to the prince's side. He had an obligation to get the prince landed, and that would require more time gleaning information. He did not wholly trust Kelryn, but his emotions and the oath-bond goaded him to believe her three promises at least. It seemed unlikely that Ritworth would attack again so soon, wounded and fatigued from his ordeal. So far, Nightfall's attempts to ply his usual sources of information had resulted in disaster: suspicion, deceit, and even outright violence. He could no longer count on the underground to supply him, but the knowledge he considered now did not require shady sources. Anyone with idle time to gossip might know what age the baron's daughter had attained and whether she had already pledged herself to marriage. Nightfall's memory suggested she and Edward would come close enough in years to raise no questions with their union, and he believed an event as huge as the wedding of a baron's daughter would have reached his attention. Now, all he needed to do was discover the details and start the process.

If only I could arrange for him to see her naked. Nightfall smiled at the thought, recalling Edward's overreaction to Kelryn in her undergarments. He headed for the nearest bar.

Prince Edward, Nightfall, and Kelryn rode quietly from Noshtillan the following morning. It seemed best to foil Ritworth as much as possible by moving as often as they could. So, Edward purchased a third horse, a handsome black. Its carriage and glossy coat suited the prince, and Nightfall approved of its color and training. Kelryn rode the chestnut; the paucity of supplies obviated the need for a pack horse. They strapped gear behind each saddle, and the spade rode atop the prince's personals.

As they journeyed along the earthen roadway between Noshtillan and her sister cities, Nightfall left Kelryn and Edward to their happy chatter. To his relief, they talked about the prince's ideals rather than about himself or his past, a topic he hoped they had exhausted. When Edward's ramblings glided into their usual impossible idealism, Kelryn gently bumped the conversation back to reality. Nightfall appreciated her efforts grudgingly, wishing he had her knack for diverting discussion without appearing to contradict or question.

Fatigue enclosed Nightfall's thoughts like a fog, making new ideas nearly impossible. Instead, he ran through the information he had obtained the previous night. Duchess-heir Willafrida had turned twenty that past winter, still without a husband. The reasons given for her lack of a spouse had been manyfold, and Nightfall had not yet quite decided which to believe. Several men stated that her common looks and plump, small-breasted figure had sent highborn men searching elsewhere. Others, like Nightfall, believed those who shopped for appearances shallow enough to court her for money alone. Most of these blamed her vanity or a personality that seemed to border on silly, the behavior that served some beautiful women well, those who relied on their looks and never bothered with social graces. One of the serving maids insisted that the duchess-heir's father had become so protective of his only daughter that he screened potential suitors to a ridiculous extreme.

Questioning had also brought forth details about a handful of suitors, the most promising a wealthy goldsmith called Hoson. Depending on whom he chose to believe, the couple had sustained an off and on relationship for two years, they were madly in love, or they had been spotted together periodically. In all cases, however, his name came up before that of any other potential future baron.

They continued toward Schiz amid a light drizzle, the clop of hooves a soothing, steady beat beneath Kelryn's and Edward's conversation. Until he visited the bar in Noshtillan, Nightfall had forgotten how quickly rumors spread in the south. Already, several people had recognized him as the squire of the prince attacked by a sorcerer. He had had to suffer through a dozen folk remedies for thwarting magic, many of which were the same as those he had heard homewomen used to protect their families from the demon, Nightfall. Yet one significant possibility had come even from that distraction. A travel-stained warrior alone in the corner of the bar had mentioned a friend who lived in Schiz. Called Brandon Magebane, the Schizian had proclaimed a personal crusade against users of magic and their murders. Apparently, he had a natal talent he did not bother to hide, one that allowed him to disenchant spells and, on rare occasions, to place this same power into objects for others to use. According to the traveler, the Magebane would spend a year or two concentrating his ability into stones or coins, enough to give his companions each a few defenses. Then, they would actively hunt a sorcerer.

That conversation preoccupied Nightfall as they headed toward the country of Schiz. Brandon's Noshtillian friend had just returned from such a venture, this one unsuccessful. It meant the Magebane's companions had used their special stones. From experience, Nightfall knew that natal talents used on oneself cost little in time or effort, just a moment of thought. Apparently, however, those who could direct their abilities against others or into items required more elaborate procedures, limited by fatigue. It might take two months or longer for Brandon to construct another of his disenchanting items, but the man Nightfall met in Noshtillan believed his partner might still have one or two stones left over from the previous pursuit. He had suggested Nightfall might purchase those remaining to help protect his master.

At the time and now, Nightfall's thoughts sprang off in a different direction. If he could attain one of those pre-

cious, perfect stones, he could use it to free himself from
the oath-bond. He smiled, the expression seeming unnatural through all the pain, physical and emotional, he had
suffered or inflicted in the last few days. Free, he could
start his life over, unburdened by the responsibility of
guarding and directing an idealist in a venal world who
flaunted money in front of thieves and begged the company of traitors. Free, he could leave Sudian and the enemy sorcerer behind, as dead as his many personae. Free,
he could become someone else again. Who, he did not
know nor what trade he would take. He felt certain only
that he had no wish to return to what he had once been.

This consideration followed him through the day of
travel that brought them to the duke's city of Schiz. Narrow streets glazed with evening gray forced Nightfall to
ride behind his master and their companion, and the horse
traffic drove pedestrians to the storefronts. Nightfall
chose the cheaper of Schiz' two inns for its proximity to
the goldsmith's shop, though his reasons seemed unclear
even to himself. Once free, he no longer needed to work
at landing Prince Edward Nargol of Alyndar, and the information gleaned to accomplish that mission no longer
mattered. Once again, he would completely rewrite his
obligations and loyalties, this time in any manner he
chose. First, he believed, he would locate Dyfrin and re-
pay a long overdue debt of gratitude to the only person in
his life who had helped him for no other reason than
kindness and no thought of reward.

The He-Ain't-Here Tavern was a red stone building
near the western edge of town with a paddock for guest
horses in lieu of a stable and a handful of rooms for rent.
Nightfall knew every detail of its interior. As the merchant, Balshaz, he had found need to travel to Schiz only
infrequently and had stayed in the more upper class inn
farther south. As polio-stricken Frihiat, a Schizian odd-
jobber, he had routinely spent his coppers in the tavern,
buying drinks for friends when he found steady employ-
ment. Well-liked for his story-telling ability, he could
usually drink even when his own purse emptied to lint.

Nightfall stripped the tack, placing it carefully into the
nearby hut with its rings and wooden stands for this pur-

pose. He over-tipped the servant on duty, as usual, hoping for a competent cleaning of their gear as well as the youngster's goodwill. Money came easily to an able thief, and Dyfrin had taught him to share his riches, at least, very well. Risking his life in the name of trust or kindness seemed another thing altogether. Every man and woman had a price. If he could meet it with money, he saw no need to bother with anything else.

Nightfall loosed the three horses into the paddock. They entered cautiously, whuffling the scent of strangers sharing their pasture. The bay set straight to grazing, and its calm soon spread to the chestnut. The black horse ate also. Still adjusting to its own companions, the black trumpeted a warning. The other five animals in the corral bolted, circling the fences in a wild run that Prince Edward's horses joined.

Nightfall watched the casual but powerful pump of leg muscles as the horses charged playfully around the paddock before settling into a herd. He yawned. The sleepless turmoil of the previous night exhausted him, and it made more sense for him to speak with the Magebane early, before Kelryn or Edward missed him. With the common room at its busiest, Ritworth would not dare to attack. So far, he had only come for them when he believed them alone, trapped or weaponless. By heading out alone in the dusk, Nightfall placed his own person at far more risk than the prince.

The oath-bond remained quiet, apparently satisfied with the assessment. Nightfall trotted through familiar streets, unused to watching the scenery pass so quickly. Frihiat's affected limp had slowed his pace to a restful coast that forced him to notice minutiae. Though in the guise of Frihiat less often than many of his other aliases, he had learned the streets and byways of Schiz so much better. Within a few turns, he came to the cottage the traveler had named as belonging to the Magebane.

Nightfall studied it for clues to the man who dwelt within. It looked exactly like so many other wood and thatch cottages, except for the delicate brown stain he had used to protect, seal, and beautify the construction. A chaotic jumble of flowers sprouted from beds on either side of the doorway, and straight rows of vegetation filled the rectangular area between his home and the one behind it. Nightfall surmised that, when it came to important matters, he would find Brandon Magebane as competent as his food garden, as frenetic as his flowers when it came to play.

Nightfall approached the door with more trepidation than he expected. His soul rode on the Magebane's talent, but only in a positive sense. If he got the trinket, he gained everything. If he did not, then nothing changed. He paused before the door in thought, trying to decide his course of action should he succeed in breaking free of Gilleran's binding. He wanted to run, free as a horse unlocked from too long a stay in a dark, dusty stable. But his conscience would not let him. Much as he hated the concept, he could no longer escape the realization that his tie to Edward had grown beyond the limits of the sorcerer's magic. He would not remain a servant, but he would see Edward landed, if possible, or safely home. He would do it, not out of obligation, but from friendship.

The concept pleased and puzzled Nightfall at once. To fetter himself with allegiances seemed as dangerous and nonsensical as tying himself to a post and waiting for Ritworth to claim him. Yet he finally understood Dyfrin's explanation for assisting a desperate, demon-child named Sudian: "When you willingly choose another's troubles as your own, you stop surviving and start living."

The door swung open, though Nightfall had not yet knocked. A man in his mid-twenties stood in the doorway. Muddy curls perched atop a head that seemed too large for his shoulders, and blue-gray eyes studied Nightfall over a crooked nose and thick lips. "Are you sunning yourself, like a turtle, on my porch? Or did you come for a reason?" Despite the words, his tone emerged friendly. In the grayness of evening, the joke fell flat.

Nightfall lowered and raised his head respectfully. "Are you Brandon Magebane?"

"I am." The stranger continued to focus on Nightfall's every movement, perhaps watching for him to cast some type of magic. Although sorcerers could not afford to trust one another to band against him, a single one could come in secret to try to catch him alone and unprepared for a fight.

"My name is Sudian, squire of younger Prince Edward Nargol of Alyndar." Nightfall imitated a shy page, forced to recite a full title despite being apprehensive in the presence of a superior. He believed this act would work better than any attempt to cow the Magebane with privileges and vanity. Any man who voluntarily riled sorcerers would not intimidate easily. "I'm sorry to bother you, sir. I was sent by a friend of yours in Noshtillan. Tall, quiet, middle-aged fellow with a scar." He drew a line from the corner of his right eye to his chin to indicate the positioning of the injury.

"That would be Gatiwan." Brandon stepped back to give Nightfall room to enter. "Come in. Come in, please."

Nightfall obeyed hesitantly, still keeping with his act. He found himself in a sitting room lined with shelves that held sundry knickknacks from all corners of the world. In contrast, the stools and crates that served as furniture seemed drab.

"Sit." Brandon waved broadly to indicate Nightfall's choice of location.

Nightfall chose a threadbare stool nearest the door, and Brandon sat on a cushioned crate.

"Now, why did Gatiwan send you?"

"Well, my master and I have gotten attacked by a sorcerer. Twice now. Gatiwan said you might have something that could help us win the battle."

Brandon laughed. "Gatiwan, dear Gatiwan. As usual, generous to a fault when it comes to my property." Though he named it a failing, he smiled to show he found it endearing rather than insulting. "He told you about the magic-breaking stones, I presume?"

Nightfall nodded. "He said you might have a few left."

"I have one," Brandon admitted. Throughout it all, his eyes never left Nightfall, though whether as habitual protection against those who might wish him dead or from suspicion, Nightfall could not guess. Brandon's tone had suggested a condition, so Nightfall remained silent, waiting for the Magebane to continue. If he needed to gather three hundred silver again, he would find a way, even if it meant stealing it back from Finndmer.

That thought set the oath-bond to a dull ache that he suppressed with the promise he would find a less Nightfall-like solution.

"Tell me what you need it for. Give me a reason to let you have it."

Nightfall considered the motivation behind the request. Under usual circumstances, Brandon collected the stones until he had enough for him and friends to challenge and, hopefully, destroy a sorcerer. Gatiwan had indicated that it took months for the creation of a stone. Therefore, it made sense for Brandon to hesitate to surrender a single one. Nightfall guessed the Magebane would respond better to cause than helplessness. "Well, we've fought Ritworth twice, and both times we came close to winning." He amended. "Actually, we're alive. So I guess we did win in that sense. But he's got this spell that kills instantly. I think if we could neutralize that, even once, we might manage to kill him."

Brandon's brows rose, and he seemed pleased by the answer. "How could I deny a stone that might bring double good: slaughter a sorcerer and save a prince?" His eyebrows returned to their normal contour, then beetled lower. "How confident do you feel about handling this Ritworth? Might it not prove better to wait a year and let me and the Magekillers handle him?"

Nightfall shook his head vigorously, seeing his last chance at freedom slipping away. "We've injured him twice, and he's hurt us. I believe it's an equal match. One small, unexpected object could make all the difference. I don't think we can hold out for a year." *In three months, I'll become a tiny, suffering piece of another sorcerer, if this one doesn't catch me first.*

Brandon frowned, the expression making his lips seem huge. He tapped a finger against their puffiness. "Very well, Sudian. Here." He pulled what appeared to be a common street stone from his pocket and offered it to Nightfall. "When you need it, squeeze it. It'll glow red. Concentrate on the source of the magic. When the stone turns blue, it's working. Once finished, it goes back to gray. It works only one time."

"Thank you." Nightfall took the stone but kept it in his hand. "Now what do I owe you?"

Brandon rose, dismissing the question with a wave. "It costs me nothing but a delay in my next hunt." Again he scanned Nightfall's reaction, apparently trying to elicit guilt should the squire take the stone without feeling reasonably certain it would give him the edge he needed.

To his surprise, Nightfall did know a mild stab of remorse. He had spoken only truth, yet he had deceived since he had no plans to use the item directly against Ritworth. Still, he had not lied completely. Once free of the terms of the oath-bond, many more means of fighting or running from the Iceman would become open to him, so it would give him the edge he needed. He only hoped it would prove enough. As free as the Iceman had been with the ice spell, Nightfall suspected it was a recent addition in small danger of becoming lost to a weakening soul-bond, at least in the near future. He put the stone in his pocket and rose. "Thank you," he repeated. "Are you sure there's nothing I can get you in exchange?"

"Nothing is necessary." Brandon headed for the door, then stopped with his hand on the knob. "Someday, Sudian, when your problem's handled, you'll come on a hunt with us?"

"Of course," Nightfall promised without an iota of sincerity. *If I ever go completely insane.* He stepped out into the night amid the mingled perfume of the flowers, and Brandon Magebane closed the door behind him.

The urge to use the gem immediately seized Nightfall, but he had learned much patience researching situations, targets, and victims. To invoke the stored talent this near its creator would risk the Magebane's wrath. Instead, he made no gesture toward the stone at all, just headed down the road back in the direction he had come. Many thoughts swirled through his mind, goading him to question situations that would have seemed obvious in the past. A year ago, he would have taken Brandon's stone and laughed at the Magebane's foolishness at not demanding payment. Or, perhaps, he would have considered all possible secondary reasons for Brandon to have refused money, from the conviction that he had placed Nightfall in his debt to the possibility the stone had other purposes than that stated.

Now, Nightfall felt the obligation he would once have glibly discarded. He had always appreciated the fear, suspicion, and danger that forced sorcerers to remain loners and not communicate with one another. He also understood the need for most of those cursed with a natal talent to remain equally isolated; the fewer who knew about their ability, the less likely a sorcerer would discover it. Yet, if he used the example of the Healer in Delfor, not all chose the same strategy as himself. Brandon Magebane had a point Nightfall could not help but consider. *Why shouldn't the gifted band together against sorcerers?* Considered in that context, it made perfect sense. The natally talented gained no advantage from harming one another, as sorcerers did, so they could work in teams without challenge. By pooling resources, abilities, and knowledge, they might drive away or destroy enough sorcerers to make life safe for them again. Nightfall had a natal talent. He gained more peace every time Brandon's Magekillers hunted. Perhaps, someday, he would pay back that favor.

Unconsciously, Nightfall kneaded the stone through the fabric of his tunic. Nothing could compare with the freedom it would buy him, a life to start over without ties or bonds to fools; and, more importantly, without a wizard controlling his soul. Yet the responsibilities would not wholly disappear. Nightfall had thought long and hard about his relationship with Edward, had already promised himself he would either see the landing through or escort him safely home. He had not dragged the gentle, young innocent to the far side of the continent to abandon him to every schemer who saw silver in theft, scam, or kidnapping. Whatever the boy's father had forced Nightfall to do by magic did not reflect on Edward. The prince deserved to see the godly side, not the demon side, of a squire he had treated well. And Nightfall found satisfaction in the consternation it would cost King Rikard and Gilleran to receive back the idealist unharmed with no way to catch or follow the master criminal they had once held prisoner. *Let them sweat in their beds every night wondering when the knife will come.*

Nightfall slipped from the main pathway into a short, black alleyway between a house marked as the tailor's and another that bore no distinguishing features. It seemed strange to moralize, especially over a spoiled prince and a situation that had started as a torture. Yet, when acting as other than Nightfall, he had considered the right path on a daily basis. Those nights he handled the evil needs and desires of his demon side left him free to become more prudent at other times and in other guise.

Nightfall pressed his back against the tailor's home, concentrating on the area around him, though the Magebane's gift and the reprieve it promised struggled to usurp all other thought. His ears and eyes told him that no one had come close enough to intrude on his moment. He was alone. Pulling the stone from his pocket, he clasped it tightly into his palm. It felt warm, though whether from some inherent magic or from absorbing the heat of his grasp, he could not guess. A red glow leeched through the cracks between his fingers, and Nightfall knew a tingle of joy. Apparently, Brandon Magebane was not a hoax or a crazy but all that he claimed. As instructed, Nightfall concentrated on the oath-bond.

Sudden pain exploded through Nightfall, and he lost all control of his limbs. He collapsed, doubling over, trying to escape agony that came wholly from within. He clung to his last abstraction, the oath-bond, little caring whether the anguish came from the stone or from the death throes of the magic. He would not lose the focus of the Magebane's gift. Nightfall managed to heave to his hands and knees, realizing as he did that the pain was fading. Now, he could separate the faint tremor of Brandon's talent from the too familiar prickle of the oath-bond. The latter had caused the pain and also chosen to quiet again. Apparently, it had risen against the threat and conquered. From all he had heard, the stone should have worked immediately, yet the oath-bond remained.

Nightfall froze, failure a shock and a terror at once. He kept calm, working through the problem logically, surmising several possible explanations. He hoped the oath-bond had gone, its buzz his imagination or an aftereffect that might gradually disappear. He tested it cautiously, picturing himself never returning to Prince Edward. He felt no reprisal. Excitement built; it seemed he truly had become free. That realization caused him to consider the prospect of abandoning Edward more seriously. The moment he did, the oath-bond leapt to life, spearing a warning through his chest that drove him to miss a breath. The stone's power had misfired, though whether from technicality or weakness, Nightfall did not know.

Nightfall rose, assessing the situation. In the tavern in Noshtillan, the man Brandon had called Gatiwan had assured Nightfall that he had never seen the Magebane's talent or his stones fail. Every time a sorcerer threw a spell, either Brandon or one of his followers with an empowered stone negated it. It now occurred to Nightfall that those who chose to hunt with Brandon probably had talents of their own they kept well-hidden. *Who would have more cause to hate sorcerers than the natally gifted?* With their powers curtailed and against several others with abilities, a weak sorcerer or one without a fast means of escape would fare poorly.

Having played both sides of many situations, Nightfall felt no pity for the sorcerers. Forever, they had preyed on the innocent, catching the talented as infants or children when possible, when they were an easy fight and less likely to understand the danger of displaying such abilities. Brandon and his people killed, but sorcerers tortured and enslaved. Those who lived by murder usually accepted that violence would end their existences as well. He had expected nothing different for himself, only wondered which way and which time the guard forces and bands of citizens would take him.

Nightfall considered the cause of the stone's failure. He sifted the three plausible possibilities from an endless procession of unlikely ones. Either Brandon had lied, Nightfall had invoked the item incorrectly, or the oath-bond had proven stronger than the stone could handle. The first and last he could do nothing about, so he considered the second in more detail. The glow suggested he had, at least, begun the maneuver in the proper manner. Brandon had told him to concentrate on the source of the magic and Nightfall had taken that to mean the oath-bond itself, although the Magebane and his hunters, according to Gatiwan, directed their power at the sorcerer hurling the spell.

Again, Nightfall pressed his back to the wall, this time crouching so a fall would not prove as painful. His senses still indicated he was alone. Once more, he clutched the stone in his palm so tightly its roughness gouged his flesh. Red light bled through the lines where his fingers met. Nightfall directed his focus to Gilleran, recalling the sorcerer at the time he cast the spell, in vivid detail. The oath-bond remained at a level just above baseline, nagging that Nightfall was leaving Edward alone too long, no longer seeing his attempt to break it as a threat. Its quiescence seemed to mock Nightfall, to insinuate that his puny efforts at escape no longer bothered it. The red glow still bathed his fingers, without even a tinge of the blue Brandon claimed would indicate the stone was functioning.

Nightfall closed his eyes, concentrating on Gilleran until his fingers ached from being clenched too long. The stone remained red, dulling as his grip loosened. The oath-bond still throbbed a steady chorus, taunting with its vibrancy; and frustration lanced to sudden rage. Nightfall slammed the stone back into his pocket, seized by an urge to pound the wall until it crumbled or his fist became mangled and bloodied. He did not translate the image into action, forcing contentment with the thought alone. He guessed the agony he had suffered came from the oath-bond striking back when it feared he might escape it. Once it realized Brandon's magic could not dispel it, it had settled back, uncaring. Apparently, Brandon had given him a faulty stone or else his ability only worked against magic in the casting. Perhaps, once set, the spell would no longer yield to the Magebane's talent.

Nightfall headed back toward the main road, feeling all the more trapped for his failure. He channeled the need to violently dispel his rage into determination. That lesson of Dyfrin's he had learned well: to wait out storms of emotion and act only with deliberate thought. Though he had heard of others who worked their scams or murders best in a wild fog of rage or a drug-induced frenzy, he considered them fools. He had done nothing blinded or driven by emotion, whether love or anger, that he did not regret. That was why he would not listen to Kelryn's explanation, not until he felt certain he could hear without love lulling him into believing the absurd or lies goading him to slaughter.

Once on the cobbled pathway, Nightfall took only a few steps toward the inn before turning aside in the direction of the duke's citadel. Now, the need to land Prince Edward became even more the obsession. One way or another, he would thwart the oath-bond and extract payment from Chancellor Gilleran, even if it meant joining and guiding the Magekillers for the expedition. King Rikard's fate would depend on his motivations for binding son and killer together.

These thoughts brought the oath-bond to a screeching crescendo that ached through Nightfall, claiming much of his rage. Harming Alyndar's officials went against the tenets of the oath-bond every bit as strongly as leading the prince into danger. He had vowed he would cause no harm nor allow harm to come to any noble, servant, or guardian of the kingdom, especially the king, his chancellor and his sons; and the oath-bond would undoubtedly see to it he kept that promise as fully as those that bound him to Edward.

Nightfall turned his mind back to his landing strategy, and the oath-bond's reminder slackened to normal. He paused to surreptitiously pluck a *shartha* flower from a cottage bed, then strode directly for the citadel. Once there, he kept to puddled areas of grayness, flitting from one to the next until he stood beneath that which he knew from years in Schiz to be Willafrida's window. In the quiet darkness, he prepared to scale the wall, first appeasing the oath-bond with the understanding that he would not steal, kill, spy, or perform any other action it might consider too much the persona he had promised to abandon. The flower had closed for the night, but wisps of tubular petals showed through the sides, promising a fat,

purple bloom come morning. The stem held the deep
green hue of health.

Nightfall placed the stem in his mouth, careful not to
bite down. He knew little about decorative plants, having
sown only edible crops in his guise as Telwinar the
farmer. However, his dealings with poisons and time on
the streets eating whatever might lessen the rumbling hollow of his gut had taught him that those plants or insects
that looked most beautiful protected themselves from
predators with toxins. From experience, he knew *shartha*
contained a mild poison that caused intestinal discomfort
and vomiting.

Catching handholds and dropping his weight, Nightfall
shimmied up the stone building. Colorful, silk curtains
rippled in the balmy breezes, the shutters open to admit
the warmth and no glass blocking his entrance. He assessed the room in a glance. Intricately carved furniture
filled most of it, in matching patterns that depicted a long
string of horses on every leg and ledge. The bedposts
held wooden horse heads as knobs, and the canopy was a
tapestry that depicted a girl in a dress composed of endless fabric sitting in a patch of blue wild flowers. Beneath
it, a young woman in a sleeping gown fluffed the pillows
and stepped daintily between the sheets. Straw-colored
hair poked from beneath a frilly cap, and the lantern light
displayed green-gray eyes and a flat, upturned nose. She
sported a rich woman's plump curves, overbalanced at the
hips so that her buttocks seemed disproportionately wide.
Though far from homely, her facial features held little attraction for Nightfall. He waited until she extinguished
the lantern and snuggled beneath the covers.

Confident of his discretion, Nightfall did not wait for
Willafrida to fall asleep before slipping into the room and
placing the flower on the night table. Once finished, he
crept back out the window, clambered swiftly to the
ground, and headed back to the He-Ain't-Here Tavern. As
he walked, Nightfall considered excuses for his tardiness.
Although he had spent less than an hour with Brandon
Magebane, and the detour by the citadel had only cost
him a few extra moments, he had obviously spent more
time away from Edward than simply stripping tack and

releasing horses into a pasture should take. He had settled on a story about having gotten stuck discussing steeds with a noble gentleman when he arrived at the thatch, stone, and mortar building. Its crookedly lettered sign bore a random shape that made it seem likely to have been a scrap from a larger project. Nightfall guessed Edward would understand and respect his decision to let a highborn talk, no matter how lengthy or dull the discourse.

Nightfall opened the door, amid a turbulent shrill of hinges that made him wince. Apparently, however, the patrons had become so accustomed to the noise that most did not even bother to turn. Inside, open windows on either side of the building admitted a cross draft that brought the smell of damp and greenery to a room that otherwise reeked of stale beer and sweat. The perfume of freshly cooked vegetables and lamb became nearly lost beneath those stronger odors, but Nightfall's hunger dredged the food scents from the others. All of the tables were occupied, many surrounded by half a dozen chairs or more. Kelryn and Edward sat with their backs to the entrance, apparently oblivious to his arrival. Nightfall did not miss the arm the prince chose to rest not-quite-casually across the back of Kelryn's chair. He felt a stab of jealously, discarded it, and immediately suffered a second warning pain, this from the oath-bond. As long as he considered Kelryn a threat, it would do so also. Four strangers, all men, sat at the table with them, probably begging news of Alyndar and their travels.

Nightfall approached, taking a position between Edward and the closest Schizian, a man he now recognized as a local stone hauler. He knew the other three as well, two builders and the cooper. All were harmless, though none could keep a secret from one end of a room to the other which explained their attraction to travelers with news, especially one dressed as richly as Prince Edward. "Master, I'm sorry it took me so long."

Prince Edward looked at his squire, smiling a warm greeting and demanding no explanation. Apparently, he had enjoyed himself enough not to notice the time. "Ah, Sudian. We saved you some food." He shoved over a platter with shredded lamb, tubers, and peas that had, apparently, served as a common plate.

"Thank you, Master." Nightfall searched for and found an unoccupied chair, using the hunt as an excuse to examine the tavern's patrons. Most were Schizian commoners familiar to Nightfall by face if not by name. Others appeared to have come from Meclar or Noshtillan, either to gather news or because they preferred their drinks in a different location now and again. Aside from Edward and Kelryn, only one man seemed not to fit. He wore a well-scrubbed leather jerkin and a tailored cloak of fine linen. A servant tended his needs, dressed in white with a red stallion embroidered on the front of his tabard. Nightfall did not recognize the standard. He scooted his chair to the table with enough noise to interrupt the talk, then seized on the ensuing silence. "Who's the highborn with the horse symbol?"

The stone hauler did not bother to turn to look. "That's Datlinst, a knight's middle son. He's been courting the duke's daughter, Willafrida; but he'll be moving on to the Tylantian joust soon like the others, I'd warrant."

Nightfall ate, looking down at his plate to keep from revealing an expression until he decided on the proper one. He had now heard of the competition for the second time, and Edward still had not mentioned it. Surely, if a knight's middle son had received an invitation, Alyndar's younger prince had not been excluded. Thinking back, Nightfall recalled several instances earlier in their travels when they had met warriors headed in various directions for special weapons training or for competitive preparation.

The stone hauler continued talking, a favorite pastime. "Now that Hoson and the others have gone, I think Datlinst thinks he has a better chance. But he can't stay much longer. The competition's in just two weeks, and it's a good week's journey to Tylantis. As it is, he probably won't find no place to settle there. Surely, all the inns are long full.

Nightfall considered carefully. With most of the suitors gone, it opened the way for him to work his plans as well; but he needed to know why Edward had no interest in a contest that could get him landed. If he could find the reason, counter it, and talk Edward into entering, he would need to cheat the prince to a win. That seemed difficult, yet no more so than creating love between strangers. For now, he left both options open. He would attempt to bring prince and duchess-heir together swiftly. As the week neared an end, he would assess how that strategy seemed to be working and make a decision. Meanwhile, he would need to uncover the reasons for Edward's apathy.

One of the builders asked the obvious question. "You're headed for the contest, I presume, noble sir?"

"Me?" Prince Edward seemed surprised by the question. "No."

The Schizians exchanged confounded looks, but they did not press. Nightfall appreciated that they left the probing to him.

Chapter 15

A dragon laughed at Nightfall's fame,
Rained curses on the demon's name;
The dragon's bones now lie in rows—
Darkness comes where Nightfall goes.
                    —The Legend of Nightfall
                      Nursery rhyme, alternative verse

Nightfall let the matter of the Tylantian contests settle, allowing Edward to take a watch, then sleeping through his own. As usual, throughout the night he remained on the restless edge of awakening.

Constructed for meeting and drinking rather than hostelry, the He-Ain't-Here Tavern kept its overnight visitors packed into two rooms. Though it meant sharing his quarters with seven more men, Nightfall appreciated that the tavern owner had decided to divide his guests by gender. Kelryn stayed with the travelers' wives, enough company for Edward to believe her safe and for her to feel no need to intrude upon the men's shelter. In truth, her welfare was of no concern to Nightfall, and he felt certain Ritworth meant her no harm at all. The Healer's description in Delfor and Kelryn's sleep-talk left him no doubt that she worked with sorcerers. Even if the Iceman was not her usual contact, she would know the right words to league with him and she surely would not hesitate to sell Nightfall out . . . again.

Nightfall assessed the men around him, curled under whatever blankets or tattered cloaks they had brought with them. All claimed to have journeyed from distant countries, three from Hartrin and four from Mitano, to watch the competition in Tylantis. Although they came from slave country, none brought any of their own. Nightfall knew by their manner and gear that these men could not afford such luxuries had they wished to do so, but he was quick to point out the respect with which they treated him.

Prince Edward seemed withdrawn. Longer than a week had passed since he proselytized about anything, and Nightfall feared he had succeeded too well at crushing the fanatical idealism, sapping the prince of any drive at all. His sleeping neighbors did not concern Nightfall. He had watched their movements, seeking a grace, offhand comment, or hidden strength to suggest they were other than they claimed, and he found nothing to worry him.

Still, the night passed for Nightfall with fretful slowness.

Nightfall, Prince Edward, and Kelryn spent much of the next day shopping for gear and rations, the squire quietly supplementing their meager money from the pockets of wealthier passersby. For the first time in his life, remorse prickled at his conscience for the intrusion, though whether born of exposure to Edward's morality or from the realization that being exploited and downtrodden no longer worked as an excuse, he did not know. He did find himself taking smaller amounts from a larger number of victims, a fairness that hardly justified his crimes, although it did ease his guilt as well as place him at more risk of discovery.

Kelryn and Edward spent large amounts of time discussing the merits of foods and fabric, which left Nightfall more than enough chances to purchase a grappling hook, rope, knives, and a container for *shartha* petals as well as obtaining capital to cover the prince's acquisitions and still leave silver in his pocket for their rooms and board. Though engrossed in his own activities, Nightfall spared more than enough attention to keep Edward safe. He could not help but also overhear much of the conversation between prince and dancer. They chatted about the pros and cons of myriad products as if they had done so together all their lives, though Kelryn had never shown interest in such talk when he had courted her. Apparently, there was much about Kelryn he had never known.

That night, Nightfall sneaked Willafrida another flower.

* * *

Datlinst left for Tylantis the following day, without any reluctance to indicate he knew about Willafrida's mysterious suitor. That satisfied Nightfall. If the duchess-heir chose not to discuss such events with Datlinst, it either meant her tie to him had not become serious or she had trivialized the gifts. No matter the reason, secretiveness would only enhance the romance of the anonymous flowers.

That evening, as dinner drew to a close, Nightfall dragged Prince Edward outside on a pretext. He chose that moment for two reasons. First, they had left Kelryn in a crowd, presumably safe, so Edward could concentrate on other matters. Second, Nightfall suspected Willafrida would already lie in wait to see whether Datlinst or some other suitor was leaving the presents. This time, he wanted to confront her directly. For that purpose, he carried a grapple and rope ladder hidden beneath his cloak.

Prince Edward and Nightfall stepped from the tavern into a hovering evening grayness that fled before their lantern and seemed to thicken as they watched. Though they walked side by side, Nightfall passively chose the direction, trying to make it seem as if Edward had done so. Most of the citizens had gone home to cook or eat and rest, but a few still wandered the streets, mostly young couples or prostitutes.

"What's wrong?" Edward asked, naturally assuming Nightfall wished to talk for personal reasons.

"Nothing's wrong," Nightfall admitted. "I just wanted some time with you away from Kelryn to make sure your needs are being taken care of. I know having her around probably sometimes makes it hard for you to talk as prince to servant, and you've been so quiet."

Prince Edward smiled, shaking his head with obvious admiration. "Always worrying about me, aren't you, Sudian? I'm fine. I'm just not certain where to go from here. I think our next action might have to be a meeting with King Idinbal or King Jolund. We can find out what dire troubles or enemies they might have and use our skills to aid the kings."

Nightfall suppressed a grin, realizing he had not wholly squashed the innocent kindness and naiveté. "Master, from what I've heard, right now King Jolund's biggest problem is a duchy that needs a duke."

Prince Edward looked away with a noncommittal noise.

Nightfall would not let him escape that easily. "Are relations between Alyndar and Shisen so strained that King Jolund would not invite a prince of Alyndar to his games?"

"I was invited," Edward admitted.

Nightfall raised his brows awaiting further explanation.

It came, though it seemed inadequate. "I've chosen not to go."

Nightfall stopped walking and stared, incredulous.

Two paces later, Edward also came to a halt, though he did not turn.

"Master, am I still barred from questioning you?"

"It's still rude." Edward remained in place. "But that's not stopped you before." Finally, he faced Nightfall. "You know I won't hit you."

Though eager to get on with the conversation, Nightfall maintained the necessary politeness, clinging to his role. Edward seemed uncharacteristically irritable, and Nightfall suspected the reason was intimately tied to his insistence on missing the Tylantian contests. "I'm not worried about hitting. I'm worried about offending."

For a moment, Prince Edward lost his regal confidence, wincing at the impact of his words. In the light of the new information Kelryn had given him about Nightfall's past, his sarcastic comment about hitting might have seemed cruel. Though the statement had not bothered Nightfall at all, he relished the discomfort that would make Edward feel more obligated to explain. "Ask your question. I won't let it, nor the mere act of asking, offend."

Nightfall started walking again with a slow, thoughtful stride. "You need to become landed. King Jolund wants to give away a landed title. Master, it seems perfect. Why would you choose not to go?"

Soon, Edward's long strides brought him even with Nightfall, and the smaller man increased his speed to keep pace with his long-legged master. "I've chosen not to go. You may question my actions for clarification, but don't challenge my motivations."

Nightfall hesitated, thrown by so many difficult words at once. "I still don't understand."

"I don't wish to go."

"Why not?"

"I don't wish to go." Rising anger tainted Edward's tone. "That is all."

"But why not?" Nightfall continued to press, not the least put off by Edward's annoyance. Like alcohol, strong emotions, such as rage, fear, and love, tended to goad people to say things propriety would otherwise gag. At best, he might discover some truer incentive beneath Edward's loyalty to himself and to the downtrodden. At worst, he would listen to another tedious discussion of manners.

"It's pointless to go," Edward's strong voice verged on a shout. "Why waste time on a contest I can't win."

The prince's words seemed so uncharacteristic, Nightfall halted in his tracks before he realized he had stopped, and it took Edward several strides to notice. "I can't believe you just said that."

Edward turned, brow wrinkled, seemingly perplexed by his own comment. Nevertheless, he stood by his words. "It would waste my time to go."

"Master . . ." Nightfall paused, finding a response as difficult as he wanted it to appear. "Are you the same man I pledged my services to? The one who set out to end generations of slavery and poverty single-handedly?"

"I am," Edward said, the anger fading into thoughtful consideration. "And I still plan to do it."

"So, as I understand it," Nightfall put the situation fully into perspective, "you're willing to fight or lecture every person in the world involved with bondage or injustice. But you're not good enough to win a joust?" He began walking again, wanting to get closer to the duke's citadel.

Again, Edward caught up swiftly. "It's not that. It's just, well, I know some of the people who'll be there, men who've fought wars. Men who consistently bested me in practice."

"Master, you're a great warrior."

The prince smiled, but his attitude seemed more tolerant than agreeable. "Your faith in me is touching, really it is. But I'm not experienced, and I know my limits."

Nightfall did not believe he had ever heard a more false statement in his life. *Knows his limits, indeed. This from a man who frees slaves without warning and expects no complaints from their owners.* This realization cued Nightfall to something deeper. Whatever kept Prince Edward from the Tylantian contest had only partially to do with the belief that he would lose. "But, Master, don't you want to know for sure? Were I highborn, I would at least wonder where I stood among the others."

"I have no need for that knowledge."

"But what could it hurt to try?" Nightfall knew he had passed the boundary of pressing too hard, but to drop the subject now might leave him no chance to raise it again without Edward immediately ending the discussion. Fresh wounds made men talkative; old anger spurred avoidance. He tensed for the tongue-lashing sure to follow his insistence.

But Edward did not yell. He spent several seconds in deep contemplation before replying. "It's my brother, you know. He's so much more skilled, it makes no sense for me to go. He's always beaten me." His voice went so soft, Nightfall had to strain to hear. "He's always made me look like a fool."

Nightfall spoke nearly as softly. "All the more reason you should go. So you can show your brother what you can do. So you can show him you've become a man, not the toddler he remembers."

"And if I wind up looking more foolish?"

"You won't."

"But if I do?"

"Then at least you tried."

Edward went meditative again, while Nightfall laughed. "What's funny about that?"

. "You're always so strong and confident. It's good to see you have some doubts for a change."

"It doesn't make me look weak?"

"Just the opposite, Master." Nightfall quoted Dyfrin once again. "A fool fears nothing and calls it courage. A hero conquers what he fears."

Edward nodded appreciatively. "Very well stated."

Nightfall refused to take the credit. "I heard it from a wise man, the closest I ever had to a brother. Sometimes I wish I had listened to him more."

Apparently noting wistfulness, Edward asked the obvious question. "What happened to him?"

"Who?" Backtracking through the conversation, Nightfall realized Edward had referred to Dyfrin, probably believing him one of Kelryn's siblings. "Oh, him." Nightfall avoided names. Caught talking about actual events from the past, he changed the subject quickly. "Nothing as far as I know. We just went in different directions. We seem to find each other every so often." He wondered if Dyfrin would have reason to attend the contests and doubted it. He had not seen his old friend in longer than two years. "Do we go to the contests?"

"Don't push me," Edward warned, good-naturedly. "Yes, I suppose we go. But you'll need to prepare my fighting gear now and on the field, things such as armor, weapons, and my destrier. And we'll need new colors. We can't represent Alyndar when the crown prince is there. We'll have to find something not already being used as the symbol of another house."

Nightfall found the details trifling, yet he guessed those with wealth needed some means of occupying the time commoners spent working to keep warm or searching for food. His first thought, to place the prince in a single, unadorned color such as flat black, passed quickly. Once Edward got an idea in his head, he acted on it swiftly and with vigor. He would want to leave for Shisen at once, and it would take at least a few days without other suitors to win the hand of Lady Willafrida. Success here might make the contests immaterial, but having the competition as a backup plan relieved Nightfall of some of the urgency wooing the duchess-heir had held. Rousing love in a day seemed difficult, but no more so than rigging several mock battles in Edward's favor without getting caught in the act. The need for a seamstress to create their colors could hold Edward here for the time Nightfall required. Now, he needed only to think of some symbol so compelling it charged Edward to his usual frenzy. "An opened shackle and a majestic eagle flying free from it." He waved the hand carrying the lantern to indicate the scene as if it stood before them. The light cut a saffron arc through the growing darkness, adding grandeur as well as possibly attracting Willafrida's attention. "In golden weave, of course. All on a background of clear sky blue."

Edward stared into the darkness where Nightfall had conjured the image, a grin creeping slowly onto his features. "We'll make it deep blue. More contrast and easier to see from a distance. I like the rest. It won't be the first emblem with a bird of prey nor the only one in blue and gold; but the motif will make it different enough." He waved a hand, as if to clear the same area for his own picture. "A captured eagle flying for freedom. How appropriate."

Nightfall believed they had come to an excellent breaking point in the conversation, and they had walked near enough to the citadel for the next stage of his plan. "Master, excuse me a moment please. I'm afraid I had a bit too much beer." He offered the lantern.

Prince Edward took it. "As you need, Sudian."

Nightfall did not wait an instant before striding, then dashing, off into the shadows. The oath-bond set off its alarm the instant the prince's form disappeared into the gloom, reminding him he had left his charge alone in sparsely traveled territory. Nightfall ignored it. He would leave for only a few moments, and his need to land the prince took as much precedence. When vows clashed, he had to choose according to situation. If he remained glued to Edward's side, the prince would never own property; and Nightfall's soul would become Gilleran's possession as fully as if the prince had died. He doubted Ritworth had tracked them yet. Even if he had discovered the town, he would have to search for specific location as well as risk attacking a prince out in the open where witnesses might come upon them.

This time, Nightfall used the grappling hook and rope ladder. It would look suspicious for a squire to know how to scale walls without such equipment, and this time he planned to reveal himself to Willafrida. He worked swiftly, swinging and flinging the grapple into place on the window ledge on the first try, tugging to embed the teeth. The time for strategy and consideration had ended. Now, it only remained to set the plan in motion. Nightfall paused just long enough to pluck a perfect flower from one of the citadel's tended beds, then scurried up the rope.

Nightfall hesitated near the top, guessing darkness cloaked him well enough to hide his identity, especially given the soft glaze of light in the duchess-heir's bedroom. He hoped the romance of a single nightly flower slipped anonymously into her room would make her curious and proud rather than threatened. He would need to act swiftly if he met anyone other than Willafrida in her room. Quietly, tensed to jump, Nightfall peered inside.

Willafrida perched on the bed, the curtain of veils dangling from the canopy closed. Through their silk, Nightfall could make out her silhouette. She wore a flowing dress or gown, her long hair piled on her head. She had struck a provocative pose, her arms back to accentuate the small breasts, the dress flopping away from a shapely leg drawn seductively to her chest that drew attention from the generous hips and buttocks. Seeing, hearing, and sensing no others in the room, Nightfall quietly climbed inside, careful to affect a light noise that would notify her of his presence without making it obvious he meant for her to catch him.

Willafrida took the bait. A stubby-fingered hand appeared from a gap in the silks and brushed them open far enough to reveal her face. Cosmetics enhanced her lips and eyes, and the scent of perfumed oils wafted to him. The sleeping gown seemed as thin and satiny as the canopy veils, its maroon complimenting the sun-darkened skin and its cut revealing the inner corners of her breasts. Her gaze found him, and her demeanor wilted. She pulled the gown self-consciously around her. "Who are you?"

she demanded, the romance broken. "What are you doing in my room?"

Nightfall pretended to appear startled, dropping the flower and turning to stare. "I—I'm sorry, Lady," he stammered, dropping to his knees and lowering his head in an exaggerated gesture of respect. "My name is Sudian. I'm just a servant. Please don't have your guards hurt me." While on the floor, he picked up the fallen flower, offering it to her with eyes averted.

Willafrida took the blossom absently. "What are you doing here? Not trying to court me, I hope. I don't associate with servants."

"Me?" Nightfall met her gaze from habit then quickly glanced away. "No. Oh, no. Me? Certainly not. My master, Prince Edward Nargol of Alyndar. I think the two of you ... I mean I ..." He trailed off, waiting for her to save him. Her reception suggested interest before she caught a glimpse of the scrawny, plain-looking man in livery she feared to be her suitor.

"Prince?" Willafrida repeated.

"Yes, Lady. Prince Edward. I believe he would wish you to call him Ned."

Willafrida sat on the edge of her bed, one hand still holding the flower, the other clutching her night gown to keep herself as covered as possible. Apparently, Nightfall's appearance surprised her enough to become suspicious. "Is he old?"

"Within a year or two of your age, Lady." Nightfall deliberately did not mention those years would fall on the younger side.

The duchess-heir became less tense and more pensive. "Is he handsome?"

"In all the world, from the northernmost tip of the Yortenese Peninsula to the southernmost beach of the Xaxonese, from the Klaîmer Ocean to the Plaxomer, if you found a man more becoming, he could, at best, be my Master's twin."

Willafrida chuckled. "Loyal, aren't you?"

"I only speak truth."

"Is he kind?"

"Lady, I was not born or debted into servitude," Nightfall stuck with the prevailing lie, though he hardly needed to embellish Edward's gentleness. "I chose to serve my master because of his goodness and compassion, no other reason."

"Very loyal indeed." Though she obviously doubted his sincerity, Willafrida continued her questioning. "Is he witty?"

Nightfall suppressed a smile and answered with truth. "He makes *me* laugh."

"I'd like to judge for myself," Willafrida said. "Where is he?"

"Below." Nightfall cringed, still avoiding eye contact. "He's a bit shy, and he doesn't know I'm here. I'll walk him by the window for you to see. If you don't find him attractive, say nothing. I'll lead him away. If you do, speak with him or not as you choose. In a few days, though, we're leaving for the contests in Shisen." With that warning to encourage Willafrida to work swiftly, Nightfall scampered back out the window before she could think to stop him.

Once on the ground, Nightfall rushed back to the ball of lantern glow that indicated Prince Edward's position. "I'm sorry I took so long, Master. I got to staring at the flower beds outside the duke's citadel. Would you like to see them?" He reached for the lantern.

Prince Edward returned it, seeming taken aback by his squire's sudden interest in decoration. "It's getting late. Shouldn't we head back to Kelryn? I'm supposed to protect her, after all."

Nightfall turned toward the citadel as he replied. "She's safe in a crowded tavern. The Iceman's not going to try to fight through dozens of men to get to her. We won't take long." Nightfall tacked on the last as if in afterthought. Though it was the obvious thing to say, Nightfall found it more important to assure Edward of Kelryn's safety than to worry about the passage of time. He did not want the traitorous dancer on Edward's mind while he met the woman he was going, Nightfall hoped, to marry.

Pretending to admire the flowers, Nightfall steered Edward gradually and casually beneath Willafrida's window, raising the lantern to give her a solid glimpse of features he felt certain would not disappoint her. In truth, it seemed nearly unbelievable to Nightfall that some woman had not already snatched Edward's hand and heart. Yet, he knew that royalty had stricter rules about such things. They became eligible at an older age, and the station of both parties played a large role in the matter. Edward, it seemed, had only just left his coddled nursery, whether it consisted of toys and nannies or books, practices, and stewards. Were it not such a cruel joke on Edward, Nightfall might have steered the prince toward a romance with Kelryn, if only to pay back Rikard for the oath-bond. A whore for a daughter-in-law might serve him right.

Nightfall's current abstraction made him distinctly uncomfortable for reasons that had nothing to do with the oath-bond's low-level hum, so he turned his thoughts elsewhere. They had tarried long enough. The next move belonged to Willafrida.

"Very nice," Edward said, the lack of expression suggesting politeness rather than interest. "I'm certain they're beautiful when the blooms open. In the day. We'll come back when it's light with Kelryn."

"Good idea, Master." Nightfall turned to head back in the direction from which they had come.

Before Edward could follow, a sultry voice wafted from above. "Hello, Ned."

The prince stiffened, obviously startled. His head whipped upward, and he squinted through the darkness. Willafrida's face poked through the window, and Nightfall could make out the regular hatchwork of the rope ladder he had left grappled to her window.

"Hello, Ned." Willafrida repeated.

"Hello, fair Lady," Edward returned in his usual friendly manner.

Before honesty drove Edward to say anything about not knowing her, Nightfall whispered the information the prince needed. "Willafrida. The duke's heir."

Edward nodded slightly to indicate he had received the message. "What can I do for you tonight, Lady?"

"Are you, in fact, a prince of Alyndar?"

"I am," Edward admitted.

"Come up and talk with me, Prince Ned."

Edward glanced at Nightfall, who bobbed his head encouragingly. "Go," Nightfall whispered. "I'm fine, and I'll take care of Kelryn." The oath-bond flared slightly, though he reassured it and himself that he had no intention of straying far from Edward, his only obligation to Kelryn revenge.

"I'll be there shortly," Edward called back to the duchess-heir. He headed away.

Surprised by the sudden change in direction, Nightfall caught up to Edward. "Where are you going, Master?"

Edward stopped, features crinkled, obviously confused by the question. "To call on her, of course, Sudian. What did you think?"

Nightfall kept his voice low. "Master, I think she wants to have a secret meeting. I think she wants you to go in through there." He made a subtle gesture with his head to indicate the window. He held the lantern so as to reveal the hemp resting among the ivy.

Prince Edward followed the direction of the gesture, finally noticing the ladder. "Oh," he said, then, more carefully, "Oh. All right, then." He hesitated. This obviously did not fit his image of propriety, though neither did refusing the request of a young, female noble. With a shrug, he strode to the base of the wall, caught the rope, and clambered to the window. Willafrida met him at the top and helped him inside.

Grinning like a slave served his master's dinner, Nightfall put out the lantern, settled his back against the wall, and waited in the shadows.

Prince Edward flushed, feeling like a sneak thief breaking into Alyndar's castle. The duchess-heir's room seemed strange and feminine; veils, canopies, and the heavy scent of oils, spice, and flowers only adding to its exotic air. The furniture and smells reminded him of his mother's private room, where she had gone to spend quiet time alone, away from his father as well as the hustle and responsibility of queendom. Flowers always perfumed the spring or summer breezes wafting through the window, and he had come to associate ginger and *deprim* with her. She had always welcomed him, even into her special

chambers; and there she had taught him the gentleness
and breeding behind the many rules his nannies made him
memorize. She would have encouraged him to treat
Willafrida with politeness and dignity.

Willafrida smiled at Edward, her silky gown hugging
the ample curves. His mother had carried extra weight,
too, though it had settled at the belly and breasts rather
than the lower regions. He had never considered her anything but beautiful, and her happy carriage did not imply
she believed herself otherwise. Nevertheless, she used
mirrors without gawking and never lorded her looks over
anyone. Now, Edward could see the inner quarters of
Willafrida's breasts and make out the nipples impressing
the fabric. His eighteen-year-old body responded without
input from his mind, and the lust without love embarrassed him. He imagined she could see his excitement
through the fabric of breeks and tunic, and he self-
consciously pulled his cloak closed.

"You're as handsome as your servant promised,"
Willafrida said, admiring his face and body as he studied
her.

The words confused Edward. "You spoke with my
squire?"

"Yes," she said. "He said you were shy."

Edward had never heard that particular word applied to
him before. In fact, he had been scolded for boldness and
discarding convention for cause so often, the description
nearly made him laugh. Yet, in truth, around women, he
did display some quiet uncertainty. "Yes, well. He's a
good and loyal servant."

"So I'd gathered." Willafrida smiled flirtatiously.

Edward felt a knot form in his gut. The idea of leaving
seemed pleasant but rude. The comment required no response, but politeness deemed it his turn to speak. If he
could not continue the thread of the current discussion, he
had the obligation to turn to trivial talk until a new subject was broached. However, before he could find even a
minor topic, she took over again.

"You're going to the Tylantian contests?" Willafrida
gestured him to sit beside her.

"Yes, I guess I am." Edward perched on the edge as invited, uncomfortable intruding on a woman's sleeping pallet. "My squire talked me into it."

"He's good at that, isn't he?"

"Good at what?"

"Talking people into things."

"Sometimes," Edward returned, finding the duchess-heir's comment strange, an obvious attempt at conversation that seemed awkward to him.

"Six of my suitors are already there, trying to win a duchy."

"That hardly seems necessary." Edward glanced around to indicate the citadel. "You have one already. Why would they need to win you another?"

Willafrida shrugged then smiled, lowering her eyes modestly. "I'm nobility, but most of them are just gentry. I think they want at least as high a title as me. You can understand that."

Prince Edward nodded, without commitment. He did not see why station should matter to a man and woman who loved one another. "I suppose so, Lady."

"You wouldn't have to enter the contests to get a title, of course."

"No, Lady, I wouldn't." To Edward, the conversation seemed inane, but he stuck with it, seeing merit in learning to chat with women. He wondered if all conversations with the fairer sex would prove as tedious and realized he already had the answer. He had loved spending hours with his mother, discussing emotions and aspirations, reading stories and poetry. His conversations with Kelryn seemed to flow as easily, and the thought of her made him grin. His first meeting with her had proven even more awkward. His throat had closed down, making words impossible, and it had taken all of his sense of honor to tear his gaze from her near-naked beauty. From that moment, he had known she was special. Though he hated the idea that Ritworth the Iceman menaced her as well as him, he had appreciated the excuse and necessity it had created. The injury that marred her grace made him cringe every time she walked, but it had given her reason to quit dancing for a time and join them. And her fast and eager acceptance of his invitation suggested that maybe, just maybe, she had some feelings for him in return.

". . . a prince need to do so?"

Prince Edward started from his reverie, embarrassed that he had let thoughts of a woman preoccupy him so much he had become rude to another. Though he had not heard most of her question, he could divine the rest. If he guessed wrong, he hoped she would attribute his error to misinterpretation rather than inattentiveness. "I'm the younger prince. I have no claim to Alyndar's throne, kingdom, or lands. I need to establish myself elsewhere, and Tylantis' duchy will serve that need well." Edward gave the proper response by nature, and the doubts did not come until after he spoke the last word. "But mostly I'm going for the camaraderie and the thrill of competition. I have little hope I'll win."

That attitude clearly surprised Willafrida as boastful certainty seemed a much more common conviction among highborn. For the first time, it took her several moments to formulate a reply. Before she did, someone knocked on the door, the sound deep and reverberating. Edward stiffened, naturally leaping to his feet. Willafrida clasped her hands in her lap and turned her head toward the sound. "Who is it?"

A solid bass wafted through the panel. "It's Milnar, Lady. Is everything all right in there?"

"Everything is fine, Milnar," she called back. "I'm just getting ready for bed."

"Very well, Lady Willafrida. I'm sorry I disturbed you." Heavy footsteps retreated down the corridor at a rapid pace.

Willafrida returned her attention to Edward. "A guard. They check on me all the time." She patted the bed, indicating Edward should sit again. "You were just telling me you have no claim to Alyndar's throne."

Prince Edward considered excuses for leaving now, but none seemed good enough this early in the conversation. Apparently, she had called him up only to chat and get to know him. It was way too soon to know whether or not they would prove compatible. "My brother, Leyne. He's the crown prince."

Willafrida made a wordless noise to indicate interest. The intensity of the sound suggested fascination with the brother rather than the conversation. Her next question enforced the impression. "Is *he* married?"

"No."

"How old?"

"Twenty-six."

Finally, Willafrida turned the conversation back to Edward. "And you?"

"I'm not married either. And I'm eighteen."

Willafrida frowned, obviously surprised at the numbers.

Edward guessed the duchess-heir had a few years on him and it bothered her. Usually, noblewomen married men a few years older or sometimes, in the case of an aging ruler without an heir, decades older. He hoped age differences did not matter too much to women, not because of Willafrida but because of Kelryn. Conversation, comments overheard, and appearance indicated the dancer was a few years older even than Willafrida. Edward's mother had taught him emotion took first precedence; and, for all his father's wealth and power, she had married for love. She had come from a rich family, and status had never held attraction for her. She more often escaped than embraced the duties of being queen.

"Does your brother look like you?"

Edward pictured Leyne. He had never thought much about comparing appearances, although he had always envied his brother's shrewd eyes and knowledge of court procedure. "In a general sense, I guess. He's bigger than me, and he's got dark eyes."

Willafrida's gaze roved up and down Edward's tall, firm frame as if to imagine someone larger.

The prince assisted the image. "Not taller, just more muscular. He's the one to watch at the Tylantian contests. I'll be surprised if he doesn't win."

"Why would the crown prince of Alyndar need an eastern duchy?"

"My brother surrender a chance to pit his weapon skill against some of the best fighters on the continent?" Edward shrugged. "He'd sooner give up food. Besides, my father is strong and healthy. If Leyne waited for him to die before gaining land and status, he might not do so until his own sons became ready to take the throne." He added jokingly, "Assuming he ever marries, of course."

"Of course," Willafrida repeated, pensive.

The door knob rattled, echoing through the chamber. Before Edward could think to move, the door swung open. A portly, frizzle-haired gentleman approaching seventy stood in the entry, flanked by three guards in Schizian bronze and black.

"Father!" Willafrida sprang to her feet, the sudden movement nearly knocking Edward to the floor.

Prince Edward recaptured his balance and rose politely for introductions.

"What?" the duke stammered. "How?"

"I can explain," Willafrida started, but the duke gestured her silent.

"I don't want to hear from you right now. Go to your bed."

Willafrida hesitated.

"Go!"

She went, and the duke's attention locked on the approaching prince. "Stand where you are!"

Edward stopped, halfway across the chamber.

"Who are you, young man?"

Prince Edward bowed respectfully. "Prince Edward Nargol of Alyndar, sir."

The title barely seemed to impress the duke. "What were you doing in my daughter's bedroom."

"Talking, sir." Edward glanced over at Willafrida who had skittered to the center of her bed, clutching a pillow to her chest.

"Talking?" the duke repeated. "Talking! You sneak into my daughter's locked bedroom like some common assassin and have the nerve to tell me you were talking?"

"We were talking," Edward said again, not entirely certain of the answer the duke wanted or, more likely, expected.

"Prince or other, no man despoils my daughter's body and reputation. My physician can determine whether you've seduced my daughter and ruined her for decent marriage. But first, I will give you a chance to state your intentions."

Humiliation turned Edward's cheeks red. He knew some relief as well. He had done nothing wrong or disrespectful to the duchess-heir, and surely the physician's examination would reveal that.

The duke went straight to the point. "Prince Edward, do you plan to marry my daughter?"

"Marry her?" Edward repeated, trying to make sense of the words. "Marry Willafrida?"

"Do you plan to marry my daughter?"

Edward replied honestly. "Well, no, sir."

The duke's face darkened to purple. He gestured to his guards. "Take him away and lock him up." He turned on his heel and strode from the room as the guards advanced.

Edward did not resist.

The booming voice of the Duke of Schiz and the wail of the oath-bond aroused Nightfall from a half-doze. He scrambled up the ladder, watching in stunned silence while the duke's guardsmen arrested his prince for no more reason than entering his daughter's bedroom. The situation made no sense to Nightfall. His mother's nightly strings of bedtime clients had ill-prepared him for considering the mere act of being found in a woman's sleeping chamber a crime serious enough to deserve jailing. Yet Edward's quiet acceptance of his punishment suggested guilt.

Nightfall waited only until the guardsmen closed the door behind themselves and Edward. He listened for the sounds of returning footsteps and heard nothing over the ear-filling clamor of the oath-bond. Finally, he slithered through the window and to the side of Willafrida's bed, resisting the urge to clutch his stomach in agony. The oath-bond felt like a burning knife, twisting through his guts. "Where's your dungeon?"

Willafrida stiffened, obviously not noticing the intruder until he spoke. "Our dungeon? It's deep. Below the ground floor. But why?"

Nightfall suspected he might have only a few moments before the duke returned to confront his daughter alone.

He stumbled from the room, batting the door without bothering to see if it fully closed. Willafrida could handle that. He had graver matters to attend.

"Sudian, wait." Willafrida's desperate whisper chased him down the corridor, but Nightfall dared not stop. Movement toward the goal of rescuing Edward dimmed the oath-bond's alarm enough to let him function. If he turned back, he felt certain it would overwhelm him, driving him to twitch and writhe until it robbed him of soul as well as vigor. Finding the hallway empty, he charged toward a corner tower at random. He hit the door running, scarcely managing to trip the latch as he did so. The panel slammed open, crashing into a waiting guardsman so hard it sent him tumbling down the stairs, armor ringing against stone.

Nightfall cursed his lack of caution and his luck. Obviously, the guard had not expected trouble from the second story and so had positioned himself to block the exit from an intruder coming from below. Seeing no merit to trying to find another stairway now, Nightfall pounded down the steps, the oath-bond seething. On the next landing, he found the fallen guard sprawled, another crouched at his side. Glad for the distraction, Nightfall charged past, leaping down the stone stairway into the gloom below.

The conscious guard shouted. "Hey! You there!" He changed his tactic to a warning to those below. "Intruder headed down! Enemy on the stairs!"

Nightfall landed with his usual cat lightness, the oath-bond too persistent to allow him to use his talent to further soften the fall. He crouched, assessing the scene at a glance. Two guards blocked the pathway between two sets of three cells flush with the wall. The cages' barred sides rose into roofs that ended five hands' lengths from the stone ceiling that served as the floor to the level above. After the last pair of cells, the pathway ended and shorter branchways headed off in each direction, in turn ending at the walls. Only one figure occupied a cell, the farthest one on the right. Nightfall did not pause long enough to conclusively identify the prisoner. He raced down the walk.

In response to their companions' warning, the two

guards in the dungeon rushed forward. Nightfall darted through the gap between them. Both grabbed for him at once. One missed cleanly. The other caught a grip on his cloak. Arching his shoulders, Nightfall let the fabric slip free and continued running. Behind him, he could hear the guards calling strategies that seemed obvious. They would prove far more bunched and ready for his escape than they had been for his sudden entrance. Nightfall did not care. The closer he got to the prisoner he felt certain was Edward Nargol, the more the pain faded. He skidded around the corner, peering through the bars.

Grimy hands clenched the steel, and sad, dark eyes peered back at Nightfall through the gaps. A man with limp, brown hair and an openmouthed expression shy several teeth seemed as surprised to see Nightfall as the squire to find a stranger where his master should stand. The oath-bond's threat intensified with abrupt and suffocating intensity. For a moment, Nightfall froze, fighting back the pain enough to function. He glanced back around to the main pathway. Four guards swept it in two groups of two, moving with readied caution. Shortly, they would trap him against the wall.

Damn. Nightfall scarcely dared to believe he had cornered himself for an unknown hoodlum. He watched, calm, as the sentries came toward him. Nightfall still carried the last of his throwing daggers in addition to three others he had been given in Alyndar. Pain drove him to hurl himself upon the guards en masse, to bite, claw, and stab in a wild frenzy until they killed him. Nightfall delved deeper to the more familiar and personal part of his brain and the cold pocket of calculation he drew upon in times of desperation.

The guards turned the corner. Nightfall took a careful, backward step, aware one more would press his back to the wall. To his right, the farthest wall of the dungeon hemmed him. To his left, the bars of the prisoner's cage loomed. He saw only one other route, a small and desperate possibility he could not ignore. As the guards charged him, Nightfall scrambled up the bars. He flung himself up and over the cell roofs, skittering from cage to cage in a dashing crawl.

"Hey!" a guard shouted. "Get him." Their footsteps pounded a wild cadence in pursuit. Nightfall leapt from the last cell, hit the floor running, and sprinted back up the tower steps. Heavy footfalls resounded through the turret, seeming to come from all directions at once. Lowering his head, Nightfall jumped over the moaning guard on the first landing, whipped up to the second floor, and caught the door handle. He ripped open the panel and raced through the corridor. The oath-bond tore and hammered at him.

This time, he found a young maid in his path. He swerved as he ran past, but his shoulder struck her, jolting her to her knees. She let out a short scream that impressed the need to work swiftly. Catching the latch to Willafrida's room, he tripped it and pushed. The door slammed open, revealing the duchess-heir sitting alone on her bed. Nightfall closed the door. "He wasn't there."

Willafrida stood. "I tried to tell you that. My father wouldn't lock up a prince in a dungeon."

Every sinew in Nightfall's body seemed stretched to the point of breaking, as if his body might explode to open his soul to the magic. "Where is he!"

"I don't know exactly," Willafrida admitted. "Calm down. He's safe."

Nightfall believed her, and the oath-bond settled to a persistent, but no longer excruciating, roar. "You're sure they won't hurt him?"

"And cause a war between Alyndar and Schiz? Are you insane?"

Nightfall forced himself to think through the dense fog of agony dampening logic. He suspected the maid's scream would bring more soldiers or family soon, and Willafrida's safety would be foremost in her father's mind. The woman in the hall might have seen which room he entered and cue the pursuing guardsmen. "What will they do with him?"

"Keep him safe until they can get someone to vouch for him. They'll send a message to Alyndar, probably."

Nightfall knew a sudden clutch of fear accompanied by a single, sharper thrust from the oath-bond that was mercifully short-lived. It would take at least a month for an envoy from Alyndar to travel, during which time Prince Edward would miss the Tylantian contests. Worse, they might have to return to Alyndar, the tenets of the oath-bond unfulfilled, Nightfall's time limit wasted in waiting and travel.

Voices in the corridor warned Nightfall of approaching danger. He cleared the distance to the window in a single bound. "Please, when I get down, toss the grapple after me." Without awaiting confirmation, Nightfall sprang to the ledge and skittered down the rope ladder. A moment later, the grapple cut a gleaming arc through the moonlight and thumped to the ground nearby. Grabbing it, Nightfall slipped beyond a tended hedge of leafy bushes, safe for the moment.

Willafrida's certainty of Edward's security appeased the oath-bond enough to allow Nightfall coherent thought, though it remained a generalized, gnawing ache. He had only one solution. He needed to affirm Prince Edward's identity and intentions by himself, without the courtly breeding that might give him the words and knowledge he needed to succeed. He would have to play the situation by the moment and hope the right attitude would come naturally. The distracting, harassing throb of the oath-bond would only make his task more difficult.

First, Nightfall knew, he needed to look calm and in control, a competent representative of the country of Alyndar. He brushed dust from his clothing, using collected moisture on the branches to wash out streaks. He wrapped the rope in neat figure eights around the grapple, placing the package on the ground. He added all but one of his knives, tucking that in a well-camouflaged boot sheath. He had learned enough from Edward's lectures to know it would not do to visit a duke's home armed. He emptied his pockets of assorted objects he carried without specific thought to what he might do with them until a problem arose. Long years of poverty and danger had encouraged such behavior. Breaking free a thorny branch, he combed his red-brown hair, arranging it neatly around his collar. He pushed all of his things beneath a bush, memorized the location, and rose. He gave his clothes one last pat, then headed boldly for the front of the duke's citadel.

Nightfall tried to look official and confident, but pain turned his walk into a listing shuffle. Nevertheless, Nightfall kept his head high and his eyes alert as he wound along the cobbled walkway to the stone porch and knocked on the carved, oak door. Lanterns lit windows on every floor from rooms that had been dark when Edward and Nightfall had first arrived.

After several seconds, the door swung ajar to reveal a plump woman in a baggy dress and an apron. "Hello. What can I do for you, sir?" She seemed nervous for a servant attending a door, apparently aware of the excitement in the household but not wholly informed of its source. He understood rumors circulated quickly among house workers, but the events of moments ago surely had not yet dispersed widely.

Nightfall cleared his throat. "I'd like to see the duke."

"Thank you, sir." She curtsied. "But Duke Varsah isn't seeing anyone this late. Could you return in the morning?"

The oath-bond's threat intensified, giving the answer Nightfall already knew. "This can't wait. I need to see him now."

"I'm sorry, sir. But . . ." The woman trailed off, glancing to her left where, apparently, someone approached.

Nightfall heard the click of mail and smiled. The guards, he guessed, would be inordinately interested in what he had to say.

"Is there a problem?" The man's voice preceded him into view, then he appeared. Nightfall recognized him at once as the first floor sentry of the tower, the one who had tended his fallen companion. The drawn face held a half day's growth of stubble, and mousy hair poked from beneath a leather and metal cap. Large blue eyes studied Nightfall from a pall of obvious astonishment. He said nothing more. The woman stepped aside to let him handle the situation, a feat he was managing poorly.

Nightfall met the guard's surprise with impatience. "I need to see Duke Varsah now."

Gradually, the guard broke free of his trance. He addressed the woman first. "Escort this man to the meeting room, please. I'll speak with the duke."

The woman opened her mouth as if to protest, presumably on the basis of policy. Then, apparently realizing the guard had placed the burden of punishment on himself, turned to Nightfall instead. "Come with me, please, sir."

Nightfall followed the woman through a wide entry hall into a room with three doorless exits, each on a different wall. A massive, block fireplace held unlit logs. Above it, the mantle held an assortment of knickknacks, most figurines of warriors in various types of combat. In the center, a small battle raged, complete with archers and spearmen. A portrait hung over it all, of a stately man in mail and a rich cloak in a frame constructed from metal and notched daggers. A plush chair faced two matching couches, and a rectangular table stood in the center of the arrangement. The latter held a chessboard, each jade or alabaster icon set in its starting position. The woman gestured toward one of the couches, and Nightfall sat, mentally valuing each item in the room to keep his mind from the inescapable throb of Gilleran's magic.

Within moments, a few faces peered at him from every doorway, then disappeared. Nightfall sat back and smiled, enjoying the show. He noticed a few guards among them whispering to confirm their guest as the same man who had led them on a strange and reckless chase through the dungeon, though surely his motivations, for the hunt as well as the returning, evaded them. Shortly, the servants went reluctantly back about their business, leaving only the sentries. Then, he overheard hissed snatches that told him the guards worried more for hiding their incompetence than for informing their duke. No harm had come of Nightfall's run through the dungeon, so they would not report it. The rapidity and ease with which so many came to agreement made him certain they had grown accustomed to covering up their mistakes and duty failures. Nightfall guessed he would soon understand why avoiding Varsah's disapproval took precedence over truth.

The guard who had met Nightfall at the door came, escorting a stout, elderly gentleman with a jowly face and frizzled hair slicked back with perfumed oil. "Duke Varsah," the guard presented.

Nightfall called on every detail of Edward's descriptions and lectures, wishing he had paid closer attention.

Even street orphans knew to stand and bow in the presence of nobility. He did so.

Duke Varsah gestured Nightfall to sit, then claimed the chair. The guard took up a position at his left hand. "What can I do for you . . . ?" He left a long enough pause at the end to indicate a polite request for an introduction.

This time, Nightfall caught the appeal. "My name is Sudian, squire to Prince Edward Nargol of Alyndar."

"Ah," the duke said. The guard nodded. From the entryways, Nightfall saw other heads bob and heard quiet whispers.

"I believe my master is here, sir."

"He is," the duke admitted.

Nightfall met the duke's eyes solidly. "You need to free him, Duke Varsah."

"Why?"

The question caught Nightfall off-guard. He recalled Willafrida's comment about vouching for Edward and hoped it would prove as easy at it seemed. "Sir, in every way, he's as good and moral a man as this world has."

The duke's brows fanned down toward his eyes. "If that's so, then there's little hope left for our world. A man who would sneak into a woman's bedroom, without the permission or even the knowledge of her father—" He broke off with a sharp, wordless sound, clearly feeling he had no need to finish the sentence.

Nightfall wished that he had. It would have clarified so much. In his world, where families felt lucky to have a single sleeping chamber, it seemed nonsensical to worry about a harmless liaison between nobles, no matter in which room it occurred. Those thoughts notwithstanding, he took it as given that such was improper behavior and worked from there. "Willafrida called for him, sir. Would a good man refuse a lady's invitation?"

The brows snaked lower. "My daughter did no such thing."

"With all respect due." Nightfall had come to enjoy the phrase. In his mind, the amount became a spectrum on which most men deserved a pittance. "I was there, sir."

The duke's face pinched further, becoming ugly. "My

daughter would never call a man to her room. That's an insult I won't tolerate, especially from a servant. Why did you come? To besmirch the name of my daughter? To try to make her unmarriable?"

The duke's responses bewildered Nightfall, and he tried to return the incident to its proper perspective. "Sir duke, I came to clear the name of the most moral and honest man I've seen or heard about. Nothing more."

Duke Varsah made a noise that implied he believed otherwise.

The solution seemed simple to Nightfall. "What does Willafrida say about the matter, sir?"

"What?" The duke's features returned to normal, more, Nightfall guessed from the discomfort of their previous position than from any change in attitude.

Nightfall pressed. "Sir, Willafrida was there as well. Surely she told you what did and didn't happen."

The duke clenched his hands, glaring. "This isn't a matter to involve my daughter. I will not even insult her purity by asking. There's no need."

Nightfall stared, his own rage growing, not daring to believe what he had heard. "Perhaps, sir, if you spoke with your daughter more often, she wouldn't feel the need to call men into her room."

Duke Varsah's jaw drooped, and he sputtered, no coherent words emerging for a moment. Apparently no one had ever spoken to him in this manner, and he had never had to deal with punishing such rudeness. "Servant, I could have you executed."

Nightfall met the angry glare with level coolness. "And incur the wrath of Alyndar. Do you really want to war with a kingdom?"

The guard remained nervously in position, awaiting a direct command. The others in the doorways ceased their whispered discussions and became more visible.

Varsah pursed his lips, weighing Nightfall's bluff. "Over a servant? I think not."

Nightfall remained notably calm, his composure a disquieting contrast to Varsah's fury and threats. He had seen Alyndar's dungeon as well as the duke's and little doubted it would prove easy to escape in comparison. He sincerely doubted the duke would carry forth on his warning of execution in his own living room. Even if he did, Nightfall was ready and willing to discover whether his dagger and skill would get him out the door. "Sir, I'm not a normal servant. I'm Prince Edward's personal squire. I hold his life in my hands on a daily basis. Do you think I was chosen on a whim, without careful forethought?"

"Perhaps not," the duke admitted grudgingly. "But I can tell you're ill-mannered and lowly bred."

Many sarcastic ways to answer the taunt entered Nightfall's mind, but he dismissed them. This was a time for diplomacy not antagonizing. In truth, Nightfall doubted Varsah could find a man less cultured or of baser stock. "Duke Varsah, my only wish is to free my master. What do I need to do?"

The duke sat back, folding his arms across his chest. His manner suggested a willingness to discuss the matter but a heldover hostility that could surface at any time. "First, we need to determine if Edward dishonored my daughter. If not, my next step depends upon his attitude. He claimed he had no intention of marrying her. I'll have to see some explanation and remorse for breaking into a woman's room at night. If I don't, his father and I will discuss his punishment. If I do find that my daughter's been violated, his father and I will have a different discussion. One that involves restitution, discipline, and, possibly, a wedding."

Nightfall considered a moment. The last had promise. Voluntary or not, Edward's marriage to Willafrida meant landing, he believed. Yet, Nightfall refused to place his trust in that last possibility. Edward choosing to marry a duchess-heir fell into a vastly different category than being forced into an intolerable union. Surely King Rikard would not let Nightfall out of the oath-bond based on a strategy that had gotten Edward in trouble, shamed the younger prince and his breeding, and gotten him married as a punishment. That thought sparked another. *Perhaps King Rikard would sanction any action that got Edward land and out of Rikard's charge.* At one time, that would have sufficed for Nightfall. Now, it bothered him. He could always take another chance at uniting Willafrida and Edward; the danger of their romance might heighten its excitement. But Edward deserved a chance at something better than a wedding at weapon point and a jackass for a father-in-law. Despite Nightfall's thoughts, he responded directly to the duke's words. "Sir, that seems fair enough. I'll wait here while Willafrida is asked whether my master forced anything on her." Nightfall hoped the young woman would speak honestly and not lie to snag a prince of such beauty.

The duke dismissed the suggestion. "The court physician will examine her in the morning."

The duke's words seemed wholly unrelated to the topic. "Examine her, sir? There's a way to tell such a thing?"

Duke Varsah stared, equally incredulous. "Of course. Physicians can tell if a woman's virginity is intact. Purity is required as a condition of most noble weddings."

Nightfall wondered if the rule extended to the men as well as the women. If so, it explained much about Edward and, especially, his reaction to Kelryn.

Varsah's manner hardened again, though less extreme than previously. "Poor Willafrida. I had hoped never to have to subject her to such a thing until her wedding day. That alone makes Edward deserving of punishment, whether innocent or guilty. Even if they merely talked as he claimed, his crime began when he invaded a lady's room."

The impact of Varsah's words struck hard. If the physician would perform his check for the first time, it meant Edward would take blame for any indiscretion of Willafrida at any time. Recalling the outfit and pose she had struck when she believed Nightfall the suitor who sent the mysterious flowers, he doubted she would pass the physician's test. Edward would take blame and punishment for another man's entertainment. "If you ask her about what happened, she won't have to suffer the physician's test."

The duke stiffened, sitting forward in the chair again. "My daughter is innocent. There's no need to question."

Nightfall turned the remark back on itself. "Surely then, sir, she would not lie."

Duke Varsah's voice gained volume. "She's a sweet girl. She might protect him out of kindness. Or embarrassment. The examination will tell the whole story. If

Edward violated her, she becomes unweddable to any noble on the continent. Alyndar will need to marry her to one of theirs, and it won't be to the rapscallion who violated her."

Now Nightfall recognized the whole story, and it confirmed his lack of faith in human nature. The duke of Schiz had found a way to turn an incident into a godsend and a promiscuous daughter into a proper princess. It was not his daughter's welfare, nor Edward's impropriety, that bothered Duke Varsah. He had seen gold, land, and title; and he leapt for those with vigor. Marriage to a prince was not enough; he had set his sights on Prince Leyne Nargol of Alyndar. Annoyance churned through Nightfall. He had not noticed the oath-bond in some time; apparently the duke's assurance of Edward's safety had appeased it temporarily. Now, it rose with Nightfall's anger, inadvertently fueling it. "No. Oh, no." He sprang to his feet. "You're not using my master to win your daughter a kingdom."

"You're talking nonsense!" Varsah shouted. The guard edged between duke and squire. The other sentries blocked the exits, hands clenched around hilts or polearms.

"My master will not take the blame for every thorn that pricked your daughter."

Varsah leapt to his feet, features purple, as if he planned to pummel his guest to death with his own hands. If the guard had not stood between them. Nightfall guessed things might have degenerated into a brawl; but the duke stopped short, still too far to hit. "Take him away! Just get him out of my sight!"

Nightfall's thoughts raced, assessing the layout and situation in an instant. He believed he could fight his way through, but not without casualties, possibly on both sides. If he failed, he either died or went on trial for murder in addition to insubordination. The former, he felt certain, would hold a more massive penalty. If he went willingly, they would almost certainly imprison him until Varsah calmed down enough to decide punishment or a representative from Alyndar discussed terms for the release of prince and squire. Although he never doubted Rikard would happily sacrifice him, Nightfall knew he could escape more easily and with less violence from the duke's dungeon than his guard-surrounded meeting chamber. From the inside, he had a better chance of finding Edward, and Willafrida's conscience might drive her down to check on him. She could find out where the duke had imprisoned the prince.

Nightfall assumed a passive, submissive position, head low, arms away from his body and out-turned. He would not give them reason to use force on him, no matter the pleasure that might bring Duke Varsah. He would rather place them in the position of protecting him from the enraged noble than the other way. The irony soothed him.

The guard in the room gestured Nightfall away from the furniture. When he obliged, sentries took a brisk formation around him. One stood in front of him, his back an eager target for a blade Nightfall would not draw. Another took a position behind their prisoner, and the remainder fell in at either side. As a unit, they marched out a different door than the one Nightfall had entered through and headed down a short corridor to a tower.

Although Nightfall's cooperation should have made the guardsmen lax, they seemed more edgy than comforted. He credited their attitude to the wild chase he had taken them on through the dungeon and opposite tower. He hoped the guard who had fallen down the steps had not been seriously injured, not from any sympathy for a stranger's welfare but from the concern that the guards might avenge their fellow with brutality or Duke Varsah, if ever informed of the incident, might try to claim he had intentionally harmed the man. No official in Alyndar would doubt the duke's accusations against Nightfall. Edward was another matter. He hoped it would take more than the physician's examination to convince Rikard that his raving idealist of a son would rape any woman. If swayed, however, he would place the blame directly on Nightfall. Though he knew little about court law, Nightfall doubted Duke Varsah could really maneuver a wedding between his daughter and the elder prince. But the duke apparently believed so; and, for now, that was all that mattered.

To Nightfall's surprise, the contingent led him up, rather than down, the tower steps. His imagination brought images of his body tossed from the parapets or of a hidden torture chamber in the highest corner of the citadel. He pushed these ideas away. Whatever happened, he would find a way to handle it. He always had. Now, he felt sorry he had ever considered bringing Edward and Willafrida together. He would not wish a father-in-law like Varsah on anyone. *Well, maybe Finndmer. But he wouldn't deserve Willafrida or a dukedom. Hell, he didn't deserve the swamp land he sold me.*

Nightfall counted five landings when the upper cone of the tower steepled over his head, the rafters littered with frayed twigs and speckled with bird feces. One of the guards opened the door, and the other eight ushered their prisoner through it. It opened onto a room with a table surrounded by several chairs, and three doors broke the contour of the wall on the opposite side.

"Together or separate," one man asked a broad-shouldered brunet who was obviously the leader.

The large one considered for several moments. "Together, I guess. Better politics."

A short, stocky guard with a crooked nose raised doubts. "Are you sure the duke wanted him brought here? The dungeon . . . ?"

The leader shook his head. "Better politics. We can always move him later. It's easier to increase than lighten sentence, once done."

One of the sentries who had not spoken loosed a ring of keys from his belt and placed one into the lock of the central door. Nightfall studied it from habit, getting a feel for the general contour. He doubted he could relieve one of the guards of his colossal set of keys without the missing weight becoming obvious, but he did not believe the lock would prove all that difficult to pick anyway.

The leader patted Nightfall's clothes from neck to ankle, then checked each obvious pocket. By the time he finished, the guard had opened the door and the others had taken defensive but nonthreatening stances. The room contained simply crafted furniture, including a bed, nightstand, and a table that held bins for washing. Prince Edward stood, staring out a semicircular window at the town. He turned.

"In," the leader said to Nightfall.

Nightfall could not imagine any room looking less like a jail cell. This chamber seemed more comfortable than most of the inn rooms they had shared over the past few months. He entered docilely, and the door swung shut behind him. The oath-bond died to a level just above baseline.

"Sudian." Edward smiled, then his face furrowed. "What are you doing here?"

"Great to see you again, too, Master," Nightfall good-naturedly belittled Edward's greeting.

"Well, of course I'm glad to see you." Edward moved to the center of the room. "I just don't like the circumstances. I'm a prisoner, you know."

Nightfall could think of no direct reply that wouldn't sound either patronizing or inane. "They haven't harmed you, have they, Master?"

"Certainly not. They've taken fine care of me."

Nightfall politely stepped around Edward to look out the window. The ground lay five floors below them. He poked his head through the hole, gauging the distance. He could fit through easily; Edward would have to wriggle and shove. The regular blockwork of the tower would make scaling it a routine effort for him, but he doubted Edward could manage it at all without equipment. He turned. "Let's go."

"Excuse me, Sudian?"

"I'll climb out through the window. Then I can get the grapple up here, and you can come down." Although he had deliberately purchased a lightweight grapple, he did not feel certain he could toss it five stories. He did believe he could climb partway and accomplish the throw from there, if necessary. At the worst, he could clamber back to the top and place the grapple in position.

"You mean run? Escape?"

Nightfall blinked, his intention surely obvious. "Well, yes, Master. Of course."

Edward sat on the edge of the bed. "I can't do that!"

"You can't?"

"No."

"Why not?"

Edward entwined his fingers in his lap, his attention fixed

on his hands. "I did something wrong. I'm imprisoned here until my father and the duke decide punishment."

Nightfall froze, shocked. This complication he had never considered. "But you didn't do anything to Willafrida."

"I sneaked into her bedroom. That was wrong."

"But . . ." Nightfall started and stopped. This line of discussion would get him nowhere. They needed to slip away before sunrise or else they would not have another chance until the following night. By that time, Duke Varsah could decide he wanted Nightfall executed or tortured and a note would be on its way to Alyndar. "But, Master. We can't stay in one place." A good reason presented itself in an instant. "The Iceman will find us." He paced, wringing his hands, trying to look as frightened and agitated as possible.

Edward looked up. "He can't find us here."

"He will, Master. I'm sure of it. By morning, every gossip in town will have some story of what happened here. Ritworth will hear." He added in sudden afterthought. "And he can fly." He made a broad arc with his arm to indicate a swoop through the window. "And what about Kelryn? You promised to protect her, too."

"Sudian, it's all right. We'll just explain to Duke Varsah, and he'll protect us all."

"No!" Nightfall spoke before he thought his reply through, but the obvious horror worked as well as any gauged response. "You promised, Master. You promised no one would know about my . . . my . . ." He whispered, honestly concerned someone might overhear. ". . . my curse."

"You mean, birth-gift," Edward corrected.

"The curse is Ritworth. And others like him. There's no gift in that. Master, please. Please don't make me beg."

Edward studied his squire with sympathetic eyes. "All right," he said at last. "We go, but it's against my better instincts. There'll be long-term ramifications . . ."

Nightfall was out the window before Prince Edward finished the sentence.

Chapter 16

A wizard hoped to slay the beast.
He conjured up a poisoned feast.
The demon fed him to the crows—
Darkness comes where Nightfall goes.
                    —The Legend of Nightfall
                     Nursery rhyme, alternative verse

Moonlight bathed the He-Ain't-Here Tavern to a red glaze in darkness, and horses stomped and snorted in the paddock. Pressed against the pasture fence, Nightfall watched patrons come and go, identifying them in the open doorway by torchlight from the common room. Prince Edward crouched beside his squire, his huge figure, light-colored silks, and golden hair too obvious a target to Nightfall's trained eye. Given his way, Nightfall would have had them ride as swiftly as possible to the joust. Abandoning Kelryn would have seemed a blessing, but he had yet to think of an argument that could bypass the prince's current obsession and convince him to leave her behind. Until he did, he would not mention the possibility as it would only cast suspicion on his motives once an appropriate reason occurred to him.

Silently, Nightfall cursed Edward's persistence and the situation into which it trapped him. Logic told him allowing Edward into the tavern would prove too dangerous, and the rising tingle of the oath-bond confirmed his doubts. It made more sense for Nightfall to enter the tavern alone to collect their gear and a woman he would rather desert; yet caution would not allow him to leave the prince in an alley, alone and hunted, either. Snagged into a stalemate, Nightfall also realized the dangerous significance of time. The longer they tarried, the more likely Varsah's men would recapture them.

Becoming impatient, Edward pressed forward. "She's inside, Sudian. Let's go."

Needing to delay, Nightfall blocked Edward with an outstretched arm. "Wait, Master." He took advantage of the sight of three men entering the tavern together. "Look there." He pointed to the strangers.

Edward glanced in the indicated direction, unimpressed. "What, Sudian?"

"Guards, Master. Probably hunting for us."

Edward shook his head, dismissing the possibility. "They're not guards. No mail and no uniforms."

Nightfall kept his arm in place, blocking Edward's path. "That's a trick, Master. I'm certain. I saw most of the duke's men. Those are guards."

Prince Edward stepped back into place, giving his squire the benefit of the doubt. "Off duty?"

"Possible," Nightfall admitted. "But just as dangerous."

Edward returned his attention to the door, though the men had already entered. "Why do you think guards would be going there now?"

Nightfall kept his gaze on the tavern door. "Good place to hunt for us, don't you think?"

Edward shrugged. "Not necessarily."

"And to get information of any type."

Edward stiffened visibly. "Do you think Kelryn's in trouble?"

Nightfall pretended to consider, knowing immediately that he could only answer in the negative. "Master, they don't know she's with us. Even if someone tells them, she has nothing to do with your visit to Willafrida. They have no reason to hurt her." Nightfall seized the opportunity. "If we go to her now, Master, we may get her in trouble. If she doesn't know what happened or where we've gone, there's no excuse for Varsah to bother with her at all."

Edward opened his mouth to protest, but no words emerged. He must have seen some common sense to Nightfall's explanation, yet it did not sit well with his honor and need. "She's still in danger from the sorcerer. We can't just leave her."

"Of course not, Master." Nightfall answered the second concern first. "We'll come back for her. We can even send word from the joust. Money, too, if you think it necessary. *After* Varsah has given up on Kelryn having any information about us." He addressed Edward's other point. "And the Iceman doesn't want her. He's after me."

Edward dropped to his haunches, obviously still uncomfortable with the idea of leaving Kelryn. He crouched in a thoughtful hush for several moments. Then, obviously having made a decision, he pulled a stylus and a curl of parchment from his pocket. He started scribbling.

Glancing about to ascertain that no one was nearby, Nightfall sat beside the prince. "What are you doing?" he whispered.

"Making a note." Edward continued writing. "We can sneak it to Kelryn somehow. At least then she knows we didn't strand her, and she can catch up to us later."

Nightfall liked the idea of a note, though he would have it say something quite different. "Master, one problem."

"Hmmm?" Edward continued writing.

"Kelryn can't read."

Edward's stylus stopped moving. He looked up. "She can't?"

"No, Master." Nightfall simply told the truth.

Shocked, Edward asked the obvious, though foolish, question. "Why not?"

"Most commoners can't, Master."

"Oh." This was apparently not a matter he had considered before.

"If she takes it to just anyone to read for her . . ." Nightfall trailed off, the complications of such a thing obvious.

Edward looked stricken.

Nightfall presented his plan then, certain Edward would be receptive to many ideas he would not have considered moments earlier. "Kelryn and I had a picture language." Again, he spoke honestly. They had invented ways to communicate with drawings or gestures. "I could write the note, and we could pay someone to deliver it to her. If anyone else looked at it, they couldn't read it."

Prince Edward handed over stylus and parchment eagerly.

Nightfall broke off the part Edward had scrawled. It

made little sense for him to use code if the note also contained written details.

"Tell her we had to leave in a hurry and we tried to get her, but we couldn't." The prince dictated excitedly. "Tell her we're coming back for her. Oh, tell her where we're going so she can follow us. And sign it from me." He pointed at the parchment. "With love."

Nightfall met Edward's gaze directly, brows raised. Times like this reminded him his master was still an adolescent.

Edward controlled his childish exuberance, his voice returning to its usual commanding timbre. "Did you get all that, Sudian?"

"Yes, Master, I heard it all." Nightfall ignored the prince's guidance, writing precisely what he pleased. He returned the stylus to Edward. "Now, I need to find a messenger." The obvious choice came to him at once. He glanced toward the tack house. "The stable boy should do. He could get our packs, too, without suspicion. I'll be right back."

Prince Edward craned to see the writing over Nightfall's shoulder. He frowned at the two illustratives. "That says everything?"

"Not everything, Master," Nightfall admitted. "I can't write as much in code as free hand, but this has all the important points she needs to know." *Like that we don't want her around us any longer.*

"I'll come with you." Edward rose.

"It would be unwise, Master." Nightfall gestured the prince back down. "The guards will be watching for the two of us together. They won't notice me so much if I'm alone."

Edward nodded, though obviously not wholly comfortable with the situation. "Sudian, be careful."

The warning seemed ludicrous; it was far more likely they would spot Edward. "I will." Nightfall slithered into the shadows. The oath-bond quivered awake, intensifying the farther he went from the concealed prince. Nightfall ignored it. He would not go far nor remain away long. Within a few paces, he came upon the tack house and pressed his back against it. He glanced toward their hiding place near the paddock. His trained eyes carved Edward's outline from the surrounding darkness with an ease that discomforted him. He would have to work fast.

Nightfall remained in place, studying the area in the moonlight briefly. Seeing no suspicious figures or movement, he opened the tack house door. First, he hauled down the gear for their horses, leaving it outside for later collection. Then, he approached the stable boy sleeping on piled straw in the corner. The youngster lay on his side, curled beneath a threadbare blanket, his breathing deep and slow.

Nightfall placed a hand on the boy's shoulder and shook gently. Drowsy, brown eyes flickered open, and the stable boy sat. Pieces of straw clung to his brown hair. He studied Nightfall for several moments. Obviously recognizing him and recalling the generous tip on their arrival, he smiled and leapt to attention. "What can I do for you, sir? Should I get your horses ready?"

"No. Thank you. We can handle that." Nightfall offered a silver.

The stable boy rose quickly, gaze locked on the coin.

"I'd like you to go to the men's inn room, get my master's pack and mine, and quietly pass them through the window." Nightfall described their gear.

The stable boy nodded. Though it must have seemed an odd request, he did not question it.

"Then, I want you to find a woman named Kelryn. She might be in the women's overnight room." Nightfall pressed the silver into the boy's hand. "She's in her early twenties. Has hair as short as mine, and it's white like an old person's."

The stable boy stared at the payment. "Is she the one I saw with you earlier today?"

"Yes. Good. Give her this message. Just hand it over, and don't tell her anything. Then meet us by the packs. No matter what Kelryn actually says, tell my master that she claimed she'd wait here till we return."

"All right." He placed the silver into his pocket.

"I'll give you another if you do that all correctly and quickly."

The stable boy grinned.

Nightfall did not bother to swear the boy to silence. So long as Nightfall mentioned nothing about their destination, the boy could say whatever he liked to protect his own innocence, even the truth. There was nothing inherently illegal about assisting patrons, especially a foreign prince; and the boy would have had no way to know he helped fugitives.

The stable boy trotted off to play his role, and Nightfall gathered the horses' gear.

As night deepened, the crowd in the He-Ain't-Here Tavern thickened, then waned to the small group of patrons who had paid for lodgings. Kelryn sat at a table by the unlit fireplace, alone, becoming more alarmed the longer the absence of Prince Edward and Nightfall stretched. She knew she could no longer assume they had just stepped out and would soon return. Something had happened to them, though whether a voluntary escape from her or trouble she had little information to surmise. She knew only that, earlier in the evening, one of the Mitanoan travelers claimed to have overheard them talking about joining the Tylantian contests. She doubted Edward would leave her without explanation, but Nightfall would do everything in his power to strand her and talk the prince into doing the same. She knew no one better at manufacturing emergencies.

Tears welled in Kelryn's eyes, smearing the color to a pasty green-brown. Love ached within her, a burden she felt certain she could never shed. Though understandable, Nightfall's hatred cut like shards of the broken swan, and she felt as if her heart had shattered with it. Truth, if he would listen, would have to win him back; but even that did not seem the answer. Although it would exonerate her, the explanation might hurt him more than just letting him believe she had betrayed him.

Memory assailed her brutally then, as it did whenever she allowed her thoughts to stray to the ugliness she could never forget: the man on the floor twisting his body to escape the agony the sorcerer gleefully inflicted. The screams that cut straight to the heart and seemed to turn her insides into liquid. The driving need to do something, anything, to stop the cruelty, and the fear that had paralyzed her into a shocked and helpless silence. The knowledge that any action on her part would only have meant death for them both did not assuage the guilt she lived with every day.

Kelryn gritted her teeth, forcing the image away before it solidified. From experience, she knew that, if the details became clear in her mind, the picture would haunt her through the remainder of the day and nightmares would terrorize her sleep.

"'Excuse me, ma'am."

Glad for the interruption, Kelryn glanced to her right. A boy dressed in the same gray linens as the serving maids stood at her elbow.

Kelryn tried to keep her voice steady. "What can I do for you?"

"Here." The boy tossed a scrap of parchment to the table. Without further explanation, he turned and headed toward the outer door.

"Wait," Kelryn said, many questions coming to her at once. She could never recall a messenger not waiting long enough for a tip, at least.

But the boy ignored the call, scurrying outside before Kelryn could shout for him again. She let him go, more interested in the parchment. Although illiterate, she knew a few words, mostly ones Nightfall had taught her; and the two had developed a sparse language of hand signs and pictograms during their courtship. She unfolded the parchment. Nightfall had used the picture code, his handwriting bold and crisp. He had drawn only two symbols. The first, a gently waving series of lines, meant love. He had penned it neatly, then slashed over it with dark, brazen lines to indicate an error. The only other marking took the shape of a guiding arrow.

Kelryn crumpled the parchment in her hands, driven to tears by the implication. She knew he intended to tell her that the feelings he had once held for her had been a mistake; and the arrow pointed for her to go away. She folded her arms on the table, buried her face between them, and let the tears fall where they would. She found herself pinned in place, hopeless beyond moving but not beyond suffering. The love symbol and its covering lines seemed like a branded impression against her eyes, a picture that would never fade. *It's over.* Kelryn tried to let go of all the promises and hopes for the future, but they clung, a fiery agony that made the tears come faster.

Why do I care? Kelryn had asked herself the question too many times to need an answer now. *He's a thief and a killer.* Yet Dyfrin's words returned to haunt her: "I think what he struggles with most is that deep inside he's a good man, fighting to become the demon his mother and the populace named him. If he committed half the crimes ascribed to him, he'd have to be quintuplets; and I know it's closer to a tenth of the burglaries and a hundredth of the murders. And every one, no matter how necessary or deserving haunts the conscience he doesn't even believe he has. Why do you think he plays so many people? With each one, he tries to escape the very thing he believes he has to be. He has no realization of how much time he spends in other guises compensating and consoling the families of those he robbed or killed. But I know."

Kelryn had listened raptly with a skepticism deeper than she would have believed anyone could allay. But Dyfrin had done so, countering every question and quelling every doubt. That he knew Nightfall as well or better than Nightfall knew himself swiftly became obvious. More eerie, he seemed to understand her to the core as well. Only later she discovered the explanation, knowledge that had cost her the man she loved, a fear that would not leave her, and evil dreams that lasted long into the day. So innocent. So simple. And yet nothing had held such a price. If Nightfall would only let her tell him, he would understand.

The burden Dyfrin had placed on Kelryn would not allow her to surrender. "Someone has to break the cycle, Kelryn; and that someone is you. I admit, I worried that you would hurt him and drive him deeper into the abyss he doesn't realize how much he wishes to escape. But now I know you truly love him. You can help him. He needs you."

Kelryn remembered how those words had made her

feel at a time when she still grappled with the realization that the man she had fallen in love with was the world's most notorious and vicious rogue. All she had ever wanted was a normal life, never to change the world or any person in it besides herself. Yet Dyfrin convinced her. Nightfall was not the wanton killer the citizens believed him; and, unlike the conscienceless mercenaries who could only be controlled or executed, Nightfall rehabilitated could become a boon to the very continent that had so long cowered to hear his name. "Why me?" she remembered asking, the burden too much for one common dancer to carry.

"He loves you."

Kelryn had thrown the answer back at Dyfrin. "He loves you, too. And for much longer."

Dyfrin had worn a pained expression that showed he understood, but the matter had too much significance to allow for doubts. "I've done what I could. I showed him the other side of life and relationships at a time when he needed it. I demonstrated that love and pain don't have to go together, that loyalty does not always lead to betrayal, and gave him as much self-worth as an impoverished street orphan could have. Without those things, he would have been lost, every bit the night-stalking demon so many believe him to be. I've done all I can. Now, he has to know that I'm not unique in the world, that others can be trusted. And he needs to learn it from a woman."

Utter panic had suffused Kelryn then, the need to run from a responsibility she had no competence to handle. She still lived amid the wreckage of her own less than adequate home circumstances. To help her family eat, she had lied about her age and started dancing at twelve. By thirteen, she had needed to sell her body as well. No matter the notoriety of the source, Nightfall's gentleness had made her feel special, and his obvious love for her had turned sex from a chore and duty into the beautiful and joyous thing she had always heard it should be. She owed him, wanted to do what she could for him, and Dyfrin understood that as he did everything else about her.

Kelryn's crying slackened to a trickle as gentler scenes from the past paraded through her mind, but realization of the tragedy that had followed their conversation jarred her back to the present. She would not abandon Nightfall until she forced him to listen and he understood what had really happened. He could believe her or not. He could react in any fashion that suited him. He could still choose to leave her, and she would handle that as it came. But she would not let him do so without first hearing the truth. Without the facts, he could only assume, and he could do little else but believe she had betrayed him. Yet, though she had considered it a thousand times, she still could not discard the realization that the truth might hurt him more.

Kelryn regathered her composure. She raised her head, studying the tavern through tear-glazed vision. No patrons remained. The serving girls wiped and rearranged the tables. The bartender restored bottles, bowls, and mugs. She rose, stretched, and headed through the door to the rooms beyond. Gathering her supplies, she went back into the common room and slipped out into the night. Any direction seemed as good as another when she had no way to know for certain where Edward and Nightfall had gone, so she followed her only lead.

The road to the eastern cities did not take Kelryn far before exhaustion overrode her. Determination had driven her until that moment; but, as the sun rose higher in the sky, the decision to chase randomly after a stranger and a man who hated and mistrusted her seemed foolish. In the cities, she was protected. Here, she felt vulnerable and alone, prey for woodland creatures as well as the bandits or rapists who menaced those who dared to travel without armed guards. And, though it made little sense for one without a natal talent to fear them, she worried about sorcerers most of all. She had seen the pain they could inflict, and the memory obsessed her.

As if to personify Kelryn's fears, a man stepped casually from the brush. He wore unwrinkled linens, finely tailored. Light brown curls fell rakishly across his forehead, and his dark eyes examined her like prey. He held a doll in his hand, apparently fashioned from the same grayish mud as the pathway. She recognized him at once as the sorcerer who had ambushed Edward in her room, the one the prince had called the Iceman.

Kelryn gasped, taking an involuntary backward step. Her heart rate trebled in an instant, and images of blood and death scored her vision until the man in front of her seemed to disappear. Terror froze her in place. She prayed for someone to come, anyone who might frighten the sorcerer away; but she stood alone on the broad stretch of road. She glanced about wildly, desperate for escape though her limbs would not obey her.

The wizard smiled. "If you're looking for a place to run, don't bother." He held the mud doll in one hand and seized its foot in the other. Suddenly, he twisted.

Agony shot through Kelryn's leg, and she collapsed to the ground as much from startlement as pain. "Stop," she sobbed. "Please stop." Ghosts plagued her, a body striped with wounds. Splashes of blood on wall and ceiling.

Ritworth released the foot. By all natural law, the mud should have crumbled in his fingers; but the figure returned to its created shape, strangely pliable in his grip. He continued to study Kelryn calmly, the smile etched in place, as if he found as much pleasure in control as in the pain he inflicted on her. "Don't try to escape. Answer my questions honestly, and there'll be no more pain."

Kelryn remained in position on the road as the pain receded, her eyes still aching from the crying jag the previous night. She drew all her courage together, forcing away the images and managing whispered speech. "What do you want from me?"

"Information."

"I don't know anything."

"Let me ask the questions first." Ritworth came closer, standing directly over her, his face cruel and his eyes reflecting a happy madness. "Where are the prince and his squire?"

Kelryn whimpered, despising her weakness. "I don't know."

Ritworth buried a fingernail in the gut of his figure. Pain doubled Kelryn over, and she snaked into a knot to escape it, without success. She screamed.

Still composed, Ritworth removed his finger, and the

anguish settled to a dull throb. "I'm going to pretend I didn't hear that and ask the question again. Now, where are the prince and his squire?"

Pain and fear drove tears to Kelryn's eyes. When she swiveled her head to display her integrity, she saw him through a blur of moisture. "Please. They left without me. I don't know where—" This time, the agony speared through her back, and she felt as if she would snap in two. She screamed repeatedly, welcoming the hovering promise of unconsciousness.

Apparently realizing he would lose his information source to oblivion, Ritworth restored the shape of the mud doll. "Damn it, woman. I'll find a pain that makes you talk if I have to inflict it by my own hand!"

Kelryn sobbed, curling into a helpless ball that only seemed to further enrage the Iceman.

"Talk, damn you. Talk."

"I—" Kelryn managed, obligated to say something. "I—just—"

Another man spoke from the brush, his voice ominously familiar. "She doesn't know, Ahshir Lamskat's son. Or should *I* call you Ritworth, too?"

The Iceman stiffened and spun to face this new threat. "Who are you?"

Kelryn's fuzzy thoughts would not let the identity of the second man come into focus. Though she believed herself rescued, something about the voice shot shivers of dread through her. She loosened her muscles cautiously, moving slowly as much from fear of retribution as from discomfort. The pain seemed to disappear as swiftly as the magic inflicting it, but one glimpse of the newcomer's middle-aged face with its neutral brown hair and ghost-pale eyes brought a crampy ache that had nothing to do with sorcery. She vomited, sick from terror and pain. Two sorcerers stood before her now, and she could not handle even one. She slumped to the ground.

"Does my name matter?" the more recent arrival said. "I could make one up as easily as you did."

Ritworth's response was a sudden harsh word accompanied by a gesture Kelryn remembered well. She cringed as he flung his ice spell at the other sorcerer.

As quickly, the newcomer pointed at a site directly in front of himself, mumbling. Where he indicated, the air seemed to shimmer like heat haze over dark earth. Ritworth's magic entered the area and slowed to a crawl, its intention visible as icicles and crystals stretching toward its target. The blue-eyed sorcerer stepped aside as the spell crept toward him. Once through the band, the magic apparently returned to its normal speed; because, an instant later, a patch of ice slopped onto the road.

Frost dusted the more recent arrival's brown bangs. "Nice," he admitted, unruffled.

Ritworth's face puckered and reddened. He threw down the mud doll, slamming the breath from Kelryn's lungs and sending bruises aching through her limbs, pelvis, and rib cage. She struggled for air as the wizards exchanged spells that came to her only as slashes of light and pinpoint sparks across her vision. When she finally managed to breathe, they stood where they had, glaring at one another, as if daring the other to attack first again.

The newcomer broke the silence. "Ahshir, I didn't come to hurt you. I have a proposition."

The Iceman's eyes narrowed. "A sorcerer make a deal with another? You mistake me for a fool."

"Listen to what I have to say first. Then you decide."

Kelryn remained in place, throbbing in every part as if she, not the doll, had gotten hurled to the packed roadway. She wanted to block out the sounds and scenes around her, to silently creep from the road and become lost in the forest. But pain held her immobile, and something about the blue-eyed sorcerer's voice soothed and drew her to trust him. If not for the memory of him towering over another, inflicting torture that sent his victim writhing and seizing in a frenzied, panicked desperation to escape, she might have given her loyalty without understanding why. Horror and hatred overcame the gentle magic he used to help persuade, at least for her.

Ritworth, however, had no previous experience with the newcomer to prejudice him. He remained coiled and watchful, but he did listen. "Speak your piece, then."

"My name is Gilleran, and I'm the chancellor of the

kingdom of Alyndar." The blue-eyed one kept his gaze locked on the Iceman.

Kelryn tensed, preparing to fast-crawl away. The movement roused pain; and she squirmed, driving her focus to his words to avoid the pain but pretending deafness. She wriggled toward the mud creation, certain only that she wanted it out of other hands than her own. Any further movement would require motivation she did not have. The constant ache sapped her of drive, and vivid memories of the agony this sorcerer could inflict all but paralyzed her.

Gilleran continued. "Both princes are headed toward their destiny: death in tourney. The king is getting older, and I stand next in line for the throne."

Terror ground through Kelryn, lost in the wild maelstrom of fear already assaulting her. Bad enough she would surely die for no more reason than befriending victims of treason. She would never get the chance to warn the innocent prince and the loyal squire she loved.

Ritworth's lips pursed. "A convenient arrangement for you," he conceded. "But how does this concern me?"

"A kingdom of souls. A quarter of the continent at my mercy." Gilleran's tone created a grander picture than his words. "An endless pool from which to replenish my power as captured souls get used to decay. More spells than I could ever use myself. Some perhaps would prove more to your liking? A fair split would make us both the most powerful men in the world. Our talents and our armies could conquer any who dared stand before us. Ultimate power and every talent-soul our property. What more could any man want?"

Ritworth glanced at Kelryn just as she scooped up the mud doll. If Gilleran spoke the truth about Edward heading toward the contests, Ritworth no longer needed whatever information Kelryn could give him. "Keep that, if you wish," he told her. "Its power is spent. Try to run, though, and you're dead."

Kelryn clutched the figure possessively. Though tight, her grip caused her no consequences, suggesting either that Ritworth had spoken honestly or only things he did to it could harm her. *Better to chance killing myself than die in the agony he could inflict.* Kelryn gradually winched her hand closed. The doll crumbled to dust, and no pain accompanied the breakage.

Ritworth addressed Gilleran next. "It sounds like the perfect arrangement. Why would you want to share?"

Gilleran shrugged. "There's more here than I can handle by myself. It's lonely having everything. Who better to split the riches with than someone who understands 'the hunger'? Who better than someone with enough power to help defend it all?"

Ritworth frowned in consideration, his interest obvious even to Kelryn, though she could not tell whether it stemmed from avarice or some mundane or magical ability of Gilleran to sway. She shivered, no longer pained, held in place only by Ritworth's warning and her own incapacitating fear. She had always considered herself tougher than most, yet the images of sorcerous slaying hammered at her courage until it became lost beneath the terror.

"Will you join me, Ahshir?" Gilleran pressed Ritworth for an answer. "Or do we battle now to the death? Your choice."

Ritworth sighed, obviously torn. "How do I know I can trust you?"

Gilleran smiled. "Watch." He walked to Kelryn. Once there, he addressed her. "Kelryn, pretty girl. We meet again." He held out a hand to assist her to stand.

Kelryn shied away, all her desperate fear returning. "Get away from me, you murderer."

Gilleran flashed a grin at Ritworth. "We're old friends." He turned back to Kelryn. "I can kill you as easily on the ground. In fact, more so. If you cooperate, I won't harm you."

He used a sincere tone that Kelryn had difficulty doubting. Then her mind filled with images of magical slashes that splattered blood and Gilleran's laughter as he butchered the screaming man pinned beneath him. Tears blurred her vision. Avoiding his hand, she obediently stood. She could escape more easily on her feet.

"This is how I bind my oaths." Gilleran made a broad, arching cut with his hand. Pausing, he mumbled a few guttural syllables. "Kelryn, this spell will hold us both to any promises we make. Here are the terms this time: If you find Prince Ned, you will tell him his loyal chancellor has handled the Iceman and he has nothing more to fear from sorcerers." He winked at Ritworth, as much, Kelryn suspected, to keep his attention on a potential enemy as to share the details of the spell. "You may say nothing negative about me within earshot of Edward, Leyne, or Rikard Nargol." He added with an evil smile. "But before you leave, you must kiss me like a lover."

Revulsion restored Kelryn's will to fight. "Beast! Demon! I'd rather eat feces than look at you."

Gilleran retained his cool demeanor. "No need to flatter, Kelryn. I had already planned to give something in return. My promise to you: this time, at least, I'll let you go unharmed and alive. And I will do what I can to see my companion does you no damage either."

Ritworth raised his brows at this, obviously displeased.

Gilleran finished, "However, should I meet you later under other circumstances, I retain the right to act as I feel prudent. Do you agree to these terms?"

Kelryn hated every part of her situation, but most of all remaining in the presence of two sorcerers. She did not doubt the efficacy of the spell; she knew too little of magic not to believe the claims of those who practiced it. Gilleran had not made her promise anything malevolent. She could not warn Edward of danger, but she could still tell Nightfall everything and let him handle the prince. This time, she swore, she would compel her lover to listen. If she did not agree to Gilleran's terms, she harbored no doubt the wizards would kill her in the most vile fashion they could devise. A kiss seemed little enough compared to what Gilleran might force upon her if she refused. "All right," she said carefully. "So long as your promise is included, I agree."

Ritworth interrupted. "Is that wise? Letting her go, I mean. She's a witness."

"A witness?" Gilleran crinkled his brow. "Witness to what?"

"She knows what we are."

"No matter. She knew before. Sometimes the knowledge of others works to a man's advantage, even when it doesn't seem so. Trust me."

"She heard your plan."

"I've been with the king nearly two decades. He trusts me. No one would believe the tramp, especially when the story she tells varies in the presence of royalty."

"Still ..." Ritworth started.

Gilleran shrugged off the argument. "If she gives me reason, I left us plenty of opportunity to kill her." He grinned at Kelryn with a corpse's warmth. "I believe she's a smart girl, aren't you, Kelryn?"

Kelryn kept her mouth closed. She would make no more promises for the sorcerer to seal with his magic.

Gilleran muttered a few more words, accompanied by some finger movements. "Done," he said at length. He nodded at Kelryn. "You're free now."

Kelryn did not wait for a second invitation. She launched herself from the path to the woods, taking three running steps before pain slammed her low in the belly and she collapsed to the dirt again. Something sparked and crackled, like a fire inside her, driving her back toward the roadway and the sorcerer waiting there. She whimpered, nearly incapacitated by the pain, rolling to find some position that eased the agony tearing through her. By luck or instinct, she wriggled back the way she had come, and the lessening of the magic's urging sent her crawling to Gilleran's feet.

"Forgot something, didn't you?" Gilleran prodded her with a boot toe. Ritworth watched in silence.

Understanding struck Kelryn then. She could not leave until she had administered the promised kiss. "You bastard," she managed, the oath-bond now only a prickle prodding her to her feet and to fulfill the promise. She stood, torn between need and loathing. She took a step toward him. Leaning over, she granted him a quick peck on the cheek that dulled the buzzing only slightly.

"Ah, well, no wonder you've lost your lover if that's the best you do for him." Gilleran reached for Kelryn.

She cringed away, though it cost her a stab of pain.

"Come now. I know you enjoy our company, but we can't stand here all day. If the Iceman decided to kill you,

I'm not certain I could move fast enough to stop him. I only promised I'd try, remember?"

Kelryn chose the lesser of evils. Determined, she planted her lips on Gilleran's, hating the perfumed smell of him and despising the taste of his lips. Her tongue touched his, and she gagged as much on the thought as the presence of his saliva. His hands explored her with fierce and shameless boldness, and it sickened her. The kiss lasted until the inner pain disappeared, leaving only the nausea. She pulled away, trying to run. But her empty stomach roiled from the experience, and she heaved dry. Dizzy aftereffects dropped her to her knees.

Gilleran laughed at her discomfort. "Do you see how I bind promises?"

"Yes." Ritworth nodded. "I'm convinced. Now we kill her."

Kelryn stiffened.

"No." Gilleran stepped between Ritworth and Kelryn with a quickness that seemed uncharacteristic. "I'm every bit as tied to my oath as she to hers. Killing her would destroy my soul. And I can't let you do it either."

Ritworth relaxed, apparently satisfied by the answer to his little test. Although Gilleran's claim proved nothing, his instantaneous loyalty to his oath, even before the partner he was trying to befriend, was convincing enough; and he had knowledge of the manner and workings of magic. "Very well, then," he said grudgingly, clearly still not comfortable about letting Kelryn go free.

Through all the fright and discomfort, a memory surfaced in Kelryn's mind, words Nightfall had used the same night he had revealed his foul past: "Accident is never reason enough to kill a man. There are better ways to handle mistakes than murdering innocent spectators." Clearly Gilleran had learned this lesson where Ritworth had not. For that, at least, he seemed the lesser evil. Though no longer the focus of attention, she rose cautiously and edged toward the forest. No one tried to stop her.

"What do I have to do?" Ritworth prepared for the process.

"Come here," Gilleran gestured Ritworth to stand in front of him, beneath an oak edging the roadway.

Ritworth moved to the indicated place. Kelryn slipped into the woods, every instinct goading her to run. But, this time, she managed to keep enough presence of mind to remain hidden in the brush. The words the sorcerers exchanged could become vital to the safety of Edward and Nightfall. She peered between branches in time to see Gilleran make the broad, looping cut he had performed just before beginning the spell he had used to bind her. This time, however, he added a guttural phrase.

Ritworth and Kelryn realized the significance at the same time. The maneuver had nothing to do with the oath-bond, nor had it when he cast the spell on her. Gilleran had set Ritworth up for other magic. Even as understanding dawned, sorcery cleaved a massive limb over Ritworth's head, and it came crashing down upon him. Ritworth dodged aside, too late. The branch slammed him across the back hard enough to snap vertebrae and pinned him to the ground. Kelryn screamed, the sound lost beneath Ritworth's louder screech of agony and Gilleran's laughter.

Now, nothing could keep Kelryn in place. She sprinted without thought or direction, dodging and ducking through trees and brush, ignoring brambles that clung to and tore her clothes and skin. At least four times she slammed into trees, once hard enough to send her sprawling, the wind knocked from her lungs. But every time she staggered onward. The Iceman's shrill cries of agony prodded her like a burning brand, and her thoughts flashed back to the night in her room: The conversation interrupted by Gilleran's sudden entrance. The wild charge that had grounded a gentle man who had become a friend in a matter of hours. The short struggle—futile. Gilleran's magical slashes had carved deep, bleeding swathes as easily as he had cleaved the tree limb over Ritworth. The physical mutilation had seemed endless, the suffering cries spiraling her into a hysteria that would not leave her, night or day. If only she had not frozen. If only she could have saved Dyfrin.

Kelryn ran until the sorcerer's screams faded into the

background swish, rattle, and bird calls of the forest. She charged through the woodlands until time, hunger, and exhaustion lost all meaning. Then, when she could run no more, she crumpled into a sobbing heap on the forest floor and prayed to the holy Father that she would some-day find the strength to fight back.

The road and forest became familiar to Nightfall and Prince Edward Nargol as they traveled eastward. After the first few days, they found themselves in the constant company of would-be spectators from every land. Night-fall appreciated the crowds. Their talk told him most of what he needed to know about the layout of the tourney fields, the specifics of the combat, and details about the competitors. Where eavesdropping fell short, he supple-mented with innocent questions, usually gaining far more than the information he sought. More than seventy nobles and highborn had received invitations. The true tally, of course, would not come until they arrived. As Edward had proven, an invitation did not necessarily mean the in-vited one would choose to participate. The elimination setup also meant that Edward would not directly battle most of the others. In fact, simple computation of the chances, without assessing skill, suggested even odds that Edward would be eliminated in his first trial. Nightfall would see to it those numbers changed quickly.

At night, they camped. While Nightfall prepared food and chatted with their many short-term companions, Edward pieced together outfits and horse decorations of rich purple to serve as their crest. He had had little choice when it came to colors; Nightfall's clothes came only in Alyndarian purple and silver. Without time to create the symbol, they would have to temporize with a solid ban-ner. Once the duchy was won, they could work out the details of a crest. This lapse seemed to worry Edward more than the contests themselves, but Nightfall guessed that had more to do with using it as an excuse to take his mind off the possibility of facing off with his brother. Nightfall found competition between the princes no con-cern at all. Surely, the officials would make efforts to keep brother from standing against brother; and, with any luck, Prince Leyne Nargol would lose early.

Nightfall and Edward arrived at the walled city of Tylantis in the late morning, though a winding line of people blocked their view even of the ramparts. Mounted guards in Tylantis' orange and bronze rode through the masses, stopping at intervals to question individuals or escort the highborn, their servants and families, to the head of the line. Within an hour, a stately guardsman in mail on a dappled horse approached Edward. "Good morning, good sir. Might I ask your name?"

Not wishing to spend the remainder of his natural life waiting, Nightfall took his cue. "My master is Prince Edward Nargol of Alyndar."

The sentry seemed pleased by the name, apparently one he had been counseled to seek. Nightfall hoped that came from the competition, not some message sent by Schiz' duke. He banished the paranoia. It would take time for Duke Varsah to notice them missing and figure out which direction they had taken. He would also need to decide whether or not to risk pitting duchy against kingdom by hunting a prince over an issue of manners.

"Participating or spectating, noble sir?" the guard asked.

"Participating," Edward replied.

"Very good, sir." The guard glanced at the surrounding crowd. "Do you have retainers or family you wish me to attend?"

"Only my squire." Edward indicated Nightfall with a sweep of his chin.

"Come with me." The guard rode off, shoulders back and head raised, obviously preferring the duty of escorting players to herding disgruntled spectators. He led Prince Edward and Nightfall directly to the gates. "Just one moment please, Prince Edward." He dismounted, shouldering through a press of guards at the gateway. True to his word, he returned almost immediately. "Come with me, please." The guards stepped aside to leave a pathway into the city. With their guide at the lead, Edward and Nightfall rode between them.

Though Nightfall once knew the city by heart, it looked

nothing like he remembered. Every open area had merged, now covered with the retinues of knights, nobles, and highborn men of every description. Massive horses, groomed to a sheen, grazed while servants and slaves scurried to tend animals and masters. Some of the buildings and dwellings he remembered had disappeared to make room for the competition. In the middle, wooden fences marked off several rings where the combats would take place, each with its own portable wooden jousting wall inside the confines. Merchants thronged the periphery, offering everything from fresh cooked meals to "strength potions" that likely contained nothing more exotic than the local food. Though rare on the green, women abounded among the fringe elements, seeking husbands or quick money for a night of pleasure before the following day's events.

The guard found a relatively open space amid the jumble of participants. "You're one of the last to arrive, Prince Edward. I'm sorry about the cramped quarters."

Edward cheerily dismissed the need for apology.

"I'll let the officials know you're here and see if I can find out who you'll be fighting."

"Thank you," Edward said.

"Why don't I go with you?" Nightfall added quickly. "I can bring the news back to my master and save you the time and trouble of returning."

Edward nodded his agreement, obviously buying that Nightfall volunteered to assist an overburdened underling. In truth, Nightfall wanted a glimpse of the competitor list as well as some guidance as to how the system worked in order to calculate every opponent Edward might face. The knowledge would make cheating far simpler.

"Thank you," the guard said, though with far less enthusiasm than an offer to help should have elicited. Obviously, he preferred carrying information to nobles, a far more pleasant aspect of his job than the outside sorting he would have to return to that much sooner. Nevertheless, he accepted Nightfall's presence without complaint. Together, they rode toward the central rings and a group of highborn elders conferring there.

The guard pulled up before them. "This is the squire of Prince Edward Nargol."

The men nodded, exchanging muttered comments and rummaging through lists. The guard threw Nightfall a good-bye gesture, then wove his way cautiously through the participants and back toward the gates. Nightfall dismounted and approached, unobtrusively reading one of the lists upside down. "Excuse me, sirs. The guard said you could tell me who my master would be fighting."

A heavyset, grizzled man with a short beard fielded the question. "Certainly. Just a moment." They conferred briefly, giving Nightfall a long look at the list while they used a stylus to cross out and shift names. From their exchange, Nightfall discovered they arranged the participants by anticipated ability then paired them, one from the bottom and one from the top of the list. That meant that the man most likely to win the entire competition fought the weakest opponent, the second fought the next weakest and so on. The strategy had sense to it not obvious on initial inspection. Though the first round of fighting would have little challenge or merit, the least competent fighters would become eliminated in the starting round, and each subsequent match should become more evenly matched and exciting. Once the pattern became established, it only remained to see where they ranked Prince Edward.

Nightfall did not wait long. They sketched in Edward's name far closer to the bottom than he liked, then counted down from the top. He glanced at the list more obviously, as if for the first time. "About half a hundred participants?" he guessed aloud. He scanned more closely, surprised to find Prince Leyne Nargol of Alyndar at the very top of the list. Obviously, Edward's awe of the elder prince's abilities stemmed from more than just brotherly adulation.

"Forty-eight," the grizzled man replied. "You're the last to arrive. All the other invitees are accounted for, one way or another. Prince Edward's opponent is Sir Takruysse sol-Chiminyo."

The "sol" indicated a bastard son, and the name seemed pure Mitanoan. Nightfall glanced over the camped nobility, selecting one at random from the crowd. "Takruysse? Isn't he that gentleman there." He pointed. "The one with the green and copper standard?"

"Green and copper?" The grizzled man shook his head without bothering to follow Nightfall's gesture. "That's Ivral's colors. Takruysse uses a background of brown and green swirled together, and his symbol's a stalking cat. Brawny knight with hair so dark black it's almost blue."

Nightfall did not recall having heard anything specific about the man on his travels. Likely, Mitanoan nobility would keep slaves, and he might find information or even disloyalty among them. At the worst, having an opponent who ruled in slave country might fire Edward's spirit. "What kind of fighting will they do?" Nightfall rephrased the question in a form suiting a dutiful squire. "What weapon should I ready for my master?"

"The first round, everyone jousts lance to lance. The winner only has to unhorse his opponent. The loser is eliminated from the contests. The winners get paired, and a flag toss determines who chooses the weapons. The decision is posted tonight, so there'll be no surprises or unfair advantage tomorrow. By the last match, we should have only the best three fighters remaining."

Nightfall repeated the math for himself. By tomorrow, the numbers would whittle to twenty-four, then twelve, then six, then three.

"Those three will all face one another, so that each will fight twice." He rattled off the rules next. "All participants should fully armor for their own safety. Deliberate attacks directed against horses will result in disqualification. Standard rules apply for weapons: no sharp edges or tips. Jousting is done from opposite sides of the wall. We don't want any serious accidents. Each man is responsible for his own equipment and his own horses and slaves or servants. We do have some sparring weapons available, but we don't guarantee quality."

Nightfall knew Prince Edward had no practice weapons, but he suspected a man who could wield a spade against enemies probably had little prejudice when it came to balance or construction.

The man finished, "Any rule not covered here will be

assumed to be as routine for tourney. All disputes about decisions must be brought to the judges immediately after the match. Personal grudges should be handled outside of the city. King Jolund reserves final authority in all decisions of any type." He smiled at Nightfall. "Any questions?"

"Just one." Nightfall smiled back. "When my master wins, who will he fight next?"

The judge allowed for Nightfall's loyalty. "When your master wins, he'll compete against the winner of . . ." He scanned the list quickly for proper pairing. ". . . this contest." He touched a finger to the names just above Edward's. "Either Baron-heir Astin of Ivral or Sir Fedrin of Trillium." He winked. "If judges could place wagers, I'd bet on Astin. Then again, I'd also put my money down on Sir Takruysse. He's won his share of contests."

Nightfall shrugged, seeing no reason to overplay his loyalty. He glanced at the sheet for a reasonable idea of who might become future competition. Each contest doubled the number of possibilities, but it gave Nightfall some direction for his research. Edward would start with a difficult opponent. With each consecutive win, the competition would get more fierce; and Nightfall hoped his cheating could carry the prince all the way to final victory. Despite his experience with devious underhandedness, he had never gotten involved in the luxury games played by the highborn. Still, he supposed, nobility needed some way to weed out the chaff, and contests of skill seemed better than comparisons of lineage. Edward, Nightfall guessed, was considered Alyndar's roots and stems. "Thank you." Turning, he headed back into the crowd.

Remounting, Nightfall took the long way back, examining the competition. Squires curried horses, oiled tack, and polished armor. Slaves and servants scurried between masters and the periphery with food, water, and small items for preparation or repair. He found Takruysse toward the center, the cat symbol and swirling colors unmistakable. His slaves had crafted a wooden lean-to in which a proud blood bay charger stood, its demeanor watchful but calm. Clearly, it had weathered many contests. The jousting saddle perched upon a stout log supported horizontally by poles staked into the ground. Silver reflected highlights that blinded Nightfall, and he shielded his eyes for a closer look at the more functional, weaker parts of the tack. The cinch strap was a braided weave of brown and green sewn onto a gleaming ring, its cleanliness suggesting it was brand new for this contest. A leather tie would draw it into place. The front and back supports, Nightfall guessed, would prove sturdy. The armor lay neatly stacked on a blanket, two collared slaves oiling and buffing, giving full concentration to the task.

Nightfall took the scene in at a glance, without pausing to gawk. He headed back toward Prince Edward, his mind a whirlwind of ideas. Thoughts of tampering with Takruysse's lance passed quickly. To hollow it would take too much time and risk, and Takruysse would surely notice the abrupt change in weight and balance even before the contest began. Whittling it down would not get past the knight's inspection. Nightfall cared for horses too much to lame one without consideration of all other options first, and he doubted he could injure Takruysse without taking his own life in his hands. He imagined he could sneak in and kill the knight, but neither his conscience nor the oath-bound promise to leave the persona of Nightfall behind would allow murder without justification. Tampering with the armor seemed possible, but remotely so. Nightfall knew nothing about its parts, construction, and donning. He considered slipping something inside it, such as bees or some kind of grainy powder; but a better plan came to him based on equipment he knew well. The saddle seemed the target; he had sabotaged cinches before. And minor preparation of Prince Edward as well would aid the success of his plan.

Nightfall returned to his master pleased by his own cleverness. Edward had dismounted, though the horse still wore saddle and bridle, the reins looped in the prince's hand. He talked with another man perched on a heavily-muscled palomino, its coat burnished and its mane cream white, unmarred by even single hairs of darker color. It stood motionless, four feet steadily braced and its ears cocked back and attentive to its rider. Nightfall focused on the stranger, drawn by the majesty of stance and appearance. The close-cropped blond hair made Edward's longer locks seem unruly though they were well-brushed. The features were familiar, and the shrewd, brown eyes clinched the identity. He looked like an older version of Edward, except for the eyes that could only have come from King Rikard. Only then, Nightfall recognized the purple and silver patterning on the silks of man and horse, the too-familiar colors of Alyndar.

"Master, let me handle the horse." Nightfall reached to take the reins from Edward. He gave each prince a respectful half-bow.

Edward waited until Nightfall had a good hold on the leathers, then released his grip. "Sudian, this is my brother, Crown-prince Leyne."

Nightfall made a gesture of deferential respect with his free hand, allowing the elder prince to speak first.

Leyne obliged, his voice the same booming bass as his father's. "Ah, yes. This is the fanatically loyal squire they're still whispering about back in Alyndar." He studied Nightfall with a measuring gaze that seemed more curious and aloof than mistrustful. Nightfall would have bet all the money in his pocket that Leyne knew nothing about Rikard's and Gilleran's arrangement. "Four months and not quit yet. That is impressive." He winked at Edward to show he meant no offense.

Edward smiled tolerantly.

Nightfall took an immediate dislike to the crown prince of Alyndar. The things brothers could get away with saying to one another had never ceased to amaze him. Nightfall set to his work without a reply, stripping saddles and bridles from both horses and hobbling them to graze.

Leyne turned his attention back to Edward. "Best of luck, brother. It's good to finally see you take some interest in competition. No matter how you fare, it'll be good experience for future tourney." He spun his horse and waved over one shoulder before heading back into the crowd.

Edward watched after his retreating brother, lips pursed and gaze longing. "I wish I could be more like him."

Cut your brain out. Bloat your self-regard. Nightfall

kept the thought to himself. Finished with the horses, he set up camp swiftly. Edward continued to stare after his brother, looking nervously out of place amid the confident band of nobles and their entourages, nearly all of which consisted of more than just a single squire. Once he spread the sleeping blankets, prepared food, and arranged the packs protectively around their camp, Edward finally addressed him.

"How much do you know about armor and jousting weapons or getting horses ready for tourney?"

Nightfall saw no reason to lie. "Nothing, Master."

"Nothing," Edward repeated, clearly disappointed but not surprised. "Well, then, I'll teach you. Leyne said the first round will be all tilting."

Nightfall's brow creased. "Tilting, Master?"

"Lance competitions from horseback." Edward sighed, apparently realizing Nightfall had not exaggerated when he claimed to know nothing about the sport. "A good choice in some ways; you'll need to learn everything at once." He considered his own words. "A bad choice for the same reason, I guess, depending on whether you learn better at once or gradually." He gave Nightfall a questioning glance.

Nightfall shrugged. "Teach me whatever is needed. I'll learn."

Edward nodded, obviously realizing the answer did not matter, nor would it change anything about the situation. "First, a trip to the weapons stock. The experienced ones will have brought equipment of their own, decorated and balanced to their liking. As late as we came, we'll have to take whatever's left of what the competition supplied, if anything. Otherwise, we'll have to borrow."

Nightfall nodded to indicate he had heard, but he did not concern himself with the problem. Once a weapon met certain specifications, the biases of individual wielders made far less difference than most would think, at least to Nightfall's mind. He preferred a perfectly balanced and tapered throwing knife, but he could fling a sharpened stick into a bullseye. Skill played a far greater role than tools, and he had watched Edward wield a spade like a sword with too much competence to believe minutiae would destroy his ability or sense of timing. "What about Prince Leyne's lance? Wouldn't he lend it to you?"

"He probably would." Though he answered in the affirmative, Edward shook his head. "I wouldn't ask."

Nightfall tendered his question cautiously, a repeat of Edward's words. "You wouldn't, Master?"

"It would be impolite. Leyne's weapons are like his queen will be: long-sought, meticulously chosen, and not to be shared." The prince hesitated, obviously as discomfited by his own choice of words as the thought of borrowing from the brother he emulated. "Did you find out who I'll fight first?"

"Sir Takruysse sol-Chiminyo." Nightfall gauged Edward's reaction.

The prince swallowed hard, features paling. He managed a mild smile, with obvious effort. "They must trust me to do well in my first competition to give me an opponent who has placed high in so many."

Nightfall thought it best not to explain the true structure of the Tylantian bouts. It would only wreak further havoc on Edward's already sagging morale. Instead, he selected words to fire up his master. "I'm not the only one who sees your prowess, Master. And the battle the Father gave you begins as well. Takruysse is from Mitano. And he keeps slaves."

Edward looked away, lost in thought. Only the tensing of his jaw gave away his mood.

"Which comes first, Master, lessons or lance-picking?"

Edward unclenched his teeth to answer. "Weapon first so we can make arrangements for borrowing, if need be, before nightfall."

Nightfall had long ago learned not to respond to the word-play on his name, although this time it seemed eerily appropriate.

Edward added apologetically. "I'm afraid we'll probably have to practice donning and doffing armor several times tonight."

Nightfall suspected the exercise would prove a chore for both of them, but he did not mind. With knowledge of the proper technique would come an understanding of the competition's weaknesses. Means to cheat, Nightfall felt

certain, would come to him as well. He would only have
to find ways to do so that would keep the judges, and
Edward, ignorant.

Leyne's name came up for the first of the five waves of
competition and Edward's for the second, which meant
Edward needed to prepare while his brother fought. Word
reached them quickly enough, however; and it scarcely
seemed worth watching even had circumstances allowed.
The crown prince had cleanly unseated his opponent on
the first charge with an easy fluency that remained the
talk of the spectators even as the second set of competitors paraded toward their assigned rings.

Nightfall had found his loophole in the form of raw-
hide bindings that secured Edward's legs to the saddle
and his gauntlet to the pommel. Though not directly mentioned in the rules, Nightfall guessed his trick would
prove unlawful and against propriety if anyone discovered it; he would see to it that no one did. He had secreted the straps as only a sneak-thief could and wet them
to hardened strands he would need to cut when he unar-
mored Edward. They would not break. The same, he
hoped, would not prove true of Takruysse's cinch. Under
cover of darkness, he had slipped past all of the
Mitanoan's slave sentries to work his trickery on the tack.
It had taken finesse to weaken ties without tell-tale fray-
ing and to just the right extent that it would not give
while cinching onto the horse, even for a second tightening.

Following the lead of other squires, Nightfall rode at
Edward's right hand as the procession wound, in two
lines, toward the roped off arenas. Unlike nearly all of the
others, they had no symboled banner to display; only the
purple cloth they both wore demonstrated that they belonged together. Yet, even without a standard, Edward
looked regal. He kept his head high, more, Nightfall
guessed, from training than temerity; and his blond hair
fluttered like gold around his aristocratic brow and
cheeks. The blue eyes, though soft, flashed determination,
and the armor added size to an already substantial figure.

At a command from a man in Shisen's colors, appar-

ently a representative of King Jolund, the squires in
Nightfall's line looped behind their masters and took new
positions at the left. Missing the cue, Nightfall trailed the
others, finding his place just as the two ranks closed together. Now, the nobles rode in pairs, competitors side by
side, and the squires sandwiched them. Although the eyes
of every participant and servant remained fixed ahead,
Nightfall violated the pomp by using the arrangement to
study Takruysse. He saw little but the gleaming, towering
form the armor lent all of the participants, and the shadows of the helmet revealed only snatches of expression
and feature. A single dark curl had escaped the enclosing
metal and drifted across his forehead. The man riding at
his right hand seemed more frightened than honored.
Nightfall hoped Edward read the slave's discomfort as
well. It might goad him.

King Jolund spoke from a dais in the center of the arenas, surrounded by rigidly alert guardsmen. "Shisen gives
its thanks to all the many visiting nobles . . ." The speech
rattled on, the king saying very little in as many words as
possible. Nightfall paid the king no heed, having overheard it all when the first wave of combatants had held
this same position. He would prattle eternally about the
seriousness of the competition, the duchy prize at its conclusion, the rules Nightfall had heard from the judges the
previous night, and the standard procedures and conduct
at competitions that he had already violated.

Some of the horses stood like statues, moving only to
swish their tails at an occasional fly. Others pranced in
anticipation or impatience. The competitors, including
Edward, listened raptly to the king, their expressions as
grave as the Father's most faithful in his temple. It
amazed Nightfall how seriously the highborn took their
games, placing on them an adherence to honor that tran-
scended life and death. To Nightfall, it only reinforced
how removed they had became from the issues of and
need for survival. Every year, while the nobles traveled
from city to country, deciding which toy lance suited their
hands most comfortably, the commoners daily made decisions as to whether to feed the weakest child and pray
both might live or the strongest and give that one a fair

chance while the other's cries faded and disappeared. Caught up in the sobriety of the moment, Nightfall could not help but consider Edward as a ruler. Given his morality and Nightfall's advice, many things would change. Fewer children would grow up beaten by mothers with no other outlet for their frustration.

Applause splattered through the audience, shaking Nightfall free of musings that embarrassed him. *I'm thinking like Dyfrin again.* He strove for the unfeeling pessimism of the demon, but it remained beyond his reach. It did not fit his current guise. For now, and until Edward won Shisen's duchy, he was Sudian.

The nobles split to their respective rings, and the audience drew in as close to the roped off areas as they dared. Nightfall rode to the sidelines with Takruysse's slave, the horses shielding them from the hordes. The two combatants split, riding to opposite sides of the arena. The crowd went silent. The slave tensed and loosened his fists, eyes locked on his master, clearly intent on the outcome.

Nightfall initiated conversation. "Your master must treat you well."

The slave tore his gaze from the baron's bastard reluctantly. "Not really." He smiled. "But if he rules a duchy in the east, I'm a free man. There's no slavery in Tylantis."

Nightfall nodded his understanding, glad Edward could not overhear. Better the prince did not consider the possibility that his losing might grant some slaves freedom, at least not unless consolation became necessary. Before he could reply directly, the slave's attention snapped back to the contest. The horses charged toward one another on opposite sides of the low, central wall.

Edward held his lance in position securely, his shield raised to take whatever blow Takruysse delivered. He seemed anxious, an unsettling contrast to Takruysse's staunch resolve. The two raced toward one another. Nightfall stared, not allowing himself the luxury of a blink. He needed to remain alert to anything that the impact might reveal or that the judges or Takruysse might call a foul. His eyes stung by the time lances met shields with a thunderous crash, the weapons tearing a line of sparks along metal shields. The collision proved too much for the damaged cinch. It snapped, dumping saddle and rider over the horse's rump. Edward rode past, barely budged, cautiously reining his horse.

The slave swore viciously under his breath, and they both rode to meet their masters. Takruysse rose, eyes wide and mouth open, as if he could not fathom how he had wound up in the dirt. The slave assisted his master dutifully. One judge came to Edward's side and the other spoke to Takruysse. The baron's bastard shrugged, speaking too low for Nightfall to hear. The judge at his side made a gesture to the other to indicate no challenge. With a nod, the one near Edward spoke. "The winner of round one, Edward Nargol younger prince of Alyndar." Sparse applause and whispers accompanied the pronouncement. Takruysse had gained a following from his appearances in previous games. Edward had only the secret love many hold for any underdog and the steadfast squire who rushed to his side and covertly removed illegal restraints.

First round won. Five to go. Nightfall knew the process would grow harder as the numbers became whittled. His frauds would have to become more subtle as the crowds and judges paid closer attention. As winning lent confidence and the duchy became more than distant dream, losers would become quicker to dispute judgments, right or wrong.

Edward chattered softly at Nightfall as they rode around the finishing competitions in the other arenas. "I can't believe I actually won. Lance has never been my best weapon . . ." He broke off as they rounded the last of the rings where a dispute had ensued, drawing the attention of competitors as well as spectators, including Prince Leyne.

The knight who had called the foul explained. "He hit my horse. That's against the rules."

The not-yet-proclaimed winner pleaded his case. "If it's deliberate, it's against the rules. I just swung a bit wide. I grazed it by accident."

The judges nodded, glancing from one to the other and whispering between themselves. A hum stretched through the crowd as each moderated the dispute in his own mind.

From what Nightfall could hear, most believed the victor should keep his win. The judges seemed uncertain, deliberating for moments that passed like hours to the competitors. If they upheld the win, the knight of lesser ability would continue in the contests, at least according to the lists. That made the claim of foul hold more weight than if the stakes stood the other way.

Clearly, Prince Leyne did not agree with the masses. He addressed the "winner" directly. "Usually, Darxmin. An accidental strike would not count against an honest man. But that same so-called accident won a match for you in Grifnal last month and in Mezzin last year. The judges should know that also."

Darxmin glared momentarily at Prince Leyne, but he did not deny or defend the charge.

Edward nodded slightly, his expression grave, his eyes round with reverence at his brother's knowledge and memory. Nightfall watched without obvious expression, wondering what advantage Leyne gained by overturning the victory.

The judges pondered several moments longer. Then, the eldest spoke, "Retire to your corners to prepare. This match will be fought again."

Applause followed the announcement of what seemed a fair compromise, even to Nightfall. It did not impugn either man's honor and would assure an honest contest. Intentionally or by accident, Darxmin would not hit the other horse again.

Leyne threw his brother a stiff, acknowledging salute, then rode off into the crowd.

Edward and Nightfall continued toward their camp, the prince smiling quietly. "Honest, capable, forthright, and bold. To what more could any noble aspire?"

Uncertain of the question, Nightfall had no response. "Yes, Master," he replied as seemed expected.

"I wish I could be more like my brother."

Not again. "Like Leyne, Master?"

Edward swiveled his head to study his squire. "Well, yes. Who else did you think I was talking about before?"

Nightfall thought it best not to say he had assumed

Edward spoke in general terms. "You're wonderful as you are. Why would you want to change?"

They pulled up at the camp. Nightfall dismounted, removing the bridle so his bay could graze without danger of looping a foot through the reins. Swiftly, he went to Edward's side to assist his dismount in armor.

"As always, I appreciate your loyalty, Sudian. But how can a man not model himself after one as exemplary as Leyne Nargol?"

Nightfall chose not to answer, instead seeking the real motivations behind Leyne's action while he meticulously removed the armor as he had been taught only the day before, beginning with the gauntlets so Edward could use his hands. "Does his highness not like Darxmin?"

"They're friends."

"How about the other knight?"

"Sir Trettram? Leyne knows him, too. They've lost contests to one another." Edward assisted Nightfall, painstakingly piling the armor to avoid further scratching or dirtying it.

This news fell outside Nightfall's experience with human nature. It made more sense for Leyne to side with the man who would prove no match for him later in the contests. He explored other possibilities, trying to force the picture into his view of reality. He worked on the theory that Leyne might side with the man whose style of fighting he knew better. "He's stood against Trettram more often then, Master?"

"No, actually, Darxmin's been a part of the competitions longer. He's just not a particularly good warrior, at least compared to most gentry."

Nightfall let the thoughts settle while he removed the last of Edward's protections from the padding beneath it. Curiosity goaded him to delve further into Leyne's motivation, but propriety would not allow it.

Edward extended the conversation to its natural conclusion. "His honor won't let him tolerate dishonesty, so he speaks out. His interference makes things better. I try to do that, too, but I always wind up in trouble because of it."

The comments brought understanding to Nightfall in

two forms. First, he conceded that Leyne might actually have mediated the situation fairly rather than tried to rig it in his favor. Second, he realized just how much Edward Nargol tried to imitate his brother and just how miserably he had failed. The situation intrigued Nightfall. He had never had a sibling. Although he respected Dyfrin more than any person on the continent, it had never occurred to him to mimic his friend's morality or actions, only to occasionally follow the advice when it suited him. He had to be what his bloodline made him, not a copy of Dyfrin. Yet, Nightfall realized, bloodline had given Edward and Leyne the same potential.

Prince Edward changed into his regular clothes while Nightfall inspected and polished tack and armor. Edward obtained the meal from one of the many vendors, and Nightfall packed away gear to protect it from damage or theft, appreciating the reprieve from cooking. He ate well, reawakening the charade of testing Edward's portion for poison. With a duchy at stake, Nightfall doubted most of the other participants would prove as truly "noble" as Crown-prince Leyne. In fact, he had not forgotten his own vial of *shartha* petals tucked away in a pocket. In any but tremendous doses, it would only cause cramps and vomiting; and he had no intention of killing anyone.

After the meal, Edward wandered to the rings to watch the remaining matches, though whether as entertainment, for technique, or to judge the competition, Nightfall did not care. He napped, preparing for another sleepless night of rigging contests.

Chapter 17

A gambler bet the tales were lies
And scorned the wisdom of the wise.
The odds were not the ones he chose—
Darkness comes where Nightfall goes.
>   —The Legend of Nightfall
>   Nursery rhyme, alternative verse

The rising and falling roar of milling crowds, merchants hawking wares, and the shouts and applause of the spectators did not awaken Nightfall; but a closer noise did. The last round of tilting had scarcely finished when a horse violated the mental boundary Nightfall's mind considered camp. Instantly fully alert, he leapt to his feet, instinctively positioning himself between Edward and the threat. He found himself facing Prince Leyne mounted on his palomino charger. The beauty of horse and rider gave them the appearance of a grand, golden statue draped in purple and silver. The identification did not allow Nightfall to relax. He still mistrusted the elder prince.

Leyne laughed. "I'm sorry. I didn't mean to startle anyone."

Edward looked up from where he sat near their gear, reading, clearly unstartled. "No harm done." He closed the book, careful not to bend pages, placed it on his pack, and rose.

Leyne swung down from his horse, passing the reins to Nightfall, obviously accustomed to instant responses to his needs. Nightfall accepted the responsibility without reluctance or comment, playing his role. He admired the horse, a highly-worked and -muscled gelding that seemed as obedient and calm as it was beautiful. Stories abounded about knight's horses, and most peasants and stable hands believed them ingrained to one owner. Dozens of tales circulated about well-intentioned stable boys stomped to death by war-horses taught to kill any man but their masters who touched them. Clearly, either high-born disseminated the stories to discourage thieves or Leyne used a different beast for war than tourney.

"Congratulations." Leyne approached his brother. "I never thought of lance as one of your better weapons, and you bested a worthy opponent."

Nightfall listened for some grain of accusation or challenge in Leyne's voice and did not find it. The sentiment seemed heartfelt, the elder prince genuinely happy for and complimentary of his younger brother.

Edward fairly beamed. His blue eyes sparkled, and the corners of his lips bowed slightly upward. However, he maintained his dignity. "Thank you, brother. I'm pleased."

Nightfall watched and judged openly, not bothering to hide his protectiveness from either prince. Physically or emotionally, he would defend Edward's well-being.

Leyne smiled, either at Edward's innocent joy or Nightfall's overcaution. "They've posted the next round. You're fighting Astin of Ivral, the baron's first son. It doesn't seem like you to pick double swords, so he must have gotten choice of weapon."

Nightfall had always considered Edward huge; however, Leyne dwarfed him for sheer muscle mass. Nightfall guessed the elder prince outweighed Nightfall, at his baseline, by double or more. With the addition of armor, the golden gelding carried an impressive burden that explained its bulk as well.

"Double swords?" Edward's words seemed more repetition than question, but Leyne explained as if the latter were true.

"Long swords. One in each hand."

"No shields, then."

Leyne smiled to show he meant no malice. "Not unless you intend to hold it in your teeth." He clapped an encouraging hand to Edward's shoulder. "An unusual choice certainly, but not one you're altogether inexperienced with."

Edward smiled, but it was strained.

"You'll do fine. The strangeness of the weapon will draw attention to the match. Win or lose, if you put up a good fight, you'll be long remembered for it. And I can't see you giving any less. You handled Captain Rahtayne and me well enough."

Edward's grin wilted into sobriety. "With two of the best swordsmen in the country pounding on me whenever I did something wrong at practice, how could I not learn defense? But I don't think I ever scored a strike against our teacher or you. War or contest, nothing was ever won without offense."

Leyne shrugged. "You'll do fine. If you expect to win every contest you enter, especially the first, you'll be forever disappointed. Pride yourself on a competent defense. If you stand long against Astin, you'll gain a reputation and a following." He glanced at Nightfall with a smile not returned, then brought his attention back to Edward. "Do you have two sparring swords?"

Edward shook his head. "Not even one."

"Long swords will go fast, and you're going to need two, preferably ones that balance well together. Why don't I pick some good ones for you?"

"Thank you. Give me just a moment, and I'll come with you. I appreciate your help." Edward made it clear he trusted his brother's eye implicitly. Nightfall felt certain Edward would follow Leyne's intuition even over the feel of the weapons in his own hand.

"You stay and relax. You've earned it." Leyne gestured Edward to remain in place and headed back to his horse. He took the reins from Nightfall. "I'll just take your squire with me if you don't mind."

Nightfall stiffened, certain Leyne had not arranged the situation as casually as it seemed. He scrambled for an excuse that would not insult royalty.

Prince Edward did not make it any easier. "Certainly. Take Sudian along. Between the two of you, you probably know me better than me."

Nightfall played his only card. "Master, I'd rather not leave you alone among so many strangers."

Edward dismissed the concern with a wave. "Nonsense, Sudian. I'm safe with this crowd. Mount up and go with Leyne."

Nightfall hesitated, weighing concern against propriety.

Seeing advantages to discovering why Leyne wanted him alone, he raised no further objections. If the elder prince tried to harm him, he could defend himself well enough. Pain accompanied the thought; the oath-bond leapt to attention and slid into a crescendo of alarm. Recognizing the offending idea, Nightfall carefully reconstructed his thoughts to indicate he would not consider hurting Leyne or any other in the hierarchy of Alyndar. He would only run from conflict. Satisfied, the oath-bond settled. Nightfall placed the bridle on his bay, then sprang aboard without bothering with a saddle. Leyne mounted his palomino.

The two men rode in silence toward the central area where the extra blunted weapons lay piled. Once there, Leyne began his dismount. Before he could reach the ground, Nightfall vaulted down and caught both sets of reins. The prince muttered something incomprehensible either in thanks or impressed appreciation. He picked through the weapons without asking or, apparently, expecting any assistance. This pleased Nightfall well enough. Even from a distance, he could tell Leyne gave at least a reasonable effort to make good selections, tossing aside many for color, construction, or balance. Whatever his intention, it did not seem to involve sabotaging Edward's chances with bad tools. That consideration, however, when coupled with the knowledge that Edward had a strong defense gave Nightfall the answer to how to rig the contest.

At length, Leyne settled on two practice swords. He carried these to a small Tylantian standing nearby, apparently the one in charge of the weapons. They exchanged words Nightfall did not hear, although he caught Edward's name among them and guessed Leyne had explained his purpose for taking two. The Tylantian wrapped the swords in cloth. Leyne balanced them on the palomino's rump, binding them to the back of his saddle with twine. He mounted. Nightfall passed the prince his reins, then leapt aboard his bay.

"This way," Leyne guided Nightfall away from the main affair, through the circling line of merchants and hangers-on, to the base of the outer Tylantian wall. Finding a quiet, grassy place, he pulled up his horse and dismounted. This time, he removed the bridle to allow the palomino to graze. He dropped the head-tack to the ground.

Nightfall followed suit. He waited, allowing the noble to speak first as Edward had taught him, though the urge to question Leyne's true motivations burned strongly.

Prince Leyne's dark eyes seemed to bore into Nightfall's blue-black ones. "I didn't bring you along to select weapons."

That being self-evident, Nightfall responded only with a nod of acknowledgment. Though mistrust goaded him to spar for dominance, if only with eye contact; he used the head movement as a way to politely avert his gaze instead. There was far more at stake here than a war of egos. To antagonize might cause a battle the oath-bond would make him helpless to fight.

"I brought you to offer you this." Leyne put a hand in his pocket and enclosed something in a meaty fist. "Here."

Obediently, Nightfall outstretched his hand to take the unseen offering. Leyne dumped half a dozen gold coins into his palm.

Nightfall could not recall the last time he had seen gold, let alone six coins at once. Though surprised, he allowed his features to reveal no reaction other than confusion. He squinted, brow crinkling. "What's this for, noble sir?" He looked up, unable to keep from meeting Leyne's stare again.

Leyne held the cold eyes with his own, his mood intense, obviously judging every word and movement. "It's yours if you leave my brother's service."

Nightfall's dislike for Leyne turned to frank hatred. In response, he flung the gold at his feet, stomping each precious coin into the dirt. He met Leyne's eyes again, this time hoping the ferocity of his infamous glare stung. He did not bother with words, certain his actions had spoken loudly enough.

Leyne's expression was unreadable. This time, he pulled a pouch from beneath his cloak and opened it so Nightfall could clearly see the contents.

Nightfall tore his gaze from Leyne and cast it upon a treasure. Gold coins and trinkets filled an area nearly the size of his head, its value priceless.

"All this if you leave Edward in any fashion you devise." Leyne shook the contents slightly so that gold shifted across gold, the sound a muffled series of clinks.

Nightfall could not help imagining the uses for more wealth than he had accumulated in a lifetime of theft and butchery. Still, no amount of gold could purchase his soul; wealth served no purpose to a dead man. He did not reach for the bag, even from habit. Instead, he raised his eyes back to meet Leyne's once more. "Noble sir, it is only because of the esteem in which I hold your brother that I don't spit on you and your money." He whirled, storming toward his horse.

"Sudian, wait."

Nightfall stopped, but he did not turn.

"Sudian, please. Hear me out."

Nightfall stepped around to face Prince Leyne once more. The shrewd eyes glimmered with joy, and neatly combed yellow hair perched high above features so similar to Edward's yet intelligent-looking where the younger prince's seemed only boyishly handsome and innocent.

"I love my brother, Sudian. You came from nowhere with a loyalty as fanatical as the most ardent priest. You can't blame me not trusting you."

Nightfall said nothing. The highborn could teach him their ways and manners, but they could not change his inner feelings. He would place blame as he wished.

"The payment." Leyne returned the pouch of gold to his cloak. "It was a test. You passed gloriously, with more honor than any knight or noble here today."

Nightfall understood that Leyne gave him the highest praise he could muster, yet it did not wholly appease him.

"Scant months ago, Ned would have turned that contest with a Mitanoan into a war of cause and conscience against slavery. Righteous rage might have driven him to kill." Leyne studied Nightfall as he spoke. "He would have credited his victory to the holy Father's will rather than his own ability. He may not believe it, but he's a reasonably good warrior."

"The best, Sire," Nightfall returned with habitual ease. Leyne smiled. "That remains to be seen. He's not better than me, I'm afraid, and I intend to win this duchy."

"Why?" Nightfall challenged. Then, realizing he had forgotten the title of respect, he continued as if he had not finished. "Sire, what need does a crown prince have for a duchy?"

Leyne shrugged as if the answer seemed too obvious for answer. "What use does any man have for a duchy? My father will live long, and I may never inherit the kingdom. Even if I do, we both believe I will appreciate my inheritance more if I understand the effort it took my forefathers to win Alyndar. Those who receive without toil become weak rulers and their offspring more so. More than one reigning line has degenerated into decadence and destroyed itself." His manner softened as he brought Nightfall into his confidence. "Besides, someday I'll probably have more than one child of my own. Who does not inherit Alyndar will still have territory to rule."

The concept had seemed obvious to Nightfall from the start. Now, he needed to understand. "Sire, you would provide for your younger children? Why won't your father do the same for my master? Surely, there's enough of Alyndar for more than one."

"First, dividing a kingdom weakens it." Again, Leyne scrutinized Nightfall, though he had surely learned all from his previous efforts. "It would be better if what I say next did not reach Ned's ears."

Nightfall nodded. "It is my mission, Sire, to do what's best and safest for my master. So long as ignorance does not place my master in danger, I promise he will hear nothing of what you tell me."

Leyne bobbed his head once as he made his decision. "My father is concerned about Ned's ability to rule. He needs to win his land and title to truly appreciate and understand its complexities. Hardship and experience teaches."

"I understand hardship, Sire."

"Yes," Leyne grinned again, this time with genuine warmth. "My father said so. Though I think he worries still over his decision to let you squire, he believed you might have a good effect on Ned. I doubted it, concerned you would either prove as unworldly in your devotion to Ned as he with his to the causes he chooses or that you had an agenda of your own in mind. Now, I can see my father was right, as always." Clearly, Rikard had not told Leyne about Nightfall's identity, which meant almost certainly that only the king and his chancellor knew the truth.

Nightfall gained a new respect for King Rikard, now sure the king had not sent Prince Edward away to die. It required a competent mind to project how such an unlikely couple as Nightfall and Edward would fare, yet Rikard had, apparently, guessed well. Whether or not Edward got his land, the king had achieved his goal. Likely, it did not matter much whether the actual landing occurred so long as Edward benefited from the association. The fate of Nightfall's soul, however, was not King Rikard's concern. "So, noble sir, it would be very much in my master's best interests to win this competition?"

Leyne laughed. "Certainly. But it won't happen." He sobered almost instantly, obviously realizing he had become insulting. "Not because of any frailty on Ned's part, of course. I believed from the start he would win that first round if he tried at all. He's better than he believes. He's just used to sparring or watching me; and, with all modesty, I'm ranked the best on the continent. But it's Ned's first contest. And he'll have me to fight, at least."

Nightfall took a chance. "Sire, if it's in your brother's best interests to win, why wouldn't you let him."

Leyne's forehead crinkled. "Let him? What do you mean let him? I'm cheering for him every match."

"Except against you, Sire."

"That goes without saying, of course." Leyne's dark eyes went pensive as understanding seeped within. "You want me to purposely lose to him?" Horror and surprise tainted the question.

Nightfall's shoulders rose and fell, leaving Leyne to work the suggestion through himself.

"That's cheating. It's dishonorable." Leyne shook his head so vigorously his yellow hair flew. "Ned would never feel good about winning in that manner. He would suffer from the shame for eternity."

Nightfall clung to the point. "Only if he knew you let him win. If he believed he had done so by his own skill . . ." He let the thought trail.

"No." Leyne's dark eyes narrowed. "I would know, and I won't forsake my honor for anyone. It's unlikely Ned will make it far enough to compete against me. But if he does, he will win with his own hand or not at all." His features darkened, and his hands trembled slightly with anger. "This, I hope, is not what you've been teaching Ned."

Nightfall remained calm. "Sire, it's my job to protect my master, not train him. I just thought, perhaps, my master's brother would help him achieve the goals your father set. Help or not as you will. My master will win this contest with his own talent alone." Again, he spun around to leave and, again, Leyne stopped him with a word.

"Wait."

Nightfall turned back.

"I will not condone fraud for any man, but I do still admire your loyalty. I wish Ned luck and you as well, and I hope you see my integrity as a virtue not an evil, though it does not work in your favor this time. I understand that those born low cannot always understand the principles of nobility."

Honor loses meaning in the face of starvation and pain. I've never yet met a priest who would not abandon the Father for his own personal gain. Dyfrin had often warned Nightfall to learn men by deeds not words. Those who claimed to be most pious and devoid of sin veiled souls without conscience and deeds of greed and cruelty they justified as gods' will. It was those most evil who generally believed themselves most good, surrounding themselves with lies to placate whatever shred of decency remained. "It's not a matter of understanding, Sire. It's a matter of circumstances. Morality, like laws, can't cover every situation." He turned from generalities to specific. "Sire, I respect your honor and am truly sorry I suggested what I did. I've never done it before, and I won't do it again."

Leyne saved face for both of them. "It seems a shame to let gold lie in the street. If we recover it together, our dishonors should cancel. Three for you and three for me, no favors involved."

Nightfall agreed to the compromise.

Nightfall spent that night swiping swords from the sleeping Astin, then whetting the blunted practice weapons to wickedly sharp edges. He finished by meticulously sanding the temper until its razor verge appeared as dull as prior to the filing. Although he had thinned the blades at either edge, he doubted the difference in balance would prove obvious enough to cue Astin. From rumors, he had learned that the baron's heir had a ritual of practicing the night before a contest and blessing his weapons prior to sleep. He believed training prior to a contest would wash luck and benediction from the blade. Whether or not he kept to his routine, Nightfall doubted Edward's opponent would notice the duplicity.

Nightfall remained edgy, which kept sleep mostly at bay, even after he successfully returned the swords to their sheaths without Astin's knowledge. The maneuver would work only if Prince Edward proved as competent with defense as he and Leyne had suggested. If not, that sharpened blade might prove his downfall, possibly even his death. The oath-bond clamped onto that worry, chiming a warning that ached through Nightfall, assuring the sleeplessness to which his own doubts had already condemned him.

The morning dawned with a light rain that daunted none of the knights. Whittled from forty-eight to twenty-four, the participants could achieve all of the contests in half as many rounds. Many of the losers had packed up and left that night, though the majority had chosen to stay from interest, curiosity, or a desire to learn procedure and technique for future events.

Edward and Leyne both drew into the first round; therefore, neither could watch the other fight. That suited Nightfall well enough. The younger prince would probably prove less self-conscious without worrying about his critical brother scrutinizing every attack or defense. The parade to the field proceeded with its usual pomp, its symmetry marred by the mixture of horseback and on-foot participants as well as the many and varied weapons selected. Nightfall walked quietly beside Edward, alert to any sign of trouble from Astin. He also examined Edward's potential future competitors, dredging up all the information he had learned about them so far. He would need to use a different trick for each one to keep from raising suspicions against Edward. The *shartha* flowers he had gathered in Schiz seemed the obvious next step.

King Jolund's speech came to an end, and the participants moved into their appropriate arenas. Edward entered first, turning completely around before Astin came into the ring. Nightfall took his position directly along the rail where the spectators grudgingly gave him room as convention specified.

The battle began with a double attack by Astin that sent Edward immediately into the defense he and Leyne had described. Repeatedly, Astin's swords skipped for vital areas, parried or blocked by deft movements of Edward's blades. The crowd applauded every jab and each deflection.

Yet, soon, the style of combat wore on everyone. Astin continued his attack, finding little need for defense since Edward tended only to his own protection. As the strokes became repetitive, the applause dropped to a few polite claps. Nightfall kept his attention on the baron-heir's swords. The small amount of light glazing through the clouds diffused across the blades, revealing nothing of their sharpening. But Nightfall knew where and how to study the blades, finding constant, regular notches cut where Astin's swords had bashed against Edward's. Over time, the steel would weaken. He only hoped Edward's patience would hold that long.

Even the last, scant applause died away as the audience waited for some new maneuvers to break the monotony. Edward ignored them, eyes following every movement of Astin's hands, face tight in concentration. The baron-heir changed his style of combat to hard, slamming strokes that Edward fended with his usual skill. The oath-bond increased in intensity as the blows became more vigorous, a warning that sharpened steel, well-aimed, could stab or carve between joints of armor. Then, just as Nightfall gritted his teeth against the pain, Astin's right-hand blade snapped. Steel flew in an ungainly arc, then tumbled to the dirt. Muttering darkly, he dropped the hilt. The crowd murmured in sympathy.

In becoming more one-sided, the battle became less so in other ways. No longer bombarded by two swords, Edward found openings for attack as well as defense. Apparently from a sense of fairness, he cast aside one of his own weapons and battled single sword to single sword. Yet, within half a dozen exchanged strikes and parries, Astin's second blade broke also, its tip digging into the arena floor.

Astin hurled down his hilt, now swearing long and loud. Edward hesitated, obviously uncertain of the rules in such a situation. He glanced swiftly around the judges. When they all shrugged in turn, he followed his own honor. Approaching the sidelines, he passed his second sword to Nightfall. Then, he returned to the battle, weaponless. He dove for baron-heir Astin, wrestling him down. Within moments, Prince Edward had his opponent lying flat in the dirt beneath him. The judges called a halt.

Edward released Astin and rose, reclaiming the sword he had thrown down.

All eyes turned toward Astin. No one waited for him to actually call a foul; his disgruntled demeanor told the entire story. The judges surrounded him. Nightfall slipped nearer to the baron-heir's side of the ring to try to catch at least a few words of his complaint. An investigation might reveal his sabotage, but there would be no way to link the sharpening with Edward. The much more likely explanation, that Astin had whetted his own blades to give himself an advantage, would surely seem far more believable. Many witnesses could corroborate that Edward had gone nowhere near Astin's camp, and the baron-heir's own servants would verify that the swords had remained on their master's hip since his personal inspection the previous night.

Astin stood, brushing off the colored silks that covered his armor. He entered a short conversation with the judges that seemed mostly to involve ascertaining that reasonable and fair procedure had been followed regarding broken blades and winning a contest with weapons other than those chosen, in this case a bare-handed match. Apparently, Edward had violated no rules in this regard because, after a few moments of griping and questioning, Astin waived his right to call a foul. Applause followed, more than at the previous contest. Edward had, apparently, already won himself a following.

"The winner of round two, Prince Edward of Alyndar." The judge gestured at Edward for the benefit of those who did not know either of the combatants.

Prince Leyne met Edward and Nightfall as they headed back to camp, his match having lasted far shorter than the double sword fiasco. He clapped Edward on the back. "Won again, little brother. That's wonderful. Keep going. You're proving all Nargols formidable opponents, no matter how young and untested."

Nightfall dropped back to let the nobles talk.

Edward smiled. "How did you do?"

"I won." Leyne did not dwell on the victory. "The next round of fighting will determine your next opponent and who chooses weapon. We'll all fight one more time tonight."

"Tonight?" Edward flexed his forearms, obviously sore from the constant jar and pound of swordplay.

"It's customary. One more battle, though this time we've few enough to only need one round to finish. That'll leave six competitors by morning and three finalists by tomorrow afternoon. Things should wrap up tomorrow evening. By nightfall, the Tylantis/Shisen area will have a new territorial duke."

By Nightfall. Nightfall smiled. *We can only hope.*

Leyne reached for the practice sword Edward had given Nightfall, and the squire turned it over to him. The prince then tapped the hilt of Edward's other sword.

"Here, let me take those back for you. You get some rest."

Edward drew the sword, though he did not hand it over right away. "Don't you need rest, too?"

"Yes. But the practice pile is on my way."

Edward handed over the weapons and watched Leyne head into the crowd. After a few moments, he started back toward camp. "This should be a learning experience for you, too. I've gotten so caught up in my own role, I've been remiss in my teaching."

Nightfall moved back into step with his master.

"I began with defense, biding time for an opening . . ."

Nightfall let his own considerations take over, disinterested in the details of a match he had observed from beginning to end. He guessed each participant's security would tighten as the goal became visible, and he appreciated that he had used the flashier, more invasive techniques earlier. This afternoon, he would poison Edward's opponent with *shartha* petals, causing waves of nausea that would weaken the other enough to assure Edward's victory. Tonight, Nightfall planned to seek out Okraniah, a street woman who had worked for Nightfall many times for pay. Whatever the job, she had always done well and remained closed-mouthed about the scam. Others would perform tasks for money, but he trusted few.

Edward continued, oblivious to the loss of his audience. ". . . a weapon, it only seemed honorable to disarm myself as well . . ."

Nightfall uttered an understanding noise to indicate that he was listening and impressed, though neither was the case. They headed back to their camp for a short rest.

The relaxation period ended too quickly for Nightfall. Shortly, he headed out to find the slave carrying a meal to Sir Aoscurit, a knight from the western tip of the Xaxonese Peninsula who was Edward's next opponent. It had proven simple enough to sprinkle powdered petals onto the meat amid the hurried jostle of the crowd. Hours later, nothing about the knight looked amiss. Edward had chosen his favorite weapon, poleax, and Aoscurit seemed miffed by that particular decision. He argued vehemently with the judges, loud enough that nearly anyone could hear. Though not a standard dueling weapon, it pleased judges and audience alike, a standout from the usual sword to shield combinations or even the grand horseback lance jousting that was becoming routine.

Nightfall wondered if argumentativeness, for Aoscurit, was a side effect of feeling ill from poison petals, though it did not matter. Whether an unrelated or associated symptom, it would only serve to further wear him down.

Waiting patiently at the inner railing, practice polearm in hand, Edward discussed the matter with his squire. "Maybe I should withdraw and choose a different weapon."

Nightfall frowned, leaning against the wooden framework to keep their conversation private. "It's too late, Master. The judges already approved your choice. Besides, you won the flag toss, not him. He can't get his pick every time, Master. It's not fair for him to expect otherwise."

Prince Edward watched the ranting display in center ring with distress. "But it doesn't really matter to me what weapon we use. And it obviously matters very much to him."

Though Nightfall did not care about the weapon, he preferred Edward used the one with which he felt most comfortable. Even with cramps and nausea, Aoscurit might prove the better using his own favorite arms. "Trust me, Master. It's an insult to you for him to insist his choice is superior. Injury always follows insult. And how will he learn sacrifice and honor if others give in to his tantrums? Let him rave."

Apparently resigned at last, Aoscurit hefted his pole, stepping into position. He seemed slightly more awkward than Edward, and Nightfall attributed this to the poison although smaller size or inexperience could have explained it as well.

"Begin," the judge said.

Prince Edward remained in place, giving Aoscurit ample opportunity and space for the first attack. The knight obliged, charging, the poleax horizontal. As he closed, he whipped the butt end up in an obvious feint. He snapped the polearm back, spinning the metal end toward Edward's helm. Edward caught the attack toward the butt end of his pole, allowing the momentum to help drive his strike for Aoscurit's abdomen. The practice weight slammed against armor, driving the knight off his feet. He crashed to the ground. Edward finished the movement, ending with the butt end of his polearm against Aoscurit's throat.

"End," the same judge said.

Edward removed his weapon and backed away.

Aoscurit sat up, ripped off his helmet, and hurled it to the ground. He shook his head at the judge to indicate no challenge of foul. He had already lost his only possible claim.

The judge raised his hand to Edward. "The winner, Prince Edward Nargol of Alyndar."

This time, the crowd cheered.

Nightfall glanced about, surprised to discover other contests had not yet finished despite the lengthy argument that had delayed their own. Prince Leyne's palomino was just winding its way from a nearby ring, a lance couched against its withers. His smile revealed his victory, and he swiveled his head to catch a glimpse of Edward's contest, now finished. He rode to Nightfall. "How'd Edward do?"

"My master won." Nightfall adopted the look of a child whose greatest wish had come true. "And you?"

"I won, too," Leyne replied matter-of-factly. "Perhaps we will stand against one another after all. If he needs me, you know where to find me."

Nightfall nodded. "Yes, Sire." He did not know the precise location of Leyne's camp, but he could find it easily enough with a short search.

Leyne rode away.

Soon after, Prince Edward emerged from the ring victorious, and Nightfall stepped up to meet him.

Nightfall set out to find Okraniah that evening, threading through the masses of camped nobles as if on a simple food-buying mission for his master. He took special care to pass Aoscurit's area, seeking some indication that he intended to cause trouble. But the knight had, apparently, raised all the objections he would before the match. His slaves diligently polished and packed his gear except for one who huddled near a ragged tent, arm clamped to his abdomen, reeking of stomach contents.

Nightfall bustled past, but not before the realization and irony struck him. Aoscurit had not eaten the poisoned food. Either he had given it to this slave or he had thrown it away and this man had plucked it from the garbage. In either case, Edward had fought a fair battle. Realization extended naturally from the conclusion: Edward had bested Aoscurit without Nightfall's assistance. And he had done it well and quickly.

As Nightfall trotted from camps to periphery, he considered the implications. If Edward had bested one of the continent's finest, he was clearly more competent than Nightfall, Leyne, the judges, or even Edward himself had credited. *How could that happen? How could every man misjudge so completely?* Nightfall discovered the answer with the barest amount of thought. That Edward had never entered a contest before seemed only half the answer. The rest came more slowly. Since childhood, Edward had practiced with, aspired to, and been compared only to Leyne Nargol, the warrior ranked the best on the continent, at least in tourney. Age and experience gave Leyne other advantages as well. In such a situation, how could any man seem more than mediocre, to himself or to others? He recalled Leyne's own words: "He's better than he believes. He's just used to sparring with or watching me."

Nightfall edged through the ring of camp-followers, ignoring the goading cries of merchants and the women's quiet displays of thighs or breast valleys. His obvious livery made him a small target for merchandise, and he slipped past and into the city with relative ease. Once past the hangers-on, he found Tylantis much more as he remembered it. Narrow streets wound between cottages, shops, and pastures, constructed before horse and cart traffic became common. As he headed north and east, the byways thinned further, hemmed by drafty homes and crumbling, ancient warehouses that blocked the sun.

Grimy, snot-nosed children peeked at him from alleyways or through crevices in cottages that appeared abandoned.

Nightfall discovered Okraniah headed, with two younger women, toward the contests. All three wore handmade dresses that clung at breasts, hips, and waists and ended short at the thighs. Okraniah kept her red-brown hair cut femininely short with a curl in the front that gave her an air of sultry innocence. Long lashes bowed from her large, dark eyes. The three headed toward him.

Nightfall leaned against the wall casually, waiting until the women approached. He kept his face and his colors in shadow, preferring that no reports of his presence find their way back to the tourney. The cut of his clothes would reveal him as a servant, which should satisfy them that he was not a local thief or danger.

From habit, they assessed him as they passed, the strangers with only a passing glance. Okraniah granted a flirtatious smile. Having played the game longer, she realized that nobles' servants often carried money or made arrangements for their masters.

Using only a brisk movement of his head, Nightfall summoned Okraniah. She said something to the others, who looked briefly back at Nightfall then continued walking.

Okraniah wandered to Nightfall. "What can I do for you, sir?"

Nightfall smiled. He pulled two silver and one of the gold coins from his pocket, sorting through them with a finger.

Okraniah glanced quickly, then stared as she recognized the gold.

Nightfall plucked out the gold and passed a silver. "There's a knight whose symbol is a walking bear, named Sir Gondol. Spend the night with him . . . and the morning. See to it he sleeps too late for the contests, and the last coin becomes yours, too." He handed her the second silver. "You never spoke with me."

Okraniah nodded agreement. Taking the money, she headed toward the fighting grounds.

Nightfall slipped quietly into the darkness. Tonight, at least, he would sleep.

* * *

Sir Gondol had chosen a sword and shield combination the previous night, and Nightfall methodically prepared Prince Edward for the match. With practice, armor found its proper positioning more easily; and Edward seemed comfortable with the classic weaponry, though he had not selected it. Nor, Nightfall believed, would he have to use it. He had seen Gondol and Okraniah arm in arm the previous night, and the woman had never failed him at any task in the past.

Nightfall had just finished with preparations when Okraniah threaded through the crowd. She feigned interest in a nearby noble while Edward faced her. As soon as he looked away, she made a subtle wave at Nightfall.

Sudden alarm washed through Nightfall. Only six participants remained, and King Jolund had abandoned the paraded entrances and repetitive lectures to allow each match to occur singly. That way, everyone could watch, and it would delay the final round until evening. Edward and Gondol had drawn the earliest position. It seemed simple enough for Okraniah to delay the knight until just past daybreak, long enough to force him to forfeit the match. Yet, apparently, something had gone wrong.

Nightfall handed Edward his shield. "Excuse me a moment please, Master."

Edward studied his shield, scrubbing at a dull spot that Nightfall knew from the previous evening would not respond to polishing. He nodded his consent.

Nightfall strode to Okraniah and pulled her aside. "What's wrong?"

Okraniah took Nightfall's hand, surreptitiously returning his coins. "I couldn't do it. I'm sorry. Here's your money back."

"What?" Nightfall made no attempt to take the silver, openly or in secret. She would never have considered defying Nightfall when she had known she worked for him. He had not expected his Sudian persona to win the same obedience, but he had believed his money would make up for the difference.

"I'm sorry. I tried my best." Okraniah looked genuinely regretful, her already big eyes looking huge.

"Gondol has some woman he's promised to. He was ready to forget her early on, but guilt got the better of him late last night."

Damn. Nightfall shook his head.

Okraniah sighed, a sad smile bending the corners of her mouth. "I'm sorry."

Nightfall met her gaze. She looked away quickly, dark eyes disappointed, though he did not ponder whether from personal failure or loss of payment. It did not matter. Either way, Edward would have to win or lose this contest by skill, and all of Nightfall's trickery might come to nothing. Ignorantly, Okraniah might have sold out the demon's soul for love. Nevertheless, he let her keep the silver. That would buy her silence, even from Gondol. Turning on his heel, he headed back to Prince Edward.

Nightfall had only traveled half the distance when Edward waved him in impatiently. "Hurry, Sudian. We wouldn't want to be late."

Nightfall trotted to Edward's side, helping him strap on the swordbelt since the gauntlets did not allow delicate adjustments of buckle and leathers. They rushed to the center ring to find that Gondol and his entourage had beaten them there. The knight stood in the center, facing the entrance, his squire and two retainers hemmed against the railing. Nightfall left Edward at the entrance then took his position beside the walking bear standard, wishing he had room to pace. He had no one to blame except himself; experience had taught him to trust no one, and he should have found some means to handle this match that did not rely on another.

Nightfall studied the competitors with a detail that made his eyes water. The armor made it difficult to judge size, but he knew from prior observation that the two seemed nearly evenly matched for weight. Age had given Gondol a paunch; yet, though not as well-defined, his musculature seemed as developed as Edward's own. The hazel eyes seemed alert and ready, measuring the prince with a scrutiny that nearly matched Nightfall's intensity. He held the sword in a relaxed position, halfway between attack and defense, and with a composure that indicated assurance as well as skill.

Prince Edward also held an appropriate stance, though wholly defensive. He crouched, legs parted for balance, and leading with his left side.

"Begin," one of the judges said.

Gondol charged without hesitation. Edward remained in place. Gondol's high stroke arched down on Edward, blocked by the shield. Edward riposted with a chest-height blow that Gondol fended. Both men bore in for the attack, hammering at one another's defenses until the arena rang with the sound of steel smiting steel. They exchanged blow for blow, either occasionally sneaking in an extra offense while the other closed his defenses. Nightfall cringed at every attack while the spectators applauded, shouted, or chanted at every movement. Although Gondol had drawn a more massive following over his career, Edward's recent devotees retained loyalty to the underdog princeling who, in their minds, never should have survived the first round.

Nightfall ogled every motion, discovering a discomforting trend. Gondol's attacks came closer to a mark than Edward's, and he seemed more competent when it came to dodging shield defenses. Twice, he managed to jab through openings to strike armor, but the judges considered neither a killing blow. In the same amount of time, Edward met only Gondol's shield or sword. As fatigue made them sloppy, the knight seemed likely to deliver a winning stroke first.

But the battle continued, long past the time Nightfall believed he could have managed to support the armor, let alone exchange sword sweeps. The audience seemed a wild wave of indecipherable sound, loving the length of the combat as much as any specific blow.

Gondol thrust beneath Edward's shield. The prince recoiled far enough to save his armor, then lunged in with a high feint. Gondol raised his shield, momentarily blocking his own vision. The instant he did, Edward drove in with his off-hand, catching the rim of Gondol's shield on his own. Edward swept his shield, dragging Gondol's along in a movement that opened the knight's defenses while closing his own. The prince whipped in with an upstroke that would have torn Gondol belly to throat if not for the armor.

"End match."

Nightfall could scarcely hear the judge beneath the screaming crowd, but the combatants apparently did. They separated while one of the judges approached Gondol and carried on a short conversation. The knight sheathed his sword and shook his head.

The judge raised his hands, and the audience fell to silence. "Match winner and first contestant for the three man finals: Younger Prince Edward Nargol from Alyndar."

Edward's followers cheered. Even Gondol's people applauded politely, although the squire and retainers rushed to aid their knight without comment. Nightfall leapt the rail, reaching Edward first for the shortcut. Taking the shield and removing the gauntlets, he fell into Edward's joyous embrace, truly sharing the excitement for the first time. The exhilaration that came with honestly winning a contest against a superior warrior seemed electrifying.

With a parting salute to Sir Gondol, Edward left the ring with his squire. "Let's hurry and get this equipment off. I want to watch the others and see what I'm up against." His own words brought a somberness that seemed uncharacteristic in the wake of his joy. Nightfall guessed the prince had just remembered he would almost certainly come against Leyne in the finals. That contest he had no delusions of winning.

Nightfall believed it might suit Edward better not to observe Leyne's competition. It would only whittle at the confidence he had gained only after four consecutive wins against higher ranked competitors. However, he saw little means to delay Edward. Those in charge would drag out the festivities as long as possible so that money continued to flow into the city. Few would leave this near the final match. The later the contest lasted, the more meals the nobles and spectators would buy for themselves and their retainers.

As Nightfall headed back to camp with Edward, he caught a glimpse of a familiar figure moving through the crowd. His mind recognized it at once, the way a rabbit knows an owl from nothing more than shadow. *Gilleran.* Nightfall jerked his head around to look again, certain he must have imagined the sorcerer's figure and movement on another man. He saw nothing but a retreating form, richly dressed in breeks and cape. The neutral brown hair could have belonged to any man. Still, Nightfall caught himself shivering from a combination of rage and fear.

Apparently, Edward detected the change in his squire. "Are you all right, Sudian?"

"Fine, Master." Nightfall redirected his attention seeking some excuse to follow the other now and ascertain his identification; but he knew he would think of no reason to leave Edward bundled in armor. He would tend the prince first, as swiftly as Edward had vocalized. Once he had Edward safely in front of the contests, he could hunt down the sorcerer himself.

The armor removal and packing left both men impatient. As the last piece fell into place, Edward gestured to the arena. "Let's go. Quickly."

Now, Nightfall finally found his tongue. "Master, if you don't mind, I'll stay and guard our belongings."

Prince Edward glanced back at the camp, obviously reluctant to waste time in discussion. "That's not necessary."

"Nevertheless, I'd feel more comfortable. Do you mind, Master?"

Prince Edward shifted his attention from central contest to squire and back. Then, apparently more interested in spectating than arguing, he shrugged. "Very well. But if you change your mind, join me at any time." With a brisk wave, he darted toward the masses.

The oath-bond scarcely responded to Edward's leaving. Taking its cues from Nightfall, as always, the magic found its caster the more pervasive threat.

Nightfall rushed to track down Chancellor Gilleran of Alyndar.

Chapter 18

Six princes fought him in the night,
Their fortress of unequaled might.
'Twas gone before the sun arose—
Darkness comes where Nightfall goes.
> —The Legend of Nightfall
> Nursery rhyme, alternative verse

Nightfall scurried across the tourney grounds, his boots leaving no mark in pastureland already trampled to mud by the crowds. The sorcerer could find no better hiding place than amid the hundreds of spectators intent upon Leyne's contest against Prince Irbo of Hartrin. However, Nightfall guessed that Gilleran had arrived for other reasons than to watch. If he came to harm Nightfall, he would likely do so in a place where few witnesses could observe or interfere, especially if he planned to perform his evil ritual. More likely, the wizard simply intended to sabotage Edward's chance to become landed, thereby obtaining the same results without effort. If Nightfall read the intention correctly, Gilleran would not act until the younger prince once again took the ring.

Caught up in his search for a specific man, Nightfall was startled by a movement to his left. He spun faster than appropriate amid so many strangers and found himself face to face with Kelryn. Her white hair formed a knotted, disheveled mane, spotted with leaves and entwined with twigs. Her hazel eyes bore a wild glint of determination.

Anger welled up in Nightfall, liberally sprinkled with annoyance. He started to turn away.

Kelryn seized his arm. "Listen to me."

Nightfall shook off her hand. He headed toward the periphery at a brisk walk.

Despite her limp, Kelryn caught him easily. She hustled to his side then stepped directly in front of him so suddenly he had to stop to keep from trampling her. He did so from instinct, wishing in the following moment that he had managed to keep moving. Instead, he stared directly into her eyes, focusing the same murderous rage into that glare that had quailed so many.

Kelryn did not back down. Her soft, green-brown eyes remained fixed on his and did not skitter away. For the first time, Nightfall had met a person more desperate than himself. "You're going to listen to me."

"No." Nightfall took a backward step, but the eyes fascinated him. He would not look away first; he never had. Yet if he did not, he would have little choice but to hear. Every sense told him they stood alone, far enough from packing nobles and screaming spectators to go unnoticed and unheard. Nevertheless, he kept his voice low. "I'll kill you."

"I don't care."

Nightfall grabbed both of Kelryn's forearms, shaking just forcefully enough to show her he meant no bluff. The gesture broke the war of wills as well. "Are you deaf or just stupid? I *will* kill you."

"Kill me, then, if you must. I don't care anymore. Just hear my story first."

"No."

"Ned may be in danger."

"I can protect the prince."

"The way you protected Dyfrin?" Kelryn fairly spat the words at Nightfall.

The question seemed nonsensical and frightening at once. Nightfall had never declared himself his friend's defender; yet duty had little to do with the ice that seemed suddenly to clog his veins. "Dyfrin? What about Dyfrin?" The thought of his mentor in danger made him rabid, concerned enough to listen to Kelryn this once. It occurred to him that she might have used the name only because she felt certain it would fully seize his attention. Yet, he had never mentioned the Keevainian to her by name.

Kelryn bit her lip, holding something back. "Dyfrin came to me several months ago. He talked about you, mostly, asked me to take good care of you. He believed I would."

"He was wrong," Nightfall returned, not daring to believe Dyfrin had been taken in so easily. Always before, he had read people with an accuracy that seemed almost miraculous, a talent Nightfall had envied.

"Dyfrin wrong about someone?" Kelryn's statement echoed Nightfall's thoughts closely enough to send a chill through him. "It would have been the first time." She raised her brows, eyes still locked on Nightfall's and without a hint of guilt or doubt. "Dyfrin seemed to read emotion as easily as expression. He always knew your problems, your thoughts, your moods. He always knew what to say to fix the pain."

Nightfall released Kelryn, as haunted by the constant use of past tense to refer to Dyfrin as by her ability to describe events and ideas she could know nothing about. He wanted to walk away, to make Kelryn believe she had all her facts wrong. But for all the hatred he harbored for this woman, he had to listen for Dyfrin's sake. Clearly, she knew things she should not, and that truth could hurt him worse than any betrayal. It could harm Dyfrin. "How could you know that?"

"He told me." Kelryn dropped her hands to her sides. For the first time, her gaze softened and Nightfall found the beauty that had captivated him into a trust that, he believed, had ruined him as well. "Marak, he was born with a talent. Dyfrin was a mind-reader."

"A mind-reader." It was not Nightfall's way to repeat things in stupefied horror, but realization left room for nothing else. A million, ancient questions died in that moment, answered by a single pronouncement that should have seemed obvious. *Dyfrin was a mind-reader.* It explained everything, from his friend's uncanny ability to select friends, enemies, and targets to his exceptional talent at consolation of even the worst kinds of pain. For an instant, Nightfall felt betrayed again. The friend whose judgment he had trusted implicitly, who had seemed loyal to the point of learning every nuance of action, expression, and behavior was a fraud.

Yet Nightfall dismissed the assessment as soon as he

made it, regret hammering him at the vileness of the thought. The mind-reading did not matter, only Dyfrin's decision to use that talent to aid, rather than harm, Nightfall. The applications for such a potent natal ability seemed endless. Dyfrin could have channeled his energies into finding the locations and protections of the world's most valuable treasures. He could have scanned every wager, discovering who really had the goods. He could have won card games and scams until he owned more money and power than any king. The possibilities became an endless parade, halted abruptly by truth. Instead, Dyfrin had lived in squalor, using his talent to rescue children and adults whom others abandoned as hopeless. Dyfrin's gift only made him all the more remarkable and generous, and it shocked Nightfall to realize that, with a similar gift to help him understand the ugliness behind the mask most people presented, Edward could have been a second Dyfrin.

Nightfall pushed aside that thought for ones more frightening, serious, and immediate. Suddenly, the other answers came, those so terrifying he could scarcely find voice to ask the questions. "Dyfrin's dead, isn't he?"

Kelryn lowered her head, eyes suddenly blurred by tears.

The description of Genevra, the Healer in Delfor, leapt suddenly back into Nightfall's mind. "Dyfrin was the man the sorcerer killed in your room." Remembered pain from the Iceman's attack made him cringe. Dyfrin had suffered more than any man should, and the idea suffused Nightfall with a pity that made him want to curl up in a ball and sob as well as a rage that drove him to vengeance and murder.

"I froze." Kelryn wept. "I cowered in a corner. I was so scared, I just couldn't do anything."

Nightfall put the remainder together on his own. Chancellor Gilleran of Alyndar had killed Dyfrin with his ritual, ripping out the Keevainian's soul for the mind-reading talent he coveted. He knew so much about Nightfall because he had read Kelryn's mind afterward, leaving her alive as a means to gather more information about him should it become necessary. In Alyndar's dungeon, Nightfall had believed Gilleran had a truth-detecting spell; but it was so much more. The idea of Dyfrin's spirit writhing in agony inside a sorcerer made his stomach flop. He gagged on bile.

Kelryn fought her own war of conscience. "If I had just done something. Anything. Maybe I could have saved him."

Nightfall shook his head. "You could have done nothing but get yourself killed as well. And probably Genevra."

Kelryn drew her head back, obviously surprised by his knowledge of Genevra.

"I met her in Delfor," Nightfall explained. "She wanted you to know she was fine and well-protected."

Kelryn smiled slightly at a bit of good news among so much bad. She met Nightfall's gaze once more.

The hatred vanished, displaced by a grief tempered only by guilt. No longer confined, love filled the aching void. Nightfall felt as if he would drop dead where he stood if he did not hold Kelryn. He caught her in his arms, and she embraced him with equal fervor. "I'm sorry," he said, the apology seeming far from adequate.

Kelryn clung, apparently needing nothing more. "I love you. I always did. I always will."

Why? Nightfall wanted to scream. *Why?* It made no sense for a woman so perfect to care about one so unworthy, and he wondered why the holy Father had so blessed him when so many good people had so little. Yet, he knew he would not have long to enjoy his fortune. Within months, Gilleran seemed likely to add his soul to the collection. Nightfall would join Dyfrin one more time, in an agony that would end one way of two: with his soul and talent spent or, upon the sorcerer's death, replaced by the eternal torment of the Father's hell. Dyfrin, at least, Nightfall believed, would find paradise. Carefully, he unwound himself from Kelryn's hold. "Kelryn, it would be better for both of us if we went our separate ways."

Kelryn jerked back, clearly stunned. "But I . . . We finally . . ." She concentrated on completing a thought. "You still don't believe me?"

"I believe you," Nightfall assured. "And I truly am

sorry for everything I put you through." He recalled the incident in Noshtillan's eatery, and realization added another depth of honesty to his already forthright account. "If I ever hit you again, just kill me. I'll let you. I promise."

"Don't be absurd."

"I'm not joking. People who hit those they love don't deserve the life the Father gave them."

"I agree." Kelryn kept her expression as somber as Nightfall's, making it clear she would not allow him to hurt her again. "But at the time you slapped me, you hated me. And you had every reason to believe you should have done far worse."

"But I shouldn't have—"

Kelryn interrupted. "Drop it. Don't dwell on it. One lapse doesn't make you evil. Under the same circumstances, I probably would have hit you, too." She waved off a response. "We have more important things to talk about right now. Edward might be in danger."

A nudge from the oath-bond turned Nightfall's thoughts immediately to this new problem. "How do you mean?"

Kelryn cocked her head, as if seeking permission to give him details. "The Iceman came to me to find you. He wound up in a fight with the sorcerer who killed Dyfrin."

"Gilleran," Nightfall said, suddenly recalling his glimpse of and search for the chancellor.

Kelryn continued the story. "He killed the Iceman." She cringed, apparently at the image of the ritual. "But first he said some things that terrified me."

Nightfall contemplated the consequences of the standoff. Gilleran's power had doubled if he'd slaughtered Ritworth and added the Iceman's spells to his repertoire. The thought sent a shiver through Nightfall. The killer freezing spell, flight, and the mud doll tortures had all become the property of an already too-powerful sorcerer. The situation seemed concerning enough, but Nightfall probed for the specifics of Kelryn's worry. "What did he say?"

Kelryn ran a hand through her white locks, the movement stopped by a stick snarled into a tangle. "At the time, he was trying to win the Iceman's trust, so he may have exaggerated or lied outright. I don't know whether he meant any of it, but he claimed to be next in line for Alyndar's throne. And he told us the princes would die in tourney."

"Die in tourney?" Nightfall spoke aloud as he considered. A few of the competitors had sustained minor injuries from practice weapons or falls from horses, but he had no reason to suspect that death during the nobles' games occurred more often than rarely. The only way Gilleran could know such a thing was if he planned to arrange it, yet that idea had its flaws as well. *If Gilleran planned to harm Edward or Leyne, why did he wait so long? Unless he had more faith in Edward's abilities than everyone else, he would have to believe he would arrive after the younger prince was already eliminated from competition.* The oath-bond continued its steady, discomforting hum, apparently still uncertain whether the danger to Edward had become concrete or serious. *As Kelryn said, Gilleran had been talking to impress Ritworth.*

"Die in tourney. That's what he said." Her gaze followed a spectator hurrying toward a private corner near the gates. A roar from the crowd indicated the end of the current match. "You should also know I'm bound to say nothing negative about Gilleran that Ned or his relatives might overhear, and I have to tell him he's safe from sorcerers now. Ritworth is dead."

"Bound?"

"Magically bound."

"Aah." Nightfall knew that spell too well.

"So *you*'ll have to warn Ned."

Nightfall saw the difficulty Kelryn missed. "I tell Prince Edward what you saw and heard, then he asks you about it and you have to deny the danger." He shook his head. "He'll think I made the whole thing up."

"I'll tell him about the magical binding." Kelryn cringed, apparently in response to some prodding from her own oath-bond. "Or you could tell him about it."

Needing to protect his own apparent loyalty, Nightfall

thought it better that Prince Edward know nothing of oath-bonding. "Bad idea."

Kelryn sighed in obvious frustration. "What do you suggest?"

"We don't put the prince in the position of choosing between our allegiance and that of a chancellor he's probably known and trusted since birth. We handle Gilleran on our own."

Kelryn looked stricken.

Nightfall amended. "Or I handle him. It's just as well that you don't get involved any more than you already have." The oath-bond intensified, rising and falling in sickening waves of warning.

Kelryn bit her lower lip, obviously struggling with words. "Marak, I know you've done many things no one else would dare. But it'll take more than one man, even one with your reputation, to handle a threat like Gilleran."

Nightfall shrugged, trying to look unaffected though he felt like a landlubber riding the deck in a sea gale. The oath-bond would keep him from harming any official of Alyndar, including the sorcerer. That complicated the matter to the boundary of impossibility. "I think you should leave while you still can."

"No." Kelryn seized Nightfall's hand. "I won't lose you a second time. Not without a fight. I've frozen twice when it came to helping others stand against Gilleran. Not again. He's an evil that needs destroying."

Nightfall considered. He would prefer that Kelryn fled to safety. Barring that, however, he might need her to battle a sorcerer he could not harm by his own vow. "Very well, then. Let the hunt begin."

Kelryn and Nightfall had not located Chancellor Gilleran by the time the last match before the finals ended and Edward headed back toward camp. As the cheers and applause thundered across the pasture, they rushed back to camp to meet Edward, trying to look casual.

Many neighbors returned first, discussing winning maneuvers with a detail that told Nightfall more than he ever needed to know. Leyne had bested Hartrin's Prince Irbo after a lengthy bout with maces and shields. An over-lord's son from Grifnal, named Sander, would face each Nargol in the upcoming finals. No matter the end results, three matches would be fought, with sword and shield. Each contestant would engage in single combat with the other two, no matter the outcome of the first match. Therefore, even should Sander best one of the princes, Leyne and Edward would fight. The victor of the duchy would have to win both of his matches. Nightfall considered the logistics. Obviously, only one contestant could possibly win two battles. The difficulty would come if each won one and lost the other. Yet, Nightfall suspected, such a circumstance would not upset any official or spectator, only prolong the excitement to the following day.

Shortly, Edward returned, expression somber as he considered the upcoming competition and, Nightfall guessed, the need to stand against his brother. As he drew closer, his gaze fell on Kelryn and a light sparked through his blue eyes. His stern look brightened into a delighted smile. "Kelryn!" He swept her into a joyful embrace.

Nightfall watched placidly, wishing the happy reunion looked a bit more friendly and less sensual. Now that he and Kelryn had renewed their relationship, the concern he held for her closeness with Edward withered to simple jealousy. The two made a spectacularly good-looking couple, and the affection they held for one another seemed obvious, at least to him.

"Kelryn, I'm so glad you found us. I've been worried about you." Edward's expression changed to one of regret. "We had to leave quickly, a misunderstanding with the duke."

Peering around Edward, Kelryn flashed Nightfall an interested look that suggested she would expect a full explanation later.

Edward continued, oblivious to the exchange. "You got Sudian's note, I presume."

Kelryn rescued Nightfall from his alibi. "I got it. I came straight here. It took me longer on foot, and I ran into some trouble."

Prince Edward disengaged to study Kelryn's features. "Bandits?" Nightfall could not see his face, but his voice indicated horror at the possibility that highwaymen had ambushed Kelryn while alone.

"No." Kelryn gave Nightfall an uncomfortable glance. "The Iceman. Your chancellor arrived just in time, though, and dispatched him. He told me to tell you you had nothing more to fear from sorcerers."

"Good old Gilleran." Edward brushed hair from Kelryn's cheek. "Always there to remind me there're kindly sorcerers as well as the bad ones."

Kelryn said nothing.

Nightfall rolled his eyes at the naive innocence to which he had grown accustomed. Kelryn had spoken her piece. Now, he hoped, her oath-bond would cease to control her.

Edward took Kelryn's hand and steered her to his blanket. He gestured her to sit.

Kelryn obeyed.

Nightfall aided Edward, who would not brag. "You came just in time. My master made the finals. If he bests two more opponents, he becomes the duke."

"Really? Congratulations." Kelryn smiled so prettily that Edward blushed.

"Now, Sudian. I'm just glad to make it this far." Edward glanced at Kelryn apologetically. "It's not likely I'll get any further, but you still might want to watch. My opponents are worthy."

"He'll do fine." Nightfall politely contradicted. "He's just a bit anxious because he has to fight his older brother."

Edward turned his squire a pointed glare, clearly prepared to lecture about the rudeness of emphasizing a master's weakness.

"Oh, dear." Kelryn sounded appropriately sympathetic. "That would be difficult."

Basking in Kelryn's attentive compassion, Edward forgave his squire and ran with the situation. "Leyne's a tremendous jouster with any weapon."

Kelryn smiled again. "Leyne didn't save my life with a chair."

Prince Edward returned the grin.

Nightfall had stomached enough of their exchange, so

full of insidious romance and compliments. "I'll get your armor and weapon ready for this afternoon."

"No hurry." Edward did not take his eyes from Kelryn. "I drew out of the first match. It's Leyne and Sander. For now, we're probably all hungry. Why don't you see what you can scrounge in the way of food?"

"Yes, Master." Nightfall trotted off to make purchases from vendors he trusted, taking a long route in the hope of locating Chancellor Gilleran amid the crowd. But the intermission left spectators and competitors milling in random patterns that made a coherent search impossible. He returned to Prince Edward and Kelryn with a reasonable dinner, not having caught so much as a glimpse of the sorcerer and with little idea of how to finish rigging the contests. Anything he did now would require a finesse he was not in the mental state to concoct and which could have serious repercussions for Edward. At least, the duke of Schiz seemed to have made the right decision in regard to pursuit, and Nightfall drew scant comfort from it. If Edward won, Nightfall guessed, the problem would rematerialize. Only this time, he would face it as a free man. The thought barely brought a tinge of joy. First, Edward would have to best Crown-prince Leyne Nargol of Alyndar. And that seemed impossible.

Prince Edward refused to miss the competition between Leyne and Sander, so Nightfall armored him up early so he did not need to rush to prepare for his own match. It bothered Nightfall that Edward would tire himself before the fight by wearing what felt like a ton of metal for longer than necessary, but it did not seem a major problem. Whoever he faced from the previous battle would also have worn his armor over the same period of time. Nightfall turned his attention to the competitors.

Leyne stepped into the ring first, with his usual confident grace. He faced the crowd with an artistic salute that set off a wild round of cheering. Sander entered soon after, a huge brunet with restless eyes. Nightfall could sense a nervousness that seemed only natural when pitted against the man favored to win the contests; but, when he faced Leyne Nargol directly, he stiffened with grim resolve.

"Begin match," the judge called.

The spectators pressed toward the ring, nearly crushing Edward, Nightfall, and Kelryn to the rail.

Leyne made the first attack, a controlled sweep for Sander's midsection that the overlord's son easily blocked. Caution stole all time and chance for riposte. As Sander repositioned for defense, Leyne jabbed for his neck. Sander parried with his sword. Leyne turned his offense into a broad, low slash that Sander caught on his shield. Obviously intimidated, Sander concentrated on defense while Leyne took leisurely pokes, prods, and cuts designed as much to measure his opponent as to win.

Then, suddenly, Sander's style of combat changed. Spurred by realization that he could not win without attacking, or by simple determination, he drove in with a series of hard, overhand strikes at Leyne's helmet. The prince raised his shield, repositioning it effortlessly to catch every wild cut.

Nightfall scanned the crowd at least as often as the fight, seeking Gilleran amid the jumble of spectators who fit every racial description on the continent. He kept track of the fight by the ringing slam of Sander's sword hammering Leyne's shield in a frenzy, a desperate move that would require a lucky opening to succeed. Yet, Nightfall guessed, it had probably won contests and wars in the past. Unpredictable attacks became difficult to fend, and the need for speed and concentration left Leyne little time for riposte.

Studying the spectators, Nightfall located a few familiar faces and crests, mostly those whom Edward had or might have battled in the ring. Others slept in nearby camps or had become known to him under different circumstances while he was in other guises. Leyne's two retainers held positions on the opposite rail, recognizable by the purple and silver livery that had become too familiar to Nightfall. He saw no sign of Gilleran, and that frustrated rather than soothed him. *Biding his time,* Nightfall guessed. *Waiting to get Leyne and Edward in the ring to-*

gether. It seemed the most obvious plan, yet Nightfall would not anchor all his wariness on that one battle.

As part of his inspection, Nightfall glanced upward. The sky seemed diffusely gray, impossible to discern clouds from the general background of slate. A movement caught his eye, and he jerked his head in its direction. Gilleran floated silently toward the ring, flying over the heads of the masses whose every eye remained locked on the contestants in the arena. Clearly, he had begun his flight well beyond sight of witnesses, quietly drifting forward, trusting the natural proclivity of people to look in any direction but up as well as the distraction of final tourney. His arm arched in abrupt and deliberate threat.

The oath-bond turned into a savage shrill of alarm that tore agony and nausea through Nightfall. Instinctively, he placed his person between Edward and any spell Gilleran might have thrown. As he moved, he drew and flung a dagger, hilt first, focusing on the need to only distract and not damage. Harming Gilleran would violate the oath-bond.

The magic struck first, creating a shimmering curtain in the path of Leyne's shield that Nightfall might not have noticed had he not witnessed the casting. The oath-bond's warning died as Nightfall realized Edward had not been Gilleran's target. Sander's sword slammed down toward Leyne's helmet. Leyne's shield shifted toward it, entered the magicked area, and slowed to an agonizing crawl. Horror filled both combatants' eyes. Then, a massive sword stroke that should have been easily fended crashed against Leyne's helmet. The metal caved in, joints separating, and the prince collapsed to the dirt. An instant later, Nightfall's dagger embedded itself in Gilleran's left cheek.

The gasps of the crowd drowned Gilleran's scream. He plummeted into an uncontrolled dive. The oath-bond boiled through Nightfall with a vengeance that sprawled him, helpless, to the ground. This time, he felt certain, it was over. He did not bother to fight it with action, just lay as still as his twitching muscles would allow, hoping the crowd would trample him to death before the sorcery claimed his soul. He had not intended to hurt Gilleran, only to stop the deadly magics that might have slaughtered his charge. But old habits died hard, and he had long practiced how to hit, not miss. His eyes showed him a blur of humans frozen in place by shock and terror. Gilleran managed to catch himself, spinning in midair and zipping off toward town. Within moments, he disappeared amid the grayness.

Apparently, the oath-bond accepted the accidental nature of the injury. It withdrew with an agonizing slowness intended, Nightfall guessed, to remind him how narrowly he had escaped its punishment. He promised it he would not attack an official of Alyndar again, in any fashion, and it mercifully dropped further, leaving only a dull ache that hammered him from head to toes. He managed to clamber to his feet, gulping great lungfuls of air, feeling as if he had run for hours with his windpipe squeezed closed.

Only then, Nightfall realized someone held and steadied him. He glanced at his benefactor and found himself staring into Kelryn's worried face. "Are you all right?"

Nightfall did not waste breath on an answer. His gaze swept the area and he saw no sign of Prince Edward. Sudden panic seized him. "Where's ... Master?" he forced from his air-starved chest.

In answer, Kelryn pointed toward the ring.

Nightfall spun about so suddenly that dizziness blanked his mind briefly. When the buzzing and spots receded, he saw Edward in the arena tending to his brother along with two other men Nightfall hoped were Healers. Sander sat amid the judges, his helmet off and his face pale as a corpse. Nightfall scanned the skies and crowd for Gilleran but found no sign of the sorcerer.

"What happened?" Kelryn whispered.

"No-win. Did something shouldn't," Nightfall explained in as few words as possible. "Leyne bad?"

Kelryn shrugged to indicate no one had announced his condition yet. Nightfall dared to hope his dagger might have saved the crown prince's life. Probably, Gilleran had planned to get close to Leyne using his title and position, then would have extinguished any life remaining. Now,

Nightfall moved cautiously toward the arena, alert to the possibility of Gilleran's return. He took Kelryn's arm to drag her along with him and hissed directly in her ear, "Keep on your guard for the sorcerer." The oath-bond's warning tingle seemed painless in the wake of its previous spearing agony, but Nightfall took its cue. He had vowed not only to keep from harming Alyndarian officials, but also that he would not cause or allow others to do so. If Kelryn attacked Gilleran, he would have no choice but to defend the sorcerer against her.

The idea stoked rage that burned with the intensity, if not the pain, of the oath-bond. He knew he lived only by the mercy of the magic, a clemency that he believed came not from any humanlike kindness from the oath-bond but from his own ability to rationalize his actions quickly and without guilt. Luck and unbreakable habit had allowed him to accidentally stab the sorcerer he had vowed with his soul not to harm. He could only hope that wound would prove fatal and Leyne's would not. The last thought brought a realization that thrilled him. Even if Leyne survived, his injury would eliminate him from the contest. Prince Edward had only one more opponent to best to become a duke in Shisenian territory, and Sander seemed shaken enough by the accident not to require Nightfall's assistance to lose.

Hope sprang from the wreckage of what had, moments before, seemed a hopeless situation. He continued toward the far side of the ring, closer to the Nargols and Leyne's anxious retainers. The fog covering his mind lifted as he approached, and he caught a clear glimpse of the suffering anguish that twisted Edward's youthful features. Suddenly, the prince howled like an animal. The sound barely carried through the wails and whispered speculation of the crowd, but it tore at Nightfall's heart, bringing tears to his eyes that shocked him. Never before had another's pain affected him so deeply. Needing to console, he leapt over the railing, avoiding the need to talk his way past the judges and guards.

Nightfall went directly to Edward's side. The younger prince continued screaming. "No!" he shouted loud enough to shatter Nightfall's hearing, as if the mere force of the words could undo the tragedy. "No! No! NO!"

Nightfall seized Edward's shoulder, fingers slipping into the joint between pauldrons and gorget, though he touched only the undermail. "Master, it's all right. Everything will be all right. Just let the Healers work."

Prince Edward spun, hurling himself suddenly into Nightfall's arms. "He's dead. Gods, Leyne is dead. My brother can't be dead!"

Nightfall rescued his fingers and trebled his weight in time to keep from falling, though he still staggered beneath Edward's bulk. He held the metallic figure of the prince feeling more like an armory than a consoler. He glanced at the Healers. One shook his head. The other lowered Leyne gently to the ground.

Edward pulled free, desperately restless. "No!" He hovered over Leyne. "NO!" He seemed incapable of other words, and now his grieving appeals thundered over a crowd gone silent. Abruptly, he collapsed at Leyne's side, sobs stealing even that last word from him, a passive occupant of his armor. One Healer left to speak with the Shisenian guards. The other hovered, helpless, but unwilling to leave one who looked as pained as Edward.

Nightfall removed Edward's helmet and gauntlets methodically, nearly as lost as his master. Though they lacked the frenzy of Edward's, tears streaked his face as well, though how much he cried for Leyne or Edward did not matter. The pain seemed permanent, wholly internal and without any input from the oath-bond. Prince Edward clung to his squire.

At length, an official in Shisen's yellow and gray silks approached. Dark hair hung to his shoulders, and he wore an expression so somber it seemed painted. "Prince Edward?"

Edward remained in place, curled to the extent his armor allowed.

The official glanced at Nightfall in question.

Nightfall took over, disinterested in talking at the moment either but seeing the need. "What can I do for you, sir?"

The man cleared his throat. Although he addressed

Nightfall, he kept his attention on the prince. "King Jolund and all of the kingdom of Shisen wishes to express its deepest regrets about the accident that occurred here today."

Nightfall nodded, flicking his gaze to the grieving prince to indicate he felt it way too soon for long-winded speeches.

The Shisenian held his expression constant, but his shifting stance revealed nervousness. Receiving no acknowledgment from Edward, he finally turned his focus to Nightfall. "We'll take care of all the arrangements for escorting His Majesty's remains home in dignity and explaining this tragedy to King Rikard."

"Thank you, sir." The response sounded unnecessary as well as inadequate, but Nightfall had no way to guess at custom, if there was a routine way to handle such a disaster.

"It is our duty, one we despise the need for but are honored to fulfill."

Nightfall hoped he was not expected to formulate an equally eloquent reply. To anticipate even eye contact from Prince Edward now seemed as cruel as it did foolish.

The official obviated the need for answer. "Please let us know if we can do anything to make the night more comfortable for Prince Edward. Of course, the final tourney will be postponed until tomorrow. We can discuss details in the morning."

The tourney. Nightfall stiffened. He had not considered the competition since that one flash of insight when he believed Leyne injured but still alive. He glanced at Edward again. The prince lay, unmoving, huddled over his brother like a menaced turtle in his shell of steel. It would take a miracle from the Father to goad Edward to fight in the morning, and Nightfall's soul hung on that need. Unable to find other words, Nightfall simply repeated those from before. "Thank you, sir."

The official saluted Edward, a respectful gesture the prince never saw. Turning on his heel, he headed from the ring.

Edward moaned. "No! No! No!" He did not resist

when Nightfall assisted him to his feet and led him, hollow-eyed and sobbing, from the ring.

The night seemed to span an eternity. Nightfall drew upon memories of Dyfrin to find the best ways to soothe an agony that seemed too savage to touch. With Kelryn's help, he managed to remove the armor from Prince Edward, without a protest. No one spoke. Nightfall knew from experience that platitudes would not console and attempts to find a positive side to the experience would only intensify the pain. Dyfrin could have read the best approach, but Nightfall had no choice but to rely on Edward's words when they finally came. Until they did, he could do nothing more than hold his master's hand and share the grief in silence.

For a long time, Nightfall sat with Edward in a gentle quiet, his fingers resting on the prince's hand. Then, Kelryn took her vigil while Nightfall tended to the duties of camp. Polishing and packing armor allowed him the movement he needed to overcome the restless need to do or say something that would only make the matter worse. Once finished, however, he retook his sentinel willingly, appeased but disappointed by the realization that Kelryn made no more progress than he had. For all his inability to trust and uncertainty with relationships, he seemed to have handled this situation prudently. He only wished he could find words to break the prince's mourning hush.

Then, as midnight shifted toward the wee morning hours, Edward's hand closed around Nightfall's, finally returning the fellowship his companions had shared so freely through the hours. A hint of life entered his eyes, though they remained focused on the stars. "I can't believe Leyne is dead." His voice sounded weak and graveled from crying.

Nightfall squeezed Edward's hand, suddenly wishing the prince had decided to open up on Kelryn's shift. She would know what to say far better than he. For now, he echoed Edward. "I can't believe it either, Master."

"I keep waiting for something to come and erase everything. In a moment, I'll awaken from a nightmare. Or,

Leyne will ride up and tell me it was a prank. Or the Healer will tell me he made a mistake."

Nightfall sighed, the distress in Edward's tone driving the tears back to his own aching eyes. "No," he said.

"No," Edward repeated softly, the word bringing back fierce memories of his desperate pleas in the arena to any god who might listen.

"I remember . . ." Edward began, the floodgates opening upon a vast array of tales and memories about Leyne, good and bad. Unfamiliar with the elder prince, Nightfall could contribute little but consolation and quiet presence to the discourse, but that seemed enough.

Edward talked about his brother until he finally lapsed into exhaustion at daybreak. And Nightfall succumbed with him.

Nightfall felt certain he had only slept a moment before strange presences in the camp awakened him. He sat up instantly, attention immediately riveted on the sound. The Shisenian official stood before him, his clothes impeccable and his curtain of hair brushed to a sheen. Two guards flanked him. The sun had fully risen, beams jutting through gaps in the overcast sky as if cutting light-holes in the clouds. "May we speak with your master, please?" the official asked.

Nightfall turned to Edward. The blond hair lay in tangles, clinging to cheeks still sticky with tears. He seemed at peace for the first time since the accident. "No, sir." Nightfall returned his gaze to the Shisenian. "Not now. It would be wrong to wake him."

"I understand," the Shisenian said, though his stance suggested he did not. "We've gathered His Majesty's things and prepared a guarded escort to leave at midday."

"Today?"

"Today." The Shisenian confirmed.

"You can't postpone it?"

"The weather is warm. It would be wrong to return the crown prince in any shape but the best we can manage." The Shisenian official prodded. "We can put off the match for the duchy for a couple days, but I'm afraid too many people have traveled too far not to finish the competition before affairs of court call them back. You understand."

Nightfall doubted it mattered if he did or not. A few things he knew for certain. Edward would prove incapable of fighting, let alone winning, a tourney this day. And his conversation the previous night made it clear he could not function, intellectually or emotionally, until his brother's body found its proper place in its grave beside that of his mother. He would insist on leaving with the funeral procession. Again, Nightfall studied Edward, the lines of anguish that still etched his youthful features, even in sleep, the fetal position he had crunched his huge bulk into in order to find a modicum of rest. Even if Nightfall managed to goad Edward into battle, even should he find the means to make the prince win, it would prove a costly success. He wanted Edward worldly, not broken by reality. The truth came hard. The continent needed a heroic leader whole far more than a vicious demon alive. The duchy would benefit little from a prince battered by circumstance into a lifeless shell unfit to rule.

Nightfall made the hardest decision of his life. "We'll accompany the escort back to Alyndar. Prince Edward will forfeit the match."

Chapter 19

The Evil One, the demon blight
Who hides in day and stalks the night.
He steals the stars and drags them low—
Darkness comes where Nightfall goes.
　　　　　　　—The Legend of Nightfall
　　　　　　　Nursery rhyme, final stanza

The funeral procession consisted of a dozen armed guards on horseback riding fore and aft of two covered carts, the first containing the jewel- and gold-inlaid box that carried Leyne and the second his belongings. Two emissaries of Shisen drove the former carriage and two guardsmen the latter. The palomino trailed, tethered to the second coach. Prince Edward, Nightfall, and Kelryn rode alongside the caravan, their conversation sparse even toward the end of the month of travel between Tylantis and Alyndar. Edward floated from states of unbearable depression, to giddy story-telling, to sentiment seemingly without pattern or stimulus. Nightfall preferred the times when he told bittersweet tales about his brother and his past. These seemed most normal.

The procession stopped frequently to ice the body, for supplies, and to rest. Everywhere, the town or village folk met them with honor and pity, free with trite phrases that quickly became more tedious than consoling. The trip bored Nightfall, leaving him with far too much time to consider his decision. He still had a month and a half in which to complete Prince Edward's landing, but he had run out of possibilities. He had no way to guess what effect, if any, Leyne's death might have on his magically-enforced task. Clearly, Rikard could have given his youngest son property at any time; according to Leyne, the winning process and the display of responsibility mattered more to the king. Yet, given the circumstances, King Rikard might want to keep his only remaining son safe at home and groom him for the ruling position he might some day take. Surely, the hammer-handed king could not risk sending the only prince away with a vicious murderer now that he had no other heirs. *Or did he?* Nightfall squinted, knowing little about the passage of titles among royalty.

The question haunted Nightfall all the way to the borders of Alyndar. As Edward's lucid moments increased to become the more common norm, Nightfall finally managed to broach the topic without sounding as if he saw Leyne's death as an opportunity rather than a calamity. The day had dawned fair, the sun strong and clouds rare, a welcome change from the rains that had followed them from Tylantis. Riding between Edward and Kelryn, Nightfall went directly to the heart of the matter. "Master, are you now Alyndar's crown prince?"

Edward remained silent for some time, clearly considering. Surely, the thought had to have entered his mind sometime before in the month since Leyne's death, yet he had no ready answer. "I don't know. By strict laws of ascension, if my father died without a specified heir, I would become king. But the decision lies with my father. He has the right to choose any noble. I have seven cousins, several of whom are far more worthy than me—"

Nightfall could not help but interrupt. "No one is more worthy, Master."

Edward shrugged, taking his squire's familiar devotion in stride, but Nightfall could see the beginnings of a smile at the corner of the prince's mouth. "Even after all this time, your loyalty is touching, Sudian." He turned his head to meet the blue-black eyes. "I wish I could tell you how much your company means to me. Aside from my mother, you're the only person who ever cared about and supported me for what I am, not from duty to my father or personal gain. Without your boldness and sincere faith in me, I'd still be off chasing shadows, accomplishing nothing more than clownishly shaming my family and myself."

Edward's eyes brimmed with tears, as they had so many times over the past month; but this time, he cried for other reasons. Reining his horse closer, he caught

Nightfall's wrist. "My causes haven't changed, nor my need to right the injustices some have suffered since long before my birth. But my paths to those goals have descended from the clouds. Here, in reality, they twist and wind for miles, riddled with mountains and barricades; but we can fight our way through or around those. Effort never daunted me when the cause was right." The grin blossomed until it seemed to light his entire face. He drew his horse closer and clasped Nightfall's forearm without jerking the rein. "Now that Leyne's gone, you're the only true friend I have. I love you, Sudian."

The words caught Nightfall by surprise, and he choked on the necessary reply, not because he did not share the sentiment but because circumstance stole all meaning from it. Edward had become like a younger brother to him, and the constant need to protect had become far more than forced responsibility or habit. The phrase "I love you" seemed shallow and meaningless to Sudian, a bridge between beatings, a random string of words that hours later might become "I hate you, you worthless spawn of demon seed." Nightfall could not help wondering what about him had changed that so many he considered good people loved him when his own mother never could. "I love you, too." For once, he left off the "master," knowing it would weaken the moment at a time when Edward needed strength. He also left off the usual series of raving compliments. Deception now would only enhance the guilt Nightfall could not escape. He had plundered Edward's emotions on pretext, and no theft of an object ever seemed as cruel. The friend Edward believed in so staunchly was a slave in magical bondage. The only man who respected the younger Nargol for himself was a lie.

As the procession arrived at the castle gates, Kelryn rode to Edward's other side. Citizens followed them through the streets, whispering their observations, as if they might inadvertently awaken the lifeless prince. Guards met the carriages, spoke in earnest with the Shisenian officials, then ushered the coaches and escorts into the courtyard. Alyndarian guards, nobility, and servants approached the carriages with appropriate pomp and dignity, preparing to reclaim their crown prince and his possessions in a ceremony Nightfall and, apparently, Edward had no interest in witnessing. Travel-worn, weary, and broken, the younger prince needed his sleep, and Nightfall found that matter far more urgent. He glanced about the courtyard, now thronged with Alyndarians quietly performing their roles in the bleak formalities.

Stable hands managed the horses, and Prince Edward, Nightfall, and Kelryn approached the castle entryway on foot. Attentive guards with poleaxes met them at the door, and the taller of the two addressed Edward. "Lord prince, King Rikard asked that you wash up and rest. He'll meet you in the North Tower chapel later." His glance rolled to Kelryn. "The guest chamber is prepared for your lady friend."

Edward nodded, and the guard turned his attention to Nightfall. "Sudian, the king asked that you go directly to the Great Hall. I'll escort you."

The idea of abandoning Edward now raised a dangerous prickle from the oath-bond. He had not seen Gilleran since the murder, and he harbored little doubt the sorcerer had returned here. Nightfall shook his head. "Please tell King Rikard I'll be along shortly."

The guardsman's bushy brows rose high enough to disappear beneath his helmet. "King Rikard requested your presence right away."

Nightfall remained composed. "And he will get it, but not before I assist my master."

The sentry glared. "King Rikard does not care for delays."

Nightfall ignored the warning. "My duty is to my master the prince, not to the king. If you'll excuse us." He headed for the open castle door, hoping his movement would naturally sweep Edward and Kelryn along with him.

The maneuver failed. Though he meant well, Edward said the words Nightfall dreaded. "It's all right, Sudian. It's bad to slight a king, especially my father. I'll do fine without you."

The oath-bond intensified. Nightfall paused in the

doorway, turned, and made a gracious bow to Prince Edward. "With all respect, Master, I am going to tend you first. The king *will* understand." He stared directly at Edward, hoping his expression conveyed his complete lack of compromise on the matter to the prince rather than the guards.

Prince Edward opened his mouth to speak, and Kelryn gave him a mild warning kick in the shin. Startled, Edward closed his mouth and glanced at her instead. Kelryn shook her head slightly, then lifted her chin to indicate they should continue forward. Edward took a hesitant step, glanced at Kelryn again, then headed toward the hallway with more confidence. Nightfall and Kelryn trailed him, the magical warning dying.

The guards exchanged glances that indicated they believed Nightfall had made the wrong decision, but they did not try to stop him or say anything more. They would report their duty done. The blame would fall on Nightfall.

Prince Edward led Nightfall and Kelryn through a series of corridors and chambers filled with vases, books, and knickknacks Nightfall assessed from habit. They pattered up a spiral staircase to the third story. Polished rings held unlit lanterns at regular intervals, and tapestries lined the spaces between them except where gilded, teak doors broke the continuity. Prince Edward paused before one door that bore the Alyndarian hand and hammer symbol with inset purple gemstones and lowered his head respectfully.

Nightfall waited for Edward to pay his respects before what was, apparently, Leyne's bedroom door. After several moments, Edward led his guests to the next room, similarly decorated except for the absence of the jewels. He pushed open the door to reveal a vast sleeping chamber that could have held all of the inn rooms they had stayed in on their travels. A wooden frame supported a bed piled high with mattresses and feathered pillows, topped by a colorful quilt with fringes dangling to the floor. Though simple in design, the four posts had been meticulously sanded so that they reflected the light from two high-arched windows into perfect patterns. The room also contained a desk, chair, chest, dressing table and closet, all obviously made by the same craftsman who created the bed frame. The table held an assortment of brushes, combs, and bottles; and a mirror lined the wall above it. Several rugs covered the wooden floor, as intricate as the tapestries wealthy men used to decorate their walls. "My room," he explained unnecessarily.

Prince Edward did not enter. Instead, he continued one door farther down the hallway, opening it to reveal a chamber nearly as large and well-furnished as his own. "Will these quarters suit you, Lady?"

At his side, Kelryn stared in openmouthed silence. For a moment, Nightfall feared she might reply that it would suit her entire village. Instead, she nodded dumbly, the words following only after a strained pause. "Very well. Thank you, Ned."

Edward turned to Nightfall. "And you—"

Nightfall did not allow Edward to finish. "—will stay with you, Master."

Edward's features bunched and crinkled. Obviously, he had planned to say something completely different. "That's not necessary, Sudian. There's plenty of room for you."

That seemed gross understatement, but also senseless. The amount of space in the castle had nothing at all to do with his choice of sleeping site. "I will stay with you, Master." He emphasized the inarguable finality of the statement with tone and expression.

Edward made a gesture of dismissal. "Go see my father, as he requested. We can talk about this later."

Nightfall made no move to obey. As usual, his need to tend to security overrode his obedience to Edward's command. "Your safety comes first, Master, your father's wants a distant second."

"Safety?" Still in the guest room doorway, Edward studied his squire. "You're being ridiculous, Sudian. I'm home. There's no danger here."

Nightfall would not budge. "Where you feel most secure, you are in the most danger. No place is certain sanctuary."

"Disobedience to my father, the king, could make all

the dangers in Alyndar seem harmless." A sharp edge entered Edward's tone. "You're acting foolishly."

Nightfall shrugged. "Master, I would rather leave you angry at me than dead. I will stay with you. And, until I return from my meeting with the king, you must promise me you won't leave your room nor open the door for anyone but Kelryn."

"What?" Edward's eyes widened. Clearly, he meant the word as an exclamatory rather than a question. "What nonsense is this?"

"Master, my only concern is your safety. I will not go until I've assured that."

Kelryn stepped in, placing a hand on Edward's upper arm. "There's no use fighting it, Ned. He won't give up, and he means well. The sooner you agree, the less time passes to upset the king." She smiled sweetly. "I'll stay with you while he's gone, so you won't get bored."

Clearly flustered by the touch, Edward lost the will to argue. Surely, boredom had little to do with his reasons for disagreeing, but to deny it meant losing Kelryn's company. "Very well. Now go. If you keep my father waiting much longer, even I can't stay his wrath. Go. Go on."

Trusting Edward in Kelryn's hands, Nightfall obeyed, without suffering any discomfort from the oath-bond. However, he knew a different sort of pain, a deep sadness at the growing bond between Kelryn and Edward. Logic told him that if he truly loved the dancer he would want the best possible life for her. With the prince of Alyndar, she would have that, as well as an ally to share her grief when Gilleran stole his soul. Nightfall headed back up the hallway to the stairs. It seemed the perfect situation for Kelryn, one only chance could arrange. Not only would Edward treat her as kindly as any man could, but he would do so with love and respect. He could give her everything, including the one thing no one else could: positive memories of the demon the whole world otherwise hated.

Yet, despite all of these things, Nightfall headed down the winding staircase with a heart that felt heavy as lead. It made no difference that he would do so willingly and to an opponent far more worthy; giving up the woman he loved ached within him, a burden rather than a choice.

Once at the base of the stairs, Nightfall navigated the corridors to Alyndar's Great Hall from memory. The walk turned his thoughts from Kelryn to considerations about the king's motivation for meeting with him. Many possibilities filled his mind, from benign to ridiculous. He discarded all but the most plausible. It made sense that King Rikard would choose to listen to Nightfall's version of the events of the past several months as being nearer reality than Edward's. Yet, it seemed to Nightfall that propriety must dictate Rikard discuss matters with his son first. More likely, King Rikard no longer found a need for Nightfall's services. Reality had stolen enough of Edward's naive exuberance to allow normal tutors to work with him, and Rikard could no longer give all his direction to his elder son. Kings tended to dispose of what no longer aided or amused them.

Nightfall's steps slowed at the realization, but he did not falter. This time, running and hiding would not save him. The oath-bond would take him in either instance. At least, if he reasoned with Rikard, he might have a small chance to rescue life as well as soul. At the worst, he trusted his ability to incite enough to believe he could goad king or guards to kill him before the oath-bond took him.

Four sentries with spears and swords stood in front of the massive door that opened onto the courtroom of King Rikard the Hammer-handed. These stepped aside as Nightfall approached. One addressed him. "Sudian, Edward's squire?"

Nightfall nodded, though he suspected the question came from routine formality. Surely, every guard in Alyndar had learned his description.

"The king has been expecting you." The sentry emphasized the word "has" to indicate a long, impatient wait. He pushed the door ajar.

Nightfall bobbed his head to indicate understanding. Without wasting more time with words, he pressed inside the courtroom and trotted briskly down the carpeted pathway between rows of benches and toward the high-backed chair that served as Rickard's throne. To Nightfall's relief, the chancellor's chair beside the seated king stood empty. The spectators' benches held no people. The only other occupants of the chamber were a dozen attentive guardsmen spread along walls festooned with paintings and tapestries. Volkmier, the competent, red-haired chief of prison guards who had threatened Nightfall after his fall from the parapets, held a position near the front of the room at the king's left hand.

Nightfall took his cues from Rikard and Volkmier. The king sat with rigid alertness, his gray-flecked brown curls in mild disarray and his fur-trimmed robe wrinkled. Nightfall suspected the lapses in demeanor had less to do with slovenliness than an unwillingness to steal time or regard from more important matters. The dark eyes told all, hard with a steely gleam that offered no kindness or mercy. Clearly, he had not called Nightfall only to request news of the past months.

Volkmier's stance seemed as unyielding as Rikard's expression, though Nightfall guessed he echoed the king's mood from duty or concern rather than any suspicions of his own. Kelryn had seen through his disguise, but she had known him as no one else but Dyfrin could. Surely, if King Rikard told anyone about the oath-bond, he would select a chief among his guards; but Nightfall felt certain Gilleran would convince him to keep the arrangement fully secret. Even without the sorcerer's input, it seemed foolish to discuss such a dangerous matter with anyone.

Nightfall stopped the proper distance from the king, knelt, and bowed his head to his chest. He remained in position, waiting for Rikard to speak. His other senses kept him keenly aware of every movement of king or guards, though he did not bother to focus. A sudden attempt to harm or kill him seemed the least of his worries now.

After a period that seemed excessive to Nightfall, Rikard spoke, but he addressed the guards rather than the man he had summoned. "Away with all of you. I wish to talk with Sudian alone."

Nightfall held his pose, listening to the hiss of movement and the gentle, scarcely audible rattle of mail under tunics. Heavy footfalls tracked the far side of the rows of benches then came together to approach the door. One by one, the sentries filed from the room. Yet, Nightfall could tell, without vision, that Volkmier still had not obeyed.

King Rikard waited until the door clicked closed before addressing his chief prison guard. "Alone, Volkmier."

Now, Nightfall heard the swish of fabric as Volkmier obviously made some grand gesture of respect. "Sire. I will not leave you unprotected."

Nightfall could not help smiling at the familiar words, glad his position hid his expression from the others.

King Rikard sounded annoyed and impatient. "I'm in no danger from Sudian. Go."

Volkmier only repeated. "Sire, I will not leave you unprotected."

"It is not a request. It is an order."

"And I am loyal to your orders, Sire. Most so to the one that I will not leave you unguarded among men I do not know. Sire, I will not leave you unprotected."

Only concern for his own fate kept Nightfall from laughing at the irony. He remained still, not even bothering to sneak a look at the insistent guardian. He could judge mood and intention well enough by tone alone.

"Very well," King Rikard said at length, sounding much like his youngest son. "Stay, then, but do not listen. Words spoken in private must remain so." Finally, he addressed Nightfall. "Sudian, guard your tongue."

Nightfall rose and raised his head, an action allowed by the king's acknowledgment. He guessed that the king intended that he say nothing in Volkmier's presence that would reveal his persona or the oath-bond, but the warning seemed unnecessary. The first he could not do as a condition of the magic; the second disclosure would do him more harm than good. He recalled the captain's warning from the parapets, the honest rage behind the vow still vivid: "If you give me the slightest excuse, I'll shoot you dead and revel in it."

King Rikard shifted, as if to flex every colossal muscle on his warrior's frame. He riveted his gaze on Nightfall's face. "Did you kill my son?"

Nightfall stared, frankly stunned. This question he had

not anticipated in any version of his speculation. "What?" Surprise shocked amenity from him, and a long while passed in quiet before he added, "Sire."

Volkmier's eyes and nostrils widened. As commanded, he feigned deafness in that he took no action nor made any comment.

Rikard repeated, "Did you kill my son?"

"Your son, Sire? Prince Leyne Nargol?" The suggestion seemed too ludicrous to contemplate.

The king became relentless, though patient. "Yes. You killed him, didn't you?" The tone was flat, indicative of a rage so massive there could be no containment.

Nightfall knew he could say nothing King Rikard would believe. Guilty or innocent, he had no choice but to deny the allegation; yet he harbored no hope that he might be trusted. "No." He met the eyes of guard and king with level honesty. "Sire, you know I couldn't have."

King Rikard rose. He spun suddenly, hands clenched, back to Nightfall. At last, it seemed, anger had driven him even beyond speech.

Nightfall waited patiently beneath Volkmier's ceaseless scrutiny.

The king knelt, fishing something from behind his seat that clanged as he moved it. He tossed several objects to the floor: first the torn, brown and green cinch strap that had belonged to Sir Takruysse, then four pieces of two different sparring swords. As each item struck the wood with a clatter, he studied Nightfall's reaction to them.

Nightfall raised his brows slightly, eyes tracing every movement. The display told him much he did not like, though it did not surprise him. Only one man could have learned of his tricks in such detail and would gather the physical evidence, one who could read his mind.

King Rikard produced one more item, a battered, bloodstained work of steel and leather that had once formed a helmet, the one Leyne had worn in the final tourney. Now Nightfall could see that someone had thinned the crown to a half or quarter thickness which explained why Sander's single blow had proven fatal.

Rikard's voice sounded choked and uncharacteristically feeble. "Do you know these things, Sudian?"

Nightfall saw no advantage to lying. "Yes, I do, Sire." Gilleran's intention and purpose seemed abundantly clear. Like so many others, he had easily copied Nightfall's methods, using the similarities to ascertain guilt. It only remained for the sorcerer to devise some explanation of how Nightfall had escaped the constraints of the oath-bond in order to murder the crown prince of Alyndar. King Rikard clearly expected clarification, so Nightfall supplied it. "Sire, I admit I rigged the cinch strap and the swords. In my situation, I believe most men would have done the same. But my later attempts to cheat failed, and my master won every contest from that time without my help." He met the shrewd, dark eyes with an expression at least as somber. "Sire, your younger son has more ability than you or he or anyone gives him credit for."

Volkmier fidgeted, obviously troubled.

Nightfall hoped the guard was responding to the confessions of fraud rather than his own words. His time with Edward suggested that royalty despised any comments that put their past judgments about anything in doubt. "As a ruler, there's nothing wrong with Prince Edward Nargol that age, a few confrontations with reality, and some lessons from his father couldn't fix."

King Rikard's eyes narrowed, but he remained too preoccupied to take offense from Nightfall's speech . . . yet. "You're avoiding the question."

Nightfall fell silent, expression open with uncertainty. "The question of the helmet?"

"Yes."

"Sire, I had nothing to do with it."

The king said nothing, only stared with a look that encouraged Nightfall to continue.

Nightfall shrugged. "There's nothing more to say, Sire. Even had I need or reason, you know I could not have harmed Prince Leyne in any way."

King Rikard relented slightly. "I don't believe you intended to kill him, only to eliminate him as competition for Ned."

Nightfall saw no cause for arguing the point. "Your

Majesty, I can't deny that I considered ways to give my master an advantage, even over his brother. But I never touched that helmet."

"No one else had cause to do so, aside from Prince Sander, whose honor I would not disparage."

"Nor I, Sire." Nightfall would not shuffle guilt onto an innocent, no matter how obvious a target. He kept his gaze steady, knowing few things bespoke guilt as completely as restless eyes. "I didn't survive this long by painting myself bullseye yellow and writing 'I'm guilty' on my forehead nor am I foolish enough to skirt the edges of magic that could—"

The king made a sudden, cutting gesture that hushed Nightfall. Clearly he had said more than Rikard wanted Volkmier to know.

Nightfall continued more carefully. "Sire, when you consider the goal as murdering Leyne rather than winning the tourney, the list of suspects becomes much longer. Whenever the answer seems too obvious, look to the source of your information."

"I've heard enough!" King Rikard kicked the helmet, sending it skittering across the floor. It crashed against the wall, now riddled with new dents. "You're a killer, and I was an old fool to trust you near either of my sons."

Volkmier tensed, awaiting a direct command.

Nightfall instinctively mimicked his actions for the same reason. When no edict followed, he broke the excessive quiet that followed the king's display of violence. "Sire, if you truly believed I murdered Leyne, you wouldn't have called me in to ask. You would only have meted punishment."

King Rikard's face purpled. "Don't gainsay my motives. Who in the Father's blackest, coldest, empty hell do you think you are?"

Nightfall dodged the question, preferring to finish the meeting before anger drove the king to irrational action. "Sire, am I under arrest?"

"I haven't decided yet." King Rikard studied the assortment of ruined objects on the floor.

"Then, Sire, perhaps I can make your choice simpler." Nightfall turned his gaze to Volkmier, meeting sharp green eyes beneath a fringe of red bangs. He had faced off with the chief prison guard twice now, neither an experience he wished to repeat. "I perceive danger to Prince Edward here. If anyone tries to keep me from him, I'll have no choice but to fight my way free in any way I can. You may lose a guard or two. At best, I'll get the quick, painless death that seems the most I can hope for at the moment." He glanced back at Rikard who had retaken his seat, obviously calmer. "If you free me, you know precisely where to find me if you change your mind."

Volkmier prodded for his next course of action. "Sire?"

King Rikard scrutinized Nightfall as if to memorize every detail. He lingered longest on the eyes, and Nightfall met him stare for stare. He had told only the truth, boldly forthright, and nothing about his story could or would vary in the future. "Dismissed, Sudian."

Volkmier frowned, maintaining the verbal distance he had promised but obviously confused by his king's choice. "Sire?"

King Rikard addressed his guard, switching to an unrelated matter to emphasize the finality of his order. "Volkmier, send someone to tell Edward I'll meet him in the North Tower chapel right away." He turned some of his aggravation inappropriately on his captain. "I need some time alone with my son. I presume you'll trust me with Ned and won't force yourself on us."

Nightfall turned and headed from the Great Hall of Alyndar without looking back.

King Rikard watched Nightfall leave, sensing rather than seeing Volkmier's alert presence still poised to protect him. Guilt knifed through his belly, and he regretted the annoyance his own befuddlement caused him to channel against one of his most loyal servants, one into whose hands he had placed the defense and defenders of Alyndar. In no mood for apologies and intolerant of displays of affection, he expressed his regret in the form of including Volkmier in his considerations. "What do you think?"

Volkmier paused, apparently trying to divine the purpose of the question. "At your request, Sire, I heard nothing."

Rikard dismissed his previous order with a wave. "Surely you have an opinion about Edward's squire."

The guard's chief hesitated longer. Then, he spoke his mind, surely realizing his relationship with Alyndar's king had gone far beyond the testing stage. "I have many opinions about him."

The king raised his brows, sincerely interested. He trusted Volkmier's wisdom as well as his physical competence, though never so much as he had Leyne's. "Speak your mind."

Volkmier assessed Nightfall. "No simple peasant's son, that one, Sire. He has a nimbleness and quickness about him that suggests an acrobat, juggler, or dancer. Or perhaps a sailor." He shook his head. "But then, too, he has a vigilance that seems innate. I've only ever seen that about a fighting man, though he doesn't appear to have the strength or size of a warrior." Volkmier put all of his clues together. "If I had to guess, Sire, I'd say a farm boy. An animal farm. The type that'd use his off-time to slip into the pastures to ride stallions and bulls for sport."

King Rikard wearied of the taboo he had created. "You may speak freely with me about the events that transpired here today. What do you think of what he said?"

Volkmier relaxed along with the conversation. His stance returned to attentive normal, freed of the rigidness he had adopted for Nightfall. "I believe him, Sire."

The short, direct reply startled Rikard. "What?"

"Sire, I didn't understand much of the conversation, so I can only judge from tone and expression." A strand of sweat-plastered orange hair slid free of his helmet to sprawl across his forehead. "But every line of his attitude, every set of his face, and, most of all, the eyes bespoke integrity."

The words surprised King Rikard. He paced around his chair, trying to process the information in the light of what he already knew. He, too, could not deny an inclination to trust Nightfall's claims, this time at least; and many of the demon's words struck home for him as they could not for Volkmier. He had trusted his chancellor too completely and too long to believe a lying, traitorous stranger first; yet, when it came to matters involving Nightfall, Rikard had already seen a side of Gilleran that seemed disparately cold. *Is it possible that Leyne's death was an accident? Could some other, a jealous noble or an enemy of Alyndar, have switched the helmet? Could it be that Gilleran drew the wrong conclusion, worse, used the opportunity to lay the blame on a man he hates?* King Rikard shook his head to clear it from a line of thought that seemed ludicrous. To believe the word of a criminal over that of a long-loyal retainer seemed madness. *Maybe, Gilleran just made a mistake.* "What if I told you Sudian was a man experienced in deception and trickery?"

Volkmier stiffened, obviously taken back. "Sire, I would have no choice but to say he fooled me; but I'm in good company." He stroked some object in his tunic pocket, roughly rectangular in shape. "Or, perhaps, Sire, I'm just influenced by this." Thrusting his hand inside the pocket, he drew out a book. The dyed purple cover and its decorative swirls in silver leaf identified it at once as Leyne's journal. "Forgive me, Sire, for bringing up such matters before the funeral, but the time seems right. Would you mind, Sire?"

King Rikard stopped before his chair, eyes narrowing with uncertainty. "This is germane?"

Volkmier explained. "Sire, it's Leyne's impression of Sudian."

Rikard dropped into his seat. Leyne's ability to assess people and their intentions had always impressed him. He wanted to hear, but the grief was still too fresh. *Leyne's words in the voice of another man, opinions that survived beyond his death.* He closed his eyes, picturing his most beloved son as the author of Volkmier's speech. "Go ahead."

Volkmier cleared his throat. "It's dated the fourteenth day of the Month of Plenty."

Two days before his murder. King Rikard felt tears sting his eyes and angrily banished them as weak and foolish.

Volkmier read: ". . . Finally met Sudian face to face. Must admit I mistrusted him at first. Felt certain those timid features and boyish dedication hid a greed only a prince's gold could satisfy. Am thrilled to know I judged him wrong. The changes in Ned are nothing short of miraculous, the kind of self-control and understanding that could only come, I thought, with decades of experience. His dangerous exuberance has gained direction, now nothing short of determination. No doubt, Sudian is the cause. I tested the promises of loyalty I mistrusted and now find them as genuinely solid as the bond between my father and myself . . ." Captain Volkmier trailed off. "He went on to talk about the contests. Do you want to hear more?"

The king's lip trembled, and he resisted speech until he felt capable of hiding his weakness. "No, not now." He reached for the book. "I'll read the rest in private, when other matters don't compete for my attention." He reached for the journal, and Volkmier passed it to his king.

Back in Alyndar's corridors, Nightfall navigated from habit, his thoughts riveted on the events in Rikard's courtroom. Hope died, leaving only the familiar, bare spark that had allowed him to survive since childhood; yet that seemed more mockery than tool. His mind found the loophole, as it always did. Once the necessary grief-sharing and services had concluded, he would find some way to talk Edward into sneaking away from Alyndar for another attempt at landing. Duke-heir Willafrida seemed his most likely possibility once again. With Leyne gone, the duke could no longer set his sights on Alyndar's eldest prince. Surely, Edward could learn to love her.

Yet, even discovering a solution did not lift Nightfall's spirits. His time with Edward had taught him the difference between living happy and merely living, and survival had become a poor motivator when it meant condemning Edward, Kelryn, and himself to lifelong bitterness. Though not quite ready to discard the possibility of another means of landing, the best solution seemed obvious. Surely, Nightfall could find a way to antagonize King Rikard, Gilleran, or his retainers into murdering him before the oath-bond took him. Then, Edward and Kelryn could make a happy life together, even without the support of Alyndar's king.

Nightfall continued toward Prince Edward's quarters, persisting in his personal war now only from habit. It made sense to know the best result at any specific time; but, when the solution was permanent and extreme, to act before necessity seemed senseless. For now, he would follow the demands the oath-bond set on him, and his own heart when possible, and hope the possibility of dying violently would remain when the time came for final, irreversible decision.

Nightfall trotted up the winding staircase. The oath-bond had remained at baseline, nagging without driving, throughout his time away from Edward. Now, as realization of the length of time he had left the prince came to the fore, it amplified to a disquieting buzz that reminded Nightfall of the danger posed by the sorcerer who had cast the spell. Having a better feel for the players, Nightfall pieced together the various motivations for creating the situation that trapped him. Gilleran's intentions had seemed clear nearly since the beginning; he had found a means to all but ascertain possession of Nightfall's soul and natal gift. Likely, King Rikard's choice of execution, even for a criminal as notorious as Nightfall, would have precluded Gilleran's ceremony. By talking the king into the oath-bond, Gilleran had assured his prize and, at the same time, placed the youngest prince at the fate of a practiced and conscienceless killer.

The king's reasons continued to puzzle Nightfall, and they seemed complex. First, Gilleran surely used his long relationship, and possibly magic, to assist the decision. Whether Rikard also hoped for the deaths of two pests or truly believed the association would benefit Edward, Nightfall still could not fathom. The private conversation between king and prince would bring answers, shedding light on their relationship. He dared to hope it would prove positive; Edward and Leyne had to have gotten their sense of justice and fair play from some source.

Nightfall had just turned his contemplations to his own fate when he heard light footsteps on the stairs above, headed toward him. The curve of the spiral staircase hid the approaching figure from view. Nightfall stopped, keeping close to the rail to leave space for the other to pass. As soon as he did, Gilleran swung around the corner, his mousy hair neatly combed and in place. A scar puckered the skin between cheek and ear. His blue eyes seemed to smolder, and a frown crept slowly down his mouth. "So. He chose to let you go. How could our good king make such an error?"

Nightfall watched the sorcerer's approach without flinching. He felt confident Gilleran would not attempt his ceremony in the castle in plain view of any guard, Nargol, or noble who happened upon it. Anything less, Nightfall felt prepared to handle. If Gilleran wished to banter words, Nightfall would give him cause to worry. "Perhaps he finally realized his chancellor is a scheming rodent posing as a man."

Nightfall thought the insult mild and unoriginal, unworthy of his reputation, but Gilleran took it far more seriously. He punched at Nightfall's face. A side step rescued Nightfall, and Gilleran's momentum staggered him. He lurched forward, catching the railing for support.

Now uncomfortably close, Gilleran jabbed a finger at the scar. "You *will* pay for this."

The oath-bond flared even before Nightfall recognized the murderous hatred that had arisen within him. Its pain stole his attention for an instant that proved his downfall.

Suddenly, Gilleran planted both hands on Nightfall's chest and shoved.

The unexpected tactic toppled Nightfall. He crashed to the stairs, their irregularity stamping bruises the length of his back. His head struck one hard enough to slap his jaw shut. White light flashed across his vision, then all coordination left him. He tumbled and rolled, scrabbling wildly for purchase and balance, the hard edge of each step a hammering agony against flesh. About halfway down, he caught hold of the railing, pulled to a jarring halt that wrenched every tendon in his arm. Though dazed and disoriented, he forced himself to look up.

Gilleran rushed after Nightfall, gaining the stair above just as Nightfall recognized the danger. Gilleran's boot smashed into his face. Pain exploded through Nightfall's nose, spidering along his cheeks and eyes to his already aching head. Though thrown backward again, he held his grip, assaulted by an agony that seemed to come at him from every direction. Rage drove him to murder, inciting the oath-bond to a frenzy that dwarfed the physical injury. Every instinct screamed at him to fight, but the magic would not allow it.

Gilleran drove another kick for Nightfall's face.

Survival won. Nightfall snatched the foot in flight, stopping it fingers' breadths from his left eye. Gilleran twisted, equilibrium lost. The oath-bond stabbed and twisted, wrenching an involuntary scream from Nightfall's lungs that he only partially choked back. He lurched to his feet, steadying Gilleran as he gently lowered the foot to the step, hating the thwarted vengeance the oath-bond had stolen from him. The instant he did, Gilleran caught him with a backhand slap that sent him tumbling down three more stairs.

Gilleran rushed Nightfall. A sound on the upper landing drew Nightfall's attention, a soft scuff amplified by the sound-funneling staircase. Kelryn bent over the railing, clutching a vase the size of her head. Desperation tempered Nightfall's joy. The oath-bond became a consuming bonfire spurring him to protect the very man self-preservation drove him to destroy. He stumbled to his feet, leaping to knock Gilleran from the path of the missile in the same motion.

Kelryn hurled the vase. Oblivious, Gilleran jerked away from what he naturally construed as an attack by Nightfall. The vase struck his shoulder, sprawling him into Nightfall. It crashed to the steps, spraying pottery chips that stung Nightfall's face and arms. Both men careened down the final stairs in a wild, clawing frenzy, landing in a heap at the bottom. Pinned beneath Gilleran's weight, Nightfall shook his head to clear it. The oath-bond pulsed and diminished in waves, and the wounds from his fall seemed to do the same. Kelryn scurried down the stairs toward them.

Gilleran stumbled to his feet. "Guards!" he screamed. "Guards!"

Apparently, the sentries had already been drawn by the

noise, because two arrived while Kelryn still negotiated the final dozen steps.

"Take him away!" Gilleran jabbed a finger at Nightfall. "He tried to kill me."

Nightfall sat up, overemphasizing his injuries to make himself seem less threatening. He tasted blood. He wiped it from his nose, managing little more than to further smear it across his face.

Kelryn defended Nightfall. "He did not. I saw it all."

The Alyndarian guardsmen studied the scene before exchanging glances. One gave Gilleran a short, stiff bow. "Sir?"

Gilleran obliged. "This servant ambushed me on the stairs. He hit me over the head with a vase, then tripped me. If I hadn't gotten hold of him as I fell, he'd have killed me."

"That's not what happened!" Kelryn shouted. "I'm the one who threw the vase."

Nightfall waved her silent briskly. Her involvement would accomplish nothing more than getting her arrested also. The terms of the oath-bond cast on her, to say nothing negative about Gilleran in any situation a Nargol might overhear, would keep her from speaking the truth. Likely the noise had or would draw prince or king; if it came to trial, both would certainly attend.

Gilleran shook his head in dismissal. "The lady is protecting him. I don't know why." He straightened his silks. "Lock him up."

The guards set to their duty, first assisting Nightfall to his feet. "Come with us."

Nightfall lowered his head, cooperative with every movement and gesture. Blood dripped from his injured nose, leaving a trail of droplets on the parquet. He continued to feign worse injuries than he had received, wishing his head would stop pounding and allow him to think. So long as the guards believed him submissive and wounded, they would treat him gently.

Soon to be left alone with Gilleran, Kelryn retreated several steps but did not run. Her stance bespoke courage, and her eyes glimmered with determination. She had promised never to freeze in the sorcerer's presence again, and she had not. Obviously torn between rescuing Nightfall and his direct command, she protested only feebly. "You're making a mistake."

Nightfall hoped Kelryn's newfound boldness would not prove her downfall. "It'll get sorted out." Nightfall modulated his voice to try to soothe her without forsaking his pained and hopeless act. In truth, he felt nearly as broken as he looked. The oath-bond's fury at his thoughts of breaching one tenet had died away, but another soon rose to replace it. Gilleran had set his scheme in motion when he murdered Prince Leyne. With Nightfall in custody, no obstacle stood between him and the younger prince. As the oath-bond rose to a tearing shriek within him, he put his misery into words for Kelryn. "My master?"

Kelryn caught the unspoken need beneath the question. "He's fine. Meeting his father on the seventh floor chapel in the North Tower."

Nightfall appreciated Kelryn's thorough description. Though no Dyfrin, she could read him better than he dared to expect.

One of the Alyndarian guards prodded Nightfall. "Come on."

"Stay alert," Gilleran warned. "He's quicker and more violent than he seems. Shackles are in order here; and backup as soon as possible."

The guardsmen exchanged looks that Nightfall read as contempt for soft nobility who over-aggrandized the danger to men trained to war. Nevertheless, they kept him between them, scrutinizing his every movement and holding their own stances well-balanced. They searched him in the hallway, with an exhaustive thoroughness that far exceeded that of the duke's men, and uncovered all of the throwing daggers as well as a myriad of seemingly harmless objects in his pockets, including Brandon Magebane's stone.

Sight of the latter object brought realization, hope, and remorse at once. When it had failed to remove the oath-bond, the spell-stone had become essentially forgotten. Now, Nightfall realized, he had carried the means to rescue Leyne from Gilleran's magic. At the thought, guilt flared, then died abruptly. The tactic would only have delayed the inevitable. Preventing one spell might have surprised Gilleran, but no more than the danger of a thrown dagger; and Nightfall could not have stopped a second attempt moments later. Experience told him the stone had no effect on spells already cast, so he doubted directing it against Gilleran's flight would have had any significant consequences.

Nightfall pretended to pay the guards little heed, though he memorized the placement of every one of his possessions. He anticipated, but cursed, the caution with which the guard placed the daggers at his belt. Though simple, a theft would prove obvious, and Nightfall would find himself facing trained guardsmen when his own weapons had come only half-free. The harmless-appearing stone slid into a tunic pocket that he could plunder in his sleep. Nightfall could regather his other equipment as easily; however, none of it seemed worth the trouble or the risk.

An unrelated idea flashed through Nightfall's mind, and the oath-bond's goading riveted his attention fully. The private meeting between king and prince, without guards, would make the perfect circumstance for Gilleran to work his evil. The oath-bond hammered at Nightfall, driving him to rip free of their grip and charge to the North Tower chapel. But, for once, common sense intervened. Now more accustomed to the magic's sting and howl, he learned to think around it, to separate physical pain from idea. If he harmed these sentries, it would start a manhunt that involved the entirety of Alyndar's guard force, all of whom would want his blood. The wild romp that had reunited him with Edward in the citadel of Schiz' duke would not work so easily here. It made far more sense for him to allow the imprisonment, slip free of the restraints and locks, then head up the parapets to the North Tower leaving no one the wiser.

Instead of placating, the consideration turned the oath-bond to a shrill whine in his ears, and knifing pains in his gut twisted more sharply. The sudden change doubled him over, and he sank to the tiled floor. Only then, he understood. Foiling manacles and shackles, picking prison

locks, and escaping from Alyndar's dungeon would identify him as Nightfall as few other actions could.

The guards halted, reaching to assist Nightfall to his
feet. Clutching his abdomen with one hand, Nightfall
gave the other freely, clasping the guard's fingers in a
weak and clammy grip still smeared with blood. He increased his weight to a reasonable maximum, feigning
frailty. Then, as the other pulled him toward a stand,
Nightfall dropped his weight as low as possible. The abrupt loss of resistance sent the sentry staggering backward. Nightfall snatched the Magebane's stone from the
guard's pocket, then sprinted down the corridor through
which they had come.

"Halt! Stop!" The other guardsman charged after
Nightfall as his companion struck the ground. "Prisoner
free! Alarm! Alarm! Prisoner free in the south hall."

Nightfall increased his speed, racing down the hallway
with little consideration to a goal. Within moments, he
heard pounding footsteps and the chitter of mail echoing
through the crisscrossing corridors and rooms. It would
take time for the many sentries at their various stations to
converge, but Nightfall felt certain it would happen long
before he reached the northern side of the castle, let alone
breezed up the seven flights of stairs.

The oath-bond's insistence became an agony that overturned his senses. Nightfall staggered, pain stealing all
sense of balance, then toppled to the floor. Momentum
sent him skidding over the polished wood floor, rugs
crumpling and sliding beneath him. His head filled with
the certainty of lethal danger to Prince Edward, and it left
no room for other thought. He continued forward, crawling the length of a doorway before gaining his feet
through some instinct or miracle he could not fathom.
The pain flashed from core to limbs in waves that quickened in narrow increments. Within a dozen steps, it had
fused into a constant, straining scream; and within a
dozen more, familiarity made it tolerable enough for
other thought to squeeze past it. Nightfall realized his
best chance lay outside the palace where larger spaces
and distance from the royal family would make the pat-

tern of guardsmen sparser. Once out, he could climb the tower.

The creation of a plan eased the oath-bond just enough to encourage more detailed thought. Weaponless and only a fair warrior, Nightfall dared not consider the possibility of battling his way out of a bastion made to thwart attacking armies. Common sense told him it would make little sense to make the front door impenetrable, then leave other holes for enemies and assassins to slip into the castle. Surely, the ground floor would have no other entrances or exits, with the possible exception of emergency bolt holes for the king's family. He did not have the time to root out such secret passages. The windows, he felt certain, would be shuttered closed or barred on the lower levels.

Nightfall whipped around a corner. Two guardsmen hastened just as swiftly in his direction, obviously as surprised by his sudden appearance as he by theirs. Nightfall did not slow. He charged them like a war horse, head low, weight high, shoulders braced. They skidded to a halt unevenly, scurrying to block off the way with their bulk.

Nightfall aimed for the closing gap between them, diving through as they positioned. Cloth and mail glided from his arms. Fingers brushed his thigh, and he kicked into a wild dive that sent him tumbling through the corridor. He restored his weight.

"Alarm!" one shouted. "Pantry hall! East heading!" The sentries whirled, pounding a hot pursuit that sounded directly on top of Nightfall.

Nightfall did not waste precious seconds glancing behind him, just galloped onward in uncertain desperation. The oath-bond's shrill punishment became an unbearable torture to which his body compelled him to surrender. But premonition as well as logic told him that, unlike death, giving in to the magic would not be an ending. To submit meant an inescapable eternity of suffering. Rescuing Edward might supply at least a temporary escape. That observation awakened something more primal. Edward was in danger. Edward was a friend. Oath-bond or none, Nightfall would use every trick at his disposal to rescue his charge.

A stairway loomed in front of Nightfall, its left side flush with the wall, an elaborately carved wooden railing along its right. The hallway continued as well, but Nightfall followed the continuation of his own logic. The lower the floor, the better protected, at least from those trying to enter or escape the castle. A glance told him neither would prove an easy run. Paired palace guards ran toward him from each direction. Nightfall soared up the stairs.

The sentries coming down the steps had slowed their pace to match the terrain. Therefore, they halted and closed ranks much more quickly and easily than their colleagues had in the hallway. Again, Nightfall tucked his chin and rushed them. This time, he met a solid barrier that made his head ring. Impact reeled him backward. His foot skimmed the side of a stair, and he toppled down four steps, stopped by the feet of the chasing guardsmen. One reached down, closing a hand around his forearm.

Nightfall froze, allowing the sentry to hoist him to shaky legs. He met a pair of hard brown eyes beneath a standard-issue helmet, the image blurred and liquid. Only then, Nightfall realized that pain and concern had driven tears to his eyes. The weakness and apparently overwhelming fear of his catch must have surprised the guard as well, because his grip loosened and his expression lost its edge. In that moment, Nightfall sprang for the rail, intentionally squashing the sentry's fingers between his elbow and the wood. The guardsman recoiled. Nightfall twisted, catching the rail supports, and flung his body over it. For an instant, he hung on the outside of the stairway handrail, guardsmen from the hallway lurching upward, those on the stairs spinning to follow his movement. Nightfall climbed, hand-over-hand, then leapt abruptly to the upper railing. He sprinted across it like a squirrel, a simple feat compared with racing along *Raven*'s bouncing gunwales. Once past the guards, he jumped to the steps and bounded to the second landing. He crashed through the door, running without bothering to orient.

The guards shouted his location. "Prisoner on the second floor. Kitchen hallway!"

Kitchen. Kitchen. It took Nightfall's mind inordinately

long to wade through the syllables to meaning. Even as he equated food and cooking to the word, the implications struck him. Of all the rooms in a castle, the kitchen would most likely have connections to the outside to prevent the need to haul dead animals, vegetables, and garbage through the castle. He ran past a series of unmarked doors and doorways. Ahead, a double set without knobs or latches perched well above the ground. From a glance, he could tell the folded hinges would allow them to open in either direction. No place but the kitchen could require the need to open doors both ways and without the use of hands. He burst through, flinging the panels to create an inlet.

A girl skittered out of Nightfall's way, obviously startled by his entrance. He skidded into a massive chamber bustling with servants in livery much like his own but tailored to lower status and protected by stained, white aprons. Cook stoves lined the walls, along with bread spoons, tongs, pottery, steelware, and forks the size of tridents. Tables filled much of the center of the room, covered with cooling baked goods, fruits, and meats. Burdened with what was, apparently, more than their usual chores, the workers paid Nightfall little heed. The crackle of fires, the thump of kneading dough, and the clatter of pans as they were filled or emptied covered his deep, rhythmical panting. The shouts of the guards, however, did not disappear so easily, though their undirected suggestions blended into a roar that revealed nothing specific to the servants.

Then, Volkmier's commanding bass rose over the uproar. "Six to the royal chambers. Four to the North Tower. The rest of you wait here and guard the exits. No one goes in. If we damage the kitchen right before the funeral banquet, it'll be my hide and your heads." A short hammer of footsteps followed. A moment later, the guards' talk resumed at a lower tone. A few of the kitchen workers glanced at Nightfall, then returned to their jobs without comment.

Momentarily reprieved, Nightfall reveled in the slowing of his heart back to its normal beat. But the comfort did not last. The pause in his mission sent the oath-bond

off on another rending cycle of torment that drove him to
action he could not immediately think to take. He followed the line of his previous consideration, eyes searching for some opening to the courtyard before his
consciousness recognized the attempt. He discovered a
bolted and locked square between the ovens that surely
served as a pulley system for heavy products drawn into
or lowered from Alyndar's kitchen. That seemed his most
likely possibility, but he doubted even the detached
kitchen staff would allow him to jimmy the lock without
some comment or warning to the guards. Optionless, he
headed toward it, halted by the sight of an elderly woman
dumping parings, rotted scraps, and entrails down a chute
near a countertop buried in cutting boards and pestles.

Not for the first time, Nightfall appreciated the smaller
than average frame hardship had given him. He crossed
the room, casually eyeing delicacies his stomach, queasy
and twisted from pain, would not tolerate. He kept his
movements relaxed, waiting only until the woman turned
her back before diving through the narrow slot.

Greased by the sludge, Nightfall slid at a speed that
alarmed him. He choked on the rancid stench of discarded and ancient foodstuffs, a minor discomfort compared to the pain assailing him. He took some solace
from the realization that, whatever threatened Edward
must not yet have killed him. Although Nightfall already
guessed the danger came from Gilleran, the dragging of
time turned it into gross certainty. Only the sorcerer
would dare play cat-and-mouse with Alyndar's prince,
probably waiting to murder until he had Prince Edward
and King Rikard oblivious and together.

A moment later, Nightfall spilled into a trough filled
with a mixture of foul, unrecognizable offal that made
him gag. Disoriented, he rolled free and to his feet, recognizing the grunt and squeal of pigs around him. He
wiped fluid from his eyes. He stood in a stable surrounded by sows guarding half-grown piglets that huddled near the enclosing fence. Beyond them, other pens
held sheep, goats, and steers. Suddenly, the sows charged
him.

Well-aware of the murderous frenzy of protective

mother hogs, Nightfall pitched over the ring of sows, rolling to his feet amid a squealing mass of retreating piglets. He clambered over the pen wall, sow teeth ripping though his breeks to his shin, warm blood trickling into his boot. He flung himself out and over the pen, slamming down on a packed pathway strewn with wood chips. Breath jarred from his lungs in a gasp, and the fall stunned him momentarily. The spark of pain seemed to course through his body in slowed motion, as if through water. His every muscle felt torn by magic; his every bone felt broken.

A shadow fell across Nightfall. Still gathering strength to stand, prodded by the oath-bond's need, he rolled his eyes up to the source. Captain Volkmier stood over him, the point of a spear leveled at Nightfall's throat. "Be still."

Nightfall fixed a desperate gaze on the red-haired guardsman, digging for his own feelings amidst the drowning presence of the magic. A trickle of wisdom told him to bait the captain to a red rage beyond thought of consequence. Death in this fashion would rescue his soul from Gilleran. But Nightfall sensed something stronger, a need that he hoped came from within, as it seemed, not just an offshoot of the oath-bond. Bound or not, he had to rescue Edward, and Alyndar, from the sorcerer's evil. He suspected Volkmier had presumed the means of his escape from the kitchen, purposefully misdirecting Nightfall with his instructions to the guards. Harboring no fear of a routine killing but driven to reckless urgency by magic, Nightfall doubted he could remain in position longer than a moment. "May I stand, sir?"

Volkmier's features opened with surprise at what was, apparently, an unexpected question. "You may sit," he said at length, the spear retreating slightly.

Nightfall rose into a crouch, keeping his hands well in sight. "I'm unarmed."

The captain ignored the claim. Without taking his eyes from Nightfall, he back-stepped to a bag on the floor. He sorted the contents without looking at them, tossing a pair of opened shackles, then manacles, at Nightfall's side.

"Put them on. No tricks. I'll check them when you're done."

The oath-bond struck him with a sharp pain as abrupt and frightening as lightning. It took most of his will to keep from skittering to his feet against the captain's order. He waited for the pain to subside enough to allow speech, then fixed his gaze on Volkmier. "No."

"No?"

"No, sir." Nightfall could not compromise. Though he could unlock the bonds once placed, the magic had become too insistent for more delays.

Volkmier did not relent. "I didn't ask a question, Sudian. Do as you're told."

"I'm trying to." Nightfall fixed the most earnest stare he could muster on Captain Volkmier, then quoted him nearly verbatim. "I was told to protect my master, and I'm bound to his service. I won't leave him unguarded with men I don't trust. I won't leave him unprotected."

"Your charge is with his father. No danger there."

Nightfall tensed to rise, goaded to thoughtless action by the oath-bond.

The spear reared back. "Don't test my aim. I've slain zigzagging rabbits smaller than your head."

"No choice." Time constraints made Nightfall's sentences incomplete. "Kill me if must. Rather die than forsake master." Nightfall sprang to his feet and raced for the exit in a straight line Volkmier could not miss. Without so much as a backward glance, he charged into the courtyard, tensed for a stab through the back that never came. Nor did he hear a clatter to indicate the weapon had been misthrown. Nightfall knew a sudden camaraderie that both, it seemed, could understand. "Look to your own charge," he shouted as he ran. "The king may face the same danger."

Apparently not fully trusting the man he had just released, Volkmier shouted to his men. "Prisoner in the courtyard. Those on duty, man the walls and gates. The rest, inside to the North Tower chapel!"

Volkmier's command was obviously intended to police Nightfall's claims and keep him from escaping from the castle grounds. Since he had no intention of doing so, their position posed no threat. It would take time for the guardsmen to enter the door, head north, and clamber to the North Tower, a delay Nightfall dared not spare. He rushed north, praying to the Father the North Tower had been appropriately named. As Alyndar's guard force rushed alternately to the periphery or the castle entry, Nightfall made a beeline for the northernmost tower.

Daylight turned the stonework into a glaze that revealed no hand or toeholds aside from sundry windows on every level, the ones on the lowest three shuttered and barred. Nightfall vaulted for the first, landing lightly on its ledge. From there, he dropped his weight as low as the wind would allow, shinnying as quickly as a menaced spider, trusting momentum and his featherweight to serve where the craft of the artisans foiled him. Each upward glance brought sunlight glaring into his eyes, the aftermath a bland sequence of lines and spots on the stonework that made grips even harder to find.

Glass paned the fourth and fifth floor windows, apparently to thwart insects. Nightfall doubted any man, himself included, could battle past the courtyard guards and scale the walls without noticeable equipment. Desperation goaded him up walls that had begun to seem glass-smooth and achingly hot from the sun. By the sixth floor, he realized he had lost a boot, and his fingers bled from the minuscule irregularities they groped to clasp repeatedly. Every leg or arm muscle ached, and the stone had abraded his cheek. His nose still throbbed from the fall, and his head pounded. Yet, these pains seemed a blessing. As he approached Prince Edward, the oath-bond had returned nearly to its nagging baseline. He drew some hope from the realization that the sixth floor windows sported no glass, shutters, or bars, just lacy curtains that flapped and spiraled in the wind. Heart pounding, Nightfall dropped his other boot and scooted upward.

The purple curtains on the seventh floor windows matched those on the sixth. Using their fluttering pattern as cover, he peeked into a massive chamber that surely accounted for the entirety of the level. He perched high over a dais that supported a glass case of books, the gold-inlaid box that held Leyne's body, three hammer-and-fist banners of Alyndar, and a colossal candelabra holding eight burning, purple candles. Prince Edward slumped on the steps leading to the dais, Chancellor Gilleran in front of him, animatedly waving his arms.

I'm too late. Nightfall's heart seemed to stop, and pain fluttered through his chest. But the oath-bond remained at its lower level. Apparently, Edward lived. A moment later, a sigh shuddered through his body indicating consciousness as well. Both men wore tailored costumes, as richly dressed as nobility in court. Nightfall assessed the remainder of the room from habit. Wall sconces held lanterns, illuminating the central as well as the outer aisles between lengthy rows of pews. At the far end of the middle aisle, an iron-studded door stood closed.

Nightfall lowered himself through the window, scrambling down the wall to the floor, briefly losing track of his charge in the moments it took to climb. Those few instants cost him surprise.

Edward called out to him softly. "Nightfall."

Nightfall whirled at the address, realizing his mistake as he did so. In his nearly three decades of terrorizing the continent, he had never once crossed personae. Now, he had allowed emotion to steal his composure. He had fallen prey to the oldest and easiest trick in the world.

"Father take me, it's true." Edward's voice became an anguished sob, and he crumpled to the steps. "I believed in you. I dared to think someone believed in me. It was all a vicious lie."

Standing over the despondent prince, Gilleran smiled his triumph.

The rising prickles of the oath-bond were Nightfall's first warning that his hatred had again intensified to thoughts of murder. Whether the news, so close on the heels of Leyne's death, had overwhelmed Edward by itself or only with some magical assistance from the sorcerer, he did not know or care. He had only two options: win back the prince's trust and turn him against the chancellor he had known since childhood or battle alone against an enemy he could not harm without destroying himself.

Chancellor Gilleran made the choice for him. "Just in

time for the finale." He recited harsh syllables with a gesture that had become familiar, attention on Edward.

Edward lay, curled on the steps, weeping with the same world-oblivious grief he had displayed for his brother. It was a touching, heart-rending tribute, lost on its recipient who had eyes only for Gilleran.

The ice spell. Desperation drove Nightfall into a wild charge, thoughts deliberately focussed only on defense. He could not clear the distance to physically disrupt the magic in time. *The Magebane's stone.* Nightfall fumbled it free as he ran, shouting to draw what little regard he could seize from Edward's unreasoning anguish. "Look!" The stone glowed red in his fist, and he turned his concentration to the death spell Gilleran had wrested from Ritworth.

Gilleran waved his hand toward Edward. An angry, blue light blazed from the stone, arching like lightning toward the magical energy. The forces met in silence, but a brilliant explosion of light slashed Nightfall's vision, flinging sparks in a multicolored rain.

Gilleran retreated with a startled gasp.

Nightfall cleared the distance between then, speaking to Edward without bothering to see if the prince was watching. "See? I had the power to escape the bond at any time. I did believe in you. *I chose to stay in your service!*" It was a necessary lie. Until he roused Edward, he could accomplish nothing but delay.

"Murdering liar! Demon!" Gilleran undermined whatever confidence Nightfall had reclaimed. His gaze fixed on the stone, now cold and lifeless in Nightfall's fist; and the icy corpse's grin returned. "You have no power at all, over it or over me." He lurched toward Nightfall.

Hatred boiled within Nightfall, and he closed before he could think to do otherwise. The oath-bond caught him a blow he could not fend, an abrupt agony that shocked through his body. "No!" he screamed. "Master, run. Save yourself." Before he could regain control of his limbs, Gilleran hammered a fist into his face that sprawled him. Rage and the need for vengeance struck as hard as the blow, bringing a whirlwind response from the oath-bond that spasmed every muscle in his body. Pain only fueled the venom, an ugly cycle he fought to escape. His body jerked into a wild seizure he felt helpless to override.

A boot tip thudded into Nightfall's chest, stealing what little breath his shuddering lungs managed to gather. Gilleran kicked him repeatedly, shouting epithets Nightfall could not decipher over the roar of the oath-bond's threat. Dimly, he recognized a series of kicks and blows, heard something crack, and tasted blood. But the physical agony seemed secondary. His mind seemed to slip away, as it had in childhood, separating thought from emotion. The battering became a familiar lull on which to focus his consciousness, its source a nameless creature that bore no relation to anyone he knew. The drive for retribution and self-defense died, unfullfillable, and the oath-bond gave him enough reprieve to feel the stabbing, aching momentos of the beating. And also to realize the pounding had stopped.

Nightfall staggered to his feet, forcing his pain-glazed eyes to focus. The cruelty had snapped Edward from trance to flying rage, and he charged the sorcerer with sword drawn. Gilleran calmly gestured, a spell different from any Nightfall had seen cast before. Logic jerked back to body in an instant. He recalled Kelryn's description of the cutting magic that had dropped a tree branch on Ritworth. Then, Gilleran had only wanted to trap, not kill. *What damage could a force that sharp do to a man?* Nightfall sprang for Edward.

Nightfall crashed into the prince just as Gilleran made the final, curt movement. Pain gashed Nightfall's side, magic opening the flesh from hip bone to buttocks. Edward collapsed, head slamming against a pew with a sickening thud. He slumped to the aisle, and momentum sent Nightfall tumbling over the seat then skidding beneath the pews. He thumped into the dais steps hard enough to jar every wound in his body. Blood smeared the wooden floor. Dizziness assailed him like an enemy, the blanket of buzzing stars that could only come from blood loss.

Nightfall's eyelids felt heavy, but he forced himself to look. Edward lolled, unconscious, on the floor, his sword a hand's breadth from his limp fingers. Near the door, the sorcerer started the ice spell again. This time, Nightfall knew he could not prevent it. He had lost, and his soul belonged to Gilleran. The urge to sink into coma, to pray to the Father that death took him first became an obsession. But survival instincts that had become more curse than friend nudged him to action. He staggered to his feet, already too late.

The door jerked open with an echoing snap and squealing hinges. King Rikard of Alyndar stood in the doorway. "Edward, I—"

Gilleran spun, redirecting his spell from surprise or desperation. White light bathed the king's head. Rikard went still, mouth open, expression fixed. He pitched backward, head striking the floor and shattering. Shards skittered down the hallway, the sound eerily benign, nearly lost beneath the thud of his collapsing body.

Nightfall's agony seemed to drop a thousand notches in an instant. Still dizzied, it took him longer than it should have to divine the reason. *The king is dead and the eldest prince. Edward is king of Alyndar. Edward is landed.* Freed from the oath-bond, Nightfall launched himself at Gilleran.

The stomp of footsteps funneled up the staircase, accompanied by the clatter of mail.

Gilleran swore, the ever-present smile becoming a desperate grimace. He whirled, sprinting deeper into the room. An accident in the chapel room that took king and prince, he could have arranged. This, he could never explain. His mad scrambling dash ran him headlong into Nightfall.

Both men sprang at once, Gilleran rising to fly for the window, Nightfall attacking in blood-maddened frenzy. Nightfall tackled the sorcerer, hands scrabbling for the throat, Gilleran twisting and swearing. The magic proved stronger. Gilleran soared upward, Nightfall still clinging and clawing for a better hold. As the Alyndarian sentries reached their king, some elbowing past to find the culprit, Gilleran and Nightfall shot through the window.

Once in free air, Gilleran fought back, planting his fingers on Nightfall's face and raking his nails over flesh. Nightfall tossed his head, saving his eyes. The movement nearly cost him his grip. Gilleran spun, kicking and flailing to free himself from Nightfall's encumbrance. The ground lay seven stories beneath them. Gilleran spiraled higher, ensuring Nightfall's death when his grip finally failed.

Nightfall hid fear behind desperation and will. His mind filled with swimming spots, and his vision gave him only whirling pictures of tree tops, guards leaning from the tower window, and the courtyard far below them. Gilleran's struggles and blood loss stole his coordination and, soon, his hold on the sorcerer. *If I fall, I die. If we both fall, we both die.* The choice was easy. Eventually, Gilleran would have to touch down, but Nightfall dared not risk the chancellor's escape. He could not bear the cost in friends' lives. He closed his eyes, concentrating on a quick prayer. *Seven Sisters, may my death, at least, not be in vain.* He opened his eyes, feeling an inner peace that he tried to believe came from divinity, though the absence of the oath-bond after so many months seemed the more likely explanation. He locked holds on Gilleran's arm and belt, driving his weight to its maximum. They plummeted.

Gilleran screamed, writhing. He pounded on Nightfall's wrists, then eeled his head and buried his teeth in the squire's thumb.

Nightfall jerked, saving his finger instinctively, but losing the arm grip. Tree limbs snapped like twigs beneath them. Nightfall dropped his weight as the ground rushed up to meet them. They spun like flotsam, Gilleran flopping to the bottom as he became the heavier of the two. Nightfall stiffened for the impact, trying one last, urgent act. He imagined himself weightless as he released his death grip on Gilleran's belt and snatched a tree branch from the air.

Gilleran crashed to the grass, limp. Nightfall closed his eyes as he continued to fall, his previous velocity unstoppable. The branch bent only slightly, bearing his meager weight. The jolting stop tore his right shoulder from the socket, and he felt something snap in his left hand. The branch held, but his grip did not. He fell again, his speed seeming impossibly slow in comparison, most of his momentum broken. He landed on Gilleran, then rolled to the ground, his last realization that the impact had not killed him. "Good-bye, Dyfrin," he managed to think before oblivion overtook him.

Epilogue

Nightfall awakened enfolded in blankets as smooth as water. Consciousness brought the throb and sting of myriad wounds, softened by the comfortable fuzziness induced, he guessed, by some sort of pain-hazing elixir. The hurt did not escape him completely, but his mind would not allow him to care, turning agony to discomfort. His arms ached worst of all. He could feel the stiff touch of a splint holding the left fingers in place. The twinge that accompanied every breath told him Gilleran's kicks had shattered some ribs, and a dull throb along his hip and side reminded him of the cutting magic that nearly killed Edward. His shoulder felt sore, but someone had restored its proper alignment.

Nightfall opened his eyes to slits, routinely cautious. Head bandaged, Edward knelt before a plush chair in which Kelryn perched squarely, her dancer's legs tucked beneath her. Nightfall found himself unable to focus on the other furnishings, although he did reassure himself that no other person occupied the room. The oddity of a crown prince on the floor struck him, but he did not bother to gather the energy necessary for speech.

Kelryn broke what had obviously been a long and uncomfortable silence for both. "Ned, I'm flattered. Under other circumstances, I could think of nothing more wonderful than becoming the queen of Alyndar."

Nightfall's eyes flicked open unconsciously.

Kelryn continued, oblivious. "But I can't marry you."

"You can't?" Edward's voice sounded pinched, with a hint of confusion.

"I'm in love with another man."

Kelryn and Edward turned their heads to Nightfall simultaneously.

Caught awake and listening, Nightfall smiled. "Is that man me?"

Kelryn's delicate cheeks flushed pink. "Yes, you obnoxious, eavesdropping bastard."

Nightfall brushed back the blankets from his head, weighing the pain and effort of sitting and deciding to remain in position instead. "Is that a proposal?"

Kelryn's face darkened to crimson. "It might be."

"Then I accept." Nightfall glanced at Edward to assure his comfort. Despite the humor, it was a delicate situation that pain, drugs, and ignorance did not allow him to handle gracefully. "That is, if my friend, the King of Alyndar, will attend the wedding."

Edward rose and sat on the bed, grinning, genuinely happy. Only a slight wistfulness about his bowing lips gave any indication of his own thwarted dream. "Attend, hell. I'll throw it. If a king can't put together a feast in his adviser's honor, of what good is the crown or the title?"

"Adviser?" The position caught Nightfall wholly by surprise. "Me? Do you think that's wise?"

Edward rubbed at the bandage on his head. "If I hope to help the masses, I'll need someone with real knowledge of their plight. You can refuse the title, you know. I can't force you to become gentry."

Gentry. The suggestion seemed ludicrous to Nightfall, and he knew he could never truly fit in with the highborn. Nevertheless, it might stir some good controversy to sit as counsel to Alyndar's king. "It's not that. It's just . . . well . . . am I still under arrest?"

Edward laughed. "First, my father's papers acquitted you of all crimes in Alyndar prior to our association. A term of the magic, apparently."

Nightfall nodded, guilty Edward's trust for him still hinged on a lie, that the Magebane's stone could have broken the oath-bond. He justified it with the realization that the loyalty existed, regardless of the means used to convince Edward. When the oath-bond ended, he could have escaped with his life. Instead, he had fought the final battle, not only for vengeance but from concern for the future of Alyndar and its king.

"The means of my father's death made it obvious who killed him. The orders of a traitor hold no weight in Alyndar."

Edward's words reminded Nightfall of another matter that needed addressing. He glanced at Kelryn who flashed him a broad smile. "You saved me from a lot of abuse on the stairs. You didn't freeze against the sorcerer this time, and I thank you for that."

Kelryn's grin broadened. "I wish I could have done more. I wish I could have been there for the fight."

"You did enough." Nightfall suspected that consisted of more than he knew. That Gilleran had not killed Edward in the time it took Nightfall to dodge the guards suggested something had delayed him. That something, Nightfall felt certain, was Kelryn.

Edward raised his brows, his question still unanswered. "So, will be you be my adviser?"

Nightfall replied from habit, "Yes, Master, I will."

Edward corrected. "My friends call me Ned. You know that, Sudian." His features creased. "Or should I call you Marak? Or Nightfall? Or something else?"

Nightfall considered only briefly. Aside from King Edward and Kelryn, all those who knew his alter ego were dead. *Except, possibly, one.* The chief prison guard, Volkmier, might have heard enough during his conversation with the king to suspect. His surviving a fatal fall, just as Nightfall had done from the parapets months earlier, had probably added the final certainty. Nevertheless, he believed he could make peace with one of the king's most faithful guardsmen. Perhaps, he already had. Finally, he addressed King Edward's question. "Ned, from this day forth, I believe Sudian is the only name I'll ever need."

And he meant it.

The Legend of Nightfall

A demon wakens with the night,
Reviling sun and all things bright.
Evil's friend and virtue's foe—
Darkness comes where Nightfall goes.

Eyes darker than the midnight shade,
Teeth sharper than the headsman's blade.
When he smiles a cold wind blows—
Darkness comes where Nightfall goes.

When shadows fall and sunlight breaks,
What Nightfall touches, Nightfall takes.
Lives and silver, maids in bows—
Darkness comes where Nightfall goes.

A demon cruel; a monster stark,
Grim moonlight, coldness, deepest dark.
Nightmares come to those who doze—
In darkness where old Nightfall goes.

Nightfall laughs, and death's ax falls.
Hell opens wide and swallows all.
He rules the depths where no light shows—
Darkness comes where Nightfall goes.

Lock up your children after dark,
Lest Nightfall find an easy mark.
For safety ends at twilight's close—
And darkness comes where Nightfall goes.

Razor claws and fiery eyes,
Leathern wings to cleave the skies.
His soul within stark midnight froze—
Darkness comes where Nightfall goes.

Those who brave the night will find.
Horror, dread, and demon kind.
He slays them all and rends their souls—
Darkness comes where Nightfall goes.

Birthed within the black abyss,
His silent gift, a deadly kiss.
Gone before the rooster crows—
Darkness comes where Nightfall goes.

Counting years like grains of sand.
Countless fall beneath his hand.
Time, his minion; night, his clothes—
Darkness comes where Nightfall goes.

Where Nightfall walks, all virtue dies.
He weaves a trail of pain and lies.
On mankind heaps his vilest woes—
Darkness comes where Nightfall goes.

Wolves and bats and beasts of night,
Spirits black that flee the light,
Cringed in fear when he arose—
Darkness comes where Nightfall goes.

He feeds on elders and children,
On soldiers, kings, and beggarmen.
He never stops and never slows—
Darkness comes where Nightfall goes.

The Evil One, the demon blight
Who hides in day and stalks the night.
He steals the stars and drags them low—
Darkness comes where Nightfall goes.

Alternative verses:

Three kings and their armies rode
To hunt the demon in the cold;
But where they've gone, no mortal knows—
Darkness comes where Nightfall goes.

A dragon laughed at Nightfall's fame,
Rained curses on the demon's name;
The dragon's bones now lie in rows—
Darkness comes where Nightfall goes.

A wizard hoped to slay the beast.
He conjured up a poisoned feast.
The demon fed him to the crows—
Darkness comes where Nightfall goes.

A gambler bet the tales were lies
And scorned the wisdom of the wise.
The odds were not the ones he chose—
Darkness comes where Nightfall goes.

Six princes fought him in the night,
Their fortress of unequaled might.
'Twas gone before the sun arose—
Darkness comes where Nightfall goes.

The Evil One, the demon blight
Who hides in day and stalks the night.
He steals the stars and drags them low—
Darkness comes where Nightfall goes.